By Helena Harte

2023

Butterworth Books is a different breed of publishing house. It's a home for Indies, for independent authors who take great pride in their work and produce top quality books for readers who deserve the best. Professional editing, professional cover design, professional proof reading, professional book production—you get the idea. As Individual as the Indie authors we're proud to work with, we're Butterworths and we're *different*.

Authors currently publishing with us:

E.V. Bancroft
Valden Bush
Addison M Conley
Jo Fletcher
Helena Harte
Lee Haven
Karen Klyne
A J Mason
Ally McGuire
James Merrick
Robyn Nyx
Simon Smalley
Brey Willows

For more information visit www.butterworthbooks.co.uk

This trade paperback is published by Butterworth Books, UK

CATALOGING INFORMATION
ISBN: 978-1-915009-42-5
CREDITS
Editor: Victoria Villaseñor
Cover Design: Nicci Robinson
Production Design: Global Wordsmiths

Acknowledgements

A book is only ever as good as the people involved in its production, and I have some amazing beings in my team. My editor, Victoria Villaseñor, is always kind and patient with my story babies. I love her so much for that!

Margaret Burris, my proof reader, has to correct my constant stream of Britishisms no matter how hard I try to erase them before it gets to her. For all you wonderful Americans reading this book, please forgive me if I haven't quite done justice to your language use - I'll never give up trying to get better!

The many wonderful readers in my ARC team: thank you so much for giving your time and thoughts so freely. Sending new offspring out in the world is always a frightening time, and your love and encouragement make it so much easier.

And of course, to all you fantabulous readers out there. Thank you for your voracious appetite. Thank you for your encouraging and enthusiastic reviews. Just, thank you. Many of you reached out to me after An Art to Love, and I was floored by your praise. I hope you love this one, and Taryn and Cassie, as much as I loved writing their story. I strongly believe that romances like this one are needed more than ever again in a world full of danger for our community right now. Keep reading and stay safe. We will prevail.

Dedication

To my wife,
a constant inspiration for
the romance stories I write.
And I adore that we get to do
so much together, especially this.

Chapter One

DEATH-DEFYING. SHE TURNED THE phrase over in her head. The last act of the final show had to be something special. Spectacular. It's what the audience paid for. Sure, there were people coming to the show for the first time, but there were also plenty coming for the second, third, and fourth time; the adrenaline junkies who got their fix vicariously by watching stunts like these. And that's where Taryn Taylor came in.

She tilted her head and looked to her right. The bright red of the Golden Gate bridge against the clear bluebird sky was like a kid's painting in primary colors. She'd always wanted to figure out a way to jump it, though the city most likely wouldn't allow it. Taryn dropped to the temporary flooring they'd installed specially for the show and did a few push-ups to get the blood flowing. Her thick leather biker pants didn't flex much, but as long as they kept her safe, she could forgive that. *Safe. Think safe.* She popped up to stand and looked across the roof and beyond to the piers of San Francisco. She was as safe as she could ever be while hurtling across the roof of the Alcatraz cell block, racing up the forty-five-degree angle ramp, and launching herself into the air for a roll before landing on a moving boat. Most of that was nothing new. Sometimes it felt like she'd done more three-sixties on her bike than the moon had gone around the earth.

Landing on the specially built platform of a speeding boat? That was fresh. And fresh was what she was famous for in the stunt world. Pushing the boundaries of what was possible on two wheels had been her trademark since she'd jumped her first row of buses. She shut her ears to the increasingly vocal niggle in her mind that questioned if this life still fulfilled her. That was just her brain's way of letting her know she should keep coming up with wilder tricks or she'd stagnate. And if she stopped, if she allowed herself to stagnate? She may as well just stop breathing.

Taryn refocused on what she was about to do, what they'd been perfecting for the past six months. The trick was in the landing, like always. Any fool knew that it didn't matter if you did four three-sixty spins if you didn't stick the landing. And then came the flair. Hit the ground with flamboyance. Taryn closed her eyes and visualized the stunt: deploy the parachute to take the sting out of the speed, a one-eighty turn, and fifty feet of a wheelie back along the boat's platform toward the island. Jump from the bike. Pull off her helmet. Take a bow. The crowd goes wild.

Easy.

Someone clapped their hand on her shoulder. "Ready?"

She opened her eyes to Andi, the stunt team's owner, and Gwen, their engineer and math guru, at her side. "I'm ever ready. But maybe I should go over your calculations, Gwen." Taryn wrinkled her nose and rubbed her chin. "If you're off by one decimal point, it's my ass that's grass. We could postpone if you're not one hundred and ten percent sure of your work."

Gwen arched her eyebrow comically high. "I told you we should have tested the parameters here, but you wouldn't do it."

She began to flick through the pages and pages of numbers and letters Taryn didn't understand, and nor did she care to. She fought to keep her laughter in her chest, and Andi punched Taryn's shoulder.

"Don't rise to it, Gwen," Andi said. "We all know you will have checked your calculations for this stunt more times than Taryn has given the big O to lady fans over the past decade."

Taryn grinned and wiggled her eyebrows. She wasn't one to brag, but the little bit of her that remembered being the ugly duckling in school reveled in her reputation. And if she pulled this finale off without injury, she'd be seeking out some nocturnal company to help her come down from the mental high.

"Every time." Gwen puffed out a dramatic breath. "I fall for your shenanigans every time. I get nothing but sleepless nights coming up to the final show, you do know that, don't you?"

Taryn wrapped her arm around Gwen's neck and kissed the top of her head. "And your insomnia means I stay alive. I know. You're my angel."

Gwen blushed adorably. "I'm not sure where my career trajectory took a detour to get me on the road to keeping you alive, but it wasn't what I had in mind when I graduated from MIT."

Taryn smiled at Gwen's sweet attempt to cover up her obvious fondness with sharpened barbs. It was one of her many charms. "That may be so, but I am eternally grateful that you stick with us." Taryn released Gwen and looked at Andi. "It's probably time for a pay raise, don't you think? She's saving you a fortune every tour. Your medical bills would be far higher if it weren't for our brilliant Gwen."

"You're teasing me," Gwen said and narrowed her eyes.

"Only about the pay raise—Andi's too cheap for that." Taryn held Gwen's gaze. "But I'd never tease you about how much you mean to us."

"Hey." Andi punched Taryn's shoulder again, harder this time. "I'm not cheap; I'm careful. My financial sense is what kept us afloat during COVID. But on that note, I actually may be able to talk about more money, for everyone." She tapped the long rectangular form in the pocket of her tight jeans.

"Is that a phone or—"

"Don't." Andi held up her hand. "Clichés aren't your style. I got an email from the Cosmos in Vegas. They want to talk about a six-month residency. And there were a lot of zeroes in the offer."

Taryn turned away and went to her bike for last-minute checks, as if she hadn't already done them twice over. "Sure. Great joke, Andi," she said without looking back. "Two weeks is my maximum in one place, you know that. That's why I joined this circus in the first place."

Andi laughed. "That's what you tell people, but it was really because you fell in love with me."

Taryn glanced over her shoulder. "I was in lust with you for two days maximum. I was in love with your Triumph Street Triple. She was a thing of beauty."

"Until you totaled her trying to impress that millionairess in Galveston." Andi grimaced. "Losing her was worse than any heartbreak I've ever suffered."

Taryn snorted, grateful for the swing from an uncomfortable topic. "Like you've ever had your heart broken. I learned everything I know from you."

Andi grinned and shrugged. "I'm getting old; I had to pass the mantle and all my knowledge on to someone."

"Old? You're forty-nine, for Christ's sake."

Gwen whistled loudly. "I hate to break up the bro-love fest, but... A Vegas residency would be amazing, Andi. You can count me in."

Taryn clenched her jaw and pressed her thumb to the front tire. "Who checked the pressures? This feels a little soft." She looked up, and Andi's expression told Taryn she was clearly unimpressed.

"The tire pressures are perfect," Andi said. "The bike is ready. The boat's ready, and I'm ready. Are you sure you're up for this? We can postpone if you're not one hundred and ten percent sure."

Taryn couldn't stop her nostrils flaring at Andi recycling her own words as a challenge. She got on her bike, turned the key and revved the engine. "You make sure the boat's in the right place, and I'll land on it."

Andi nodded and smiled the way she did when she knew she'd hit her mark. She tapped her watch. "Less than twenty minutes to the closing act. Let's leave Taryn to her final preparations." She winked at Taryn. "And we'll talk about Vegas tomorrow."

Andi took Gwen's hand and led her from the roof, leaving Taryn to mutter and curse to herself. She checked her earpiece and comms with Banjo before pulling her helmet on.

"Hearing you loud and clear, Tar," Banjo said, coming into Taryn's ear as if she were standing right beside her. "The boss is on her way down to the boat right now, and Sally is whipping the crowd into a frenzy. The wind's dropped to three knots with gusts up to eight. Considering the location, the conditions couldn't be any better."

"Perfect." Taryn filed away the imminent Vegas conversation as something to deal with later. If she wasn't fully focused on this stunt, she wouldn't even be around to have that chat tomorrow. She broke into a grin as adrenaline and anticipation tore around her bloodstream, priming and pumping her up for another daring stunt. Was it a cliché when it was the truth? She'd check with Andi when they were sharing their traditional post-show bottle of Jack with Gwen.

But right now, she took the bike across the roof and stopped at the base of the long ramp that curved up into the sky. The last few feet of the TransAmerica Pyramid poked out above the ramp's edge, providing the optical illusion that she could launch off the roof and land on its spiky peak. That feat would only be slightly more risky than the one they were about to attempt. Simulations and dry trial runs had gone well. Taryn could get the required speed across the distance of the roof and the ramp to do the spin and clear the island to land on the boat, and Andi had been able to drive the landing platform at the perfect velocity to meet Taryn and her bike. But they hadn't recreated the stage elsewhere, and they hadn't practiced for real here on Alcatraz. Taryn hadn't wanted any footage to leak before the final night. She wanted her first time to be the audience's first time, much to Gwen's chagrin. Taryn completely trusted Gwen and the computer program she'd built; it was easily as good as a live trial, and she'd been able to run the trick hundreds of times to ensure every element of the stunt was error-free, calculated to the umpteenth decimal point of velocity, distance, wind speed, body mass—every minute detail. All Taryn had to do was maintain her weight and keep her cool.

"How's it looking up there?"

Banjo's voice filtered into Taryn's consciousness, and she turned the bike toward the edge of the roof overlooking the stage and the gathered crowd. "All good."

"Ready for your close-up? Dee and Fig are almost done."

Taryn glanced at the closest of the many video cameras positioned all across the roof and then back down to the stage where the twins were wrapping up their BMX high-wire set. "I will be." She removed her helmet, placed it on the tank, and pulled the visor down to use as a mirror. Then she ran her hands through her wig to untangle it before she blew a kiss to the camera. "How do I look?"

"Stunning, as always," Banjo said. "You must be the only motorbike rider ever to be able to look that good after pulling their helmet off. I look like I've been pulled through an aviation engine by my ankles whenever I take my skidlid off."

Taryn laughed at Banjo's colorful description. "I'd like to be able to disagree, but I can't." She twisted around and tugged at the straps of the parachute over the back of the bike seat, but there was no need. It was snug. "Maybe if you just shaved off all your hair?"

Banjo guffawed so loudly, it nearly deafened Taryn.

"As if that's ever going to happen. My hair is my best feature. Take my mane, and I've got nothing."

"Hey, that's bull crap. Take it back, or I'll tell Sally what you said."

"You wouldn't."

"I would. We're all beautiful, Banjo. Take it back, or I tell your wife, and she will kick your ass." Taryn knew it was easy for her to say—she'd been blessed with great genes and bone structure—but she hated the whole world's obsession with socially imposed beauty.

"Fine. I'm just as gorgeous as you are. If the person looking has been poked in the eye with a white-hot knitting needle and is squinting through blinding sun and ruby rose-tinted glasses.

You're on in 5, 4, 3, 2, 1."

Taryn gave her widest smile toward the camera. In her peripheral vision, she saw the video of her head and shoulders forty-feet high on the screens surrounding the stage as the crowd erupted into a raucous cheer and began to chant her name.

"Taryn Taylor, everyone! Give the people a big wave, Taryn."

Sally came through Taryn's earpiece, and she did as requested.

"Are you ready to give these lovely folks the thrill they've been waiting for?"

"Yes, I am." Taryn put the bike in first gear and pulled the throttle hard. The back tire rebelled against the constraint and swayed from left to right, creating a plume of dark, pungent smoke behind her.

The volume of the crowd's excitement ramped up a couple of notches, and their excited energy solidified to trace a soft caress along Taryn's spine. Moments like these were what she lived for. She looked at the distance between the ramp and the Bay she was aiming for. And they were worth dying for.

The video feed switched to Sally. "Lovely audience, are you ready to have your breath stolen from your lungs?" She held her hands to her ears then covered them up when the crowd's answering response almost shook the foundations of the old prison. "Andi Anderson, are you in position?"

Andi, at the helm of the specially made boat, appeared on the giant screens. "Hell, yeah!"

The audience clapped and stamped their feet, creating a tribal rhythm that reverberated around the island and thundered up Taryn's soles, vibrating her core.

"Taryn! Take it away!"

While Sally continued to work the crowd to a feverish frenzy, Taryn secured her helmet and spun the bike around to head to her starting position at the far corner of the cellblock. She got into place and walked the bike back until the rear tire hit the edge of the custom-built, thirty-foot travelator and clicked into place, lifting the rear wheel from the floor. She clicked into first gear and accelerated gently to test the system.

The bike didn't move, the engine growled into action, and the travelator matched the speed of the back wheel, sending the front wheel into suspended motion. Gwen was a true genius. The piece of equipment she'd invented purely for this trick would allow Taryn to reach sixty miles per hour without moving. When Gwen, their engineer, released the catch holding her in place, she'd be able to get up to the required 153mph by the time she hit the ramp.

"Taryn holds the world record for a no-hands wheelie with two thousand feet and eleven inches, and if we ever give her a long enough break, she wants to smash the world record for longest distance covered while doing a headstand on her motorbike."

Taryn signaled she was ready and began to accelerate. She flicked through the gears, eased to sixty in less than four seconds, and held the bike there. She took a long, deep breath and exhaled quickly. Now she was in position, and she couldn't wait to ride.

"Are you ready to give this crowd the thrill of a lifetime?" Sally yelled.

Fire tore through her blood, and her heart pounded against her ribs. "Hell, yeah. Hit it."

At the command, Gwen released Taryn's back wheel, and the bike zipped along the travelator. She gripped the handlebars tight to compensate for the jolt from static to sixty, then accelerated across the smooth surface of the cellblock toward the ramp. In her periphery, she saw the white water from Andi's boat but kept her gaze fixed ahead. Frosty focus on her body, the bike, and the ramp was the only way she could complete this stunt without injury.

The digital speedometer clicked over 145mph, and Taryn twisted the throttle just a touch more. She hit the incline at 153 and started the climb. Everything but the ramp disappeared from sight. The stage, the tiny dots of color that were the audience, the island, the Bay; all of it gone as she fully extended the throttle to maintain her speed. She felt the G-force trying to tug her back to earth, so she leaned close enough to the tank to kiss it.

And then...

Weightlessness as she soared through the air, slicing through it like a samurai sword, effortless and just as lethal. At the peak of the forward momentum, she pulled back on the handlebars and leaned into the spin. She fought against the force trying to push her head back as the bike completed the rotation. When she emerged from the revolution with her speed decreasing rapidly, Taryn focused on the platform as the boat came into view and she softened her grip on the handlebars. Too stiff and she'd snap like a matchstick. Too soft and she'd bounce off the bike and into the Bay.

Andi was exactly where she should be, and even from her aerial perspective, Taryn could see her as clearly as if she was overlayed on one of the many, many computer simulations. She was going to make it.

The bike headed inexorably on its downward curve, its trajectory perfect in relation to the boat platform. She readied herself for the intense impact, and sure enough, as she landed both wheels simultaneously, the shock shot through every cell, bone, and muscle in her body. The bike's parachute deployed by virtue of the pressure sensors on the platform—another piece of engineering genius from Gwen to be grateful for—and the resultant tug and dramatic reduction of speed sent Taryn forward on the seat. Her helmet stopped just shy of the bug shield before the parachute released, and she was back in control of her machine.

She saw Andi fist-pump on the deck before Taryn spun the bike around, pulled back into a wheelie, and shot toward the far end of the platform. She hit the brakes and leapt off the bike, leaving it to slide elegantly into the safety net that had been pulled up as they headed back to the island. Andi would forgive her the extra theatrics, and the bike always had a fresh paint job ready for the next show anyways.

Taryn pulled off her helmet and took a bow to the camera at the edge of the boat, keeping her more exuberant reaction inside to share with Andi when the director switched the video feed back to Sally onstage. The crowd's whooping and hollering widened her smile before Sally cut in, sounding even more excited than the audience.

"And you're off-air," Banjo said. "That was fucking amazing, Tar."

"Thanks, buddy." Taryn was already turning to celebrate with Andi when she was hoisted into the air.

"That was next level, T." Andi's grin matched her own. "You were like a god up there. I thought you were gonna sprout fucking wings. And that landing was textbook form." She squeezed her even tighter. "Goddamn!"

Taryn hugged Andi back just as hard. "Jesus, Andi. I've never felt anything like that before. It was... it was transcendent. I can't even begin to put it into words."

"No words, T. Just feel it. I bet it's soaring around in you like a fucking shooting star."

Taryn laughed and scrubbed the top of Andi's head with her knuckles. "A meteor! I've got a fucking meteor bouncing around my insides."

Andi dropped Taryn to her feet and wrapped her arm around her neck as she tugged her toward the front deck. "I don't know what the hell we're gonna come up with to top that."

"What about jumping over the Statue of Liberty?" She gestured to the TransAmerica Pyramid. "Or I could see how far I can ride up the side of that?"

"I was kidding, T." Andi shook her head and chuckled. "Let's enjoy this one for a while."

That sounded suspiciously like Andi was looking to slow down, then she remembered Vegas and the six-month residency on the table. "Sure," she said with no conviction.

That was tomorrow's conversation though. Taryn threw her arm around Andi's waist and let the enormity of what they'd just achieved settle into her bones. Her aching bones. Christ, why could she feel that already? Never mind, half a bottle of their traditional Jack D would soon obliterate that awareness. And one of the cute fans who'd be waiting at the docks for autographs would take care of the rest.

Chapter Two

"Cassandra Kennedy, M.D. That's what you should get."

"Why? In case I forget my name and occupation when I'm following you down a drunken rabbit hole?" Cassie batted Rachel's arm before continuing to flick through the laminated pages of art on a side table. "And we're not here for me; we're here so you can cover another piece of your ever-disappearing skin." She glanced at the flesh Rachel had on display—almost every inch of it colorfully covered in all manner of what she considered to be great art. Some of it was. Some of it…wasn't.

"Come on. We can do both. I bet there'll be someone free to ink your virgin canvas." Rachel nudged Cassie's shoulder gently. "It'll be good for you to try something new."

Cassie rolled her eyes. "Why is it that I feel like your special project sometimes?"

Rachel wiggled her nose like an intolerably cute rabbit. "Because although you're only in your mid-thirties, you act twenty years older, and it's my mission in life to constantly remind you that you're on this big ball of dust to have some fun. All work and no play make Cassandra a dull woman, old way before her time."

"I have fun when I'm out with you." Cassie felt herself pout, quite unbecoming of a middle-aged professional. She was middle-aged, wasn't she?

Rachel bounced on her heels and smiled widely. "You do! You have bags full of the stuff. Which is why we should do it more often, and it's why you're going to get your first tattoo right now."

Rachel tugged her toward the desk, where a cute short-haired woman looked simultaneously bored out of her mind and vaguely amused by their performance. No doubt, hundreds of tattoo-tourists passed through these doors without having the courage to permanently transform their skin. And Cassie would proudly be one of those people. "While I appreciate your commitment to the cause," she leaned closer to Rachel and whispered, "and while I'm sure this is a perfectly hygienic establishment, if I ever get a tattoo, it'll have to mean something." She stepped back and gestured to Rachel's whole body. "Like yours. You've got a whole story going on, with your sleeves, and your back, and your legs. And it's wonderful, it really is. But that's a you thing."

"And staying away from germs and diseases is a you thing," Rachel said.

"No. I'm pretty sure that's an everyone-who-wants-to-live-a-long-life thing." Although the thought of catching a deadly virus from an unclean tattoo needle was another good reason to stay away from them.

"What about being spontaneous?"

God, Rachel's persistence was dialed high today. "I can be spontaneous. Just yesterday, I spontaneously chose churro-flavored ice cream instead of my regular Cherry Garcia." Cassie looked at the woman behind the counter, who was sporting a more amused grin now. She was rather cute, really. She was rocking the super cool queer vibe, though Cassie doubted a highly practical doctor would hold her interest for longer than the average ZimTak video. A wicked image crossed her mind when the woman opened her mouth to speak, and Cassie spotted a ball on the end of her tongue.

"You shouldn't force your girlfriend into something she clearly doesn't want."

"She's not my girlfriend, Zed," Rachel said with far too much horror in her voice for Cassie's liking. "Also, she's no girl. She's thirty-five, an accomplished doctor at the Spring Willow Memorial hospital, and she owns her own apartment in an exclusive part of town. In spite of the fact that she is currently acting like a complete square, she's actually a lot of fun, especially when she's buzzed. And she's totally single."

Cassie choked on her mortification. "Rach." That was all she could manage. Any potential additional response melted away the instant Zed focused her intense gaze on Cassie and her smile turned from mildly amused to "I'm a hot sex god; let's get to it on a tattoo chair, and I'll make your wildest fantasies come true."

Rachel nudged her. "Earth to Cassandra." She waved her hand in front of Cassie's face. "Zed asked if you'd be going to Infinite over the weekend."

"What?" She narrowed her eyes at Rachel. There was little chance she could look at Zed without thinking more impure thoughts about the piece of metal in her mouth. "Uh, no. I mean, I can't. I've got a double shift." She mentally flipped through the list of doctors who might be interested in swapping shifts on the weekend before Independence Day. It didn't take long; there was no one on it. She'd only been scheduled to work Saturday until this morning, then Fischer begged her to cover his Sunday, and she'd acquiesced. Damn it.

"I'm there most weekends," Zed said.

"Maybe another time?" It had been a while since Cassie's last confession to the lesbian gods, and no matter how many quick orgasms her trusty bedside vibrator provided, they were no match for the real thing. And boi, Zed was the real thing. It was times like these when she idly questioned a career that kept her social life to a bare minimum.

Zed nodded and gave Cassie another panty-melting gaze before she turned to Rachel.

"Since you've failed to convince your hot friend to get a tattoo, should we get the lines down on yours?"

"Yay, let's do it." Rachel pulled Cassie beyond the desk and into the back parlor area.

Three victims were in various stages of torture, their pained expressions solidifying Cassie's determination not to get a tattoo, or certainly not to get one without copious amounts of sensation-numbing alcohol in her bloodstream. Drinking to excess had never held much appeal, especially given her past, but it served a purpose here and there. If she ever got the nerve, if she could ever quell her anxieties over how sanitary the average tattoo shop was, a half-bottle of something around a hundred proof would be one of those occasions.

While Zed prepared a table, Rachel leaned into Cassie. "Do you really have a double shift this weekend? I thought we were going out."

Cassie glanced at Zed, busy preparing her tattoo gun and ink, and once again rued her decision to help out a fellow doc. "We were. But Fischer put a guilt trip on me about spending quality time with his wife and kids, and I folded." In her defense, his family was really cute, and in his shoes, she would do the same.

Rachel snorted. "Having a family doesn't make his non-work time any more precious than yours, Cass. You need to squeeze the sponge too. You work too hard. I don't want my favorite doctor burning out, and neither do the rest of the nurses." She bumped Cassie's shoulder. "You know you're everyone's favorite, don't you?"

Cassie smiled. Being their favorite wasn't important; she wanted the nurses to feel appreciated since they often did the lion's share of the work while the doctors got all the kudos. But the warm feeling that spread across her chest let her know it mattered a little. "That's nice to hear."

"And that's not just because you anonymously donated your Christmas bonus and had HR split it between all of us." Rachel winked and gave her a conspiratorial grin.

"What?" she asked, trying to sound surprised or innocent or anything other than busted.

"Your poker face needs some serious practice, Cass. So you would have met up with Zed? I knew she'd be perfect for you."

"And you were right, as usual. That's why you're my

self-appointed wing woman." Cassie appreciated the clunky segue back to slightly more comfortable territory. Her growing physical attraction to Zed as she watched her muscles flex wasn't *that* comfortable. But it was preferable to discussing her helping the nursing team with money, something everyone needed more than words in the growing financial crisis. Eve at HR had promised to keep it quiet, but Rachel had a way of getting information out of even the most reticent of prey. Eve never stood a chance; once Rachel put her mind to something, nothing got in the way of her goal. Cassie just hoped it wasn't common knowledge. She didn't want the other doctors to cast judgment on her motives or for the nurses to feel obliged to treat her differently. She resolved to talk to Eve when she was next on duty.

Zed beckoned them over and handed Rachel her iPad. "What do you think? Is this what you had in mind?"

Rachel tapped her fingers to Zed's forehead. "This—this is why I will only ever let you ink me." She looked again at the sketch on Zed's tablet. "It's exactly what I want."

Cassie peered over Rachel's shoulder to get a closer look at the morivivi flower and bee design. "Wow, that's beautiful."

"Isn't it? Have you changed your mind?" Rachel asked.

"You're entirely too invested in turning my body into Zed's work of art." The words were out of Cassie's mouth before she fully realized how they could be twisted.

Zed chuckled and locked her gaze on Cassie again. "I'm a busy woman, but I could squeeze you in whenever you wanted..."

Cassie bit her lip. The thought of being squeezed anywhere by Zed was becoming more appealing by the second. Her hormones were out of control; it really had been too long for her to be behaving like a horny college kid. "That sounds delightful, and if I do decide to get a tattoo someday, you'll be my first call but--"

"*I* better be your first call, *Cassandra*," Rachel said and swatted Cassie's shoulder none too gently. "Losing your tattoo virginity is something you should share with your bestie."

Cassie raised her eyebrow and tilted her head slightly. "You think you're my bestie?"

Rachel put the iPad down and crossed her arms—quite the feat considering the size of her breasts, which was something Cassie tried hard *not* to consider.

"I *better* be your bestie. Who else is vying for the title? Is there someone I need to beat down?"

Cassie laughed. "You'd beat someone up to be my bestie?"

Rachel pouted then looked uncharacteristically serious, the kind of serious she usually reserved for work situations when there were copious amounts of blood, tears, and general terror.

"I'd do anything for you," Rachel said.

A wave of gratitude washed over Cassie, and she pulled Rachel into a tight hug. They teased each other so much that Cassie sometimes forgot how important Rachel was to her. She blinked back the hot burn of tears, sure that Zed would find them a total turn-off, and released Rachel. "And I'd do anything for you. Which is why I'm here to keep you entertained while you have your fragile skin punctured at a rate of three thousand stabs per minute—I watched a TED talk, before you tell me I know nothing about tattooing."

Rachel cleared her throat. "I need the little girl's room before we start."

Cassie didn't miss Rachel's glassy eyes before she turned away. Cassie looked up to the ceiling to stem her own unbidden reaction, then she focused on the catatonic expression of the guy in the adjacent station to Zed's. He looked like he'd gone into shock, which wouldn't be surprising since his tattooist was bouncing his torture tool against the poor guy's cranium. When she noticed he had ear buds in, she surmised that he could've simply zoned out to some death metal music.

"What kind of doctor are you, doc?"

Zed's gentle question drew her attention back to the sexy tattooist and away from the vulnerability bubbling just below the surface of her skin. If she had let Zed loose with her tattoo gun, who knew what manner of emotions would escape. "Emergency room."

"Ah, you like the non-stop action?" Zed's smile took a wicked turn.

"I like to help as many people as I can." Judging by Zed's reaction, Cassie's answer had been sharp. She wasn't about to explain to a complete stranger what had really driven her to that specialty; those details were double digit date material, and with her career, Cassie rarely made it to date one, so her demons were safely hidden. "And it keeps me moving all day, which is useful because by nature, I'm a bit of a sloth when it comes to physical activity." She smiled but Zed was busy printing Rachel's tattoo template. *That* didn't take long to mess up.

Zed glanced up and winked. "It's obviously working; you look great."

So not *totally* blown.

"Okay, I'm ready for your next masterpiece." Rachel sat on Zed's chair, pulled off her T-shirt and lay down.

Cassie couldn't decide if it was good timing or not. Who knows what other ways she would've found to upset Zed if Rachel had left them alone much longer. Which was why she found casual hook-ups easier. It was virtually impossible to have a real conversation over the ear-bursting music that was ubiquitous with every dance club in Vegas, and thus it was virtually impossible for her to self-sabotage her chances with a hot butch. And since she usually made her excuses and left before breakfast, there was rarely any awkward post-coital conversation either.

She pulled up a spare chair, sat beside Rachel, and held her hand while Zed did tattooist-type things with a razor and sterilizer. She'd noted Zed breaking out a needle from sealed packaging, *and* she pulled on black latex gloves. Maybe this place was sanitary enough for her to consider getting inked, though the black skintight gloves begged for a more sexual application.

God, settle down. Metal Mickey, her thumb-sized vibrator, would be certain to get a workout this evening. Cassie glanced at the gentle curve of Zed's bicep as she began to trace the outer edges of Rachel's mandala, and she knew exactly what she'd think about tonight too.

Rachel wiggled her fingers. "You're staring, and you're hurting my hand," she whispered.

Cassie shushed her without speaking and relaxed her grip. She assumed Zed hadn't heard over the sound of a million buzzing bees coming from her tattoo gun. "How come you're so relaxed when everyone else looks like they're getting enemas? Anybody would think you were having a gentle massage instead of needle torture."

When Zed paused for a second to get more ink, Rachel said, "It just doesn't hurt. Everyone has different pain thresholds, and mine seems to be quite high. Which is lucky considering this is an addiction."

Zed returned to her canvas. "Sorry, Cassie, I have to ask you not to talk to Rach much. I need her completely still, or this will end up looking like a bad Keith Haring homage."

Cassie wrinkled her nose. "Sorry. I'll be quiet."

"Thanks." Zed rewarded her compliance with another sexy smile.

She watched, morbidly fascinated by the combination of artistry and surgery, and lost track of time, almost hypnotized by the precise and repetitive movements of Zed's pain pencil. Her pager sounded loudly in her pocket, and she pulled it out.

Rachel wasn't nearly as subtle and groaned theatrically. "Oh, come on. You didn't tell me you were on call."

Cassie pushed up from her seat. "I'm not. It must be something bad."

Zed stopped and looked up, her expression serious. "A shooting?"

"I don't know yet." Cassie frowned. It had been over five years since the Mandalay Bay massacre, but that kind of thing was hard to let go of. She shuddered at the memory and pushed away the vivid images of the hundreds of injured concert-goers she'd seen that night. "Rain check on lunch, Rach."

"Do you need to go too?" Zed asked.

"No. Only hotshot doctors get dragged away from their downtime," Rachel said and relaxed back onto the table. "I'll call you later."

"Sure." Cassie left, and the dry heat outside took her breath away, whooshing down on her like she'd opened the door on an oven the size of a skyscraper. She speed-walked to her car as best she could in four-inch pumps. When she got in, the upholstery of her seat all but seared her flesh and the steering wheel was almost too hot to touch. This damn hell city needed a subterranean parking lot and roadways.

The traffic was reasonably favorable, and she made good time. She screeched to a halt in her personal space and resumed her speed walk to the staff entrance. Cassie took a cleansing breath before she swiped her ID to enter. Whatever was waiting for her behind these doors, she could handle it. Just like she handled every other emergency this city had thrown at her in the past eight years. And *emergency* emergencies, where she and every other available doctor were called in, tested her mettle and made sure she was still at the top of her game. She wouldn't admit it out loud, but they were kind of thrilling in a macabre way, like she was battling the devil for human souls.

Cassie rolled her eyes at her ridiculous self and flung open the door, ready to face the melee. She was barely two steps into the building before Lucy, one of the longest-serving nurses at the hospital, grabbed her arm and tugged her into the doctor's lounge to change into scrubs.

"Thank god you got here so fast," Lucy said.

"What's happening?" Cassie opened her locker and changed faster than one of the magician's assistants on the Strip.

"Suspected fuel tank explosion at Harry Reid." Lucy held the door open and talked as they walked. "Two hundred and sixteen passengers, twelve crew, and the captain and co-pilot."

"Lucky they weren't at full capacity, I suppose." Cassie tucked her tank into her pants.

"They were on the runway, about to depart for Barcelona, when something exploded. Around a quarter of the injured have been brought to us, and we've already lost three."

Cassie straightened her top when they stopped at the main ER doors.

"Ready, doctor?" Lucy handed Cassie a pair of surgical gloves.

She nodded, pulling the gloves on. "Ready."

Lucy held her card to the access panel, and the doors opened. The cacophony of people yelling orders, screaming in pain, and crying in desperation swept over her, and in her head, she turned the volume down to a manageable roar. These were the days that reinforced why she'd chosen to be a doctor. As a seven-year-old, she may not have been able to save her brother, but she could damn well save these people now.

Chapter Three

TARYN LEANED AGAINST THE bar and took in the sprawling spread of the Vegas club. Neon lights, writhing bodies, bass-thumping music, and a high-level hum of constant chatter. She loved every element of it. Meeting new people was one of her favorite things about constantly being on the road, and the first night in a new city never got old. It didn't matter how similar their life experience was, no two people ever seemed alike. They could've had almost identical childhoods in the same area around the same time, and yet there'd always be differences, sometimes subtle, sometimes blindingly obvious. For Taryn, the variety really did give life its flavor.

She ordered two Jack and Cokes, then scanned the women sitting in hunting packs around tall tables on the perimeter of the dance floor. More than a few caught her eye, and they exchanged nods, smiles, and hungry looks. She'd only just gotten here, so it was way too early to be thinking about who she might go back to the hotel with. The bars in San Francisco had scratched her itch, so to speak, so she could definitely take her time choosing a playmate tonight.

Andi patted her shoulder heavily. "*That's* a fancy-pants bathroom. Every cubicle has one of those expensive Japanese toilets that do everything except give you an orgasm."

"Huh, I've got to see that. Drinks are on their way." She gestured to the dance floor. "The women over at tables two, three, and five look like they've been in forced celibacy for a month and are determined to make up for it tonight."

Andi followed Taryn's gaze to the tables that actually were painted with numbers. "Do you think they have bingo nights where you win whoever is sitting in those seats?"

"It's Vegas; anything is possible." She clapped Andi on the back and headed to the restrooms.

They didn't disappoint. She and their team had done shows in Vegas a few times, and so much of it changed in between visits that it was like coming to a new city every time. There was always some big new attraction designed to take your breath away, and for this club, the illusion of never-ending mirrors and toilets that cost more than the average car were this year's extravagance.

When in Vegas... She made use of the facilities and indulged in a pleasant and cleansing butt bath. When she opened the door, one of the women from table five blocked her exit.

"Hi, handsome," the woman said.

Taryn held her laughter at the woman's comical, stage-sexy whisper and smiled. "Hi, yourself." She peered over the woman's head and held up her hands. "Do you mind?"

The woman stepped aside and let Taryn go to the giant basin along the length of the wall where a four-foot-wide faucet produced a waterfall to wash her hands. Metal-tipped stilettos clipped across the stone floor, before the woman stood so close Taryn could feel warm breath on her neck. Instead of being hot, it was a little like an over-excited dog hanging over her shoulder, desperate to be taken for a walk. But desperation was never sexy. Taryn found women most sexy when she had to work for it, at least a little.

She raised her hands, and the air dryer kicked in. Hot wind caressed her skin, and she took a little longer to dry off than usual in the vague hope that the woman would decipher her disinterest and move on. But no, the woman wasn't to be dissuaded so easily.

"Are you and the woman at the bar sisters?" the woman asked.

"Ha. She *wishes* she had my genes."

"Yeah? True Religion is a great brand. And your ass is made for them."

Taryn didn't know whether the woman was trying to be funny,

whether she'd misheard her, or whether she was simply a little less intelligent than the average turkey. Her lack of a grin suggested it was the latter. "Did you know turkeys stare up at the sky when it's raining? Do you think they're trying to figure out how clouds work, or do you think they're contemplating the existence of a higher being?"

The woman frowned, which was an improvement on the come-hither expression that had been creeping Taryn out.

"They are *definitely* considering the existential nature of their position in the food chain, and thus in time and space, and most likely, are wondering about all the other selves they have floating around in the multiverse."

Taryn snapped around to the sound of this new voice faster than she'd shot over Snake River Canyon. When she focused on the woman who accompanied the words, Taryn let out a low sound of appreciation, then covered it up by clearing her throat. The woman raised her eyebrow and smirked, making it obvious Taryn had been unsuccessful.

"I thought you'd never get here." Super-chic woman linked her arm through Taryn's and began to maneuver them to the door. "Sorry, honey, this one's taken. Happy hunting."

She didn't say another word as she navigated out of the bathroom, through the maze of corridors, and back to the bar. Then she released Taryn's arm and turned to leave.

"Wait," Taryn said in far too high-pitched a voice. She coughed to find her usual tenor and tried again. "Wait. I owe you a drink. I think you just saved my life." She grinned widely and wiggled her eyebrows. Her policy of having a few hours of fun before choosing a potential playmate had just gone out the window.

"Not necessary. Erin's a bit of a vampire. I save everyone I can."

She turned to leave again, but Taryn caught her wrist gently. She couldn't let this vision of selfless virtue go without trying to get to know her. "Please. I'd want to buy you a drink even if you hadn't rescued me." Which seemed ironic and totally against Taryn's usual

MO, but confident, powerful femmes were her Achilles heel, and in her social circles, they were rare.

Super-chic woman looked at Taryn's hand around her wrist, and Taryn released her immediately. "Sorry. I shouldn't have grabbed for you. Let me buy you a drink to apologize."

She looked amused again. "Is a drink your answer to everything?"

"Depends on what the question is. There's something else you'd prefer to be offered?" Taryn asked.

She gave a small smile then gestured toward the bar. "If you insist, I'll have two mojitos."

"One for the apology and one for the lifesaving, or do you think I'd drink a mojito?"

She shook her head and motioned over her shoulder to a younger woman at table thirteen. *Damn. Unlucky for me.*

"One for me and one for my best friend. And no, I couldn't imagine you sipping something so elaborate."

Taryn rubbed the back of her head. "I'm not sure whether that's an insult or a compliment."

She merely tilted her head and gave another small smile. Her tiniest gestures were loaded with promise, and Taryn was reminded again of how much she enjoyed all these opportunities to meet new people. She hadn't met someone as interesting as this lady for a while though, and certainly not someone who didn't fawn all over her from moment one. "Can my friend and I join you both?" It was clear super-chic lady wasn't about to dump her bestie, so Taryn's only approach had to include her buddy too. "I'm Taryn, by the way."

She held out her hand, surprising Taryn with her firm grip. "Cassandra. Cassie to my friends."

"Can I call you Cassie?"

She arched her eyebrow. "Not yet."

Cassandra's lips twitched, obviously knowing damn well the effect she was having. Taryn hadn't played a beautiful game like this for so long. She wasn't certain she remembered the rules, but she was never one to back away from a challenge. Especially when said challenge came sheathed in a silken black dress. "So would you deign to let me and my buddy join you?"

"Where are they?" Cassandra asked.

Taryn pointed her thumb in Andi's direction without making eye contact with her. She already knew what her expression would be. She was like a proud aunt, the cool one who taught you how to surf, or play pool, or in this case, charm the ladies. Maybe she was more of a preacher, and through her teachings, her methods lived on. Yeah, she'd probably like that more.

She watched Cassandra's gaze travel from Andi's face to her patterned brogues and back again. She shrugged, though it wasn't a shrug, per say. Her movement was far too delicate for that, but Taryn couldn't think of a better word, and she wanted to focus all her concentration on the game she'd been drawn into.

"One drink. I'm going back to my table to tell my friend that our night has temporarily been hijacked."

If it hadn't been for the wink before Cassandra turned and sashayed away, Taryn might have questioned whether her persistence was unwelcome. Cassandra had a way of smacking away her smug self-confidence with barely a word, let alone a back-handed slap. It was like Taryn was on the deck of a ship in a massive storm, and she couldn't get her footing.

It was fantastic.

Taryn strode as briskly as she could to Andi without breaking into a sprint. She ordered more drinks and quickly filled her in on her encounter with the enigmatic Cassandra.

Andi looked around Taryn's shoulder to the table Cassandra and her friend were seated at. "Her friend is half my age."

"What does that matter?"

She poked Taryn's chest. "I have limits."

"Since when?" That was news to Taryn.

"Since always." Andi wrinkled her nose as if some evil odor had just floated up her nostrils. "My sister has a daughter about the same age. I have a strict over-thirty policy."

"I don't care. Maybe she looks younger than she is. Maybe she's had seventeen face lifts, and she's really eighty-three. Do you have an over-eighty policy too?"

"No. That would be ageist."

Taryn punched Andi's shoulder. "Let's go." She picked up the tray of drinks.

"You're an eager beaver." Andi made a show of her reluctance to rise from her seat. "The view is pretty spectacular from here, you know?"

Andi flicked a glance to the tables of cougars and baby tigers courting their attention, and Taryn caught the eye of the vamp Cassandra had called Erin. Andi would've snapped her up. She considered dumping Andi with her and chancing her luck solo with Cassandra and her friend—not for a threesome though. Cassandra seemed far too elegant for that kind of action, and Andi was right; her friend did look young. Too young for Taryn even. She preferred women around her own age or older.

"Taryn." Andi gave her a light shove, and the drinks slopped on the tray. "The view. It's just fine here."

Taryn took a backward step in the direction of Cassandra's table. "Didn't you see her? She's gorgeous."

"Sure. She's beautiful. But so is every single one of the women at those tables, and most of them are more my target audience."

Taryn chuckled and chanced another step. There was no way she was missing out on the chance to get to know Cassandra. "Audience? Are you planning to take them to bed or to see one of our shows?"

Andi shrugged. "Probably both. We're gonna be here a while. Maybe it's time for me to start looking for my permanent pillion passenger."

She hadn't seen that coming. Andi had always seemed determined to live the life of a bachelor until she died. Taryn made a mental note to bring that up tomorrow when they were both sober. "Come on, man. You've got six months to hunt for your perfect partner. I'm going with or without you, but I'd rather you come, you know that. We'll come back tomorrow night, and I'll follow your lead." Taryn hoped that trail wouldn't take them to the vampy Erin.

"I'll hold you to that." Andi made a shooing motion. "Come on then, lovesick pup."

If she'd had a hand free, Taryn would've punched Andi. Hard. She knew well enough that Taryn had more or less given up on looking for love. Unless you were lucky enough to fall for one of the team like Banjo and Sally, short-term engagements were all any of them could hope for. Unless they were prepared to give up their career and live the traveling life, like their old MC had. But Taryn had no intention of relinquishing her wanderer's lifestyle, especially when it gave rise to meeting someone like Cassandra.

Taryn sauntered toward Cassandra's table with as much casual nonchalance as she could muster, which wasn't much if her racing pulse was anything to go by. The adrenaline rush spiking through her veins surprised her a little, but when she locked eyes with Cassandra again, the surprise turned to comprehension. There was something in the way she held herself that involved more than her looks, as stunning as she was. And it was the way she used her facial features to say more in one second than Taryn could say in ten minutes. Taryn had an overall, and totally unfamiliar, sense of being off-kilter. Going to clubs, meeting new people, taking them back to her hotel or trailer had gotten easier and easier the more time she spent with Andi. And though she hadn't exactly been a slouch in her previous life, her status as a stunt driver usually afforded her an aura of awe and reverence. Fame goggles, Andi called them, and that meant that Taryn had all but forgotten what it was to actually charm someone into her bed.

Andi nudged her forward—Taryn couldn't believe she'd paused to stare—and Taryn placed the tray on Cassandra's table. She handed out the drinks, and they exchanged introductions. It was clear from Rachel's reaction to Andi that Andi wouldn't have to worry about compromising her over-thirty policy. Rachel couldn't have looked less interested, and though she was pleasant enough about meeting them both, she continued to scan the club for whatever she was really looking for. Great. Neither bestie wanted to be there, which could make her conversation with Cassandra suffer. Maybe she should just send Andi off to the vamp set and see how she fared alone.

Taryn took the empty stool beside Cassandra and pulled it even closer before sitting. She rolled up her sleeves then raised her glass. "To meeting interesting new people."

They clinked glasses and said the same words but not with the same feeling as her and Cassandra. At least it sounded like Cassandra meant it. Taryn puffed out a breath and took a sip of her whiskey; she needed to remember how easy it was to talk to women if she simply relaxed and was herself.

"What brings you to our less than fair city?" Cassandra asked.

She took a long sip of mojito and licked her lips, temporarily rendering Taryn mute. Andi kicked her shin under the table.

"How do you know we're not locals?" Taryn prided herself on not standing out like a tourist wherever they went. She'd traveled the country enough to not look out of place almost anywhere.

Cassandra pursed her lips and pointed her straw toward the vamp tables. "If you were, Erin wouldn't have draped herself over you like a winter coat."

Andi snapped her attention to where Cassandra had indicated. "You were in the bathroom three minutes, man."

Taryn waved her off. She didn't want Cassandra thinking she was some kind of player. "She practically jumped on me. And unless she's blind drunk, I bet she's all volume and no content."

"And you're not used to those kinds of approaches at all." Andi chuckled and continued to surreptitiously stare vamp-Erin's way. Maybe she wasn't ready to think about settling down tonight after all.

Cassandra raised her eyebrow. "You certainly have a unique way of letting a woman know you're not interested."

"Unique and not mean?" Taryn asked. "I don't go out of my way to be an asshole, but she just set herself up for that response."

Cassandra looked toward Erin and smiled genuinely. "As you've already astutely deducted, Erin is a few colors short of a rainbow. She tends to hook her company based on her looks rather than her mental acuity. But I've never seen her go home alone, and she keeps coming back, so she must be happy enough."

Cassandra's response wasn't an answer to Taryn's question, much like her comment about Taryn not drinking something fancy was left in the air. "So you think I was mean?"

"No," Cassandra said and placed her hand over Taryn's. "I think you were amusing."

Though Cassandra's hand was chilled from holding her glass, her touch sent a predictable and inevitable fiery thrill up Taryn's arm. She shivered and gooseflesh flashed along her skin. Taryn caught Cassandra's tiny smirk and eyebrow twitch at her reaction.

"What did you say?" Andi asked.

Taryn had been so caught up with staring into Cassandra's eyes, so brown they were almost black in this light, that she'd nearly forgotten they weren't alone. She reluctantly turned her attention to Andi. "Something about turkeys contemplating the meaning of life."

Andi rolled her eyes. "Great, I can imagine the rest. I disagree with Cass. That was mean."

"Do you think they really do? Turkeys, I'm talking about," Rachel said.

"I think anything's possible." Taryn gazed at Cassandra. What would it take to make Cassandra going home with her tonight likely? She couldn't get a handle on whether Cassandra would indulge in sex immediately after meeting someone. But goddamn, she wanted to find out.

"Anything?" Cassandra asked.

"Sure." *Challenge accepted.* "If you really want something to happen, you just have to put it out into the Universe, and the Universe will provide." Taryn was a hundred percent certain that would get an arched eyebrow from Cassandra. She seemed like more of a scientific than spiritual type.

Cassandra gently shoved Taryn's shoulder. "I don't believe that *you* believe that for a second."

"Really? And what makes you think that?"

Cassandra narrowed her eyes and nibbled her bottom lip. "I think that you're someone who isn't afraid of hard work. You're someone who isn't about to let the Universe decide whether or not you achieve something, whether or not you get what—or who—you want."

"Ha!" Andi gave Taryn's back a hard smack. "She's got you all worked out, T." She grinned at Cassandra. "What did you say you were, Cass? A shrink?"

Cassandra's expression made it clear she didn't appreciate Andi shortening her name, but she didn't comment. Nor did she respond with her occupation. Taryn decided not to push for the answer since she was in no hurry to share her career information either. People were always quick to cast judgment on what she did for a living, and it was usually polarizing; they were either impressed or aghast. She was deemed either fantastically brave or incorrigibly stupid. How amazing it must be to fly through the air at four hundred miles per hour! Or, how reckless you are to risk your life for a passing thrill.

Inexplicably, Cassandra's opinion mattered, and Taryn didn't want to be on the negative end of it.

"Is your friend correct? Do I have you worked out?" Cassandra looked directly at her.

Taryn took a small sip of her whiskey. One more slurp, and it'd be gone. Cassandra had only deigned to have their company for one drink, and Taryn had no idea if she'd done enough to secure an extended invitation, or if what she'd done had already guaranteed a swift end to this enjoyable interlude. Well, she was enjoying it if no one else was. In her peripheral vision, she saw Andi sending long glances toward the vampy tables, and Rachel seemed only interested in Cassandra's scintillating contributions. For which, Taryn didn't blame her in the least.

"I think it takes one to know one, Cassandra," Taryn said, feeling her way by the minuscule changes in Cassandra's expressions, "but I also think that would have to be the topic of conversation over dinner in a much quieter environment."

Her response seemed to amuse Cassandra. She sucked on her straw, and Taryn swallowed, unable—and frankly, unwilling—to push away the image of Cassandra's lips on hers.

"Since you seem to be one for unique approaches, is that your way of asking me to dinner?"

Boy, Taryn was enjoying this repartee. "Do you *want* me to ask you to dinner?"

Cassandra carefully placed her drink on a paper coaster and leaned back in her chair. "A safer question then. If the government decided to wipe the earth clean of Sin City, what would be the one thing you'd petition to save?"

Taryn laughed at the absurd but very original question and the way in which Cassandra had chosen not to answer *her* question. She could honestly say she had never been asked something like that in the cold light of day, let alone in the dark, sexy corners of a club. She found it refreshing. "Do I look like someone who fills in petitions and lobbies?"

"Everyone cares about something."

Cassandra had arched her eyebrow in the way Taryn was coming to understand meant she wasn't impressed. She didn't know how many of those Cassandra allowed before bailing on a conversation, so she didn't tell her that there were few things she cared about enough to rouse to action. And she had a feeling that Cassandra was talking about deep and meaningful things, rather than motorbikes and good food. "Fine. If I could only save one thing, it would be the Bellagio Fountains. I'm not one for staying in one place too long in case I grow roots, but I can watch those fountains all night."

Cassie nodded as if she approved, but it wasn't clear which bit she appreciated.

"Do you not have a place you call home?" Cassandra asked.

Taryn shifted on her chair, and she felt the hot bore of Andi's eyes on her. The amusing conversation had shifted to more serious lines, and that had never been part of Andi's teachings. She might've been tempted to go off-book if Andi hadn't been there, but she didn't miss the slight clench of Andi's jaw. Taryn smiled and emptied her glass in one gulp. "Another drink?" Now seemed the right time to figure out whether this might go any further.

Cassandra looked between Taryn and Andi, clearly seriously considering her answer. Rachel leaned close to Cassandra's ear and whispered something impossible to catch. As if in league with the two of them, the DJ cranked the music to ten decibels the wrong side of *perfect for conversation*, and Taryn had a sinking feeling that she'd blown her chance with one of the most fascinating women she'd ever met.

"No."

Cassandra's answer hit like a fall to earth from a failed jump, and Taryn diverted her eyes to the throng of semi-naked bodies on the dance floor. There were plenty of women here who would go back to a hotel room for a few hours of nameless, guiltless sex. Or maybe she would go back alone and service herself while thinking about Cassandra's voice, the way she moved, and the way she expressed herself without words.

"But you could take me out to that dinner date," Cassandra said.

Taryn grinned and snapped her gaze back to Cassandra, whose expression was amused once again. Clearly, she loved to play games with her women. "What kind of place would a woman like you expect to dine at?"

"Certainly nowhere with plastic cutlery if that's what you were hoping to get away with," Cassandra said.

Taryn laughed. "What has given you the impression that I'm cheap?"

Cassandra gestured toward Taryn's legs. "I think you might spend all your money on those jeans Erin loved so much."

Taryn had zero idea what the best restaurant in Las Vegas was right now—everything changed so fast—but she'd find out, and she would get their best table. To hell with what it might cost. *They don't put pockets in shrouds*, her grandmother used to say, and with Taryn's occupation, she could have less time to spend her earnings than she would ever know.

She unlocked her phone and slid it toward Cassandra, who tapped in her digits. Their fingers touched when Cassandra returned Taryn's cell, and she stood. "I'll text you to arrange something for Taco Bell—no cutlery needed at all there."

Taryn got up and dragged Andi away with her, though she was desperate to stay and continue their conversation. She checked her display and smiled at the name with her number.

Cassie. Taryn hadn't blown it after all.

Chapter Four

"Why?" Rachel put her hands on her hips. "That's my burning question. That's all I want to know. Why would you not just drag that hot piece of butch home and ride her all night long? Did you see her arms and chest? She looks like she bench presses cars. How long has it been? Have you lost your confidence? Is that what stopped you? Have you forgotten how you to get on your back? Or your knees?"

"Whoa!" Cassie held up her hand. "I don't think this is the appropriate location for a conversation of this nature. Especially at that volume. Do you?" She gestured to the numerous patrons in the Starbucks, some of whom had blatantly turned to wait for Cassie's answer while others pretended not to listen but were clearly eavesdropping.

"You'd rather I wait until we're in the on-call room? Or on the ER floor?"

"I think I'd rather wait until never, thanks." Cassie avoided the mixed looks of intrigue (from the men), disgust (from the parent with the three young kids), and amusement (from a cute queer person of indeterminable presentation in the corner). Why didn't one of those sinkholes appear when she needed one? "You've adopted an accusatory tone that isn't like you at all."

"My tone is exactly this accusatory whenever you blow a perfectly fine opportunity to get laid," Rachel said, quieter but no less judgmentally. "It's just that you haven't heard it before because you have never acted so inexplicably."

"Bench presses cars? Do you think? I thought she was athletic, not bulky."

"I don't care what label you put on her; her chest looked like it was made of concrete." Rachel nudged her shoulder. "And stop avoiding my question. You know I won't stop until I get a satisfactory answer."

Cassie wasn't sure she *had* a satisfactory answer, other than having work the next morning wasn't conducive to an all-night session with a stud like Taryn, who was very much her type and had seemed on precisely the same page as Cassie regarding the short-term nature of any possible hook-up. She'd been perfect in every way. But Cassie had found herself wanting...to play. "I wanted to make her work for me. She's the kind of person who only has to look at a woman, and she'd come running. I wanted to see if she'd rise to a challenge."

Rachel blew out an exasperated breath. "What if she's only here for the weekend? You've ended up with that ridiculous double shift for Fischer, so you won't be able to go out for dinner. That means you won't be able to come back to work *post-dinner*, barely able to walk, to tell me all about it."

Cassie wrinkled her nose. Damn. She hadn't thought about her lack of weekend when she'd been caught up in the game.

"You didn't think about that, did you?" Rachel rolled her eyes. "You've gone way too long between doses, and that's affected your cognition."

"Then we weren't meant to have sex. Anyway, that kind of flirtation can sometime be more stimulating and satisfying than actually getting down to it."

"If that's what you really think, you've been doing it wrong. Or women have been doing you wrong. Whatever. You better hope she's on a longer vacation, or you're going to have missed out on what was bound to have been *the* most sensational sex you've ever had."

"What makes you think that?" Cassie asked. "How have you determined the quality of the sex Taryn was capable of?" She didn't want to acknowledge the disquieting feeling that Rachel was probably right, which was more disgruntling because Rachel might also be right about Taryn not being around beyond the weekend. Very few Americans came to Vegas for longer than a weekend unless they were there for a conference. Cassie began to root for Taryn being a delegate at the AVN Adult Entertainment Expo currently running at Caesar's Palace.

"Can I take a name?"

Rachel gave her name and placed their order. Cassie paid with her phone, then they moved to the end of the other line to wait.

"It's a standard mathematical equation, actually," Rachel said.

Cassie pulled back her wandering concentration but still checked her phone messages. There were none. Should she expect a phone message or a text? Nobody really called anymore, but she would've liked to have heard Taryn's low, husky voice again. "What is?"

"You asked how I could predict the planet-exploding sex Taryn was capable of. It's applied science."

Cassie smiled. "Do explain."

"Hotness ratio plus intelligence quotient multiplied by sense of humor index. The larger the number, the more impressive the sexual performance." Rachel held her hands up as if she'd just finished explaining the concept of gravity to the world for the first time. "See?"

Cassie fiddled with the cinnamon shaker on the prep table and nodded, affecting as sage an expression as she could offer. "I can't honestly argue with that logic. I'm assuming you have case studies to back up your hypothesis?"

Rachel winked and grinned wickedly. "Many, many case studies—of people from all gender presentations, backgrounds, and cultures."

"Then I definitely can't argue with *that*; I've seen you in action enough times to know your sample size is statistically significant."

Rachel looked pleased with herself. "You know it."

The barista called Rachel's name, and they collected their

drinks and walked back to Cassie's car. Cassie contemplated what it was that had caught her attention in a more engaging way than any other woman she'd spoken to, and then bedded, over the past couple of years. Most likely, it was what she would forever call the turkey conundrum. After hearing such an original riposte to a come-on, Cassie hadn't been able to stop her own response. And it wasn't often she got to come to the rescue of any butch, let alone one as spectacularly handsome as Taryn. She checked her phone one last time before heading back to the hospital for the rest of her shift. Still nothing, but it had been less than twenty-four hours. Someone like Taryn probably had strict guidelines about the minimum time that would have to pass before she contacted a woman. Especially one that had made *her* wait first. Cassie just had to hope it wouldn't be too long or too late for her to accept the dinner date.

The next few hours passed with the usual admissions, none of which were particularly trying. She was taking a restroom break when her phone rang, and she answered it without checking the number.

"Hi, Cassandra. It's Mom."

Cassie closed her eyes and clenched her jaw then looked at herself in the mirror. Rookie error. She'd been far too quick to answer the call in the hope that it would be Taryn. "I'm at work, Mom. I can't talk. What do you need?"

"Why do you automatically assume I need something?" her mom asked. "Can't I just call my daughter without you thinking I want something?"

Because you always need something. Cassie couldn't recall her mother ever calling simply to check up on her, or see how her job was going, or if she'd met anyone new. The usual Mom questions never passed her lips. Or at least they hadn't since Cassie's brother had died. "Of course you can. But I'm on shift, Mom." She glanced at her watch. "I finish in four hours. Can I call you back then?"

The ensuing silence was a predictable precursor for the request

Cassie knew would be the real reason for her mom's call.

"I'm going to be out later. Hopefully. I've got a date, you see."

Another date. Another man her mom hoped to snare and squeeze dry. But she'd *need* something, of course. Would absolutely *have* to have this thing or her life wouldn't be worth living.

"Only my date is in Tucson, and I—"

"Tucson! For a date? Mom, that's a five-hour drive." Cassie pinched the bridge of her nose. She didn't have time for a stress headache. Hadn't she learned enough techniques that she shouldn't be so easily triggered?

"I know how long it will take, Cassandra. I'm old, not stupid."

And there was the "poor me" portion of their conversation. Her mom had a three-point plan every time she called, it seemed. Next up would be the guilt trip. "I know you're not stupid, Mom."

"I just realized that I don't have enough money for gas. My social security doesn't come in for a week, and I had to take the dog for vaccinations this week. Not all of us have six-figure salaries, Cassandra."

A salary for a job she'd worked damned hard to achieve, with no support from her family—what was left of it. "Will a hundred cover you?"

"Gas prices have rocketed, Cassandra."

So she wanted money for more than just gas. "How much do you need, Mom?"

"Three hundred would work for me. I'll pay you back when my check comes through."

Her pager beeped to indicate a new arrival that needed her attention. "Mom, I have to go. I'll put the money in your bank when I hang up."

"No! Put it in my PayPal account, please."

Cassie stretched her neck from side to side to ease the growing tension. So her mom's account was overdrawn, and she didn't want her play money swallowed up. "Sure. I'll do it after I've dealt with this patient."

"Could you do it before, Cassandra? I know how forgetful you can be."

And there was the little dig she ended their exchanges with. *I think you forget I'm still here, Cassandra. I think you forget who raised you, Cassandra. I think you forget how I gave up my dreams to have you, Cassandra.* Yeah, Cassie was super forgetful, but she couldn't forget the sound of her brother's screams on the night of his death. Sometimes, she really wished she could. "Sure, Mom." Of course the potential heart attack or stabbing victim bleeding out could wait while she dealt with her mom's *real* emergency.

Cassie ended the call and made the money transfer as she rushed back to the ER. She held her ID card against the access panel and pushed the door open to see the hospital's medical director, Harold Barr, leaning against the nurses' desk.

"What traffic have you had through the doors so far?" he asked.

"Just the usual for a Saturday afternoon," Rachel said. "Chest pains mostly from indigestion rather than heart attacks, stomach issues generally from over-indulging in the casinos' all-you-can-eat buffets, and contusions from alcohol-related tumbles."

Rachel caught Cassie's eye and blinked twice: their coded signal for "Rescue required."

She slipped her phone back in her pocket and headed toward the desk, ready to deflect Barr's unwanted advances. No matter how many times Rachel shut him down, he kept coming back for more, somehow expecting Rachel's standards to have slipped low enough to entertain him. It wasn't his outer appearance that turned her off—he was quite the handsome man, even Cassie would admit that—it was his inner ugliness Rachel wouldn't accept.

"What brings you down here, Harold?" Cassie asked and smiled.

He looked at her, his lustful gaze crawling over her body like a cluster of spiders.

"What a waste," he muttered.

That was ground-breaking and original. As if she hadn't heard that one before. "The latex glove shipment? Indeed it was." She flashed the back of her hand in his face. "But it's not as if any of us have long nails. The quality wasn't good enough, and everyone was having trouble with them. They weren't protecting anyone from anything." She pulled a pair of gloves from her lab coat pocket and stretched them to twice their length. "You can't cut corners on protective equipment. It puts the lives of our team at risk, and you wouldn't want that, would you?"

"Of course not."

The look in his eyes contradicted his words. He'd done nothing but cut budgets and shave corners to make savings, mostly to justify his phenomenal wage. Of course he'd risk the lives of staff if it saved him money and made him look good to the hospital's board.

"So we can expect a return to our usual supplier then?" Cassie pulled the gloves on and snapped them hard against her skin. She fought against a satisfied smile when he flinched and began to back away from the desk.

"Of course. I got your memo. David was supposed to be dealing with that." He gestured over his shoulder. "I'll go and do that for you now."

"Not for me, Harold for all of us. You wouldn't want a slew of litigation suits for neglectful management, would you?"

His nostrils flared, finally giving away his irritation. "No, Cassie, we—"

"Dr. Kennedy," she said. "Only my friends call me Cassie."

Chapter Five

CASSIE. TARYN LOOKED AT the name on her phone screen. How many times had she opened her contacts and hovered her thumb over "Call Cassie" since last night? Too many. The problem with being off-kilter was that she had no idea *when* she was supposed to call. Or if she was supposed to text. Or WhatsApp. There were too many options, and Taryn didn't know which to choose or when. Would Cassie think she was too desperate if she called the next day? Was it a test to see how interested Taryn really was?

"What is going *on* with you?" Andi gave her a hard shove. "I haven't seen you stare at a screen like that since you discovered lesbian porn on the internet."

"I think you're mistaken. *You're* fascinated with that particular delectation. I've always been happier doing than watching."

"I like watching *and* doing," Andi said and chuckled.

Taryn shook her head at Andi's wicked laugh. The light turned to walk, and they crossed the road into the shade. Their hotel wasn't far from the Cosmos, but the hundred-degree heat made the distance feel interminable. Taryn shoved her phone in her back pocket and pulled her shirt away from her chest, already slick with sweat. Just another two hundred feet, and the cool air of the casino would blow away her discomfort. The Florida heat she'd grown up with was preferable to this dry heat that reached down her throat and sucked the moisture from the inside out, but that was about the only thing she missed about the place her family called home.

They were met at the door by a regular-looking woman in business attire who introduced herself as Polly. "Ms. Parks is looking forward to meeting you both." Polly began to walk along the main casino floor and gestured for them to follow. "She's followed your work for several decades, Ms. Sullivan, and she was thrilled when Ms. Taylor joined you."

Taryn poked Andi in the ribs when she frowned at the timestamp. "You old dog," she whispered.

"Screw you, butthead."

Andi swatted at her, but Taryn darted out of reach easily. "See? So slow."

Andi grimaced. "You'll keep."

Taryn grinned then scanned the place as they continued between two rows of fully occupied poker tables. Barely ten a.m., and every one of them had an alcoholic drink beside them. She could smell smoke and despair even though the new carpet scent was still relatively strong. Taryn regularly gambled with her life, but that was with the backing of genius mathematicians and incredibly talented engineers. This kind of betting was rigged for the house to win, and luck could be a cruel lady.

Polly stopped at a wall covered with tropical flowers, and Taryn exchanged a questioning look with Andi. Polly looked upward, and Taryn followed her gaze to a discreet camera tucked beneath the head of a bird of paradise. She wanted to ignore the second reminder of home, but it made her realize that it'd been a while since she'd spoken to her brother, never mind her parents. Maybe she'd call him later.

A cleverly concealed door opened to reveal an elevator, and Polly beckoned them in.

"That's neat," Taryn said as she rested against one of the four bamboo seats inside.

"Ms. Parks insists on privacy and discretion," Polly said. "There are a lot of unusual security features in these buildings, and many of them are of a similar design to government locations."

Taryn raised her eyebrow and frowned at Andi, who simply rolled her eyes and looked at Polly. The casino floor had to be secure, sure, but Pentagon-style security for the offices seemed excessive. Taryn didn't like this residency idea much; maybe she was just looking for faults and weird shit she could use to dissuade Andi from going through with this. The multi-million dollar offer on the table meant that Andi was probably prepared to ignore all manner of faults and weirdness.

The LCD display on the wall zoomed from zero to sixty-nine in a matter of seconds.

"Is this the top of the hotel?" Andi asked.

Polly nodded. "And this is currently the tallest hotel in Las Vegas."

"Is that why it's sixty-nine floors? To beat another hotel?" Taryn asked. If the hotel owner had been a privileged old white man, she might've thought he chose that number for its obvious Sin City-related connotations, but she didn't expect that of a woman. Which was likely highly discriminatory of her. Woman, man, non-binary: sexual innuendo crossed all boundaries.

"Ms. Parks was born in 1969. It's simply a design touch to amuse her."

The fancy doors opened into a vast, open space with wood flooring. The sounds of the casino had disappeared the moment the elevator had closed on the ground floor, but this floor was almost eerily silent. Polly pointed to a shelving unit on the wall, which was neatly lined with around ten rows of slippers that looked like ballet shoes. Each row was marked with a different shoe size.

Polly slipped off her block pumps and took a pair from a lower shelf. "Would you be kind enough to change? Ms. Parks appreciates silence where possible."

Taryn let out a long, slow breath and clenched her jaw. Andi seemed to avoid her gaze and swapped her Vans without question. This was getting stranger by the second. Why was it unimaginable wealth invariably came with unimaginable foibles? Was there a giant company somewhere responsible for inventing the most unusual habits just for stupidly rich people to adopt?

When she didn't take a pair from the shelves, Polly touched her forearm gently.

"I know it must seem a little eccentric, Ms. Taylor, but how boring would the world be if we were all carbon copies of each other?"

Taryn rubbed her hand across the back of her recently cropped hair. *When in Rome...* It wasn't like she and Andi hadn't done more bizarre things in far-flung places across the world.

Andi took Taryn's size from the racks and shoved them at her chest with a "don't mess this up" kind of look. Andi's apparent eagerness to seal this deal didn't sit right, but she hadn't admitted anything other than wanting a big payday for the team. With this and Andi's declaration last night about settling down, Taryn was beginning to wonder if Andi was having some sort of existential mid-life crisis.

She exchanged her kicks reluctantly and gave a childish grunt before following Polly across the wide expanse of nothingness—very quietly—to a set of huge iron doors with a lion's head door knocker the size of Taryn's head. Polly looked upward again. This time, the camera was hidden in a bundle of bamboo sticks protruding from the ceiling.

The doors opened outward with a soft hiss, and the sight inside took Taryn's breath away. Now *this* she could get on board with. The room was about eight hundred square feet, and the entire floor, ceiling, walls, and windows were *glass*... That was beyond freaking unusual.

"Andi Sullivan and Taryn Taylor, Ms. Parks," Polly said.

Taryn and Andi stepped onto the glass floor without hesitation, and they both looked out the windows to the tiny tableau of life playing out far below them, like Lilliputians. "I've never wanted an office, but if I ever changed my mind, this would be *exactly* what I want," she whispered as she looked around and took in the space. And that's almost all it was: space. In the center of the office, perpendicular to the wide wall of front-facing windows, there was a large wooden desk with a view across the desert to Red Rock Canyon. But it wasn't the typical old-man, power-hungry mahogany desk; it looked like it had been created from the largest piece of driftwood ever collected. It had so many curves, knots, and features that Taryn wanted to get on her knees and run her hands all over it. That reaction was generally reserved for motorbikes and women, in that order.

And behind the desk...

Taryn was well-versed in what it would take to be Andi's perfect woman—she'd been her wingwoman long enough to have seen Andi's many, many attempts at finding her. Long, auburn hair; brown eyes; tan skin; bigger than average breasts; tall but still a couple of inches shorter than Andi's 5'10"; intelligent; sophisticated; good-looking; successful in her own right; self-assured; oozing confidence; fit and curvy—not skin and bone... Taryn could go on.

By some alchemy, it appeared that every single one of Andi's desired traits had been used to birth Ms. Parks. Andi had never mentioned settling down until last night. And she'd never talked about a resident show until a week ago. But now, standing in this insanely unique and breathtaking office, *everything* fell into place. Taryn threw Andi a sidelong glance to tell her she was on to her tricks, but Andi's gaze was transfixed on the simply stunning woman rising from behind her desk to greet them. They'd be talking about this later, but for now, Taryn resolved to remain open-minded.

Ms. Parks crossed the room because apparently, Andi's ability to move her legs had been suspended along with her ability to speak. Or maybe she'd stayed in place just to watch Ms. Parks effectively glide on air. Even without pumps, her walk was all sashay and sexiness. Taryn could practically see Andi melting into a puddle of butch appreciation and adoration. Taryn would have to be responsible for any negotiating, apparently.

Taryn moved to hold out her hand, but Andi suddenly jerked into action and stepped forward, her own hand thrust out. Taryn pressed her lips together to suppress her laugh when Andi seemed to do a little bow.

"Thank you for coming so soon after your last show," Ms. Parks said. "Which was spectacular, as always, but that final stunt onto the boat," she turned to Taryn, "was your best yet."

Her voice was honey and feathers, her expression open and inviting. Taryn could almost see herself falling at her feet even if she hadn't been nearly two decades older than her. That might be an age gap she could ignore for a woman quite so alluring. Taryn took her hand and shook it gently. Ms. Parks' skin was softer than the most sensuous mix of suede and silk. Taryn held on longer than she perhaps should have, but she'd caught Andi's nostrils flare at the prolonged contact and chose to poke the bear. If she was going to get Taryn here on false pretenses, then she deserved to be messed with.

Taryn did a little bow of her own and gave Ms. Parks her most luminescent grin. "That's really nice of you to say. We're all only as good as our last stunt." She glanced at Andi and quirked her eyebrow. Andi hadn't been an active part of their last show due to an injury sustained when they were practicing a trick with both of them on the same bike. Andi's nostrils flared so wide, Taryn thought flames might emerge from them.

She released Ms. Parks' hand and stepped back. "This office is amazing. Can I ask what your motivation was?"

She gestured to the ceiling. "I've never liked the idea of being trapped in an office but the business demands it. This way, I still feel close to nature and not enclosed. Would you like something to drink? You both look hot," Ms. Parks said with an infinitesimal twitch of her lips.

Taryn couldn't help her own twitch elsewhere in response, but she dismissed it quickly. God only knew the effect Ms. Parks was having on Andi. "Mineral water would be great, thanks."

"Same for me, please," Andi said.

Ms. Parks glanced around them to Polly. "Polly, would you mind?"

"Of course, Ms. Parks." Polly excused herself, and the doors hushed shut behind her.

"Please, sit." She returned to her desk, and they followed her to the oversized armchairs positioned on the opposite side of her desk.

Taryn hadn't been in many offices, but she knew that standard practice was to place the desk between the occupant and their visitors as a symbol of power. This way, there was nothing between Ms. Parks and them other than the obvious sexual energy radiating from Andi. Taryn might not like this idea of a residency, but she was definitely warming to Ms. Parks and would like to get to know her. Not in the same way Andi wanted to, though she wouldn't reveal that to Andi just yet—she still had to pay for dragging Taryn here under false pretenses. If they had a different relationship, Taryn might be offended that Andi hadn't felt comfortable enough to talk about the real reason she wanted this gig. But Taryn knew that Andi herself would probably be struggling with the real reason, and until she'd reconciled herself with it, there'd be no way she could talk to anyone about it, even Taryn. They were kindred spirits that way, which was probably why they'd established such a quick and easy friendship from the start.

"Polly said you've been a fan of my work for a long time," Andi said.

Taryn didn't flinch at Andi's deliberate omission. She deserved it after the stunt dig.

"Oh, I have," Ms. Parks said and crossed her legs slowly. "Ever since you were a young rider emulating Evel Knievel's stunts. I thoroughly enjoyed watching you come into your own to create your own show and team."

In her peripheral vision, Taryn saw Andi's jaw slacken at Ms. Parks' deliciously seductive movements. Her ability to combine that with a professional exterior impressed Taryn, and anyone who brought Andi's cockiness down a few levels was already awe-inspiring. No matter how slick and smooth either of them believed themselves to be, it occurred to Taryn they could be undone by the subtle power of an ultra femme. It was a strange coincidence that both she and Andi had met their living versions of kryptonite within twelve hours of each other. *Cassie.* Taryn resisted the urge to check her phone again since she'd set it to do not disturb. She might not be on board with this residency idea, but she wasn't about to be a rude asshole.

"Thank you," Andi said.

Taryn smirked when Andi blushed enough to rival the Vegas heat. Polly re-entered just in time to cool her off with chilled mineral water, which she gave Taryn and Andi before giving Ms. Parks a glass of something sage green. It looked thick enough to plant something in it.

"Thank you, Polly." Ms. Parks took a sip slash chew of her drink and turned back to Andi. "I absolutely must have your team as my first residency at my new hotel." Her dazzling smile lent a certain veracity to her words.

"How many hotels do you have, Ms. Parks?" Taryn asked when Andi didn't respond immediately. Damn, it was taking her a while to regain her composure. Taryn would dine on this for a long time. She couldn't wait to tell Banjo and the rest of the team, though they probably wouldn't believe the great lothario Andi Sullivan could be rendered dumb by anyone.

"Please, call me Bernice. This is my fifth, but it's the first one with enough real estate to be able to create the stadium you need, if that was going to be your next question."

Taryn grinned at her astute assessment. "I *was* wondering why now."

Bernice leaned back in her chair and nodded. "It's something I've been wanting to talk to Andi about for many years, but there hasn't been a suitable area of land available this close to the Strip for a long time."

"I never liked the Excalibur," Andi said. "It always seemed too immature to be in Vegas."

"I agree completely." Bernice rolled her eyes.

Andi leaned forward. "Were you present when they demolished it?"

Bernice matched her motion. *The dance is on*. Taryn relaxed back in her chair to watch while she sipped her exquisite-tasting water.

"Present?" Bernice chuckled. "I pushed the detonator. I would've laid some of the explosives if my safety team hadn't deemed it too dangerous." Her eyebrows raised almost imperceptibly.

Andi raised her chin. "And you like danger, I guess, since you've seen so many of our shows?"

"I do."

Taryn wasn't sure she'd be able to get Andi on her feet to get her out of the office. The more Bernice talked, the less solid Andi became. The transformation was almost visual it was so obvious.

"I find your willingness to risk your lives for the benefit of the audience absolutely intoxicating." She shrugged, elegantly, of course. "I believe it's the twenty-first century equivalent of the gladiatorial arena, don't you think? Only the most courageous survive."

Taryn nearly shouted *Bingo!* Pandering to Andi's ego and comparing her to a second century Roman gladiator had Andi puffing out her chest and straightening her back. Her arm muscles strained at the stretchy cotton shirt she wore, and Bernice flicked her gaze appreciatively over the display. Taryn considered leaving them to it; they were clearly going to have sex, and Taryn wasn't sure if any business matters would be concluded until they had.

However, Bernice hadn't realized that Taryn was the one who needed convincing this residency was a good idea, and while this office environment was extremely pleasant, she was still caged indoors, not moving, and not getting anything done. And if Taryn disliked—no, hated—anything, it was wasted time.

"Our team is used to a nomadic life, and we're concerned that a six-month residency might make them soft and sloppy," Taryn said, hoping her words doused the fire enough to get back to topic. "Do you have any thoughts on that?"

Andi shot her an irritated look but then seemed to relax. She knew damn well Taryn had reservations, and that's exactly why Andi had asked Taryn to come with her.

"I can easily arrange for the concerned members of your team to talk with the Cirque du Soleil performers from any of the six resident shows in Vegas." Bernice smiled sweetly. "They had similar concerns before they settled into their own rhythm. I believe their newly found financial stability diluted their fears. There are several hundred Cirque artists living their lives quite happily here." She paused to take another chew of her drink. "And I take safety extremely seriously. While I adore the illusion of wild and risky stunts, I know how important a competent safety team is. I would be more than happy to finance a large safety team, recruited by you, of course, to ensure the health and well-being of your artists." She looked pointedly at Taryn. "And that would include their mental health."

Bernice was so damned likeable. She was offering twice the regular pay plus bonuses and healthcare. The schedule was favorable and not too demanding if they took on a few more riders, or "artists," as Bernice had called them. She'd penciled in regular dark days for the team to take breaks. She was offering a plot of land just outside the main hub of the city for them to set up base, as well as providing condos in the hotel for the management team, if they wanted them. Taryn was the only one who had reservations. Everyone else was a hundred percent behind Andi's proposal. Taryn was self-aware enough to know her reluctance was personal and had nothing to do with the business side of this offer. She'd left home and everything she knew behind in order to travel the world, to roll like a stone and gather no moss. The thought of staying anywhere longer than two weeks made her incredibly uncomfortable, and she wasn't certain exactly why. Six months might not seem like long to most people, but time was a slippery mistress, escaping through cracks of inaction and complacency. Taryn's desire to achieve, to live, to dance, to squeeze every last drop of life from every single moment of her existence sat in direct contradiction to plopping down in Vegas for twenty-six weeks and *settling*. One hundred and eighty-two days. She wasn't about to do the rest of the math, but that was a lot of hours and a lot of seconds.

"What do you say, T?"

Andi's look of hope and excitement sealed the deal. Who was Taryn to stand in the way of the whole team making some serious money and taking a break from the road? There was potential, she supposed, in having that amount of time to build some serious stunt sets and perfect some awesome set pieces.

Taryn glanced at the ground hundreds of feet below her silly, soft slippers. *Leap, and the net will appear*. Except she'd never wanted a net. The thrill of the unknown rocketed the blood through her veins. But this wasn't just about her. This was about her team, her chosen family. "Let's do it," she said. Relief and gratitude swam in Andi's eyes—along with a hint of tears? What the hell was happening? It was like the earth was changing course. *Fuck it. Let the chips fall*.

Chapter Six

"INCOMING FROM THE RUN show. Compound fracture, right leg," Henri, one of Cassie's favorite paramedics, said as they looked up at her. "Trauma room?"

"Yes, please," she said and indicated for Rachel to follow them.

As Henri wheeled in the groaning acrobat, they smiled at Rachel. "Looked like you were having a good time at Infinite last night. Was that your mom with you?"

Rachel frowned and helped Cassie and Henri transfer the patient to the bed. "Ah, they mean your new stud's best buddy. Not my mom."

"Rachel." Cassie fixed her with a serious expression. Henri's worship of Rachel from afar was cute, but she wasn't about to give it space right now. Nor did she want to discuss her "new stud," particularly since Taryn still hadn't contacted her. "Thank you, Henri. We'll take it from here." She arched her eyebrow at them for good measure.

They grabbed their stretcher and backed away to the double doors. "Good luck, buddy," they said and left.

"Can you tell me your name?" Cassie began to slice through the skin-tight, flesh colored leggings. The intricate design disappeared around the wound, soaked in scarlet blood.

The patient grunted. "Edison...Wisener."

"Okay, Edison, do you know how much you weigh?" Cassie visually measured his wound to be around two and a half inches.

"A hundred and twenty-six pounds," he said around puffs of pained breaths.

"Rachel, 285mg of gantamicin, 2g of cefazolin on the IV, and

15mg of morphine."

"No contamination?" Rachel opened the cabinet to retrieve the regimen.

"No. Everything looks clean." Cassie glanced up from his protruding ankle. "What happened?"

"I lost my grip on the wire mid-air in the final scene and landed awkwardly at speed." He clenched his jaw when Rachel inserted the IV into his arm. "I've landed worse than that a hundred times and only got a sprain."

"Repetitive use and trauma can weaken the bone," Cassie said to herself more than to Edison.

His breathing slowed as the painkiller kicked in. "How long will it be before I can get back to training?"

Cassie almost laughed at how comically wide Rachel's eyes opened. "I have no idea, I'm afraid. I need to make sure you and your leg are safe first. We'll get the orthopedic surgeon to look at you, and they will be able to advise if any bone reconstruction is necessary. After that, you'll have a period of rehabilitation. You can't rush any of it." She inspected the three-inch wound and tilted her head slightly. It didn't look like he would need much skin or soft tissue reconstruction, though that wasn't her area of expertise so she wasn't about to give him any indication of how long his recovery might take. "But you shouldn't be thinking about performing again just yet."

Edison grabbed her wrist. "You don't understand, doc. I have to get back on stage. It's my life. Thousands of people depend on me."

She patted his hand and smiled. Rachel uncurled his fingers and placed his hand back at his side while Cassie began to stabilize the fracture. People depended on doctors and nurses like her and Rachel; they didn't depend on frivolous circus performers. And she really couldn't understand why any of them did what they did anyway. She'd been on shift when the Ka fatality happened. And even though Cassie didn't treat that acrobat because she never made it to the hospital, Cassie felt the loss of life was senseless and avoidable. It seemed to her that the audience paying for these shows almost hoped accidents would happen, and that pushed the performers to do even more daring and risky stunts. Over the years, she'd treated quite a few of the Cirque team from the various resident shows. She didn't deny that they seemed to be responsible and took their preparations and performances seriously, but Cassie couldn't help but see it as a lack of respect for life.

She completed her work, told Rachel to page the on-call orthopedic surgeon, and exited the trauma room.

"Time to go home, Dr. Kennedy."

Nurse Dinah tapped her watch just as Dr. Hinton entered the ER, rubbing his gut and looking like he wanted to be anywhere else but there.

"Too many burgers?" Cassie asked.

He nodded. "Burgers. Cake. Hot dogs. Chips and dip. And soda, of course, because, well... here." He gestured around the ER then covered his mouth like he might be sick. "My metabolism isn't as bulletproof as it once was."

"Amen to that," Dinah said. "Getting old sucks."

Cassie rubbed Dinah's shoulder. "Pah, you're not old."

"Old enough to be your mom, child," she said and winked. "Now get out of here and get some rest so you're fresh for tomorrow's dire and dying."

Cassie smiled and gave Dinah a hug before leaving. She'd gladly have taken Dinah as her mom. Dinah was always talking about her children and grandchildren as if their existence powered the sun. What would it be like to have that kind of relationship?

She went into the doctor's lounge to change and thought about her mom and how her date was going. If she knew her mom at all, she'd already be testing out the springs on her date's mattress. She shuddered at the thought and quickly redressed.

She made her way through the quiet back corridor and headed

into the steady warmth of the Vegas evening heat. The fog of hundreds of spent fireworks hung in the air. It somehow made her hungry and reminded her that she hadn't eaten since breakfast over sixteen hours ago. A little exercise and a bowl of Singapore noodles sounded like the perfect end to the day, though it'd be the start of tomorrow by the time she got home.

As she walked to her car, she pulled her phone from her bag to place her pick-up order. A text from an unknown number had come in. *Taryn?* The thrill of anticipation made her wait until she'd gotten into her car and locked the doors before opening the message.

Hey, Cassie. It's Taryn. We met at Infinite last night. I'm hungry— are you free for dinner?

She was hungry too, but there was no way she was going to meet up with someone now. Cassie checked the time to see Taryn had sent it four hours ago. It was too late anyway, and she was due back at the hospital in less than eight hours. She quickly placed her food order, fixed her phone to the dash and started the car, trying to temper her immediate desire to call. There was no doubt that Taryn would still be up. No one came to Vegas for early nights and cocoa.

Cassie joined the steady flow of traffic to head home. Excitement fluttered in her stomach like a horde of butterflies. She'd played it so cool at the club, but that wasn't really her style. If she liked someone enough to sleep with them, she let them know and she took them home. No games. Simple. And simple had worked well for her. She got her itch scratched, and her loneliness would recede into the shadows for a while. But Taryn hadn't scratched an itch as much as caused a different one; one which Cassie wanted to explore for however long Taryn might be in town. She just had to hope that Rachel was wrong, and Taryn was here for more than a moment.

At the stop light, she hit call and relaxed back in her seat. Taryn probably wouldn't hear it over the music in whatever club, casino, or show she was in, but the call would register, and she'd know that Cassie was hungry too.

"Hi."

Taryn sounded surprised, and as Cassie had predicted, loud music thumped steadily in the background. "Hi. I just finished work and saw your text. I thought I may as well call."

"I'm glad you did. Uh, I guess it's a little late for dinner?"

Cassie liked the hopeful sound in Taryn's voice. "As it happens, I do have to eat, but no, I can't come for dinner tonight. Have I missed your window of opportunity? Are you heading home tomorrow?"

"No," Taryn said quickly. "It looks like I'm going to be in town for a while."

"Ah, so there's no rush for dinner then?" The light changed, and Cassie took a left so she could pick up her noodles from Chang's.

"I didn't say that."

The background music hitched up a few decibels before receding again. "Sounds like you're at a club. Call me Monday."

"No, no. I mean, yes, I'm at a club, but I can still talk. If you want."

Cassie hadn't expected the sweet hesitancy from a woman like Taryn. She'd been slick and polished, and she was the kind of red-hot lesbian who would never have to go home alone. Surely she'd be on the prowl tonight; a possible dinner date with Cassie hadn't been a promise of exclusivity by any means. "Are you sure?"

"I'm sure. I want to. Let me find a quiet spot, and I'll call you back—on video."

Cassie angled her rear-view mirror to inspect herself. She looked surprisingly good after a twelve-hour shift. "Give me fifteen minutes to get home."

"Okay."

Taryn ended the call, and Cassie pulled up outside her favorite carry-out place. Yan waved through the window and held up her bag of food before making his way out to her car. She dropped the window. "You're a superstar, Yan," she said, taking the bag and giving him a twenty-dollar tip.

"You spoil me, Cassie."

She smiled. "And you spoil me with your curb service."

"Only the best for our favorite doctor." He squatted on the pavement. "Have you met a nice lady to take care of you yet? I guess not, or this order would be for two, huh?"

His eyes crinkled, showing his age and his kindness. His genuine smile never failed to cheer her spirits, which could be hard after some of her shifts. "I meet lots of nice ladies."

He shook his head. "Your patients don't count, Cassie."

She glanced at her phone, aware that Taryn would be calling back soon. "I'm waiting for a call from someone I met last night. Does that count?"

"That depends. Is she going to pamper you like the queen you are?"

Cassie smiled widely. "You're such a charmer, Yan. If only you weren't married—"

"Or a man. Or old enough to be your grandfather." He stood up and patted the roof of her car.

"You're in better shape than most thirty-year-olds." And she wasn't flattering him. She'd seen him at the park doing pull-ups and handstand push-ups like an Olympian.

He gestured back to his restaurant, where his wife, Jade-Lai, smiled and waved. "That's because I've had a *very* nice lady looking after me since I was sixteen."

"I can only be envious, Yan. Give Jade-Lai my love."

He stepped back and pressed his palms together. "Zàijiàn."

"Yep, see you soon," she said and headed home, as eager to get back for Taryn's call as she was to dig into Yan's special noodles.

A few minutes later, she was at home and in the bathroom adjusting her hair and adding a little extra makeup. Though it had been ambiently dark at the club, she'd been wearing full makeup, and that was something akin to a suit of armor for a knight, a literal mask to separate her doctor persona from her club persona. There had been mornings after the nights before, but those women still hadn't seen her without makeup. *Ever*. Likely the last person who had was her mom, and she'd impressed upon her that being seen without "a full face on" wasn't advisable until at least a year into a relationship. She put no stock in her mom's advice, but since Cassie's engagements didn't last beyond one night, let alone one year, she hadn't yet had the opportunity to ignore it.

Still, a little extra makeup to face Taryn was a layer of protection she wanted tonight. She couldn't place her finger on why that was, and she didn't have the luxury of time to analyze it, so she headed to the kitchen to pour a glass of wine to accompany her meal. Yan had included chopsticks, as usual, and she decided to eat from the carton and not dirty a plate. Good for the environment, she figured. Cassie dropped onto her couch, angled her phone on the coffee table, and took her first bite of food. The flavors exploded on her tongue, and she moaned quietly. Why cook when she had some of the best chefs in the world available by app?

She was halfway down the box, eating way too fast to avoid heartburn, when her phone rang. She leaned over and hit accept before tucking her legs under her butt and relaxing into her chair. Taryn's face filled most of the screen, but Cassie could tell she was in the Bellagio from the Chihuly glass flowers on the ceiling. "Classy place. Is that where you're staying?"

Taryn shook her head. "We were here for the show and stayed on in the casino to play some poker."

"We?" Her question surprised her. What did it matter who Taryn was out with?

"Me and Andi, and Banjo, and Fig—"

Cassie laughed. "Are you just making names up?"

Taryn shook her head and grinned. "I understand why you'd think that, but no. For reasons I have yet to divine, a lot of my friends have bizarre monikers."

Her smile was TV-perfect, but this close to the screen, Cassie noticed she had a small scar at the top left of her slightly crooked nose. She could be forgiven for not seeing it last night, but she didn't want to stop studying it now that she *had* spotted it.

"You've noticed my war wound, haven't you?" Taryn touched her nose.

Cassie's interest had clearly been none too subtle. "Sorry. Was I that obvious?"

"Well, your eyes narrowed and your brow furrowed like you'd seen something incredibly ugly. And you didn't look at me like that last night, so I'm assuming the dark club favored my good side." Taryn covered her nose and part of her face with her hand. "I could zip down to the Venetian and buy a carnival mask to cover it up if I'm putting you off your food."

"Oh my god, no. I didn't mean it like that." Though she had no doubt that Taryn would look insanely hot in full carnival garb at a masquerade ball.

"Phew. I thought me and my ugly mug had blown it again."

Taryn's smile grew wider, and her laugh lines deepened. Cassie's breath caught at the sight of such a genuine expression. She enjoyed life, but she couldn't honestly say she'd ever laughed like that. "You don't actually believe that, do you?" She knew only too well how people used humor to disguise chinks in their self-belief. It had been her go-to coping method all through her college scholarship.

"Of course not," Taryn said and wiggled her eyebrows. "I'm fantastically handsome, and my scar only adds to my overall ruggedness *and* adds a touch of mystique."

"Handsome but not humble." Their verbal sparring picked up where they'd stopped at the club, although Taryn had her on the back foot this time. Cassie liked it both ways and instinctively drew the comparison that their sex would be equally fun.

"You think I'm handsome," Taryn said in a sing-song voice. Then she brought a huge novelty glass into view and sucked a bright red drink through a curly straw.

Cassie had to stop herself from asking if Taryn wanted some late-night company. She might've been the one to suggest dinner, but now Cassie was the one wanting to skip straight to dessert. "That's a very... interesting drink you've got there."

Taryn wrinkled her nose. "I hope you're not someone who likes to label and box people. An innocent and naïve fancy cocktail doesn't care whether I'm butch, femme, aromantic, gender-fluid, or a giraffe, you know?"

Cassie took Taryn's playful grin and dancing eyebrows to indicate that she wasn't being serious. "Not at all. I'm fond of my box, but I don't seek to do that to anyone else."

"What's in your box?"

"I've got stilettos, and lipstick, and fluffy pillows, and there's always a cute and handsome pretty boi opening all my doors. I'm quite comfortable here, thank you."

Taryn shook her head slowly, and her eyes half-lidded. "You're funny. Beautiful, and very funny. It's a winning combo."

Cassie's body responded to the huskiness of Taryn's voice and her unmistakable expression of desire. She adjusted her position on the couch, but that didn't stop the insistent throbbing between her legs. "Speaking of winning, do you need to get back to your strangely named friends at the poker table?"

Taryn pouted. "Are you bored already?"

"Only a little, but I'm happy to keep on talking just so that I can look at your *almost* perfect face." Cassie winked and assumed Taryn was happy to continue their conversation. "How did you do it?"

"Mostly genes—"

"The scar, smartass. How did you get your scar?"

"High school volleyball. It was a championship game—"

"Who did you play for?" Cassie didn't follow high school volleyball, of course, but she had the urge to do a little light stalking and quite liked the idea of seeing what eighteen-year-old Taryn looked like.

"Western Christian. But don't hold that against me; it was a lifetime ago, and I had no choice." Taryn waved her hand at the screen and took another long suck on her cocktail. "Anyway, this giant girl on the Gulliver Prep team—I swear she was in her twenties—goes up to spike what would've been the winning point, but I jumped up and got my face in the way instead of my hands. Incidentally, I was close to making the Olympic team that year."

"Close only counts in horseshoes and hand grenades," Cassie said even though she was dutifully impressed. She had never been athletic, but she admired those who were. And while sports had never been her thing, teasing Taryn was better than any sport she'd ever tried.

"Ouch. First, you call me ugly and now you're calling me a failure. Is your treat 'em mean and keep 'em keen approach just for me or are you this cool with all your friends?"

"Friend... Is that what you want to be?"

"I thought I'd already cleared that hurdle, *Cassie*."

She tilted her head and nodded. "Was your sacrifice worth it? Did you win?"

Taryn looked smug and raised her chin as if she were about to greet the president. "I lifted the cup that year, yes."

"Then you're not a failure." Cassie smiled, and they were both silent for a moment, looking intently into each other's eyes.

"Aren't you going to eat your food before it gets cold? Or is it sushi?"

Cassie looked down at the half-eaten carton of delicious noodles. Taryn had been so entertaining that she'd completely forgotten it. She raised her chopsticks and motioned to the screen. "Maybe you should get something to eat too, and then we can say we're having dinner."

"No way. I promised you Taco Bell, and I always deliver on my promises." Taryn wagged her finger at Cassie. "Also, you're not getting out of our dinner date that easily. If I don't eat anything, then you can't count this as our dinner date and be done with it."

Cassie frowned. "I'm beginning to think that you have some serious self-esteem issues despite your blatant confidence. Why would you assume I might want to be done with you?"

Taryn shook her head and closed her eyes briefly. "I said 'be done with it,' not with me. You misunderstand me; I can tell you're quite the predator, Miss Cassandra, and I won't be taken advantage of. I have to buy you dinner before you do anything untoward."

Cassie hadn't laughed this much with anyone for a long time, if ever. Not even with Rachel. "Fine. I'll wait to take advantage of you, if you insist." She really didn't want to wait. She glanced at her watch and reminded herself that she had to be back at the hospital in less than seven hours. "As utterly stunning as you are and as uniquely stimulating as this conversation has been, I'm afraid I have to retire to bed."

Taryn rolled her eyes. "Damn it, woman, will you ease up? I told you, I'm not letting you take me to bed until we've been on a real date."

Cassie leaned closer to the phone and arched her eyebrow. "*You* weren't invited," she said and ended the call, thoroughly enjoying Taryn's expression of mock shock. She got up and put her uneaten noodles in the fridge. She saw herself smiling like an idiot in the black gloss door as she closed it. Taryn was a lot of fun, and Cassie was already looking forward to their dinner date almost as much as she was looking forward to getting her into bed... Almost.

Chapter Seven

TARYN PICKED UP HER phone from the bedside table without opening her eyes. After Cassie had playfully hung up on her last night, she'd over-indulged in a few too many brightly colored and highly alcoholic cocktails. The conversation had left her on a high, the likes of which she couldn't rightly say that she'd ever experienced from the mere exchange of words. Great sex always left her on a euphoric high, but it was often short-lived and easily forgotten.

Taryn already had a sneaking feeling that Cassie wouldn't allow herself to be so easily maneuvered into the distant recesses of her memory—even if they never slept together, their verbal banter would sway prettily in her mind like wind chimes. But she was determined to get that dinner date *and* sex, preferably for more than one night. Since she was trapped in Vegas for six months, she might as well spend her downtime with a woman as beguiling as Cassie.

"Answer your phone, goddamnit," Andi called from the living room.

She shook off her musings and looked at the screen, hoping it would be Cassie. It wasn't. Her brother's face invaded the pixels, and her thumb hovered over the decline icon.

"Taryn!"

Andi's exasperated call removed her indecision, and she accepted the call begrudgingly. "Hey, Cinderella. Why are you calling me at this hour?" Taryn asked. "Actually, why are you calling me at all?"

He chuckled. "You better not let Mom hear you call me that. How's my ugly sister?" He poked his finger at the screen. "Still not done anything about your busted nose, I see. Why don't you pop home before your next show? I could squeeze you in for a quick rhinoplasty. It'd make Mom and Dad so happy."

Taryn resisted the urge to touch her slightly crooked nose and smiled, recalling Cassie's fascination with it early this morning. "No. It's too good a conversation piece. And you know how I feel about perfection."

Ralph rolled his eyes. "The desire for perfection paid for your medical degree, sister."

"Which is why I don't use it, *brother*."

"So I can't tell Mom you're finally coming back to join the family business?"

Taryn shook her head. "Why do you ask me that *every time* we talk? You make me want to screen your calls."

"Because Mom insists that I ask you every time I call, and I don't want to lie and tell her that I've asked you if I haven't."

She tutted. "Fine. No, I'm not coming home." She wasn't about to share that she'd been having a mini existential crisis about how fulfilling her current career was and had even been thinking about the degree she hadn't bothered to use. It was just a weird blip, though she couldn't see how a six-month residency was going to help her meandering thoughts. Whatever happened, she would never be using her medical degree to perfect privileged plastic people.

"Where in the world are you at the moment?" he asked and waved his finger to indicate behind her. "That doesn't look like your trashy trailer."

Taryn half-snarled. "My trailer isn't trashy. It's homey."

"Sure." He turned his phone and gave her a little tour of the room he was in. "*This* is homey."

She frowned. "It looks like no one lives there. I bet your cutlery is still shrink-wrapped and your furniture still has the price tags on it."

He flashed an expensive smile. "How would my many late-night callers know how rich I was if I didn't leave the price tags on?"

"I wouldn't imagine you let them stay long enough to care." Which was hypocritical since her constant stream of carnal companions didn't get to spend too much time in her space either. But that wasn't a choice as much as a by-product of her career and lifestyle.

"And I suppose you've settled down with a lovely woman, had three children, and own a Prius."

She raised her eyebrow and put her hand over her heart. "You wound me, brother. I could never have a Prius."

"Because it's electric, and you prefer your vehicles to guzzle gas?"

"Because it's ugly. You know how much I appreciate the lines of a well-designed car, and the Prius does *not* fit into that category by a country mile."

"I know you appreciate them almost as much as you appreciate the lines of a woman."

Taryn shrugged. She couldn't argue with that observation. "As much as I love our little conversations," she glanced at the time on her phone, "especially when I've only had four hours' sleep, did your call have a purpose, or did you just want to irritate me?"

He grinned—the genuine one that made him look like her six-year-old pain-in-the-butt but cute-as-a-button brother—and nodded. "I've got some vacation time, and I thought I might come and see you. It's been a hot minute since we had a big fat steak and some beers together."

Taryn narrowed her eyes. "Who told you?"

He fluttered his eyelashes and feigned an innocent expression. "Who told me what?"

"That I'm in Vegas."

"Are you?" He pressed his hand to his chest. "I had no idea. Remember earlier? I asked you where you were in the world. I had no idea you were in my favorite city."

"Bullshit. Spill, Wreck-It Ralph." She registered his flicker of anger and was only partly ashamed that it made her happy.

"I messed up *one* time," he said. "I'm looking forward to you being menopausal, and then maybe you'll finally forget that."

"Ouch. You shouldn't wish menopause on your worst enemy, brother." Taryn reached for the room's remote control and opened the blinds. She smiled when they cracked open to reveal a bright blue sky. Sunlight streamed in, and she stretched out, feeling like a solar panel ready to recharge. Four hours' sleep was more than enough, and she and Andi had the biggest show of their lives to plan. She didn't have time to lose. But she never did. Who wanted to waste days like today lying in bed alone?

"Can you get me a room for the week in your slick new hotel or not?"

She swung her attention back to him. "Not until you tell me who your spy is."

He frowned and held up his phone. "I don't need a spy. You're all over ZimTak."

Damn Banjo. She always had that phone in her hand, sticking it in everyone's face, too busy capturing the moment to actually *be* in the moment. "The show's already been announced?"

"No. It's mainly been teasers. 'Big news coming soon,' and all that guff. But I recognized the new hotel. I've been wanting to stay there since it was announced."

"Mom and Dad are letting you have a full week's vacation? Is the business faltering?" Taryn didn't want to be a part of it, but that didn't mean she wanted them to fail.

"Far from it. We've never been busier." He shrugged. "The twins and Gary are like Mom and Dad, as you know; they're workaholics. But all work and no play would make my life too gray. I'm taking the whole family's vacation time this year."

"Okay. I'll see what I can do, but no promises."

"You're a superstar, sis. I'll call you when I'm at the airport." He winked and hung up.

Taryn smiled. Of all her siblings, Ralph was the one she could bear spending the most time with. Gary and the twins were carbon copies of their parents in more than just their attitude to the work, but Ralph was the youngest, so he'd been allowed a little more freedom to color outside the lines. They'd even let him have a gap year to travel the world before starting college. She suspected it was because they didn't want him following in her footsteps and leaving the family business altogether, and that they hoped he'd get it out of his system before knuckling down to find his way in the family business. So far, their plan had worked.

Taryn got up and pulled on some sweatpants before heading into the living room. The sun streamed through the floor-to-ceiling windows, and Andi lay flat on her back on the chaise longue, clearly enjoying the heat. "You look like a cat sunning itself."

"I'm quietly roasting." Andi pushed up on her elbows and looked at Taryn. "Everything okay?"

Taryn wagged her finger. "Oh no, you're not avoiding the inquisition any longer." She pushed Andi's legs off the weirdly uncomfortable piece of furniture and sat down on its edge. "You dragged everyone out last night because you knew I wanted to talk, but there's no more escaping."

Andi blew out a breath and flopped back onto the couch. "Fine, *Mom*. What do you want to talk about?"

Taryn punched Andi's thigh. "You know exactly what I want to talk about: the real reason you're making the team stay in one place for a six-month residency."

"*The team* seems happy about this little adventure." Andi looked at her leg but didn't rub it. "Seems to me *you're* the only one unhappy about this gig."

She shrugged. "Sure. Everyone's happy with the remuneration package, especially the health insurance. Chaney's already been to the specialist for dodgy—"

"See? I even got Bernice to include pre-existing conditions."

"And that's great," Taryn said. "But you should've told me the real reason you brought us all here."

Andi pushed up to a sitting position and looked out at the Strip. "And what's the real reason, Columbo?"

"You're showing your age with that reference. And I'd never be seen dead in a rumpled raincoat."

Andi laughed, but she didn't make eye contact. The pieces of the puzzle were starting to form a comprehensive picture: Andi was feeling old. "The other night, you said you were thinking of finding your ideal pillion passenger. I think that you've already identified who that might be, and *that's* why we're here. Bernice." Taryn held up her finger when Andi opened her mouth to speak. "Who, incidentally, I totally approve of. She's perfect for you."

Andi swung around to face Taryn and gave a half sneer. "Seemed like you thought she was perfect for you yesterday."

Taryn chuckled. "I was just fucking with you, because you've fucked with me." She gave Andi a heavy shove. "I thought we were in this together. Why didn't you tell me what was going on in your head?"

Andi rubbed her chin. "Because I'm not sure what's going on in there myself. A lot's been happening lately, and it feels like I haven't had time to think—really think—about any of it. We're always in motion: doing a show, planning a show, or thinking about a new stunt."

"I love that motion. Our hearts have a finite number of beats, buddy, and I want to make sure every one of mine counts for something. You've always been the same; that's why we've made such a great team all these years. What's changed for you?"

"Trig's death hit me harder than I wanted to admit."

Andi's words dropped like a giant rock into a small pond. Taryn swallowed hard and took a second to compose herself. It had been a long time since she'd allowed herself to think about Trig. "I was close to her too." She smiled, thinking of all the stunts the three of them had done together. And in Trig's honor, they hadn't done the triple trio three-wheeler at a show since her death three years ago. "She died doing what she loved, Andi, just like she said she wanted to." Taryn tilted her head slightly. "I mean, she didn't have the audience she would've wanted for her final moments, but that was probably for the best. That would have been an insurance nightmare."

In this business, dark humor was often the only way to deal with tragedies like Trig's, and Andi laughed lightly. "You're not wrong. She liked the spotlight even more than you."

"Hey now—"

"I'm kidding," Andi said. "I know it's about way more than that for you and always has been. And I know Trig going out in a blaze of glory on Route 66 would have been one of her top three favorite ways to die, but I think I'm becoming more aware of my mortality. It's a privilege to grow old that a lot of us in this business don't get."

"Don't you think you're being a bit maudlin?" Taryn bumped her shoulder. She and Andi had indulged in hundreds, maybe thousands of conversations over the years, but they'd never talked about what either of them would do after this. It was as if there was a tacit agreement there would *be* no end, and that they both expected to die in their little circus. "Are you really thinking of retiring?"

"Retiring. Slowing down. Finding someone to share the rest of my life with. All of those things, I think." She pressed her head against the glass, and her breath steamed the window. "But also, none of them. You're partly right; I wanted to meet Bernice. She's been on my radar for a while—her success and power in a male-dominated industry caught my attention years ago. She reached out a couple of months back, and we've been emailing about this business opportunity ever since. But I also just wanted to take my foot off the gas for a few months and get my perspective locked down. I'm not about to do anything spontaneous, and I won't make any life-changing decisions before I talk to you, okay?"

Taryn pulled Andi back from the window and draped her arm over her shoulder. "Buddy, I want you to be happy. If you want my help to figure it out, I'm here for you. And I promise I'll stop bitching about you forcing me to stay."

Andi smiled. "Do you ever wonder what it might be like to settle down?"

"Did you, when you were my age? And that's like asking a wave if it gets tired of crashing against the rocks. This nomadic life is in my bones. I can't imagine becoming a number on a population sign."

"I guess I didn't in my thirties, no. But this isn't in your blood," Andi said. "Your family are generations and generations of doctors and surgeons in Florida. Your parents don't even have passports! And you could be doing amazing things for so many people with your skills. I've always thought you'd leave eventually and go back into medicine."

Taryn resisted the urge to push up from her seat and leave the conversation now that it had gotten heavy. She let go of Andi but pressed her ass into the cushioning and forced herself to remain there. "That was my parents' dream, never mine. You know that," she said, trying to keep the irritation from her voice.

"I'm sorry; that was out of line."

"Asshole." Taryn shoved Andi off the chaise longue and onto her butt.

Andi jumped up and shook her head. "You little butthead; you're gonna pay for that."

Taryn scooted off the edge of her seat and backed around the giant glass coffee table. "Doesn't your arthritis render your threats empty, old woman?"

"I'm never gonna be too old to kick your ass, you young pretender." Andi advanced, a huge grin on her face.

Taryn plucked the head of a rose from the flowers on the table and threw it at Andi's head. "You've got to catch me first." She took off back to her room. She slammed the door and locked it just before Andi launched herself and landed against the hard wood. It shuddered from the force.

"Chicken," Andi yelled.

Stunted Heart

Taryn responded with some convincing clucking between uncontrollable laughter. Her bromance with Andi had been her North Star for so long, Taryn couldn't imagine her not being around. She pushed away from the door and headed for a shower. Nope, Andi wouldn't desert her. They'd spend six months here, and it would clear their heads. Andi could work off her fascination with Bernice, and knowing Andi, that wouldn't take too long. No woman had ever fascinated her as much as a well put-together mass of metal and pile of pistons.

And Taryn? She had Cassie to get to know, and she already couldn't wait. Taryn was certain that their residency would fly by in her company, and then she, Andi, and the rest of the team would get back on the road and back to the life they both loved.

Chapter Eight

"I THINK I KNOW who your mystery woman really is," Rachel said as she scrolled on her phone.

"What are you talking about?" Cassie rolled her eyes. Rachel was a good friend, but her melodrama could be a little tiresome sometimes, and it reminded Cassie how much younger she was. "She's not a mystery woman. I just haven't gotten around to asking her any questions yet." She applied her eyeliner and fluttered her lashes at her reflection. "That's going to change tonight."

"Here she is. Do you want to see?"

"Sure." Cassie focused on the phablet Rachel held out to her. "I thought technology was supposed to get smaller as it got better."

"Small isn't always best." Rachel wiggled her eyebrows and grinned wickedly.

Cassie laughed and waved her away. "Are you certain you're showing me the right picture? Or have you been drinking on the job?" She pointed at the screen. "I don't know where you were looking on Friday night, but you couldn't have seen Taryn at all if you think that's her. Look at all that hair! And the makeup. And that's a *lot* of leather."

"That's because she's a stunt rider." Rachel thrust the phone closer to Cassie. "It's her. Look at her eyes and face shape... And those lips."

She made a noise that sounded like a post-orgasmic contented sigh, and Cassie put her hands over her ears. "Ew. I never want to hear that again."

"Look again. Her name's Taryn Taylor."

"I don't know what Taryn's last name is, but maybe it's just a coincidence. That can't be her." Even as she said it, Cassie didn't believe it. Taryn was an unusual name; it couldn't be a coincidence. When Rachel looked like she might begin stamping her feet like a spoiled child, Cassie took her wrist and pulled the phone into a better viewing position. She didn't think the overhead hospital lights could transform a hot butch into a stunning femme, but they were making it hard to study the image with the intensity Rachel demanded. "Fine. She has similar features and longer hair. Maybe they're sisters."

Rachel wrinkled her nose and pulled her arm away. "Who gives two of their children the same name? I'm telling you; it's her." She tapped the screen a few more times. "I looked at the stunt team's social media, and they're in Vegas. Didn't Taryn say she might be staying longer for work?"

"She did." Cassie popped her makeup back in its pouch and zipped it up before dropping it into her bag.

"And what work is it?"

"I have no idea. We didn't get that far."

"Mm... What about this? Do you recognize her?"

Cassie glanced at her watch, wishing she was running late so she could extract herself from this weirdly interrogative exchange. Unfortunately, her Uber was ten minutes away, so she had plenty of time. She looked at Rachel's phone and saw the older woman who'd been with Taryn at the club. Her arm was draped over Taryn Taylor, and now that Cassie concentrated, there was more than a passing resemblance. "Okay, I see it more now."

"Ha! I told you." Rachel danced a little victory jig. "Ask her where she gets her wigs from. Sara's daughter is about to have chemo, and she wants a recommendation."

"Sara's daughter? She's only fifteen, isn't she?" Cassie asked, and Rachel nodded. Damn cancer had no respect for anyone. "Does she have adequate insurance?"

"The co-pays are expensive, and her cleaner salary can't cover much. So she's attending that new clinic on West Twain Avenue in

Spring Valley. They provide a lot of free and reduced fee care for people in need."

"That sounds amazing. Will you text me the details? I'd like to visit and see if I can help."

Rachel smiled and rubbed Cassie's shoulder. "That's sweet of you, but when do you have enough time to give any away for free?"

She had a busy schedule, like most people, and with regular visits to her mom, her free time was incredibly limited. "Maybe I could make some time."

"If you discover how to make actual time, you'd be a rich woman, and then you could work there for free."

Cassie shrugged. "Let me worry about that and just send me the details, okay? Anyway, how do you know it's a wig and she just hasn't cut her hair short for a change?"

"It's a hunch." She flipped through her phone some more. "Look at this."

Cassie watched Taryn smile at the video camera—yep, it was her Taryn; she'd recognize *that* smile anywhere, and her nose had the same slight bend in it, although Cassie couldn't see a scar. Then she pulled on her helmet and drove to what looked like the far end of a roof. The camera panned out to show where Taryn was headed, and Cassie recognized San Francisco's skyline. Her heart jumped into her mouth as the rest of the video played out, ending with Taryn landing on a *moving* boat. Her stomach roiled, and her heart took up residence in her mouth. She pushed Rachel's hand away. "I've seen enough."

Rachel narrowed her eyes. "You're still going to dinner with her, aren't you?" When Cassie didn't respond immediately, she grasped her by the shoulders. "You're not interviewing your potential wife; you're going for dinner and then you're going to have amazing sex. What she does for a career is irrelevant to your needs. Yes?"

"You're so base," Cassie said and grinned. "But yes, her career is irrelevant."

"Good." She released Cassie's shoulders and patted her ass.

"Now, go get that itch scratched."

Cassie pushed her bag into her locker and headed out of the doctor's lounge to the waiting Uber. She greeted the driver, whose aftershave bordered on overpowering, and shimmied into the back seat.

"Strip traffic is bad tonight. It'll take about twenty minutes," the driver said.

"Thanks for letting me know, but there's no rush." From what she'd learned of Taryn, Cassie decided she wouldn't mind waiting and would probably prefer it just so she could watch Cassie strut toward her in stilettos. She pulled her phone from her purse, googled Taryn Taylor, and began to watch more videos.

When the driver eventually got to Sparrow & Wolf, Cassie pushed open the car door, grateful for some fresh air. The driver's scent had been so strong, it'd almost given her a headache. The restaurant door was opened for her by a boy who didn't look old enough to be out this late, and then she was greeted inside by the maître d'. He gestured behind him, and her eyes settled on Taryn. She smiled, smoothed out her skirt, and prayed the stone-tiled surface would be kind to her heels. She didn't want to be rushed to her own ER or fall inelegantly at Taryn's feet. Cassie wasn't averse to being at Taryn's feet, of course, but she'd want to be there after a slow, seductive crawl down the length of Taryn's body.

From the hungry expression on Taryn's face, Cassie had been right; Taryn did indeed enjoy watching her catwalk-like approach.

Taryn stood and held out her hand. "Are you sure you want to eat here? Taco Bell is only a few minutes away." She looked at Cassie's shoes. "I could carry you if you didn't want to walk in those lethal weapons."

Cassie took Taryn's hand and swept her gaze over her upper body, which was sheathed in a snugly fitting, navy-blue button-down shirt. She couldn't see the chest muscles Rachel had observed, but she did wonder whether Taryn would *actually* be capable of carrying her.

Taryn quirked her eyebrow and folded her sleeve up to her elbow. "Are you checking out my body to see if I can make good on that offer, or are you just objectifying me generally?"

Cassie licked her top lip slowly and deliberately. "Both. I'm multi-tasking."

Taryn shook her head slowly. "You're killing me." She glanced toward the bar. "Can I get you a drink while we wait for our table? Unless of course, you want to skip dinner and get room service."

Cassie perched on the edge of a bar stool. "I'd like a mojito, please."

Taryn got the bartender's attention, and their drinks quickly followed.

"Do you drink anything other than Jack and Coke?" The smell of whiskey had long been a trigger she avoided, but her mom's budget didn't run to the good stuff even if her tastes did. She swallowed the reminder with a taste of her own drink and refocused on Taryn and her sparkling eyes.

"I occasionally drink bright red cocktails." Taryn tilted her head. "Would you rather I drank something else?"

"No," Cassie said, a little too quickly to convince herself. "No. Why would you ask?"

Taryn shrugged. "Maybe I imagined it, but you had a strange look in your eye for a millisecond. I'm sorry; you probably just don't like my shirt. Were you hoping for an evening gown?"

Cassie smiled, which she did a lot around Taryn. Feeling so at ease with someone was a new and unfamiliar experience, but she liked it. A lot. She also wasn't used to someone being able to translate the emotions in her eyes. That was less comforting. "Whiskey has always been a problem in my family." Why not be honest? Like Rachel said, she wasn't interviewing a potential wife and thus having to hold back the unpleasant family history until a year in. "But it's fine, truly. And I love your shirt." She ran her fingers over Taryn's collar then tugged gently on her tie. Her mind took a sharp turn to imagining Taryn naked *but* for the tie. *Yum*. She met

Taryn's gaze and saw undiluted desired reflected in her stunning eyes. Cassie hadn't fully appreciated their color in the club or during their video call, but now she was mere inches away from them, she didn't want to look away from their beauty.

"Ms. Taylor, your table's ready."

"Uh, yeah, that's great." Taryn blinked repeatedly then hopped off her stool and held out her hand again.

Cassie accepted the chivalrous gesture with her best demure smile.

The waiter scooped up their drinks onto a silver platter, but Taryn removed her glass and put it back on the bar. "I don't want that," she said. "I'll order something else upstairs."

Cassie put her hand on Taryn's forearm. "There's no—"

Taryn pressed her finger to Cassie's lips. "There's every need." She winked. "Especially since I'm hoping you'll want to kiss me later."

Touched by Taryn's thoughtfulness, Cassie leaned close to her ear and whispered, "I already want to do far more than kiss you."

Taryn cleared her throat, and a short breath escaped her mouth. "Devil woman," she whispered back hoarsely.

They followed the waiter, took the elevator to the eleventh floor and were seated with a prime view of the Bellagio fountains below. After the waiter had left them with the wine and drinks list, Cassie gestured across the road. "You were serious about those fountains, weren't you?"

Taryn frowned for a moment before she grinned and nodded. "I was. I'm impressed you remembered though."

"Of course I did. It was the weirdest question I've ever asked someone, but weird seemed to be the order of the evening given the turkey conundrum." That, and she'd replayed every moment of the night with varying scenarios, all of which ended up with them in bed.

Taryn's smile widened. "They *are* a conundrum." She looked out the window. "And those *are* spectacular, don't you think?"

Taryn looked back at her with such innocent curiosity and enthusiasm that Cassie couldn't help but agree, even if she hadn't really thought about them that much. "I suppose they are."

Taryn filled two glasses with mineral water and handed one to Cassie. "I think that's one of the problems with staying in one city. You take everything in that place for granted and don't stop to appreciate the beauty you're surrounded by."

"Is that why you don't have a place you call home?"

"I didn't say that."

"But you didn't *not* say it either. In fact, you and your friend got positively squirrelly when I mentioned it. It was quite the conversation killer, as I recall." Cassie eased back in her chair and took the pressure off, though she did enjoy the effect she had on Taryn.

Taryn clasped her hands together and placed them on the table. "Not having a permanent residence freaks a lot of people out." She unfurled her hands and fiddled with the multiple sets of silverware in front of her. "I didn't want to freak you out..."

"What else about you do you think might freak me out?" Cassie asked. "You said you'd be staying in Vegas for work—what is work?" Given that their coming together was purely for sexual release, she shouldn't have been hoping for honesty. But for some reason, she wanted to believe that Taryn wasn't a player who would say anything she thought a woman wanted to hear just to get her naked. She'd been told all manner of nonsense by women in the clubs who had no idea that Cassie didn't care one iota what they did for a living, what relationship they had with their family, or even that she was just an experiment. But she wanted Taryn to tell her the truth. She was having too much fun to have it ruined by being lied to.

"Tell me what you do for a living, and then I'll tell you."

Taryn's eyes twinkled, and Cassie was once again drawn to study them. "Your eyes are beautiful," she said, "and I'm an ER doctor."

Taryn half-choked on the mouthful of water she was swallowing. "Uh—"

Cassie tilted her head. "What's wrong? Fantasy or phobia? I've had both reactions."

"Nothing's wrong." She dabbed the corners of her mouth with her napkin, and then the waiter returned for their order. "Sorry, we haven't looked yet."

Cassie held up her finger for his attention. "If this was the only time we were ever going to come to this restaurant, what would you recommend that we simply must try?"

"Do you have any dietary restrictions?" he asked. They shook their heads. "And how hungry are you?"

A wicked smile twitched at the corners of Cassie's mouth, and she arched her eyebrow. "We don't want anything too filling," Cassie said. She had every intention of having Taryn for dessert.

"In that case, I would recommend our seafood platter."

Taryn looked at Cassie, and she nodded her approval.

"That sounds perfect. I'll have a glass of whatever wine you'd recommend to accompany that dish, please," Taryn said.

After the waiter left, Cassie smiled. "What if the wine he recommends is three hundred dollars a bottle?"

"Then you bolt, and I'll stay to wash dishes all week."

"Which brings us nicely back to your reaction to my career."

"It wasn't your job that had me sputtering. It was the way you combined your compliment with your career, as if telling me I had beautiful eyes was something I heard every day."

"Don't you?"

"No," Taryn said. "People don't tend to pay much attention to my eyes."

"People?" Cassie asked, making a quiet note of the flicker of sadness that accompanied Taryn's response. "Is that your unique way of telling me you're pansexual?"

"I wish you'd let me swallow before you drop your dry one-liners." Taryn chuckled and put down her glass. "Would it be a problem if I *was* pansexual?"

"Of course not. You're here with me right now. Why would I care who you've been with before and who will follow me?"

"You're okay with knowing other *women* will follow you?"

Cassie snorted. "You think I've already fallen in love with you and want exclusive rights to your body? Why don't *women* pay attention to your eyes?" she asked without waiting for a response to her first question, which was vaguely rhetorical anyway.

Taryn rubbed her temples and shook her head. "My brain is going to explode. I can't keep up with you."

Cassie leaned across the table and whispered, "I really hope you can, or this is going to be a short evening."

Taryn ran her hands through her hair. "Why do I feel like you eat bois like me for breakfast?"

"Breakfast, lunch, dinner, and all the snacks in between," Cassie said and wiggled her eyebrows.

"Jesus, you're incorrigible." Taryn held up her hands when Cassie opened her mouth to respond. "Which I love, *obviously*. I've just never met anyone quite so...*everything* before. Okay. Let me talk for just a minute. I'm part of a stunt team, and we've just secured a residency at the Cosmos. *Women* get a bit overexcited at those shows, and when they hang around after to meet me, they don't spend too much time gazing into my eyes. They just want a night with Taryn Taylor, stunt rider. No, I don't think you've fallen in love with me but yes, I *do* think I'll be able to keep up with you in the bedroom. And thank you for noticing my eyes." Taryn leaned back in her chair and blew out a breath.

The waiter returned with a bottle of wine, which he uncorked and then poured a little into Taryn's glass.

"Would you try that for me?"

Cassie held up her hand. "I know nothing about wine, only whether it tastes good to me or not."

"That's enough for me," Taryn said.

"Okay." Cassie took a small swallow and savored it for a

moment. "Very nice."

The waiter poured them a glass each and placed the bottle on the table. "Your food will be but a moment."

"So what's with the wig? Part of hiding the real you?"

Taryn narrowed her eyes. "You knew who I was?"

"I found out tonight. Remember my friend Rachel at the club?" She waited until Taryn nodded. "She saw an article about the new show and recognized you. She couldn't wait to share her amazing discovery." Cassie traced her fingers over Taryn's hand. "So before *you* freak out, no, I didn't know who you were when we met, and I'm not here just to spend a night with 'Taryn Taylor, stunt-rider.'" She put air quotes around the last few words and smiled, waiting for Taryn's reaction. It seemed like she wasn't quite at peace with the adoration she spoke of, which was intriguing and unusual. Taryn was an attractive woman, and she clearly knew it, and yet, she didn't seem entirely comfortable with how that and her apparent fame affected her ability to engage with women.

"You're not a glamorous stalker then?"

Cassie shook her head. So she was going with humor to cover her discomfort. It was far better than a lie.

"I wear a wig to keep my work and personal life separate, like I have two distinct parts of me. A small part, the Taryn that wears a wig, is the stunt personality." She gestured to herself and ran her hand through her hair again. "This is the real me. No wigs. No makeup." She shrugged and gave a little frown. "No mask. Is that too much? I feel like I'm oversharing."

"It isn't too much. It's perfect." Cassie stared into Taryn's eyes for far longer than she should for a one-night stand, but she couldn't help herself. "Rachel showed me your last stunt at Alcatraz," she said. Thinking of something so risky and dangerous pulled her focus from Taryn's ridiculously gorgeous eyes. "If I had a weak heart, it might've finished me off." But instead, her heart raced at the thought that one of those stunts could kill Taryn just as she was beginning to get to know her. And damn it if she didn't like everything she'd already seen. And she couldn't wait to see more. Much more.

"Cassie?"

Cassie snapped to attention. "Sorry, I zoned out for a second."

"Sorry if I'm boring you."

"Not at all. It's just been a harder day than usual." It was only a white lie, since Barr had spent a few hours hanging around the ER trying to schmooze Rachel, who had repeatedly begged for her to intervene. She was more than happy to shoot him down, but she did have to be careful how snippy she was since he was her boss.

"Isn't every day in the ER difficult?"

"Of course. But some days are worse than others." Another difficult call with her mom had been the worst part of her shift. She'd somehow spent the money Cassie had sent a couple of days ago and wanted more. Dealing with her ongoing guilt had wiped her out, and if it had been anything other than this dinner date with Taryn, she would've canceled and headed home for a hot bath and her comfy bed.

The waiter returned to serve their food, and they began to nibble at the giant plateful of food.

"Okay, let's talk about your day. I hear talking about things is supposed to help."

Cassie chuckled and shook her head. She wasn't ready to share that part of her life. Maybe she never would be, not with Taryn. This was all temporary; what would she care about her past? And discussing her alcoholic mom was far from quality pre-pillow talk. "Maybe later. What were you saying?"

Taryn narrowed her eyes but seemed to understand that Cassie didn't want to talk and didn't push.

"Later. Okay."

Taryn folded each of the sleeves of her shirt one more time. Cassie had noted at the club and today that she folded and unfolded them regularly, like it was a habit or a tic. Maybe it could tell Cassie something about Taryn that she hadn't yet learned, but thus far, Taryn had pretty much been an open book. "So what were you saying?"

"I was saying that Andi had thought the National Park Service wouldn't authorize use of the island for this trick, but she pulled it off somehow. Promises and money go a long way in this business."

"You sound rueful." Cassie had observed an indeterminable flicker of emotion in Taryn's words. "Are you tiring of the game?"

Taryn frowned. "It's not a game; it's a career."

Cassie held up her hands. "Sensitive much?"

Taryn exhaled slowly. "It's this residency. A lot of promises have been made to our team. I just hope they'll be delivered."

"Why would you think that they wouldn't? Don't you trust the person you're dealing with?" Cassie hadn't expected the serious turn in their conversation, but she was genuinely interested in the subtext of Taryn's words.

"I want to, but there's a lot of pressure on me and Andi. If the show doesn't get the audiences Bernice is expecting, she could pull the plug, and all those promises are washed away like leaves in a storm."

"I don't know anything about your business, or any business for that matter, but don't you have a contract?"

Taryn shrugged. "Yeah, but people can always wriggle out of contracts, can't they? And there's more than just dreams and promises at stake with this show."

"How so?"

"I think Andi's falling in love with Bernice. If something goes awry with the residency, that could impact their relationship."

Cassie dipped a giant prawn into a rose-colored sauce. "I'm sure if their relationship is strong enough, it can survive something like that. But you seem to be getting ahead of yourself and thinking worst-case scenario. From what I know of you, which isn't a lot, sure, but you seem to be a glass brimming over kind of person. What's making you so pessimistic about this?"

"Andi means a lot to me. She took a chance on me when

everyone else thought I was just flopping around trying to find myself."

"How old were you when you met?"

"Twenty-eight."

Cassie almost choked on her prawn. "Twenty-eight! I thought you were going to say you were fourteen, and she rescued you from the streets."

Taryn rolled her eyes. "Wow, thanks for the understanding."

"Oh, come on. Don't be like that. You have to admit that's amusing." Cassie leaned across the table and placed her hand on Taryn's shoulder. The feel of her hard muscles bunched beneath her shirt initiated a particularly pleasant reaction, and Cassie bit her lower lip. "Sorry. Tell me how Andi took a chance on you."

Taryn pulled back, crossed her arms, and shook her head. "No. All personal information privileges have been revoked."

Cassie arched her eyebrow and gave Taryn a stern expression. Well, as much as she could be stern in the circumstances, but Taryn seemed to respond to her icy demeanor as if it triggered something sexual in her. It was a response Cassie was becoming particularly fond of. Having that kind of effect over a hot butch like Taryn was intoxicating. Her hard exterior relaxed visibly, and she softened like a marshmallow over a campfire. Yes indeed, it was an extremely nice reaction to elicit.

Taryn covered her eyes. "No. Don't bring out the big guns. That's not fair."

Cassie laughed gently. "I'm sure I don't know what you mean," she said and arched her eyebrow even higher when Taryn peeped between her fingers.

Taryn's ensuing moan sent a throb through Cassie's body. How fun it was to get that response without even touching her.

Taryn kept her eyes covered and pointed in Cassie's general direction. "That. The eyebrow thing. It's crazy what it does to me."

"Tell me how Andi saved you, and I promise I won't do it." White lies were okay when it came to flirting, she decided.

"No eyebrow warfare. Promise?"

Cassie crossed her fingers under the table. "Promise."

Taryn dropped her hand and narrowed her eyes. "A lady never lies."

"Ladies always lie," Cassie said. "And so do gentlemen. And so do not-so-gentle persons and all the rainbow of versions in between and beyond."

"But you promised. And you're a doctor. You swore a Hippocratic oath to do no harm."

Cassie's shoulders shook with the laughter she was trying hard to keep inside. "'Eyebrow warfare.' 'Harm.' You're throwing some loaded terms around for a little brow wiggle."

"It's not the size of the wiggle, it's the catastrophic effect said wiggle has on a defenseless woman like me."

"Ha, you're about as defenseless as a lion."

Taryn grinned and played with her hair. "I do like my mane."

"And you like being thought of as king of the jungle too."

Taryn's expression turned serious, and her eyes darkened. "How about I take you to my hotel room, and you can make your own mind up about what I might be king of?"

Cassie throbbed at the husky drop in Taryn's voice. She looked at the seafood platter, barely touched because they hadn't stopped talking to breathe, let alone eat. She raised her hand to get the waiter's attention. "Could we get this to go, please?"

The waiter inclined his head. "Of course," he said and took the plate away.

Taryn remained silent, but the hungry look in her eyes said more than words could cover.

"What? I'm planning on working up quite an appetite over the next few hours," Cassie said.

"A woman after my own heart," Taryn said.

"Not your heart—just your body." Cassie arched her eyebrow and enjoyed Taryn's gulp. Just her body. But maybe not just once. Taryn would be here for a while. What would be the harm in a regular tryst when their chemistry was this explosive?

Chapter Nine

TARYN COULDN'T GET THE door open fast enough. She fumbled the card key, and it dropped to the floor. When she bent over to scoop it up, Cassie grabbed her ass. The strength with which she squeezed surprised Taryn, and she jumped forward, knocking her head against the wall. She scrambled back up and held the plastic card out. "I've got a concussion; you better operate the heavy machinery."

Cassie took the card and pressed her body against Taryn's. "We better get you straight to bed before you collapse."

Taryn wrapped her hand around Cassie's neck and pulled her in, desperate to finally kiss her.

Cassie put her finger between their lips and shook her head. "No public displays of affection."

Taryn stepped aside while Cassie opened the door. "What do you call that grab-ass move?" She held the door open and enjoyed watching Cassie slip past her. Her rear view was almost as alluring as the front.

"That was a necessity," Cassie said and turned around.

"So is this." Taryn closed the door with her foot, swiftly covered the short distance between them, and took Cassie in her arms. She guided her to the wall and crushed her lips to Cassie's.

Cassie dragged her fingernails through Taryn's hair and returned her kiss with a hard and hungry passion that swept through Taryn's body, and she tingled from her lips to her toes.

Cassie pulled away and whispered, "Rach thinks you can bench press cars; does that mean you're strong enough to pick me up?"

Taryn gave a small smile and pressed herself harder against

Cassie's body. "Yeah. Easily."

Cassie wriggled her hands between them, placed them on Taryn's chest, and pushed away. At least she tried to push her away, but Taryn stood firm.

Cassie moaned quietly and pressed her fingers into Taryn's chest. "You're very hard."

"I bet you say that to all the bois," Taryn murmured before she scooped Cassie up in her arms and headed to the bedroom. All that working out was good for more than just her long-term health. Carrying a beautiful woman to her bed was something she'd enjoyed being able to do since she'd started building her body seriously. Likely it was a product of watching so many movies when the guy picks up the beautiful woman. There was just something so primal about it.

Cassie ran her nails along Taryn's neck and kissed the side of her face. "That's a nice view."

Taryn growled at her touch. "Me or the Strip?"

"Both."

Taryn walked across the living room to the floor-to-ceiling windows and looked down at the chaise longue. "I've been wondering what that ridiculous piece of furniture is for. Maybe it's specifically for sex with a view." She wiggled her eyebrows. "Andi will be back in a couple of hours. I'd have to put my tie on the door if that's what you wanted."

Cassie fingered Taryn's tie and shook her head. "I want you to keep this on during sex, so I'll pass."

"I do have a desk close to the window in my room."

Cassie dragged her fingernail over Taryn's bottom lip. "Sex on a desk... Isn't that too cliché?"

Taryn turned from the window and continued to the bedroom. "I love a good cliché." She bounced Cassie in her arms. "Like this, for instance. Carrying a beautiful woman to bed." She kicked open her door and then shoved it closed with her ass. "And maybe one woman's cliché is another woman's fantasy." Taryn moved to the side of the bed and gently lowered Cassie to it. She got on her knees and trailed her fingers from the top of Cassie's foot and along her leg. As tempted as she was to get down to it, she resisted the urge and continued over the edge of Cassie's dress up to her hips. She rested her hand there and looked up at Cassie. Her hair was spread out across the comforter, its dark brown a stark contrast against the snow-white sheets. In the light provided from the glare of the Strip's neon and the soft glow of the bedside lamps, Cassie looked stunning. The rise and fall of her chest was almost hypnotic, and Taryn licked her upper lip, the taste of Cassie's mouth a sweet promise of what the rest of her would taste like.

"Are you my fantasy or am I yours?" Cassie asked and tugged Taryn's tie.

"Both," Taryn said and grinned.

"In that case..." Cassie pushed up and turned ninety degrees on the bed. She pulled her dress up onto her waist and put her heels to either side of Taryn's head. "Dinner was foreplay, handsome." She hooked her finger beneath her thong and pulled it aside, opening herself up. "Show me what you can do with that pretty mouth of yours."

The scent of Cassie's desire hit Taryn's nose, and she swallowed hard. She didn't respond. No more words were needed. She placed her hands on Cassie's hips and pulled her closer, then she tugged Cassie's thong off and dropped it to the floor. Taryn lowered her head and slowly traced her tongue from the bottom to the top of Cassie's sex. Cassie pushed her hips up to meet her, and Taryn eased off. She kissed Cassie's inner thighs and worked her way down to the crease, making sure to blow hot breaths onto Cassie's hardened clit.

"I told you..."

Taryn smiled at the way Cassie no longer controlled her tone. Her husky breathiness just made Taryn want to tease her longer. "You told me what?" she asked, back in the familiar top position for the first time in *any* of their previous encounters.

"No foreplay."

Taryn laughed gently, her lips hovering over Cassie's sex. She was about to respond when Cassie somehow managed to grasp a handful of her short hair and press her closer. Taryn couldn't tease herself anymore, let alone Cassie, and she clamped her mouth around Cassie's clit and began short, firm strokes. Cassie sank back into the bed, so Taryn tried longer, more gentle strokes. Cassie's grip in her hair tightened, and she pushed her hips up into Taryn's face. *There it is.* She kept up the exact pace and pressure in slow circles. Cassie moaned and swore, pressed Taryn in deeper, pushed her hips up harder. Her other hand grabbed one of Taryn's and she squeezed. Their fingers interlocked, and their connection solidified.

Cassie's movements became more rapid, her curses louder until she arched her back and cried out, "Oh God, Taryn."

Taryn continued to suck, and Cassie thrashed on the bed. She wanted every last drop of her pleasure, and she wasn't letting go until she had it. Cassie's breaths got shorter and faster, and she gripped Taryn's hair tighter.

"I can't..."

Sure you can. Taryn didn't let up until Cassie rode another wave of pleasure and cried out Taryn's name again. She could get used to that; the way Cassie rolled it off her tongue made it sound godlike. And while she'd always loved making a woman lose herself in the throes of passion, making a woman like Cassie lose herself was even more exhilarating.

She ran her tongue along the folds of Cassie's lips and savored her sweet taste before she brought her hand down and dragged her finger over Cassie's clit.

Cassie clamped her hand around Taryn's wrist. "Whoa, hotshot. Not so fast." She sat up on the edge of the bed, pushing Taryn gently. She rocked back on her heels and bit her bottom lip, eager for more. Cassie undid Taryn's tie then slowly worked her way down her buttons. She pulled Taryn's shirt from the waistband of her trousers then took the tie and draped it around her neck before pushing Taryn's shirt over her shoulders. Taryn shivered under Cassie's touch, and the soft material of her shirt felt like a full caress as it dropped lower. Cassie leaned closer and helped her tug it from her arms before she tossed it across the room onto an armchair.

Cassie's lips twitched. "No bra?"

Taryn flicked her eyes down to her chest. "No need."

"A wig and padded bra?" she asked.

Taryn nodded, finding that her choices being questioned made her uncomfortable. It was as if her genuine self was being scrutinized, and she was falling short. She didn't want Cassie thinking she was fake. "I provide what the audience wants. That has nothing to do with right now."

Cassie narrowed her eyes and frowned, looking a little baffled. "I know." She ran her fingers across Taryn's cheek and rested one of her long nails on Taryn's bottom lip. "I'm sorry you can't be you out there."

Taryn clenched her jaw and glanced away, unable to bear the personal probing. Invariably, she kept her wig and tank top on with her after-show hook-ups; Cassie's comment made her realize she hadn't had a genuine interaction with a woman since joining Andi and the team. What did that say about her?

Cassie dragged her nail across Taryn's lip, and the direct pull to her core set her on fire and pulled her away from unwanted, meandering thoughts. Cassie was the most interesting woman Taryn had met in an awfully long time, and she wanted to be present for every second of it... And genuinely *her* for every moment too.

"Taryn," Cassie whispered. She reached down and expertly unfastened Taryn's belt with one hand. "I want to be inside you."

Taryn faltered for a millisecond. That was new.

"Is that okay?" Cassie stilled her hand and waited.

Taryn nodded and got to her feet. Cassie's head was crotch height, and Taryn was overcome with a wicked thought about how incredibly sexy Cassie would look from this angle with her lips wrapped around Taryn's silicone shaft. She was more than mildly disappointed that she'd left it in her trailer.

Cassie looked up and arched her eyebrow as she began to open Taryn's trousers. "Something particularly naughty on your mind?"

So Cassie had mind-reading abilities too. Taryn looked down on Cassie's upturned face, unable and unwilling to part with the mental image that had formed. "I'm not sure I should say it out loud."

Cassie drew down Taryn's zipper and pushed her trousers over her hips. Taryn lifted her feet, shuffled out of them, and kicked them away.

"I want to hear it," Cassie said.

She pushed Taryn's shorts down slowly, her nails creating paths of hot need along the length of Taryn's legs. She blew her warm breath toward Taryn's core, and the mere whisper of air made her throb harder. "I was thinking about how beautiful you'd look sucking me off."

Cassie gave a wicked grin. "You don't mean sucking this, do you?" she asked and flicked her finger over Taryn's clit.

Taryn jumped and moaned at her touch then shook her head.

"Say what you mean," Cassie whispered against the hair covering Taryn's sex, before she pressed her lips closer and kissed her clit lightly.

Taryn swallowed hard, trying to concentrate enough to form a sentence, words, something more than silence and longing. Anything.

"Say it," Cassie said, more firmly. She placed her hands on Taryn's hips. "I'm not doing anything else until you tell me *exactly* what you mean."

"I was thinking that I wished I'd packed my dildo. I want to see your mouth wrapped around me, sucking me off." Taryn was simultaneously glad she'd managed to get it out and terrified that it might end the night. Not everyone was into toys or that kind of play.

Cassie stood, and Taryn's heart thudded against her chest. It wasn't something she could roll back and pretend she didn't mean.

"Another time," Cassie whispered.

She moved around Taryn and turned her so that she faced the giant windows. It really was a stunning view, but it had nothing on the beauty of the woman with her. Cassie pushed Taryn's shoulders; the back of her knees hit the bed and buckled, and she flopped onto her back. She looked down at herself then up at Cassie, still clothed, who was looking at her like she hadn't eaten for a week. Taryn only got this naked to shower, and a wall of vulnerability hit home.

"Are you sure you're okay?" Cassie asked. "I don't have to touch you."

Taryn sat up, put her arms around Cassie and drew her down to join her on the bed. The gentle weight of Cassie's body against hers was comforting and settled the nerves that had appeared out of nowhere. "I want you to."

The maroon satin material caressed Taryn's skin as Cassie slipped over to her side. She drew her hand over Taryn's stomach and up to her breasts. Cassie looked deep into Taryn's eyes, searching for permission, and Taryn nodded. Cassie lowered her head and traced her tongue over Taryn's nipple, hardening it with every stroke. Taryn closed her eyes at the sensation. She hadn't realized she even liked that.

While she continued to nibble and lick, Cassie grasped Taryn's other breast and pinched her nipple gently. Taryn bucked her hips and had to stop a giggle. Who knew her little breasts were this responsive?

Cassie stopped what she was doing and looked up. "You're so sexy."

Taryn couldn't hold Cassie's intense gaze, so she let out a soft laugh and dropped her head back onto the bed. "So they say," she said, immediately regretting the flippant remark, which also left her wondering why the hell she was thinking so much. Sex was usually so simple, but there was nothing simple about this encounter. Maybe she should've just kept most of her clothes on, like usual. It was like some sort of invisible barrier had come down when she'd undressed.

Cassie shook her head and arched her eyebrow. "*They* don't see this though, do they?"

No, no. This was too much. Taryn shifted and flipped Cassie onto her back. She caught the hem of Cassie's dress and pulled it up and over her head. She ignored the knowing look in Cassie's eyes as she bent to kiss her. Cassie lifted her head to meet her halfway, and their lips smashed together, hungry and hot, consumed in the passion. Taryn cupped Cassie's breasts in her hands, and Cassie arched and moaned in response, and her desire fed Taryn's desire. Back on top, back in control, Taryn ceased thinking and simply felt. The touch of Cassie's hot skin against hers; the softness of Cassie's lips; the fullness of her breasts; the heat of her pussy against Taryn's thigh as she rode herself against it while they kissed as if it might be the last kiss of their existence. And Taryn relaxed into one of the things she did best: sex. Simple, no-brainer sex.

***

"Is this where you'll be staying while your show is here?" Cassie asked as she traced her nails along the dips and curves of Taryn's stomach.

"Thankfully not. I have an RV." She kissed the top of Cassie's head, and the scent of citrus hit her nostrils. The smell of their all-night sex had faded slightly, but it still hung in the air and made her smile.

Cassie tipped her head up to look at her. "You don't enjoy this kind of luxury?" She fell back onto the vast mattress and sighed contentedly. "What size is this anyway? Emperor queen king gigantic? It's practically the size of my ER."

"I didn't say that." Taryn shifted onto her side and ran her fingers down Cassie's arm. She interlocked their fingers for the briefest of moments then caught what she was doing and extricated herself. She moved her hand onto Cassie's hip instead, a much safer, less intimate option. "But how do you know my RV isn't even more luxurious than this?" She would've motioned around the room, but she was far too entranced with touching Cassie.

"Ah, I see. You have one of those movie star trailers that are just as good as a five-star hotel?"

"Actually, no. It's an eight-year-old Jayco Precept. But it's my little piece of real estate wherever I park it." She tore her gaze from the gentle rise and fall of Cassie's chest and glanced around. "These places are so sterile. They have no personality. If you're lucky, you get some art on the walls and some fancy cushions. But I couldn't stay here for longer than a few nights. I'd miss my stuff."

Cassie turned to face her, and Taryn moved her hand onto the side of Cassie's waist. "What 'stuff?'"

"You know, things I've collected as I've traveled over the years." She shrugged. "I shouldn't spoil the surprise. Half the excitement is in the anticipation."

"There you go with your unique invitations again." Cassie fluttered her eyelashes. "Is that your way of asking for round two?"

Taryn scrunched her nose. "I thought we'd already had round two. And rounds three to seven."

Cassie tapped her nose and laughed. "Cocky much?"

"It's not that I was counting but—"

"Oh, you were counting," Cassie said, her voice husky and low. She tilted her head slightly and gave Taryn one of her special looks. Taryn had already labeled them special because they elicited certain reactions instantly, and she had absolutely no control over them. Nor did she want control. "That's a look that makes me want to start at one all over again." She nibbled on Cassie's finger playfully. "But yeah, if you wanted to, you'd be more than welcome to visit my trailer for an official round two...and however many more rounds you wanted. Unless you've got a strict one-night-only policy." Taryn grinned, but goddamn, if she didn't hope with all that was holy that wasn't the case.

Cassie arched her eyebrow. How could a mere eyebrow twitch make *all* her bits twitch right back in response?

"Even if I did, I'd be tempted to make an exception for you." She bit her bottom lip and shook her head slowly. "Last night was... Well, we can't have you getting more cocky. Suffice it to say, that if time and schedules permit, I accept your invitation."

Taryn sat up to avoid Cassie sensing any disappointment in the vague nature of her response. She wanted to be sure they could make time in their schedules. "I need coffee. Would you like anything?"

"Coffee sounds perfect. Should I get dressed?"

"No!" Taryn cleared her throat. "I mean, no. Not unless you want to. I was going to order room service unless you have to rush off." She jumped off the bed and glanced at the clock hanging over it. As if she needed a reminder of how transient time was right now. Or ever. She should've taken it down.

Cassie didn't smile, but her expression made it clear she was amused. "I don't have to be at work unless they page me in an emergency."

"Did we travel back in time to the 80s? Hospitals still use pagers?"

Cassie stretched back to the table at her side of the bed, and her back arched, forcing her breasts into the air, proud and tempting. Her hips pushed toward the ceiling, and her glistening sex screamed for attention. She didn't take quite as long as Taryn would've liked to retrieve the old-fashioned pager unit she then held aloft.

"Lots of hospitals still use them. The signals get through easier than a cellphone, or something like that." She arched back and replaced it.

Taryn put her hand under her chin and physically pushed her jaw closed, cartoon-like. "You're incredibly flexible."

"BodyBalance."

Taryn swallowed and tried to moisten her sudden case of dry mouth. "What's that?"

"Weren't you ordering coffee and breakfast?"

Taryn smacked her forehead. "It's hard to concentrate when you're pretzeling yourself all over my bed." She picked up the hotel tablet, opened the hotel's restaurant app, and handed it to Cassie. "Order whatever you want. Would you get me a coffee, fresh OJ, and a sesame bagel with cream cheese and salmon? I'm going to freshen up."

"Of course." Cassie took the tablet and propped herself up on the giant, fluffy pillows.

Taryn padded to the bathroom. She closed the door and rested her head against it. Was she in trouble? She went to the sink and splashed ice-cold water on her face and chest, but it did nothing to dampen the fire Cassie had ignited. God, she hadn't had sex like that since she was in her twenties, and while that had been equally as energetic, it had nothing on the intensity of last night's intimacy. Was that where the distinction lay? There was an undeniable tenderness borne from the instant connection they shared. Taryn wasn't about to go all fate and destiny on Cassie, but she hadn't gelled with anyone like this since Andi, and that had never been sexual.

A soft rap on the bathroom door refocused her attention on the here and now.

"Breakfast will be half an hour," Cassie said. "How about I freshen up with you?"

Taryn yanked open the door. "I think that's a great idea," she said and pulled Cassie into her arms, trying not to focus on how good she felt there and instead concentrating on how many times she could make Cassie come in the shower before breakfast.

Chapter Ten

FISCHER'S COMPLETE LOOK OF surprise reminded Cassie of the goldfish she'd briefly had as a kid. The same opening and closing of its mouth and nothing coming out of it other than bubbles.

"Are you sure?" he asked.

His frown deepened the lines on his forehead, making him look older than his thirty-six years, though she supposed his three kids might be mostly responsible for that effect.

"I'm sure," Cassie said and smiled brightly.

"You have plans." His repetition was robot-like. "You never have plans."

She widened her smile, feeling rather pleased with herself that she did indeed have plans. "I know. Isn't it wonderful?" She tapped on the screen and ended the call before Fischer tried guilt-tripping her about how important it was for him to spend time with his family. Cassie was pretty certain he wouldn't have been able to say anything that might change her mind. After spending eighteen solid hours in Taryn's company and, as Rachel had rightly predicted, having *the* most mind-blowing and stamina-sapping sex she'd ever had, she couldn't wait to see Taryn again and repeat the whole experience.

She was about to pop her phone into her bag when Rachel's face appeared on the screen. Cassie checked the time; she had ten minutes before Taryn was due to pick her up, so she accepted the call on speaker.

"Fischer is going bananas because you wouldn't take his shift," Rachel said.

Cassie shrugged. "Let him. This is the first time I've ever said no.

I really don't know how he manages to keep his position. Maybe
he should consider a different career that doesn't keep him away
from his family."

"Ooh, I like this new Cassie. Is Taryn's influence to blame? If it is,
I want to shake her hand personally—if you ever let her out of bed.
I assume that's what your plans include?"

Cassie felt her cheeks flush, and she was glad she wasn't on a
video call. "Why ever would you think that?"

Rachel's dirty laugh echoed around Cassie's kitchen/dining
area. "You're blushing right now, aren't you? I can hear it. When do
I get to see her again?"

Cassie tucked a wisp of hair behind her ears and applied her
lipstick, a new berry color she'd picked up on the way home from
the hospital last night. She'd chosen it specifically with Taryn in
mind but didn't overthink it. She wanted to keep Taryn interested
so she could get a solid supply of salacious sex while Taryn was
around. She wasn't going to be here forever, so Cassie didn't want
to waste any opportunity to jump back into bed with her. This kind
of casual sex didn't come along too often, and she'd have to go
back to stolen nights of passion in between hundreds of hours at
work. Work she loved, she reminded herself. Work she was driven
to do to make up for the death of her brother.

"Cassie? Are you still there?"

Cassie pushed the intrusive thoughts out of her head. "Yes,
sorry. Why do you want to see her again? You met her once, and
I'm not sharing, if that's what you had in mind."

"Pah." Rachel snorted. "You know I like my lovers curvy and
pretty, and while Taryn does look great in a wig, you said her body
was all hard and flat, and that's not for me. No, I just thought it might
be nice for us all to go out and get to know each other properly."

Cassie raised her eyebrows. "I'm still not getting it. Why do you
need to get to know her?"

Rachel groaned loudly. "For a doctor, you can be incredibly
dense sometimes. I'm your best friend, and Taryn is your new

girlfriend. I need to make sure that she's worthy of you."

"Not my girlfriend on two counts. One being we're just fucking and the second being she's a grown woman, not a girl." Cassie patted a tissue to her lips and pouted at herself in the mirror. Yep, that would be sure to get Taryn hot and horny. "So there's no need to see if she's 'worthy' of me. She's fantastic in bed, and I'm going back for as much as I can get while she's in town. It's that simple." And Cassie also wanted to get on the other side of an orgasm. She wanted to draw the pleasure out of Taryn and witness what she looked like on the receiving end in the throes of passion. A pillow queen Cassie was not.

"Oh," Rachel said.

"What do you mean by 'oh' in that surprised tone of voice?"

"Nothing, it seems. Except we've had plenty of candid conversations about your conquests, and I've never seen you light up quite like you did when you were telling me about Taryn."

Cassie shook her head. "*You'd* light up if you had more orgasms in six hours than you'd had in six months too." She couldn't ignore that their conversation had been intensely stimulating too, but it had all been a lead-up to the sex, nothing more.

"Mm, okay."

Cassie's phone vibrated to indicate another call. She murmured her disappointment when she saw it was her mom and not Taryn to say she was early and was outside waiting.

"Are you okay?"

"Yeah." Cassie pushed her phone along the countertop, deciding whether to answer it. "It's my mom calling."

"Let it go to voicemail."

Cassie smiled at the vehemence of Rachel's instruction. She was the one person in the world who Cassie had ever talked to about her mom, and even so, she hadn't gone into all the detail. She'd just said she was a bit of a drunk who was always asking for money. She hadn't told Rachel why her mom was an alcoholic or why Cassie felt like she had to support her even though she'd had no support as she'd navigated her childhood and teenage years. No one but her knew the whole story, and Cassie was almost positive no one else ever would. What was the point, really? "You know I have to answer."

"I know you *think* you have to answer," Rachel said. "But you don't *actually* have to."

"I'll see you at work tomorrow. Have a great day." Cassie hung up before Rachel could protest further, then called her mom back.

"I thought you might be screening your calls and ignoring me."

"Good morning to you too, Mom." Cassie regretted calling back and half wished that she could occasionally believe Rachel's statement that she didn't always have to be at her mom's beck and call.

"Whatever. Maybe it's a good morning for you, but I can tell you now, it isn't for everyone."

And by everyone, her mom meant only her. "What's happened?" Cassie asked, fighting to keep the judgment from her voice. A text pinged in.

I'm outside. Come see why you needed to wear jeans.

Cassie picked up her cell and headed toward her office at the front of the apartment.

"My car's broken down, and I'm in the middle of bumfuck Egypt. The tow truck guy says the engine's gone and is offering me fifty dollars for scrap."

While her mom droned on about the latest in a long line of emergencies, Cassie clamped her hand over her mouth when she saw Taryn astride a motorbike with a second helmet in her hand. She waved up at Cassie, and Cassie shook her head, quickly giving a thumb's down before she texted her. *No way I'm going anywhere on THAT. You can leave it in my garage, and we'll take my car.*

"The guy's got a car he's selling, and it looks great, but I don't have the cash on me or in the bank, Cassandra."

The unspoken request wiped the smile from Cassie's face.

"How much is he selling it for?"

Come on. Live a little. I promise not to do any wheelies or go over the speed limit.

"It's only five thousand dollars," her mom said. "And it's white, my favorite color and great for the Nevada heat."

Cassie exaggerated shaking her head then arched her eyebrow, though it would be lost over distance since Taryn probably wouldn't be able to see her full expression from three floors down.

It's my car or I'm not going anywhere.

Even with the unexpected nuisance of her mom's call, Cassie still found excitement in the option of going nowhere with Taryn. That would mean Taryn would have to come up to her apartment and entertain her here instead of whatever she had planned.

"Five thousand is nothing to you, Cassandra. You wouldn't leave me out in the desert with a stranger and no way to get home, would you?"

You better have a cool car or I'm not going anywhere either.

Cassie looked back out the window to see Taryn leaning against her motorbike with her arms crossed. She'd bet Taryn had a pouty face on, and she smiled at the thought. She also bet that Taryn would be impressed with her car, and the impromptu morning sex session receded into the horizon. "Put the guy on the phone and I'll get his payment details." Five thousand was far from "nothing" to her, but Cassie wanted to find out where Taryn was taking her, and she wanted to get on with enjoying her plans for a change. She indicated the phone to Taryn and held up five fingers to show she wouldn't be much longer.

"You're a good daughter. I knew I could count on you."

Cassie closed her eyes. She only heard those words when she was giving her mom something or getting her out of another hole. She spoke to the tow truck guy, noted down his bank details, and made the transfer on her phone. When she brought her cell back to her ear, her mom had already gone. The definition of insanity is doing the same thing over and over and expecting a different result. So maybe one day, she'd take Rachel's advice and not be there to play rescuer.

Cassie went back into the kitchen to grab her bag and car keys then locked up and headed downstairs. She motioned toward Taryn when she exited the building and the heat wrapped around her like a heavy blanket. "How can you wear leather on a day like today?"

"Safety first." Taryn patted the seat of her enormous bike. "Are you sure you don't want to ride in style?"

"I'm sure." She nodded toward the parking structure beneath the apartment building. "You can leave your bike down here."

"I need to see your wheels first, miss. I have a reputation to uphold and sponsors to appease."

"Fine. Come with me, hotshot." Cassie hooked her arm through Taryn's elbow and tugged her back toward her building. Taryn's leather jacket felt supple and warm against her skin, and she leaned into her. A few nights ago, they'd had sex with Taryn just wearing a tie; the image of them doing the same with Taryn wearing only this leather jacket made Cassie throb. The thought that she would be making that happen later today made her smile widely.

"What's making you smile so big?" Taryn asked.

"The thought of having sex with you later and you wearing *just* that leather jacket." Oh, the freedom in that sentence alone made her even more excited to get home. "Are you sure you don't just want to go upstairs right now?"

Taryn stopped and swung Cassie around. She wrapped her arms around Cassie's waist and kissed her hard and deep. "I have other plans that don't involve much clothing, but when we get back, I'd be more than happy to oblige your fantasy."

Cassie placed her hands on Taryn's chest and was once again impressed by how firm it was. "I have a long list—how much time do you have?"

Taryn grinned. "Time is a slippery mistress, and you only have a finite number of heartbeats, so I can't answer your question with any degree of accuracy. I do know that while I'm here in Vegas, any spare time—if there is such a thing—is all yours."

Cassie frowned. "Let's talk more about that in the car when—"

"*If* we're going in your car." Taryn removed her arms from around Cassie's waist and gestured toward the garage shutters. "Let's see what you're hiding."

Cassie strolled toward the parking structure and opened the shuttering. "I think you're going to be mildly impressed," she looked Taryn up and down, "though you might find it a little tight for your height." They went inside, and the temperature cooled considerably in the concrete depths. "We can put the top down so you don't bang your head."

"Huh, we'll just get sunstroke instead."

"You can always keep your helmet on if you want to avoid that."

Taryn laughed. "That might make me look a little ridiculous, and—"

"You don't want to lose any sponsors by not looking super cool? I understand." Cassie swatted Taryn's shoulder, and she simply shook her head. Cassie liked making Taryn speechless. "Here we are." She pressed her key to unlock the doors and threw her tote bag in the backseat. "Cool enough for you?"

Taryn looked vaguely impressed. "A Fiat 124 Spider... Not bad. But haven't they stopped making them because they're so unreliable?"

"That makes this one a classic, and she's never let me down. I had the leather seats swapped out for regular bucket seats, of course. No one in their right mind wants leather in Las Vegas..." She flicked a hungry look at Taryn. "Not seats anyway." She got in, started the engine, and flicked the switch for the roof to retract. "What do you think? Is it good enough for a hotshot like you to be seen in?"

Taryn nodded and put her hands on the edge of the driver's door. "Sure you don't want me to drive?"

Cassie arched her eyebrow, and Taryn held up her hands and

edged away before jogging around to the passenger side and jumping in.

"I want to get wherever we're going in one piece, thank you," Cassie said, enjoying the all too quick view of Taryn's ass.

"You should know that I've never had a single accident on the road. I'm a great driver." Taryn reached across and ran her hand over the steering wheel. "I know how to handle an Italian lady like this."

Cassie batted her hand away. "If the other night is anything to go by, I'm sure you know how to handle any woman, regardless of their nationality."

"Americans are my specialty though." Taryn dropped her hand onto Cassie's thigh and squeezed gently. "Are there cameras around?"

"Yes, there are." Cassie licked her lips and hit the roof button to cover the car again. "But they won't see anything this way." She reclined her seat and lay back.

Taryn gave a low growl and unbuttoned Cassie's jeans. She slipped her hand inside and moaned again when she found Cassie already wet beneath her silk panties. She leaned closer and pressed her lips over Cassie's, and Cassie grabbed a handful of Taryn's leather jacket, pulling her in.

"You can't do this on your motorbike," she whispered, just about able to speak over the insanely incredible feeling of Taryn's finger over her clit and the soft leather in her grip.

"Oh, we can." Taryn kissed Cassie's jawline and down her neck to her collarbone. "If you ever let me take you out on it, I'll show you how."

Cassie closed her eyes and gave her complete attention to the pleasure building under Taryn's fingertip. Her mind drifted to laying back on Taryn's bike in the middle of the desert while Taryn expertly guided her off the cliff and into a river of desire. She half-opened her eyes; she didn't need to imagine something sexy—sexy was happening right in front of her, and she gave herself over to it, to Taryn, who looked at her as though she was Cleopatra to her Marc Antony. She couldn't recall ever being looked at quite so intensely, though she hoped they wouldn't suffer the same fate.

It didn't take long before she was pushing her hips up and down in time to Taryn's rhythm, riding the wave to its crest. She peaked and fell into her orgasm and clamped her mouth over Taryn's to consume what would've been a scream loud enough to echo off the walls and wake the neighbors' sleeping cats.

Taryn removed her hand, sucked on her middle finger, and grinned. "You taste like heaven."

Cassie rolled her eyes and fixed her clothes. "You're too smooth." She took the top down again, drove out of the garage, and pulled up alongside Taryn's behemoth of a bike. "You better put that in my space, or it'll be melted by the time we get back."

"Yes, ma'am." Taryn saluted and jumped out of the car.

She pulled off her jacket to reveal a tight tank top with a female pirate on the front. Her arms weren't huge, but they were ripped and defined, and Cassie sighed happily, thinking about all the good use she would put them to over the coming months.

"Like what you see?" Taryn tensed, and her traps practically exploded around her neck.

"Very much so."

Taryn grinned and tossed her jacket on the backseat. She unstrapped a small canvas duffel bag from the back of her bike and dropped it with her jacket before straddling the bike and making it roar into life. Cassie watched the muscles in Taryn's chest, shoulders, and arms ripple with the effort of straightening the bike, and Cassie pressed her thighs together to quell her responding throb. Taryn made a perfectly balanced U-turn and disappeared down the driveway. She leaned back against the headrest. This beat covering Fischer's shift any day of the week three times over. She briefly thought about her mom; she shouldn't have just paid out five thousand dollars to a random guy. For all Cassie knew, it could've been her mom's latest squeeze, and they just wanted some good-time money. She pulled her phone from her bag and quickly thumbed a WhatsApp message asking her mom to send her a picture of the car. Predictably, the text didn't deliver, confirming Cassie's fears. She had a feeling her mom had two phones and only switched this one on when she wanted something. Cassie put her phone down and tried to put her mom out of her mind. She was having another rare day off, and she had fantastic company. They were on an adventure, and there would be more amazing sex. Her mom was the last thing she wanted on her mind.

Taryn jumped back in and smiled. "Do you mind if I put my phone up here for you?"

Cassie shook her head. "Go ahead."

Taryn placed her phone on the dash mount. "That's your route, captain," she said and relaxed back into her seat.

Cassie had no idea where they were going, and she didn't really care. Even though she was the one driving, it felt like she was just along for the ride. Cassie ceded control and set off. It didn't matter where they were going; the world just seemed a lot more fun with Taryn alongside her.

Chapter Eleven

CASSIE PULLED INTO THE gravel parking lot, turned off the engine, and stared at Taryn. "I can't swim."

Taryn placed her hand over Cassie's and smiled. "You won't have to unless we sink."

Cassie's eyes went wide. Taryn recognized fear when she saw it, so she squeezed Cassie's hand gently.

"That's not funny." Cassie pressed back into her seat and shook her head. "Boats aren't really my thing."

"Because you can't swim or is there something else?" Taryn wasn't about to push Cassie into anything she didn't want to do but facing fears could be incredibly cathartic and empowering.

"I think the urge to avoid a watery death is enough, don't you think?" Cassie smiled, but the edge to her words indicated her discomfort.

"Okay." Taryn shifted in her seat and put her hand on Cassie's shoulder. Her skin was warm, but she was covered in goosebumps. "We can turn around and head right back to your place if you want, or .."

Cassie turned to face her and arched her eyebrow. "Or?"

There she goes with the sexy eyebrows again. "Or you can put on a life vest and take a gentle ride with me. Being on water can be super peaceful and tranquil." Taryn paused to see if Cassie might protest, but she simply stared at her with wide, trusting eyes. "No one around for miles and just the big blue sky above you. No imposing skyscrapers and honking horns. I think you might like it." Taryn herself hadn't experienced peace on the water, or anywhere else for that matter. Always being on the go was kind of the antithesis of tranquility, and she'd been hoping to tear around Lake Mead in the most powerful boat they had for hire. But she'd *heard* the water could be serene.

"You're *almost* convincing." Cassie got out of the car and pushed her door closed. "And you *almost* sound like the voice of experience, but I'll bet dollars to donuts that you've never taken a sedate boat ride in your life, and you were hoping to tear around this lake at top speed." She rested her hands on the edge of her door and looked at Taryn with a serious expression. "And I've just ruined your plans."

"Whoa, no way." Taryn jumped out of her seat, jogged around to Cassie, and put her hands on Cassie's waist. "My plans aren't ruined; they've just changed." She nodded toward the car. "Just like they were when you made it clear you didn't trust me to keep you safe on two wheels. We just changed to your cute little Fiat."

Cassie opened her mouth to protest, but Taryn placed a finger on her lips.

"No," she said again, gently. Cassie had been nothing but ultra-confident and sassy to this point. A small show of her vulnerability had Taryn wanting to hold her in her arms and tell her everything would be okay. "We can hire the biggest, slowest boat they've got, and we'll putter around the lake at a snail's pace. No problem." She let Cassie go and retrieved their bags from the back seat. "Come on. Let's change into something more comfortable for this weather."

Cassie didn't look a hundred percent convinced, but nor did she look paler than a full moon, which Taryn took as a good sign. She held out her hand, and Cassie took it and squeezed firmly. They began to walk toward the main building.

"Are you sure you're not going to think this is a waste of your time?" Cassie asked. "Something about what you said back at my place—about having a finite number of heartbeats—makes me feel like you want to make the most of the time you've got."

Taryn gave a sidelong glance and frowned. "Doesn't everyone?"

Cassie narrowed her eyes. "Not in the same way. I've only ever seen you in motion. Even when we first met at the bar, your leg was tapping away under the table like you couldn't keep still. Do you ever relax?"

Taryn held the main door open, and Cassie entered. "I'm relaxed now."

"Okay, smart ass." Cassie punched her shoulder lightly. "Do you ever watch movies or lie in bed to read? How many hours of sleep do you get every night?"

Taryn raised her eyes to the ceiling. She didn't *want* to lie, but it felt like something important was riding on this conversation, and she didn't know what it was. "Don't get me started on sleep. It's a waste of time. And the ratio is totally off. I feel like evolution has slowed down a little and is being lazy, don't you think? Who decided that you should sleep one hour for every two you want to be awake and living life? Who wants to spend a third of their life asleep?"

When they got to the counter, Taryn looked at Cassie. Her eyes were wide and her eyebrow arched high.

"So it's something that you're quite apathetic about?" She laughed and shook her head. "Wow, that was some rant." She engaged the woman on the other side of the counter. "To sleep or not to sleep, Fern?" she asked after reading the name tag on her chest. "What's your take?"

Fern wrapped her arms around herself. "Sleep is amazing, and I *love* my bed so hard. It's like being wrapped up in a cloud and floating above the earth for eight hours."

Cassie nodded. "The opposite end of the scale, okay." She chuckled. "Let's talk more about this out on the water. It might keep my mind off drowning."

"You don't like the water?" Fern asked.

"I like water," Cassie said. "To drink and to shower or bathe in. Anything where I can't put my feet flat on the floor is terrifying."

Fern placed her hand on Cassie's forearm. "Oh, you'll be fine.

You can wear a life preserver." She glanced at Taryn and grinned widely. "And I'm sure that if you were to fall in, your handsome wife would jump in and save you in a jiffy."

The fact that neither of them corrected Fern amused Taryn, and she shot a small smile toward Cassie. Having a wife would be the equivalent of a mortgage and owning a patch of dirt. One love, one location. She shook her head. A wife was the furthest thing from Taryn's mind.

"I've got a booking under the name of Taryn Taylor." Fern looked up for confirmation, and Taryn nodded. "But I have a feeling you might want to change your vessel considering your wife's aversion to the possibility of going overboard. Perhaps something a little more sedate?"

She slid across a laminated sheet of paper with photos of their boats, along with their engine size, speed, and the number of people they held.

"Unless you're trying some sort of exposure therapy type thing, where you try to overcome the fear by immersing yourself in the thing you fear?" Fern asked.

Taryn smiled. "No, we're definitely not doing that. It was a mistake, that's all." She pointed at the picture of a pontoon. "We'll take that, please. But we'll need it all day. Is that possible?" With the slower vehicle, there was no way they'd make it to the cove she'd found on Google in the time they had booked with the other boat. She looked at Cassie. "You do have all day, don't you, wife?"

"I'm not on call, if that's what you're asking, so yes, you can have me all day."

Cassie quirked her eyebrow so quickly that Taryn barely saw it, but her body registered its response happily, and so quickly that she felt like Pavlov's dog. Taryn let out a long breath. It was going to be torture waiting to have Cassie until they were at the cove in the tugboat they'd ended up with. Having Cassie all day was definitely something to look forward to though.

"That is no problem at all." Fern began tapping the booking out on her computer. "We don't get too many tourists wanting the slow boats."

Taryn and Cassie shared another amused look that they'd been taken for tourists. But while Cassie was a local, Taryn was a tourist wherever she went. Cassie had mentioned that she was born and raised in Henderson so she wasn't a tourist at all, but she didn't seem to mind that any more than she had being mistaken for Taryn's wife.

Taryn handed over her credit card and driver's license and asked where they could change. Cassie went in the small cubicle first while Taryn and Fern completed the booking.

"Go through that door when you're ready, and I'll radio Jen to meet you and take you to your boat." Fern winked and handed over a map of the lake.

Taryn smirked when she saw that Fern had circled the cove they were headed for.

"It'll be nice and quiet today. Hardly anyone out there." She tugged a giant Yeti on wheels from around the corner and left it at Taryn's feet. "And here's the picnic you ordered. Have a wonderful time."

"Thank you, ma'am." Taryn pulled the cooler to the glass doors Fern had indicated then switched places with Cassie to change into shorts. They left their bag with Fern and headed out to the boat.

"What's that?" Cassie pointed to the Yeti when Taryn pulled it along with her.

"Supplies for the trip." She grinned. "I know how you like to work up an appetite."

They met Jen at the dock, loaded up the boat, and took off—very slowly.

Cassie had positioned herself in the exact center of the boat. She fiddled with the zipper on her life preserver then tugged on the straps.

"Talk to me about your aversion to sleep." Cassie stretched her neck as if looking over the edge of the boat. "Keep me focused on anything other than that." She shuddered and waved her hand toward the water.

"But then I have a question for you, okay?" Taryn turned back to concentrate on driving the boat even though Fern was correct, and there didn't seem to be another vessel on the water.

"Is this quid pro quo? You'll only tell me something if I promise to give you something in return?"

Taryn enjoyed the hint of playfulness returning to Cassie's voice. Her sudden fear had been unsettling and unexpected, though most people had their phobias, whether or not they were logical. "It wasn't that, but since you mention it, that does sound like more fun." She waited for another quick-fire comeback, but it didn't arrive. Taryn wondered if she'd done the right thing in practically forcing Cassie to confront her dislike of water. "I think sleep is a waste of time, like I said, especially when there's so much to do. We've evolved so much that I really don't understand why we haven't adapted to recover and repair faster than we do. I think we could be solar-powered; a minute in the sun for every hour we're awake and no need to sleep. *That* would be a significant step in evolution."

Cassie's laugh soothed Taryn's guilt somewhat.

"Have you put your theory forward to NASA or the American Association for the Advancement of Science?" Cassie asked. "It seems like something they should seriously be considering. I think Bill Gates would be really interested in funding the relevant studies."

Taryn glanced over her shoulder, and Cassie's bright smile made her grin. "I take it you like your sleep?"

"Not quite as much as the boat lady, and I can't remember the last night I had eight hours wrapped in a cloud, but yes, I like my sleep." She gave a contented sigh. "There's nothing like folding yourself into soft cotton sheets after an exhausting shift in the ER."

"Ah, but is it the sleep you like, or is it just because you're so heinously tired after running around working a double shift that your brain *thinks* it likes the sleep? But really, is it because your body has no choice, so it's conning you into thinking you like sleeping?"

"I'm not sure there's a difference there. And if it's happening unconsciously, I'm not sure I should concern myself with the question. Plus, sleep isn't a passive act—your brain is busy clearing up toxins and debris from your mucky day."

Taryn laughed. "Now I'm imagining cleaners wandering around my cortex with mops and buckets. I wish they'd stop hanging out by the water cooler gossiping and just get it done quicker so I could get on with a full day on less sleep."

"And now I'll never think of sleep the same way again. But sleep deprivation isn't good for humans. That's why it's often used as torture."

"Whoa, that took a turn for the macabre." *Going this slow was torture enough.* Taryn eased off the throttle just as she realized they were picking up speed. Her unconscious clearly wasn't happy about the lack of velocity, something her body wasn't used to.

"Sorry. Must be the mood my current environment is putting me in." Cassie laughed, but it didn't sound genuine.

Taryn adjusted the throttle to idle and turned around on the swivel seat. "Cass, you really don't have to do this if you don't want to. We can put the Yeti in the car and drive out to the canyon. Would you prefer that?"

Cassie shook her head and got to her feet slowly. She edged closer to Taryn and took the seat beside her. Taryn took Cassie's hands in hers and ran her thumbs over Cassie's knuckles.

"No. I want to do this," Cassie said quietly.

Her serious expression convinced Taryn, and she continued to look into Cassie's eyes long after the window of polite gazing had closed.

"You really do have the most beautiful eyes." Cassie pulled her hand from Taryn's and ran the back of her fingers over Taryn's cheek. "Did you get them from your mom or dad?"

"Hold your horses." Taryn leaned against Cassie's caress. "Quid pro quo, remember? It's my turn."

Cassie rolled her eyes and leaned back in her seat. "You're a stickler for the rules, Taryn Taylor."

"Rules keep naughty people like you in line."

Cassie arched her eyebrow. "I never would have thought you were a rule follower, especially with your aversion to staying in one place for longer than a few nights."

Taryn shook her head and gently tapped her finger on Cassie's nose. "There you go again, trying to fish for more information before you've given up some of your own. Though I don't know which rule book specifies everyone has to live their life within four walls—*but* I won't get drawn into that until you answer something for me."

Cassie put her elbows on her knees and leaned closer. "Ask away."

"Can you tell me why you never learned to swim?"

Cassie immediately moved back, and her expression hardened. She focused on the horizon ahead and didn't say anything for a few seconds. Taryn made no attempt to fill the silence though she wasn't used to any periods of quiet between them. If she thought back over their time together so far, the only time they weren't engaged in constant conversation was when they were sleeping or having sex. But this emptiness seemed necessary. If Cassie didn't want to talk about something, Taryn expected her to simply say so and they could move on to a safer topic.

"No one ever taught me."

A gust of wind lifted the canopy edge slightly, and in the streaming sunlight, Taryn saw Cassie's eyes were rimmed with tears. She placed her hand on Cassie's knee gently. Her reaction had caught Taryn off guard. The fun and sexy date she'd planned had started with promise but had taken a serious turn since they'd pulled into the parking lot. "We can talk about something else..."

"Do you *want* to talk about something else?" Cassie asked.

"No judgment, obviously. We're just supposed to be having fun, not having serious conversations like this."

Taryn placed her finger under Cassie's chin and lifted it slowly. Cassie looked up into Taryn's eyes and smiled, but it wasn't the carefree smile she'd gotten used to seeing. "I don't remember setting out expectations or legislation around what we could and couldn't do, can or can't talk about." Of course she hadn't anticipated this date going quite as sideways as it had, but that didn't mean she was in any hurry to escape it. "I can do serious too, when the need arises." She pressed her lips to Cassie's forehead then pulled back. "I've been told I'm a good listener." Which was the exact opposite of what she'd been told, but Andi had only meant it jokingly. Mostly.

Cassie looked at her and didn't seem convinced. "Okay. Maybe just a little seriousness then."

Taryn winked, engaged the throttle again and continued on their course, figuring that Cassie might feel more comfortable talking if Taryn wasn't staring deep into her eyes. She knew that'd be the case for her; there was no way she'd be able to concentrate on anything other than Cassie's beauty if they were face to face.

"I won't bore you with all the details," Cassie said, "but my dad left when I was seven, and my mom kind of lost interest in raising me after...after that."

The hesitation in Cassie's voice indicated there might be more to it than she was saying, but Taryn wasn't about to push. Whatever pain Cassie was carrying with her, it was hers to reveal as and when she saw fit.

"What about you?" Cassie asked. "Where did you get your fearlessness from?"

"From both my parents, I guess. They were pretty fearless when it came to setting up their business and attempting state-wide domination." Taryn laughed. She'd never really thought about it. "Though I have to wonder, a trait has to start somewhere, doesn't it? Maybe I made myself fearless."

"I don't know if that makes your parents sound scary or impressive. Maybe both. What do they do?"

Now it was Taryn's turn to feel a little uncomfortable with the direction of the conversation, which was absurd. Cassie had grown up with an apathetic parent; comparing their situations was like comparing avocados and pears, similar shapes but that was all. "They turn rich individuals into perfect plastic people—or at least, what they see as perfect."

She glanced at Cassie, who looked like she was trying to work out what she meant.

"Ah, they're plastic surgeons?"

Taryn nodded then cut the engine so they could bob around in the water a while and she could get a drink. She went to the cooler and pulled out a bottle of water. She had beer in there too, but somehow, she intuited that Cassie would want her in total control of her faculties, even to drive this slow-ass snail tugboat. "Can I get you something to drink? I don't think it would look good for a doctor to let herself get dehydrated."

"Water, please."

Taryn handed Cassie her bottle and got another one out, along with a bag of Ruffles. She sat in the corner bench seat and stretched her legs out. "Join me?"

Cassie got up gingerly and navigated her way slowly to the back of the boat. "Lift your legs."

Taryn did so and Cassie sat on the bench then pulled Taryn's legs over hers. She snagged the chips, and they crunched through a few without speaking.

"Both of your parents are plastic surgeons?" Cassie ran the heel of her palm along Taryn's quad. "Your legs are so strong."

Taryn took a long drink of water and enjoyed the feel of Cassie's skin against hers. "I'm *not* one of their plastic people projects, in case you were wondering." She tensed her thighs and smiled at the little squeak of pleasure it elicited from Cassie. "This is all totally natural and borne from damn hard work."

"I didn't think you were anything else." Cassie moved farther up Taryn's leg, and her fingertips explored under the edge of Taryn's jean shorts.

"Seems like you're getting more comfortable on the water," Taryn said and put her hand over Cassie's.

Cassie shrugged and pulled her hand back along Taryn's thigh. She traced the edge of the muscle around Taryn's knee instead.

"To answer your question, yes, Mom and Dad are both plastic surgeons—very successful plastic surgeons—as are all my siblings."

"*All* your siblings?"

"Two brothers and two sisters, who are twins. I'm the second youngest."

"You're one of five kids? Must've been a crowded house."

Taryn thought of the seven-bedroomed mansion her parents moved into just before they brought Ralph into the world. It would probably seem obscene to Cassie. "Not so much. How about you? Do you have siblings?"

Cassie looked away abruptly but not before Taryn had seen the blackest of clouds descend over her usually bright eyes. The little seriousness they'd agreed on seemed to be inadvertently leading them along an ever-darkening path.

She cleared her throat. "That's not something I want to talk about it," Cassie whispered.

She seemed to hold something else back. Was it something she didn't want to talk about with Taryn, or something she didn't want to talk about period? Again though, Taryn wasn't about to push. They'd been having a lot of fun together over the past week, and she didn't want to risk that by trying to force a clearly difficult conversation, didn't want to risk losing her friendship. Taryn had thought staying in one place was going to be difficult, but their time together was making it almost too easy.

"My younger brother, Ralph, is visiting for a few days. He gets in next week. Maybe you'd like to meet him?" She didn't know why she'd think Cassie would be interesting in meeting a confirmed bachelor who generally had no etiquette with women outside the bedroom and the consultation room, but she was trying to steer the conversation back into safer waters.

"Does he look like you?" Cassie asked.

"Why?" She didn't manage to keep the suspicion from her voice. When they were in their twenties, she'd lost out on too many potential lovers to Ralph for it to be a series of amusing anecdotes.

Cassie gave a sidelong glance. "Why would you want me to meet him if you're worried that he's going to sweep me off my feet?"

"Old habit," she said. In truth, she hadn't felt threatened by him for years. Especially since Andi had taken her under her wing and mentored her to stud-dom. And even if he had gone out with them, there were always more than enough women for them all. But Cassie wasn't one of those women, and apparently that mattered. Maybe she'd think about that later, but more likely, she'd ignore it.

"Well, now you've made me want to meet him just to see who could make you feel insecure."

"Hey, nobody said..." Taryn shut up when Cassie grinned at her. Something made it all but impossible to bullshit this woman.

Cassie shifted sideways and tucked her leg under her butt so that she could face Taryn, all evidence of her recent wobble gone from view.

"So now you're a stunt rider in a traveling human circus. Interesting." She arched her eyebrow. "How did that happen?"

"Mm." Taryn tilted her head back and looked to the sky. "I thought you said we were only getting a little serious."

Cassie slapped Taryn's thigh lightly. "Quid pro quo, remember? I gave you something a little serious, so now it's your turn."

"Now who's a stickler for the rules?" She bunched her thigh muscles under Cassie's hand and smiled when she saw the resulting shot of desire in Cassie's eyes. "I did all the training. Went to med school and got fully qualified."

"Wait—what? You're actually Doctor Taryn Taylor?"

Taryn scrunched her nose and shook her head. "I haven't renewed my license for a long time, so it's really just a piece of fancy paper and a title."

"Wow." Cassie said nothing else for a few moments. "You've got to be the first stunt rider who's also a qualified surgeon."

Taryn shrugged. "It's not something I've ever been interested enough to find out. I didn't want to be part of that life, so I ignore it mostly. My mom keeps hoping that I'll come to my senses, and she's desperate for that to happen before I maim myself or get too old and no longer have steady hands." She avoided Cassie's intense gaze. It had been a long time since she'd talked to anyone about this. And she liked it that way.

"So with your parents and your siblings, do they cover the whole body?"

Taryn nodded. "More or less." She knew where this line of questioning was headed even though she hadn't had this conversation for nearly a decade back when Andi quizzed her about it. Andi had taken some convincing that Taryn wanted to be a career stunt rider and that she wouldn't desert them when she got bored. Problem was, Taryn *had* begun to tire of the work. Hence the Alcatraz jump; she was pushing the risk envelope in an attempt to rediscover her initial passion.

"What were you going to specialize in?"

Cassie continued her exploration of Taryn's legs and was working her way down Taryn's calves; she was pleased she'd taken the time to shave everything that morning. Taryn rolled her eyes. "You don't want to know."

"Oh, I can assure you I do."

Taryn narrowed her eyes, and Cassie arched her eyebrow. It was like a facial arm wrestle to see who faltered first. "Fine. Designer vaginas."

Cassie clamped her hand over her mouth but that did nothing to stop the burst of laughter. "A lesbian who didn't want to work with lady bits all day, every day. There's got to be a joke in there somewhere. It certainly has to be a first."

Taryn shook her head. "I expected a more mature reaction from a medical professional," she said and smiled widely. "Think of it as *over*-exposure. If I was working on them all day, maybe I wouldn't want to play with one all night." She pulled her legs from Cassie's lap and swiveled around so that she could take Cassie in her arms. She drew her in for a long, deep kiss then firmly pressed her palm between Cassie's legs. "And I would *never* want to get tired of playing with you."

Cassie tilted her head slightly. "You with the smooth lines," she said before she wrapped her hand around Taryn's neck and kissed her hard.

Taryn pressed her body against Cassie's, and they moved to lay on the bench. Funny thing was, that hadn't been a smooth line. Taryn actually *didn't* want to tire of playing with Cassie, but she reminded herself this was just a little vacation of sorts from her normal life and its rolling schedule, moving from place to place. Just the way she loved it...right?

Chapter Twelve

"Is THIS GOING TO be payback for the boat?"

Cassie couldn't help the shudder that started at her scalp and ran all the way to her toenails. It'd been a few days since the trip that had alternately terrified and thrilled her, but apparently her body wasn't about to forget that she couldn't swim and had put herself at risk. She chuckled. "Payback? That's a rather negative way to frame something that I think is going to be very good for you."

Taryn grinned wickedly. "You're very good for me. We could stay here for the next few hours instead."

"Are you scared of what I've arranged?" Cassie took Taryn's leather jacket from her and placed it on a wall hook.

"Pah. I know we haven't spent that much time together, but you should know by now that word isn't in my vocabulary."

Cassie rolled her eyes and indicated for Taryn to follow her to the kitchen. "You're so macho."

Taryn winked. "I'm trying to keep my stunt-rider persona in place. What would people think if they suspected I got scared?"

"I don't care *what* other people think." Cassie took two flasks from a cupboard and filled them with filtered water from the fridge.

Taryn shrugged. "I have to. But since you're unimpressed with my bravado, I should probably tell you that I think fear is healthy. A little fear means you don't get complacent. Complacency leads to mistakes, and they can be fatal."

Cassie pinched Taryn's cheek. "Ah, look at you, showing me you're human. And I was almost convinced you really were fearless."

"Well, I don't have any *fears* as such, especially not illogical ones, like spiders. Being respectful that something you're doing could kill you isn't the same as being fearful."

She'd had this conversation with Rachel; Taryn's occupation shouldn't bother her, because this was short-term and there was no emotional investment. So she didn't respond. "Did you bring something comfortable to wear?"

Taryn lifted her backpack, and Cassie twitched at the way her muscle tensed as she did.

"Yes, and I'm incredibly suspicious." She lowered her bag again. "But if you're going to keep looking at me like that, I have to repeat my earlier suggestion that we just stay here, and you can explore whatever feelings are arising in response to my body."

She tensed deliberately this time, and Cassie laughed. "Since this sex we're having is centered on me receiving, I need time to rest."

Taryn pouted and turned away. She began to wander around the living room. "Have you just moved in?"

Cassie put the bottles in her bag and watched Taryn move around her space, almost tiptoeing as if she was afraid to break something. "Why would you think that?"

Taryn gestured around the room. "Because it feels like a show home. Everything's so clean and white...and perfectly in place. No family photos. No vacation fridge magnets." She ran her fingers over the six-foot high metal sculpture of two women entwined like two trees. "Apart from this; this feels like a piece you actually chose for the place."

"That's a Jamie Nelson original. But I didn't choose it; I had it commissioned." She joined Taryn at the piece and touched it gently. "A friend I went to medical school with sent me photos of an exhibition he went to in Boston. The artwork was so stunning, but it was completely sold out. I got in touch with the artist directly and described what I wanted. And this is what she came up with." This sculpture was her favorite thing in the whole apartment, and when she was close to it, it brought out strong emotions. Usually it was a sense of loneliness or longing, but today, she was having a more sexual response. Due to Taryn's proximity, no doubt. And Taryn was right about the lack of personality in her apartment. Even if she hadn't quite gotten around to being so blunt, it was certainly what she was hinting around the edges of.

"It's beautiful," Taryn said. "It must've cost a fortune."

Cassie shook her head. "Not as much as you might think. She only believes in people paying what they think her art is worth."

"Really?" Taryn didn't look convinced. "That seems like she might be taken advantage of."

Cassie laughed. "I've heard that her wife ensures that doesn't happen. And for commissions, you tell her how much you'd like to spend, and she creates something commensurate with that number." She stared at the sculpture; she almost always saw something new or slightly different every time she really took the time to look at it. "I still think I got a steal." She pulled her gaze from the piece and concentrated on Taryn. "But to go back to your original question, I haven't just moved in. I like clean lines and no clutter. It's just who I am." She shrugged then glanced at her watch. "You need to change so we can get going. If we're late, they won't let us in."

After Taryn had done the fastest wardrobe change Cassie had ever seen, she led the way out of her apartment and down to the garage. Taryn got her bike and parked it in the visitor spot that was unusually free, then she joined Cassie in her car. Cassie pulled out and headed toward her local gym. It wasn't far at all, but it was way too far to walk to in the stifling July heat.

"I feel like I might be under-dressed for the theater."

Cassie glanced at Taryn and smiled, enjoying keeping her guessing. "Who said we were going to the theater?"

"Nobody. I'm grasping at straws because you're being so cloak and dagger. But that's the only place I can think of that won't allow latecomers." Taryn leaned back in the passenger seat and stretched out.

Cassie risked a look at Taryn's long, mostly naked and delightfully muscled legs and briefly questioned her desire to take her to BodyBalance instead of just working her out in the bedroom. But they'd get to that after, without a doubt. She pulled into the strip mall parking lot, and they got out of the car.

Taryn took both their bags. "I'm not having my nails painted." She pointed to the salon Cassie had parked directly outside.

"Why not? I think you'd look great with hot-pink lacquered nails."

"Huh. It might look great," Taryn directed her glance below Cassie's stomach, "but I don't think *she'd* appreciate any kind of long nails."

"You wouldn't have to have false nails." It was ridiculous how much she enjoyed watching Taryn squirm. "We could just paint your little stubby ones."

Taryn put her hands on her hips and stopped in the middle of the sidewalk. "Still a hard pass. I know I rock long hair, but that's for my stage persona. Hot-pink or any other color nails are not for the real me."

Taryn's unusual seriousness made Cassie think she might've overstepped the banter line. She put her hand on Taryn's arm. "I promise not to force you to have your nails painted as 'payback for the boat.' But I am going to make you come work out with me." She hooked her arm over Taryn's elbow and tugged her toward her gym. When she stopped them outside the gym door, she unhooked herself and pulled Taryn close. "I'm quite fond of the *real* you, by the way. I wouldn't change a thing."

A flash of something crossed Taryn's eyes, and Cassie was struck with the notion of *learning* Taryn. Her eyes, so unusually colorful and beautiful, were also so incredibly expressive.

"That's actually nice to hear," Taryn whispered. "Outside the stunt team, I haven't spent this much time with someone since med school. Not a lot of people get to meet the real me."

They stayed that way, staring deep into each other's eyes until the door swung open. "Come on, Cassius Clay. You know how they get if you're late to class."

Cassie pulled Taryn through the door. "Sorry, Nellie the Elephant. Can you dump our bags in the locker room so we can head straight up?"

"Sure."

Taryn handed over their bags, then she followed Cassie upstairs to a small dimly lit room filled with yoga mats and lots of people. Great. Lying down and doing lots of stretching while breathing in and out.

"Cassius Clay and Nellie the Elephant?" Taryn whispered. "What's that all about?"

"Nell doesn't call anyone by their actual name." Cassie guided them toward a couple of empty mats at the front of the room. "It's a strange habit, but I kind of like it. It's rare she calls me the same thing twice." She shrugged. "But Nellie the Elephant is the best I can come up with. She doesn't seem to mind my lack of imagination."

"What would she do with my name?"

"Good question, but you're only going to find out if you keep coming." Cassie gently bumped Taryn's shoulder.

She chuckled. "Then I'll probably never know. This kind of... I was going to say, activity, but I don't think yoga counts as anything like active."

Cassie shook her head. "First, this is BodyBalance, not yoga. Second, I bet you've never tried yoga so you shouldn't judge. And third, I think at the end of this hour, you will have changed your close-minded opinion." She sat down on the edge of her mat and gestured for Taryn to join her.

Taryn flopped to the floor, acting like the testy teenager she currently felt like. "We'll see about that."

Cassie arched her eyebrow. "I did something with you that made me uncomfortable, but you can go and wait in the car or go home if you really don't want to try it."

Taryn rolled her eyes. There was no way she wanted to leave

Cassie but lolling around on the ground to soothing music was going to be quite the challenge. "I'm sorry. I'll shut up and give it a try." But she didn't have high hopes for any level of enjoyment.

Cassie gave a small smile and shook her head. "If you can open your mind as well as your body, you might just benefit from slowing down a little. Your obsession with time isn't all that healthy."

Taryn held up her hands. "Whoa there, doc. Will I have to pay for this therapy session?"

Cassie punched Taryn's bicep. "You couldn't afford therapy with me. Seriously though, we'll see how you feel at the end of the class."

Taryn mock-saluted. "Yes, ma'am."

The coach, or whatever they were supposed to be called, got everyone's attention, and an instant hush fell over the room. Immediately, Taryn felt like a naughty kid who wanted to laugh and pass notes during class, and she wished there'd been some empty mats in the back of the room. That's what she got for being late. She doubted she'd ever accompany Cassie here again, but if she did, they'd have to get there earlier so they weren't close enough to smell the coach's cologne.

The next fifty minutes were absolute torture and not for the reasons of boredom and lack of movement Taryn had expected. The coach had her twisting and stretching her body into all kinds of positions that it really didn't want to, all kinds of positions that made her muscles scream. She'd thought she was strong, but when Cassie was making a pyramidy-lungey-twisty-prayer thing look simple, Taryn's quads and glutes were shaking like Jell-O, and she had to keep taking a knee for a break.

"Push out your sit bones and let's do a forward fold," the coach said in their husky ASMR-type whisper. "Reach down toward your toes and press your chest to your thighs like a pancake."

Taryn looked at the coach to see them folded over like a piece of paper, their face between their knees. Was the human body supposed to be able to *do* that?

"And it doesn't matter what kind of pancake you are. Whether it's an American one, or a French crêpe, just try to get your chest as close to your thighs as possible."

Taryn let out an anguished groan even though her face was at least six inches away from her knees. "I feel more like a Yorkshire pudding than a pancake," she whispered to Cassie, who was also impressively folded over like a perfectly pressed Gap shirt.

Cassie turned her head slightly to face Taryn. "What?"

"A British Yorkshire pudding. Made of the same batter as a pancake but it rises like a dome." When Cassie still looked puzzled, Taryn shook her head. "Remind me to show you a photo later."

"And that's all the work for today. Let's relax onto the mat. Get into whatever position you're most comfortable in and feel your body against the floor."

Taryn gratefully flopped onto her back. "Jesus Christ," she whispered.

Cassie chuckled lightly. "Bit more of a challenge than you thought it would be, huh?"

When she saw the cautioning look from the coach, Taryn simply nodded and said nothing else. Instead, she followed their instructions, closed her eyes and tried to feel every vertebra against the floor, took big breaths in through her nose and blew them out slowly from her mouth. And she was overwhelmed with a sudden urge to...to cry? What the hell? If this is what slowing down did to her, she didn't want any part of it.

She spent the rest of the meditation section thinking about the stunts they'd be performing at their residency. The new take on the Globe of Death that she and Andi had come up with was going to be their grand finale each night. They'd built the double globe two years ago but had never taken it on the road; it was too cumbersome and time-consuming to build and take down for the short-run shows they did. But this residency was giving them the chance to finally let the world see it. Taryn couldn't wait. Her, Andi, and six more of their top riders zipping around the two giant balls at sixty-five miles per hour, with the whole rig lifted thirty feet into the air.

Yeah, *that* was the kind of feeling she lived for. She felt a tear slip from her eye and quickly wiped it away. She glanced over at Cassie, but her eyes were closed and her breasts were rising and falling slowly, indicating she was fully into a meditative state. Taryn looked up at the ceiling. Did it qualify as Peeping Tom behavior if you were already engaged in lots of hot sex with the person you were staring at?

The coach closed the session, and Cassie touched Taryn's arm gently. "Are you okay?"

"Uh, yeah, of course I am." Taryn rolled onto her side to get up, already a little stiffness creeping in.

"How did you find it? Not too tedious, I hope?"

Cassie took a long drink of her water, and Taryn watched her lips, the slope of her neck, and the plunge of her breasts into her snug tank top. "Not tedious at all, actually," Taryn said and pulled her errant eyes from their ogling. She stood and offered her hand to help Cassie up.

"Really?" Cassie didn't sound convinced. "This way."

"Really." Taryn followed her out of the room, after they'd thanked the coach.

"You'll come with me again?"

Taryn thought of the unbidden surge of emotion and chuckled. "We'll have to see how much I ache in the morning." They trotted down three flights of stairs to the locker room. Taryn stopped dead when they rounded the row of lockers and came face to face with a row of shower heads with no curtains or separation. "No cubicles? You're killing me." As if watching Cassie bend herself into all manner of twisty, sexy positions hadn't already gotten her wound up so tight, she thought she might actually explode. "I didn't get that sweaty. I'll shower when I get back to the trailer."

Cassie arched her eyebrow. "You're not coming back to my place?"

"I didn't want to assume." She gave Cassie a wicked grin. She'd been praying that Cassie would invite her in after this torture was over, but she really hadn't taken it for granted.

"Oh, you didn't? I thought we'd established an unspoken ritual: a fun time outside the bedroom and an even more fun time *inside* the bedroom. Do you want to break our winning streak?"

"I really don't. I'd hate to be responsible for that. I mean, I don't know who we're competing with, but I guess that doesn't matter." Taryn smiled and thumbed toward the shower area. "Maybe I could shower at your place?"

Cassie pressed her lips together like she was stopping herself from a fit of laughter. "I don't want your sweaty ass on my lovely upholstery. Why can't you shower here?"

Taryn bit her lower lip. Cassie's challenge couldn't have been clearer. She should be able to control herself, shouldn't she?

"Are you shy? Is that what it is?" Cassie persisted. "Don't you want the other women to see your sweet ass?"

"Huh." Taryn turned her nose up and gave her best look of indignance. "Is it sweet or sweaty? I'm not sure it can be both."

"Yet somehow you manage it." Cassie began to peel off her tank top and wiggled her eyebrows.

"I don't have a towel," she said, rapidly running out of excuses.

Cassie indicated the pile of neatly folded, white bath sheets stacked on a shelf in the back of the changing room. "Use one of those." She tilted her head and whispered, "Don't you trust yourself?"

Taryn shook her head and tried to reclaim some control of both herself and the situation. Cassie made her feel like a marionette dancing on her strings. "It's you I don't trust." She scanned the room. Most everyone else had grabbed their personal stuff and left; only a few looked like they were about to shower. Their presence would keep Taryn's hands on her own body instead of on Cassie's, where they would most assuredly want to be once they were both completely naked and under a hot stream of water.

She pulled off her clothes, jumped under a shower head in record time—a product of living in a trailer for years—and smiled. "Come on, stinky."

Cassie looked vaguely shocked and offended before she fell into laughter. "You did not just call me stinky." She stripped off her gym gear, slowly for maximum effect, and stepped into a shower three up from where Taryn was standing.

Taryn gulped when Cassie turned the water on and tilted her head back so that the jet sprayed over her neck and breasts.

"I'll stay over here so you're nice and safe." Cassie pumped some shower gel from the wall dispenser and rubbed it onto her skin, slow like she was in a body product commercial.

Taryn glanced around. The other two women were seemingly oblivious to her extreme pain or simply too polite to make it clear they knew exactly what was going on. She positioned herself at an angle under the shower head so she could wash but maintain discreet observation of Cassie's show.

Cassie locked her gaze on Taryn and didn't let up. She lifted each of her breasts and spent far too long cleaning beneath them. She trailed her hands slowly over her stomach. She turned her back to Taryn and ran her hands along the length of her legs, bending over just like she had in the forward fold, and Taryn could've exploded right then.

"Oh god," Taryn muttered and turned her faucet to cold.

The external temperature change did nothing to reduce the furnace burning between her thighs as Cassie continued her performance. If this was the first time they'd met, Taryn might've mistaken Cassie for an exotic dancer or Vegas show girl, not a highly respected ER doctor. Taryn closed her eyes but not for long; she couldn't stop herself from taking in every last inch of sexiness Cassie was displaying. She almost wished she could be videoing the revue to use later—over and over and over again. Cassie really did have everything Taryn could want in a woman *if* she ever thought about settling down. Which she definitely wasn't. There was too much other turbulence in her personal and professional life right now to be adding that wildly left-field thought into the mix.

Cassie turned around again and arched her back to wet her hair, jutting her breasts toward Taryn.

"Come on..." Taryn whispered. "You're not playing fair." She glanced to her left, and only one of the women remained, but there was also an influx of people into the changing room, presumably for another class.

Despite the chattering, Cassie remained in the zone, her every motion slow and deliberate, intended to drive Taryn to distraction with desire. Finally, Cassie turned off her shower. She ran her hands over her body with the dual purpose of flicking off excess water and stoking Taryn to boiling point.

"All done?" she asked and smiled as if she were totally unaware of the effect she'd just had on Taryn.

Taryn shook her head. "I'm far from done," she whispered huskily. Cassie would soon find out what revving her up like this would result in, though it was clear that was exactly what Cassie was hoping for.

Cassie shrugged her shoulders and padded back to her locker with a knowing smile and a killer sway. "Better be quick if you want a ride..." Cassie glanced over her shoulder, "home."

Oh, there was going to be some riding, all right. Taryn was ready to go all night. She turned her faucet back to a warmer flow and showered quickly. While she'd been watching Cassie, she'd neglected to actually clean herself, and she didn't want to waste any precious time doing it when they got back to Cassie's place. If she had her way, she'd be inside Cassie as soon as her front door was closed.

Taryn grabbed a towel and used it to dry her hair as she wandered back toward Cassie. She registered Cassie's nostrils flare, the tiniest twitch of her eyebrow, and the way she nibbled her bottom lip. God, it felt good to be this desired, this *seen*. Cassie finished dressing and sat a breath away from Taryn as she air-dried and folded her dirty gym clothes carefully and put them back into her bag. The locker room was silent and empty but for them, and Taryn glanced at Cassie. She was leaning back against the lockers, her eyes firmly fixed on Taryn's body.

Taryn half turned away. "Stop undressing me with your eyes."

"I don't think that statement can apply since you're parading around buck naked." Cassie pointed to Taryn's clean clothes. "Would you like some help *dressing*?"

Taryn raised her eyebrows. That would be something no woman had ever done. "How can that seem as sexy as the thought of you *un*dressing me?"

"Let's find out."

Cassie rose but Taryn held up her hands. "Don't you come anywhere near me, devil woman, or I won't be able to control myself."

Cassie gave her a wicked grin and whispered, "That's what I'm hoping for."

"Nope. Not yet." Taryn pulled on her clothes unassisted then grabbed their bags. "Take me back to your place before you melt me into a useless puddle of need."

Cassie hooked her finger in the deep V of Taryn's shirt and pulled her in for a hard and passionate kiss. She placed her hand on Taryn's chest, pushed her back, and dangled her car keys. "Your carriage awaits, my lord."

Taryn liked the sound of that. She liked the sound of *everything* that came out of Cassie's mouth. She hadn't been this completely captivated by a person since... She blew out a short breath and followed Cassie up the stairs. Since never.

Chapter Thirteen

"YOU'RE GOING OUT WITH her again?"

"I don't know whether you're happy or sad about that," Cassie said. "There's a lot to unpack from your tone of voice." She got in the back of the Uber and told the driver to head to Cosmos.

"I'm conflicted, since you ask."

Cassie laughed at Rachel's dramatic pout and the way her mouth practically filled the whole screen. "And why are you conflicted?"

"Well, on the one hand, I'm impressed that you're finally heeding my teaching and getting out in the world more than once a month. But on the other hand, I'm a little jealous that you haven't invited me to come with you."

Cassie kicked herself. She'd been so busy creating time to spend with Taryn by turning down extra shifts at the hospital that she *had* been neglecting Rachel. And that wasn't cool. "I'm sorry. I'm being a bad friend. There's a party to celebrate how well the residency is going in a couple of weeks; I think you're working, but maybe you could swap shifts with someone. It's at Bernice's hotel, and I think Taryn could arrange a room if you wanted."

"Now you're being a good friend again. I wouldn't want to come tonight anyway; isn't it a double date?"

"A triple date, actually. Taryn's brother is in town, and she says that he's bound to have hooked up with someone and won't be going alone. I should've checked. *You* could've been his date."

"Yes, you should have." Rachel wagged her finger at the screen and tsked. "Especially if there's a family resemblance."

"Apparently there is, but it's a bit of a sore spot for Taryn. I think her whole family is a sore spot, to be honest."

"Huh. What does that make yours?"

Cassie glanced out the window and thought about her mom, who'd been avoiding her calls since she'd bought her the emergency car. She knew what her mom was doing: not answering so Cassie had no choice but to visit. "Out of bounds and not a good topic for conversation."

"You haven't talked about your mom?"

"Would you talk about my mom with the person you were having amazing sex with? I mentioned she wasn't exactly a Hallmark movie mom, but I shut the conversation down. We're not really having the kind of relationship where we share the negative parts of our life." It wasn't exactly true. Cassie was beginning to feel like she could talk to Taryn about her messed-up family and maybe about her brother eventually. Their time together was so easy, and that was something precious to Cassie because the rest of her life *wasn't.* "Anyway, weren't you the one who told me that all that stuff didn't matter because we were just having sex?" she whispered after she caught the driver's overly interested expression in the rear-view mirror.

"That was when you were only having a one-night stand. You seem to have strayed into friends with seriously hot benefits territory."

Cassie pressed her left earbud twice to lower the volume. She didn't think the driver could hear Rachel, but it didn't hurt to be more discreet given the topic. Cassie didn't want to be a story her driver would tell his buddies later. "You think that's a bad thing?"

Rachel shook her head. "I didn't say that, but I don't want you to get hurt, Cass. You're protecting yourself, right?"

Cassie couldn't help but giggle. "I'm not going to get pregnant, Mom, no."

"You know what I mean, smart ass. I've never seen you interested in anybody beyond one night..." Rachel widened her eyes as if that would fill in the blank she'd left.

"You're worried I'm going to fall in love and get my heart broken when the tall, dark, handsome not-a-stranger-anymore leaves town?" Cassie didn't expect Rachel to respond in the affirmative, but she nodded. "Are you serious? I'm not a brooding, overly emotional teenager, Rach. I can have no-strings sex and really not get attached."

Rachel shrugged. "Good. Then I can relax, and you can keep on having some real fun. I'm proud of you."

"You remember I'm your elder, don't you?"

Rachel tapped repeatedly on her phone screen. "And *you* remember who had to drag you out of your house every month for a booty call?"

"That sounds so wrong." Cassie shuddered at the thought of having sex with her friend—all that long hair in the way. No, thank you.

"You'd be lucky to get me into your bed." Rachel's pout was even more pronounced this time.

"I would. You're right." Cassie smiled then scrunched up her nose. "But I still never ever *ever* want to."

"I think that makes you hair-ist. Is that a word? Are you a femme-o-phobe?"

"I like what I like, and I've always been that way. Sorry, not sorry." Cassie looked up when the Uber slowed and was surprised when she saw they'd already gotten to the hotel. "I'm here, so I have to go. Let me know if you get the night off so you can come to the launch party, and I'll ask Taryn to arrange a room for you, okay?" She waited until Rachel nodded. "And I'll make it up to you, I promise."

"You don't have anything to make up for, Cass. I love that you're out there having fun. If anyone deserves it, you do."

Cassie blew her a kiss and ended the call. It was sweet of Rachel to be so forgiving, but the guilt still nibbled at Cassie for practically forgetting all about her friend while she'd been carried away with Taryn. She paid the driver and got out of the car, resolving to send a special basket of Rachel's favorite goodies to her house.

Taryn waved to her from the edge of the fire fountains near the main doors, and Cassie's breath caught. Taryn was dressed in a light gray three-piece suit with a forest green shirt and gray tie, a perfect combination. The green shirt made Taryn's eyes even more striking, if that were possible. As she walked toward her, Cassie noted Taryn's hair had been freshly cut and shaved, making Cassie want to wrap her hands around Taryn's head and pull her in for a hard kiss. Her expression must have broadcast her desire because Taryn gave her that cute, lopsided grin she sported when she was unguarded and shy.

Taryn brushed the lapels of her jacket when she was only a few feet away from Cassie. "You like?"

"I love. That shirt color makes your eyes really pop." When she was within reach, Cassie tugged Taryn closer with her tie and kissed her. "You look good enough to eat."

Taryn gently shifted Cassie's hair over her ear. "I'd suggest that we skip dinner again, but my brother's come a long way to see me."

"I can wait. Anticipation can be a powerful aphrodisiac."

"Then I'll probably explode when I finally get you to bed tonight." Taryn half-turned and offered Cassie her arm. "Ralph's brought someone with him from Miami, and he's acting strangely, so I apologize for him in advance."

Cassie squeezed Taryn's bicep as they walked. "I'm sure everything's going to be fine."

Taryn grumbled quietly. "I hope so." She glanced at Cassie. "Thank you for coming. It means a lot."

She looked away before Cassie could get a read on her. Taryn seemed to be uncharacteristically nervous and on edge. "Thank you for inviting me."

The hotel doors slid open automatically, and Cassie let out a breath as she took in the ambitious expanse of the lobby. She'd googled the new hotel when Taryn had invited her for dinner, but neither the website nor the press photos did it justice or prepared her for its magnificent magnitude. The hotel name gave away its theme, as did almost all Vegas' strip hotels…but wow.

"What do you think? Over the top or absolute perfection?" Taryn squeezed her hand.

Cassie met Taryn's gaze and smiled. "You or the hotel?"

"Perfection might be a push, but the way you devoured me with your eyes when you got here made it clear that I'm looking pretty good tonight." Taryn wiggled her eyebrows. "I meant the hotel."

Cassie looked up at the ceiling that *wasn't* a ceiling but some kind of projection of outer space and shook her head. "I think it's one of the best concepts Vegas has come up with in a long time. I think it's amazing, actually. And I'm not easily impressed."

"I'll take that as a compliment." Taryn motioned to the right.

"Why? Did you design it?" Cassie asked, trying to keep her teasing smile from growing bigger.

"Oh no, I'm not talking about the hotel. I've brought the conversation back to me, and the fact that you keep agreeing to spend time with me means that I must've impressed you."

Cassie swatted Taryn's chest. "You're incorrigible. Isn't tonight supposed to be about your brother and your friend?" She looked around. "And why are you leading me toward a wall of flowers? I mean, they're pretty, but shouldn't we be getting to the table?"

"You'll see," Taryn said with a dramatic sweep of her hand.

When they were within six feet of the wall, two previously invisible doors slid open to reveal an elevator. "Ooh, fancy," Cassie said stepped inside. Once they were moving, Cassie turned to Taryn. "You seem a little nervous tonight. Anything you want to share?" It seemed a possibly invasive question to ask, but the time they were spending together *out* of bed was beginning to cement an unexpected friendship between them, and Cassie found herself caring about what was going on in Taryn's head as well as her body.

Taryn gave an almost imperceptible smile as if, perhaps, she was sharing the same thought. "If we keep sharing our feelings,

I'm going to have to start thinking of you as more of a best friend."

Cassie grasped the back of Taryn's neck and let out a distracted sigh at the feel of her buzzed hair. *Focus*. "Would that be such a bad thing? If we're being honest, I've got room in my life for a really good friend."

There was a hint of sadness in Taryn's expression briefly before she blinked it away and nodded. "As long as we can continue having fantastic sex. I'd hate for serious conversation to get in the way of," she swept her hand between them, "this."

"I promise it won't." Cassie got on her tiptoes and kissed Taryn's nose. "Spill."

The elevator made a pleasant sound to indicate their arrival, and they stepped out onto another equally impressive floor.

"We don't have enough time for me to really go into it, but you're right, I *am* nervous." Taryn held out her arm again, Cassie tucked in, and they headed toward the restaurant. "Andi seems to be falling hard for Bernice, and I'm praying that the feeling is mutual, even though I don't know what that might mean for the team...and for me. And I always get a little antsy around my brother when I haven't seen him for a while because he feels obliged to pass on everything my parents say about my career choice and their wishes that I'd come to my senses and take my 'rightful place' in the family business." They reached the restaurant. "Maybe we can talk about it later," Taryn said quietly.

"Okay." Cassie wrapped her other hand around Taryn's bicep. "But thank you for telling me. I'll be right by your side." If there was one thing Cassie could empathize with, it was family pressures, which reminded her again that she couldn't avoid visiting her mom for much longer.

"I like you there."

Taryn glanced at her with a smile so bright, it could've lit up the Universe, then she addressed the maître d', and he guided them to arguably the best table in the restaurant, which was to be expected since the owner of the hotel was dining with them.

Bernice looked exactly as Taryn had described her, and Cassie couldn't stop a modicum of jealousy. From what Taryn had said, she and Andi shared similar tastes in women, and her description of Bernice had already stirred an unusual sense of rivalry even though Taryn made it clear she preferred her women a couple of decades younger. Still, Bernice didn't exactly look her age, and in the right light, which this space was definitely providing, she could easily pass for someone in her early forties.

Taryn made introductions for everyone then held out Cassie's chair. She took it, and Taryn inched her closer to the table with ease. Cassie watched Taryn remove her suit jacket before taking her seat. Her shirt sleeves stretched over the muscles of her arms, and Cassie smiled, thinking again just how much she adored a strong woman. And knowing how much stamina was in Taryn's arms in particular made her smile even wider.

When she and Taryn were settled, two waitstaff poured champagne for everyone. Cassie knew nothing of wine or champagne, but even she recognized the distinctive Dom Perignon label. If this was how the evening was beginning, she was already thankful to Taryn for making it clear the meal and drinks were complimentary.

"You've created something truly spectacular with this hotel," Cassie said.

Bernice smiled. "Thank you. I wanted it to be totally different from everything else on the Strip—themed but sophisticated."

"You've definitely achieved that." Cassie ran her finger along the condensation of her champagne glass. "And I really hated the eyesore they called the Excalibur."

"Wasn't it just awful?" Bernice said.

Cassie nodded. "I don't think I've ever met anyone who actually liked it. I'm not quite sure how it managed to stay open as long as it did."

Bernice shook her head. "Me neither. But you really like this place?"

Everything about Bernice to that point had exuded confidence. The way she shook Cassie's hand; her clothes and makeup, stylish, simple, and classic; and the unhurried way she spoke. But her final question hinted at an unexpected humility and genuine interest in the opinion of others. Cassie imagined it would be hard to stay in touch with everyday people when surrounded by such opulence and wealth. "I really do," she said, with complete honesty though she might've lied even if she didn't like it.

Andi draped her arm around Bernice's shoulders and grinned. "My little demolition expert hit the explode button on the ugly place."

"That must've been something," Cassie said.

"It was strangely cathartic." Bernice laughed as if the notion were absurd. "I had a bad experience there as a kid, and I never forgot it. Blowing it up was like decades-old payback." She shrugged and waved her hand. "Anyway," she gestured upward to another impressive ceiling display that moved like the room was slowly spinning, "if I hadn't become a successful businesswoman, I would've become an astronaut. Here, I get the best of both worlds."

Two waiters returned pushing carts of appetizers, which they carefully placed in the center of the large table. Silence alternated with small talk while everyone dug into the fabulously presented food. Cassie murmured her appreciation around mouthfuls of something delicious which she couldn't remember the name of, and Taryn placed her hand on Cassie's thigh.

"You're not supposed to make sounds like that outside the bedroom," Taryn whispered.

"You seemed to like the sounds I made in the car. And on the boat. And in the shower. And—"

"Okay, I get it. You know what I mean though. How am I supposed to keep my hands off you when you're making noises like that?"

"You're supposed to store it all up for when we do get to the bedroom. Or wherever."

Taryn jutted her chin toward the restroom sign. "Andi says the bathroom stalls are bigger than the average hotel room. Maybe we could squeeze a little something in between courses?"

Cassie arched her eyebrow and enjoyed the instant visible effect it had on Taryn. She leaned close enough so that her lips brushed Taryn's ear. "As desperate as I am to have you inside me, I'm sure your friends and family wouldn't be impressed if we disappeared for half an hour. You'll wait because you know I'm worth waiting for," she whispered.

Taryn dragged her fingers along Cassie's thigh before letting her go. "Dammit."

Andi gave Taryn a shove. "I'd say get a room, but I think you'd take me up on it and leave us enjoying this bounty by ourselves." She glared at Taryn. "Which would be so rude."

Taryn raised her hands. "We're not going anywhere, I promise."

Ralph clinked a knife against his glass. "Just in case the temptation becomes too great to resist," he said and winked at Cassie, "and why wouldn't it?"

Taryn grumbled. "You know I'm mentally punching you right now, don't you?"

Ralph grinned. "I do, and I know why. But you have nothing to fear...anymore—"

Cassie ran her hand over Taryn's cheek. "You have nothing to fear regardless." She saw the historic wounded expression in Taryn's eyes. "My interest lies only with you."

Taryn took Cassie's hand and kissed it. "Then we should hit the tables while lady luck is with me."

Ralph tapped his glass louder. "Excuse me, lovers, I'm trying to say something important here."

Andi laughed. "That'll be a first."

She and Taryn fist-bumped, and Cassie saw the understanding between them. Clearly Andi knew all about Taryn's sensitivity when it came to Ralph and women.

Bernice placed her hand over Andi's. "Come on, sweetheart,

let the poor man speak. He's terribly outnumbered and must be feeling rather overwhelmed."

Cassie saw the knowing glance between Taryn and Andi. From what Taryn had said, there was no doubt Ralph was incredibly comfortable among so many women. As obvious as the quip was, Cassie assumed that neither of them said it out of respect for Jessica, the woman with Ralph, who'd barely said a word since Cassie and Taryn had joined the table.

"I'm perfectly happy, thanks, Bernice. But yeah, Taryn, let me speak!"

Taryn rolled her eyes and shrugged. "It better not be about family stuff."

Cassie felt Taryn's leg tense under her hand, and she squeezed gently. "I'm right here," she whispered. Taryn half-smiled, clearly expecting the worst.

Ralph tilted his head slightly. "It is, and it isn't." He put out his hand when Taryn shot him a warning look. "It's about new family, sis, don't panic." He looked at Jessica, his expression soft and caring. "You're going to be an auntie. Jessica's pregnant."

"What?" Taryn's mouth fell open.

Cassie waited for more words but when none were forthcoming, she filled in the gap. "Congratulations. That's amazing."

"It is. Yeah, it really is," Taryn said after everyone else at the table had made the appropriate noises that were expected when someone announced that kind of news.

She got up and went around the table, and Ralph stood to envelop her in an embrace that went on for so long that Cassie almost felt like she was intruding on an intimate family moment. The others around the table sipped their drinks and looked everywhere but at the sister and brother hugging it out.

When they eventually parted, both had glassy eyes, and they swiped them away in unison as if were swatting flies from their face. Standing side by side, the resemblance was so striking that they could've been twins.

Ralph patted Taryn on the shoulder. "I wanted you to know first."

Taryn retook her seat and frowned. "You haven't told Mom and Dad?"

He shook his head. "No. Jessica hasn't met them yet either. I wanted you to be the first to meet my future wife too." He nudged Jessica gently, and she placed her right hand on the table.

Cassie hadn't realized Jessica had kept her hand hidden until she saw what was on her ring finger—a huge diamond ring set in a white gold band that she wouldn't have otherwise missed. "That's beautiful."

"See, sis? Nothing to worry about." Ralph ginned widely. "Good family news, yeah?"

Taryn nodded. "Great family news, bro. I'm really happy for you both."

Taryn's sentiment sounded genuine enough, and from the look on Ralph's face, he heard what he needed to hear, but she still seemed to be radiating a slight discomfort, like she didn't know what to do with the news other than say what was expected of her. She'd promised Cassie they'd talk about it later, but her reaction was intriguing, because Cassie couldn't think why Taryn *wouldn't* be happy for them.

Bernice had another bottle of Dom Perignon brought to the table, along with their version of a non-alcoholic champagne for Jessica, and she switched out her untouched glass from the first bottle. Conversation flowed as easily as the wine, and Cassie settled into the evening, taking time to get to know Ralph and Andi in particular, both of whom had seemingly endless embarrassing stories of Taryn. Though she had plenty to retaliate with, and the laughter emanating from them all warmed Cassie's heart. She'd never been part of a large group of friends, not even in medical school; her focus had been solely on completion and success, to the detriment of fostering any lifelong friendships. But she'd been on a full-ride scholarship and could ill afford to blow it. That and her guilt drove her to eliminate anything and anyone that might distract her from her goals.

"Do you have family close by?" Jessica asked, looking at Cassie.

She half-smiled and nodded, the warmth in her heart chilling instantly. "My mom lives in Henderson." She could see Jessica waiting for more, and she also caught Taryn's wide-eyed glare at Ralph, who placed his hand on Jessica's.

"Taryn said you're an ER doctor. Do you think it's good to know the gender of the baby before it's born?" he asked.

The subject change was far from subtle and still potentially incendiary, but Cassie appreciated it, nonetheless. "That depends on your expectations and motivations, I suppose. Does the gender matter to you?" She couldn't help asking the question even though she knew she probably shouldn't. What had so far been a rather pleasant evening could turn on a dime depending on Ralph's or Jessica's answer, especially if *they* hadn't talked about it yet and had differing views.

The look the two of them exchanged said more than words could. Ralph's behavior was the antithesis of how Taryn had described him, and Cassie wondered if that might be the crux of Taryn's low-level consternation. Did it bother her that he seemed to be in love when she was used to him being such a player?

Ralph and Jessica shook their heads and smiled. "As long as it's breathing and its heart is beating when it pops out, it doesn't matter," Ralph said.

"And we don't want to put any societal expectations on a little human. I think Ralph's question should've been more about the tests you can have to check our baby is healthy," Jessica said.

"I'm sure your gynecologist will be the best person to ask those questions. I know how to put people back together in an emergency. That's always been my area of interest." And that was for reasons she didn't want to discuss with a group of strangers. Cassie looked at Bernice and then Andi, eager to turn the conversation away from herself. "Have either of you ever wanted kids?"

Andi half-choked on her champagne and had to slap her own

chest. "Never. I'm too big a kid myself to be responsible for a tiny, defenseless person." She gestured toward Taryn. "She was as close to me having children as I ever got, and thankfully, she was big enough and ugly enough to take care of herself when she came into my life."

Taryn scoffed. "You were more like an older sister who led me astray than a nurturing mom-figure."

"Ingrate," Andi said. "I nurtured you plenty, but you were always more of a tough love person."

Taryn inclined her head. "Fair. What about you, Bernice? Have you ever been tempted to make a mini boss?"

Bernice laughed. "I don't have a maternal bone in my body. But in almost every business magazine interview I've done, I've been asked if I sacrificed having a family to be as successful as I am." She rolled her eyes. "No matter how many times I told them that children were never in my life plan, that same question kept coming."

"And we're back to gender expectations," Jessica said.

Taryn raised her glass. "Here's to people being people and doing whatever and *whoever* makes them happy."

"I'll drink to that," Andi said, raising her glass in one hand and bringing Bernice's hand to her lips with the other.

They all clinked their glasses, and Cassie met Taryn's intense gaze before they thankfully moved on to less sensitive topics. Cassie smiled and engaged in the group conversations, careful to keep quiet at any mention of family. But as the evening wore on, she became more relaxed. Part of that was due to the champagne that never stopped flowing, but mostly it was due to Taryn's attentiveness. Her gentle looks and tender touches were so unfamiliar and unexpected, but Cassie absorbed each one of them like they were water for an unquenchable thirst. A thirst that had crept up on her while she'd been busy just having fun.

Chapter Fourteen

GWEN TIGHTENED THE FINAL bolt on the seat adjustment and stepped aside. "She's all yours."

Taryn grinned and straddled the bike. She settled back and placed her feet on the pedals, making sure her legs were angled perfectly before she rocked the bike off its center stand and onto both tires. She put both feet flat on the floor and rocked from side to side to reacquaint herself with its weight.

"Are you sure you want to test this bike on the globe?" Andi asked, the concern evident in her expression.

Taryn nodded. "It's not like I've never ridden it before, is it? I've been using the Pulsar over the Triple R back at the ranch between the shows."

Andi tilted her head. "Yeah, but there's a difference between razzing around the tracks with no one watching and putting it in the double globe."

Taryn looked at Andi and frowned. "I don't understand your reluctance. This is what we do. Testing out the limits of the bike in the most extreme environment we're going to put it in is how we've always operated." She grinned and turned the engine. "Is Bernice Sexpot making you soft?"

Andi punched Taryn's shoulder hard enough that Taryn grasped the handlebars to steady the bike. "Don't be an ass...and a hypocrite."

"What's that supposed to mean?" Taryn asked and gently twisted the throttle.

"You and the sexy doc. You made all that noise about not wanting to stay in one place so long, and you've settled right into a new reality nice and easy. Am I right?" Andi and Gwen fist-bumped.

"Being in love isn't so bad, Tar," Gwen said as she crouched down to inspect something on the back tire.

"First, I'm not in love, thanks, Gwen. Cassie and I are just having a lot of fun and even more sex—"

"*That* would be the definition of being in love if you're lucky enough," Gwen said. "Ask Fig. If we don't have sex at least every other day, she starts asking me if I've fallen out of love with her."

Taryn didn't know what to do with that piece of philosophy, and she wasn't about to start asking a twenty-eight-year-old about their sex life. "And just because I'm not complaining about it doesn't mean that I'm happy about staying in this neon-infested desert for more than a few days."

Andi grinned widely and shook her head slowly. "The fact that you've just reacted that strongly tells us a very different story to the one your words are trying to give us."

Taryn revved the engine instead of responding. Maybe she was protesting a touch too much.

"See?" Andi and Gwen laughed. "There's no shame in changing your mindset."

"A damn fine woman will do that for you," Gwen said.

Andi nodded. "Amen to that."

"So Bernice is the pillion passenger you were hoping she was?" Taryn asked, happy to turn the focus on Andi's blossoming relationship.

Andi's wide smile and the way her face softened gave Taryn the answer without words. She'd never seen Andi like this, so she had nothing to compare it against, but it was clear something had definitely changed for her. In her own way, Andi had loved many women in the time Taryn had known her, but this looked like *love* love. It was something Taryn hadn't felt either, but she'd seen enough movies to know what it was *supposed* to look like: wistful, faraway gazing; softly spoken sweet nothings; and a general marshmallow appearance where once had been a stone wall.

"I think so." Andi shifted on her feet and kicked at the glossy concrete surface of the stadium. "Maybe it's too early to say it out loud—I don't want to jinx it."

Taryn tried to disguise her grin at Andi's body language. Seeing her like this was so alien. "Do you know if she feels the same?"

Andi snorted. "Are you kidding? Like I'm going to outright ask if she's in love with me."

Taryn slapped the bike's fuel tank. "Ha! You are in love then?"

Gwen moved closer to Andi and draped her arm over her shoulder. "Do you want some advice, boss?"

Andi groaned. "Do I have a choice?"

"No. You don't," Taryn said before Gwen could respond.

Gwen removed her arm from Andi's shoulder and gave Taryn a look that might've been intimidating if she was another foot taller. "I don't have to share my thoughts with you, no. But it might save you some unnecessary pain."

"Fine. Let's hear it," Andi said.

"My advice is, don't play games and don't waste time." Gwen waved her wrench with each word then crossed her arms.

Taryn chuckled but couldn't agree more with Gwen's sentiments, particularly the second one. The earlier you learned that time was finite and precious, the more fulfilling life could be. "You're not even thirty yet; do you get to lecture someone approaching a half century on this ball of dust about the importance of time?"

"I do when it's related to something Andi has zero experience of." Gwen put her hands on her hips and glared at Taryn. "And neither do you, so maybe you'll learn something if you listen too."

Taryn held up her hands. "No knowledge is bad knowledge. I'm always open to learning new things...even if I have no intention of using them." Because she didn't need to know any more about real love than what she knew of it from books and movies, did she? She and Cassie *were* just having fun while Taryn was in Vegas with the show. She reminded herself that what they were doing was only ever supposed to be a short-term thing, and she was simply enjoying being around Cassie. The sex was amazing, and the conversation was great, and Taryn was having the best time she'd had outside of the shows for a long, long time. Perhaps ever. That didn't make it love.

"You're the only one you're fooling, Tar." Andi looked at Gwen. "What do you mean about games though?"

Taryn opened her mouth to retort, but Gwen shushed her.

"I mean, don't waste time playing them. If you think that you love her, tell Bernice you think you love her. If you know you love her, tell her that you love her. What's the worst thing that could happen if she doesn't feel the same way?"

"I could get my heart broken," Andi said.

Gwen laughed lightly. "A broken heart is a loving heart, and I'd rather have one of those than be closed off to all the possibilities love has to offer." She twisted the ring on her wedding finger. "You can't feel it all unless you give your all."

Taryn didn't allow her natural inclination to scoff to escape. What Gwen was saying sounded idealistic, but who was she to comment when Gwen and Fig seemed to be living proof of soulmates.

Andi nodded slowly. "It's not just about me though. If I fuck this up, it could ruin the show for everyone, and there's a lot of excitement around the paycheck for this gig. And for the potential of future gigs."

Taryn rocked the bike back on its center stand and got off. She faced Andi and waited for her to make eye contact. "I reckon I can speak for everyone about this; we've all been happy touring the world, doing what we do and getting paid pretty well for it. And we'd all be happy to do it again." She shrugged. "Of course the money we're getting for the Cosmos residency is great, but what we do has always been about more than the money. It's about family and friendship. You showed me that when you first took me in. And for some," she gestured to Gwen, "it's been about finding their soulmate. *If*—and that's a big if, based on how Bernice was hanging all over you and your every word the other night—*if* she doesn't feel the same, and that makes it too hard for you to continue the show here, or she kicks us out, so be it. We'll rally and pull together like the family that we are." Taryn took a step forward and prodded Andi in the chest gently. "You don't get to use us as an excuse for not risking your heart. And you don't get to prioritize us over your potential lifelong happiness."

Gwen clapped. "When you come out with a speech like that, you're damn right that you can speak for all of us."

Taryn pulled Andi into a full bro hug and slapped her on the back. "If you've found your pillion passenger, buddy, you need to tell her so you can start planning the rest of your lives together." She pulled away slightly and tapped Andi's chest again. "This only gets a finite number of beats. You know I believe that. Don't waste any of them."

Andi pulled her back in for a full embrace. "I'll tell her. And maybe you can take your own advice too," she whispered only loud enough for Taryn to hear before shoving her away abruptly. "Okay, enough chat. We need to get you in the globe with that bike."

Taryn frowned but didn't say anything. She *did* take her own advice. She lived in the moment every day and wasted no time. She was constantly moving, working, having fun. She was never still. She ignored the voice that began to wonder if time with Cassie was the thing she somehow needed more of.

Chapter Fifteen

CASSIE PULLED INTO THE gravel drive of her mom's property and got out to open the chain link gates. She'd gotten back in her car, pulled in, *and* closed the gates before her mom emerged from the trailer. Cassie noted the absence of the new car she'd bought. *So that's going to be the first bone of contention.* Part of her wanted to jump back in her Fiat, smash through the gates, and drive away. Not just for today but forever. She'd hated not being able to talk about her family with Taryn and her friends a few days ago; everyone else had talked freely about their loved ones, good and bad, and Cassie had felt disingenuous through her reticence.

Her mom's giant boxer pushed past her in the doorway and bounded up to Cassie. As she gave his head a rub, great globules of his saliva dropped onto her sneakers. She'd anticipated it, of course, and had duly worn an old pair of running shoes she kept for only these visits.

"Come on, boy." She headed toward the trailer, steeling herself for an unpleasant couple of hours—if she could last that long.

"Isn't it about time you treated yourself to a new pair of sneakers?" her mom asked.

Cassie tried to smile, but her mom's appearance made it difficult. Four in the afternoon and she was still in her PJs, heavily stained with food and drink, plus the odd cigarette burn, no doubt from falling unconscious drunk and still smoking. A cigarette hung from her mouth, and she had a glass of whiskey in her hand. How many had she already had before Cassie got there? And had she drunk extra because she would find this visit difficult to cope with too?

"And what's going on with your face and hair? You're letting yourself slide, girl. You're never going to attract a man if you can't be bothered to fix your hair and makeup." Her mom tutted and shook her head, her lips curling in disdain. "You never know who you might meet at a gas station, you know?"

Cassie clenched her jaw and tried for another smile, only half caring whether or not she was successful. Her mom knew full well that Cassie was gay and had never shown any interest in attracting any man, let alone the type she might meet at a gas station.

"I taught you better than that, didn't I?"

"You did, Mom. Sorry." Cassie closed her eyes briefly and gave Buster another pat on the head. She didn't think any of her mom's lessons had actually been useful, least of all the ones about how to gussy herself up *just* for the benefit of potential lovers.

Her mom stepped back into the trailer. "You better come in. You're making the place look messy." She turned away and the screen door swung shut.

Cassie looked through the door then down to Buster. He glanced up at her and whined. If she could read animal expressions, she figured Buster's was a desperate plea to escape. Her mom never took him for a walk; the only exercise he got was running around the yard. When she'd once asked why she'd bought a dog, if not to get out and stretch her legs, her mom bluntly responded that Buster was for security and nothing more. Her mom wasn't abusive, thankfully, but her idea of caring for the dog was just providing the basics of food, water, and shelter—if he was lucky and made it inside the house while she was still conscious.

"What the hell are you waiting for? Are you coming in or not? I don't want the neighbors seeing you out there looking the way you do," her mom yelled. "I'll get my makeup bag and brushes. You know where the coffee pot is."

Cassie blew out a long breath. Yep, she knew where the coffee pot was. She'd been making coffee for her mom since she was eight and could reach the counter with the help of a folding stool.

She pushed open the screen door and stepped inside. The odor that assailed her nose almost made her gag. Particles of wet dog, cigarettes, and rotting food set off her olfactory nerve like a cheese grater on her skin.

She walked around the cream couch—at least, it had once been that color before being subjected to dirty dog feet, fallen cigarette ash, and countless spills of whiskey and beer—and opened the blinds. Cassie was about to push the window up when her mom returned.

"What're you doing? The a/c is on. D'ya think I'm made of money?" She batted Cassie's hands and shooed her away. "Make yourself useful and brew a pot."

Cassie rolled her neck and tried to think of the soothing tune of a meditation track from BodyBalance but came up empty. She'd bet the Dalai Lama would have trouble meditating his way out of this ugly environment. "I thought some fresh air would be nice. It's stuffy in here."

"The only stuffy thing in here is you." Her mom gave Cassie a shove. "Go. Coffee."

One look at the coffee pot had Cassie wishing she'd brought in her to-go mug from the car or grabbed something cold from the gas station. "Do you have bottled water?"

Her mom's lip curled in disgust. "What do you think this is, the Bellagio? What's wrong with coffee?" She picked up her glass and knocked the rest of the whiskey back. "Or did you want something stronger?"

Bile rose to the back of Cassie's throat. How could her mom encourage her to drink and drive after what had happened to her brother? "Too early for me, thanks, Mom." She opened the cupboard door to retrieve a couple of mugs and pressed her lips together when her fingers registered the thick greasy film on the metal handle.

"Barely been here a minute and already you're handing out the judgments left and right," her mom said. "Anything else you want to criticize about my house and the way I live, Ms. Perfect?"

Cassie closed her eyes and focused on the blackness of her eyelids. She followed a little starburst from top to bottom before opening her eyes again. "I'm not judging anything, Mom." She wanted, of course, to question how her mom's barbs were any different, but she didn't. It wasn't worth the argument. It had taken her a while to understand that, and it had been a tough lesson to learn as a child. One of many. Therapy had been essential in college to discover how dysfunctional her family situation really was.

She pulled two mugs down, thick with dust and grime. The thought of putting her lips to one made her nauseous.

"You got someone in the car with you?" her mom asked as she stomped into the kitchen, her sliders slapping loudly on the linoleum floor.

Cassie glanced over her shoulder. "Of course not." She hadn't brought anyone home when she was a kid. She'd been too ashamed and embarrassed. That hadn't changed, so she wasn't about to start now. Her mind drifted to Taryn and what she might think of this place, of her mom. Would it lessen her opinion of Cassie somehow? She hoped she wasn't giving off too many happy vibes after all her time with Taryn. Even if Taryn wouldn't judge Cassie because of her mom, she couldn't imagine getting to a place where she'd want to introduce them to each other. It was getting harder to remember that Taryn wasn't going to be a permanent fixture in her life; Taryn would be gone soon enough, and Cassie already knew her life would be poorer without her. So she definitely wasn't about to waste any of the time she *did* have with Taryn by sharing her with her mom. "Why do you think I've got someone with me?"

Her mom gestured at the mugs on the counter. "Two. You've got to know I don't want one." She wrinkled her nose then busied herself refilling her glass. "Although I don't know why I expect you to remember anything about what I like given how little you visit me nowadays. Too busy with your fancy hospital friends to worry about your old mom." She swept her gaze over Cassie once again. "I don't know what you do with your time, because you clearly don't spend it looking after yourself." She tugged at Cassie's T-shirt. "This is too big for you. Or are you hiding something? Are you pregnant or are you getting fat?" Her mom pulled the material tight over Cassie's body then let out a dramatic puff. "No. That's good, I suppose. You've still got one thing going for you. Though it's probably about time you made me a grandma. Your clock's running, girl. Don't be one of those stupid women who think they can have a baby in their forties. Who wants a doddering old bat at their parent-teacher nights? You were lucky. I always looked amazing when I went anywhere for your school events." Her mom stood a little straighter and fluffed up her hair. "All your male teachers couldn't take their eyes from me and the girls." She pushed up her breasts and smiled.

Her mom's stained teeth were evidence she'd let her standards slip, but honestly, Cassie couldn't remember her mom coming to anything school or college-related. As with so many things, her mom had simply invented a new history to suit her internal view of herself. And there was so much in her mom's monologue to unpack, Cassie felt overwhelm already creeping up her ankles, threatening to take hold. "I'm probably not going to have children, Mom, so you don't have to worry about that." The thought of subjecting a child to her mom would be enough of a contraceptive for anyone.

"Why? I'd be a wonderful grandmother. Look at how you turned out: a doctor, no less." She thumbed toward the street. "Everyone else around here, their kids are working at the Dollar General or Walmart, stocking shelves and schlepping around the warehouse working nights. Not my baby. I taught you to want more from your life. *I* pushed you to college and that scholarship. You would've been flipping burgers at McDonald's if it hadn't been for me."

Cassie stretched out her fingers and stared at her nails, which reminded her that she and Rachel were due a visit to the salon. She needed to focus on anything other than the absolute nonsense coming out of her mom's mouth. The only thing her mom had pushed her toward was the makeup and condom aisles. She'd never shown any interest in Cassie's academic pursuits, and it had been a kindhearted high school teacher who had guided Cassie through the scholarship application process. Oh, how Cassie had fantasized that Ms. Greggs would intervene and adopt her. How many times had she dropped to her knees and prayed that Ms. Greggs would take Cassie away from her mom to live with her? She'd even sketched out the house they lived in, decorated her bedroom, and imagined their conversations in the car on the way to school every day.

"And this is the thanks I get." Her mom threw up her hands. "All that money you've wasted on *therapy* could've bought me a nice house in a nice neighborhood. But instead, I have to live out my days, scraping by on social security and the bits of money you send when you're in a good mood. And I can't rely on that because you always seem to be angry at me for one reason or another that I can never understand."

Cassie shuffled the mugs on the countertop and fought to remain calm. The therapy she'd had meant she was just about able to maintain a relationship with her mom, which she made increasingly difficult. The hours of counseling also meant Cassie could remain in control of her emotions and triggers and not let her mom draw her into something toxic. "Speaking of which, where's your new car?"

Her mom tutted loudly. "That took longer than I expected. For you to throw that in my face. But I guess you haven't even sat down yet."

Cassie shook her head. "I'm not throwing anything in your face, Mom. I just wanted to have a look at it and make sure you're happy with it."

"Huh, because you're a car mechanic too now, are you? If you were that concerned with my happiness, you'd buy me a new car with one of those ten-year warranties. If you cared enough about my safety when I'm driving alone on long, deserted roads, you wouldn't settle for a junker that could break down in the middle of the night and leave me vulnerable to attack by an axe murderer."

Why her mom was driving around in the middle of the night on those kinds of roads was an issue, but it wasn't one Cassie could confront, or she'd be accused of mothering her mother and thinking her too old to still enjoy herself. She did think that an axe murderer wouldn't stand a chance when faced with her mom's rage. "I didn't know you needed a new car, Mom."

"How could you know I need anything? You're never around." She glared at Cassie for a long moment. "Fred's taken it. He needed it for work."

"Who's Fred?" she asked before she could stop herself. Conversations with her mom were too exhausting. It was like a chess match where she had to think four or five questions ahead and know how her mom would react to them. Cassie dropped her shoulders and relaxed slightly when her mom's expression brightened a little.

"My new man," her mom said. "And what a man he is. Let me show you a photograph. I'll get my phone."

Her mom tottered off, giving Cassie the opportunity to give one of the mugs a quick wash. She also managed to empty the coffee pot and wash it and the filter before her mom returned.

"Isn't he handsome?"

Her mom thrust her phone close to Cassie's face, and she noted it was a brand new model that would be costing her a hell of a lot of money each month. Cassie moved back slightly and focused on the screen. She schooled her expression. Yes, Cassie was gay, but she could appreciate and recognize a good-looking man when she saw one. But the craggy-faced specimen captured in millions of pixels in front of her was not what she would call handsome. Beauty was in the eye of the beholder, of course, but this guy's face was all kinds of wrong, probably from in-breeding. And even in a two-dimensional image, there was a hard and hostile expression in his eyes. Cassie imagined he and her mother would clash and have epic, destroy-it-all arguments. She couldn't help her errant mind wondering what it might be like to see a picture of her own father. Did she have his eyes? His smile? Her mother had destroyed all photographic evidence of him, and Cassie had been too young when he last held her in his arms to remember any of his features. She saw him in dreams sometimes, but they were soft, and there was no definition to his face. Why couldn't she remember him?

"Cassandra." Her mom gave Cassie's shoulder a rough shove. "He's gorgeous, isn't he? Is that why you're speechless? I bet you want him for yourself, don't you?"

Cassie smiled widely at the preposterous notion. Her mirth slipped at yet another refusal from her mom to accept Cassie's sexuality. *Even if I was straight, I wouldn't touch him if the fate of the planet depended on it.* "What does he do for a living?"

Her mom's expression hardened again, and she dropped her arm. "What does it matter what he does for a living? Why is that your first question? Why can't you just be happy that *I'm* happy?" She took a long swig of her drink and wiped an escaping droplet from the side of her mouth. "I haven't been happy since your father left."

Cassie turned away and began to scoop some cheap, no-name coffee into the filter paper, wishing she could remember if she'd been happy in the first seven years of her life before he'd left. Had they been content? Her mom said they'd always been dirt-poor, but Cassie couldn't know that with any certainty. But even if they had, they could've been rich in other ways. Love didn't cost anything. Had her father held her in his arms when she'd just been born and felt a love so intense and overwhelming, it had brought him to tears?

"I bet my son would've liked to have seen me happy."

Cassie rammed the coffee pot so hard into the holder that it hit the rear wall of the machine and smashed all over the countertop. Her mom hadn't sunk this low before, and that was saying something.

"Shit, Cassandra. What the hell are you doing?" Her mom took a step closer before she halted abruptly. "You're bleeding."

Cassie looked down at her right hand and saw blood pulsing from a long cut between her thumb and forefinger. She calmly moved to the sink and turned on the faucet to wash away any remaining shards, then she yanked off a couple of pieces of paper towel from the roll and pressed them over the wound.

Her mom remained motionless and unhelpful, as she had done the many times Cassie had injured herself as a child. It was little wonder she'd ended up in medicine, even without everything else that had pushed her in that direction. Cassie lifted the paper to inspect the damage; it wasn't too deep, but it would need stitches, which, ridiculously, was a relief. "I have to get to the ER and have this stitched."

Her mom swallowed another mouthful of whiskey. "Of course you do." She waved her hands wildly at the mess in her kitchen. "Cause chaos and then disappear. That's just like you."

Cassie swapped out the bloodied paper towel for fresh sheets and ignored the groundless dig. She had no idea where her mom's memories of their interactions derived, but they weren't from reality, and her therapist taught her she couldn't battle with figments of her mom's imagination. "I'll clear this up before I leave."

Her mom wobbled her head like a turkey. "Good. And make sure you get all your blood. Fred doesn't like the sight of blood."

"Of course." Cassie began the clean-up operation, predictably unassisted by her mom, who stood by tutting and shaking her head.

"Of course you'll get all the blood or of course Fred doesn't like the sight of blood?"

Cassie frowned and swept the broken glass into a paper bag

she'd found under the sink. "You'll never know I injured myself, Mom." *And it'll be cleaner than when I got here.*

"Huh, I'll know every time I want to make coffee and can't."

Cassie didn't respond. Her mom didn't drink coffee.

"Don't give me that look. Fred likes coffee, and now I won't be able to make him any because *you've* broken the pot in a temper."

Exchanges like this caused Cassie to occasionally question the validity of her therapist's advice *not* to engage. How could her mom ever learn what an unpleasant human being she was if she was never challenged? Teaching her mom how to be a better person wasn't her job. Her job was to concentrate on herself and her own healing. But would she ever be healed if she continued to pick at the wound by maintaining a relationship with her mom? "I'll buy you a new one."

"When?"

Cassie finished wiping the countertop and crumpled the top of the paper bag closed. "Right now." She pulled her phone from her pocket and searched for the exact model in front of her. "They sell replacement pots—"

"You may as well replace the whole thing," her mom said. "You've probably damaged the machine as well with the way you slammed it around."

Cassie smiled over gritted teeth. "Sure." She showed her mom the sales page on her cell.

"That's an old model." Her mom snatched the phone and scrolled down the screen. "Fred likes his milk hot and frothy. Don't they have a machine that does that?"

Cassie pinched the bridge of her nose. *Of course Amazon has a machine that does that.* Amazon sell machines that do everything. But why would she want to spend hundreds of dollars on something for *Fred's* benefit? The man in the picture her mom had thrust under her nose did not look like a man who liked hot and frothy milk. He seemed like more of a strong and black coffee kind of guy.

She swapped out the rudimentary dressing again and unfurled the paper bag to put the bloodied towel inside. The cut was obviously deeper than it looked, but her mom still showed no concern for anything other than her own needs. Cassie didn't expect anything else, of course. Wasn't that the definition of insanity? To expect a different outcome from the same action?

Her mom handed Cassie's phone back. "That one. And I need it today. Fred should be home tonight, and he'll want his coffee. You don't want me telling him that you're the reason he can't have his coffee at night."

Or what? He'll come find me? But there was something more ominous in her mom's words than her usual drama, like she might even be harboring a little fear. God knew what kind of a man Fred was; Cassie was glad she wasn't hanging around to find out. She looked at her phone to see her mom had chosen an eight-hundred-dollar barista express machine—quite the upgrade from the thirty-dollar unit Cassie had just broken. Was she making her mom worse by pandering to her outrageous sense of entitlement? Yes, Cassie could afford it, but why should she?

Because she didn't want an ulcer, that's why. And no, she didn't want Fred turning up at the hospital demanding she satisfy his caffeine addiction. Cassie popped the contraption in her basket and selected same-day delivery. "It'll be here between five and seven p.m."

"It better be." Her mom tilted her head slightly and smiled. "Maybe you could order some nice coffee too. That would be a nice gesture for him."

Cassie pushed her phone back in her pocket and held up her bloodied hand. "I really have to go before I need a transfusion." She grabbed the paper bag from the counter and headed toward the door.

"Aren't you being a little over-dramatic? It's barely a scratch."

Cassie resisted the temptation to go back to her mom and open up her sliced skin like a mouth. "All this blood says otherwise.

And I don't want to upset Fred by spilling it everywhere, do I?"

Buster bounded up, placed himself between her and the door, and let out a loud groan. Dogs had never really been on her radar as something to keep her company, and her apartment didn't allow them anyway, but the pleading look in his eyes could've made her reconsider.

"She doesn't want you, Buster. You'd be too messy for her perfect, ordered life. Come here."

Buster ignored her mom, as did Cassie, and he continued to stare up at her expectantly. She opened the door, and he tore outside.

"When will you be back?" her mom asked.

"I don't know, Mom. I'll have to check my schedule." She might be working a lot less overtime since Taryn showed up, but Cassie wasn't about to start sacrificing that time to facilitate more contentious visits with her mom. The fun and sex she was having with Taryn felt like some of the best times of her life. Being here were the worst.

"So it'll be months again, will it?" Her mom crossed the kitchen and stood with her arms crossed in the living area.

Had it been months since her last visit? "I honestly can't say, Mom. We're short-staffed." Which wasn't a lie. It was just that Cassie had stopped being the go-to person to fill the gaps.

"And those anonymous people at the hospital are always more important than me, aren't they?"

Cassie blew out a long breath. Yes. Yes, they were. The people who ended up in the ER because of work accidents were more important than her mom. The ones who did really stupid things to get themselves admitted just so they could spend the night in a hospital bed were more important than her too. And especially important were the ones who found themselves in Cassie's care because of the careless actions of those around them.

"Goodbye, Mom." She closed the screen door behind her and hurried to her car, where Buster waited patiently by the driver's side door. "I'm sorry, boy." She rubbed his head, and he wiped his slobbery chops against her jeans. "Come on. You better go in." She'd opened her mom's gates a hundred times while Buster was untethered in the yard, but there was a glint in his eye that made her think he might've finally decided he'd had enough and was ready to make a run for it, especially if Cassie refused to take him in her car.

"Buster! Get your fucking sorry self back here right now."

They both looked back to the house at the unexpected shrieking, and Cassie's heart sank at having to leave him there. Her mom yelled again, and after one last sorry look, he loped off toward her. Cassie began the process of gate opening and closing, careful not to make eye contact with her mom. She could also feel the nuclear heat of her glare; she didn't need to see the bubbling rage that was maybe hatred too. Cassie drove away, avoiding the multiple holes in the rough road, wishing for all the world that she would never have to return.

Chapter Sixteen

TARYN HELD THE DRIVER'S side door open, and Cassie stepped out.

"This shouldn't take long," Cassie said.

"You said that your friend's daughter was here for more chemo?" Taryn closed the door behind her.

"I think of Sara as a colleague rather than a friend."

Taryn looked surprised. "Really? If this is what you do for your colleagues, your friends are very lucky."

Cassie frowned. "What makes you say that?"

"You don't think that what you're doing is a big deal?" Taryn asked and smiled.

Cassie popped the trunk and pulled out her purse. "Do you think it is?"

Taryn chuckled. "I do. I think you've got a huge heart." She pulled Cassie into a soft embrace and kissed her forehead. "It's quite endearing."

"I'm pretty sure not many people would want to be friends with me." Cassie pulled away and locked her car. "Friendships take time to nurture and maintain, and time is something I don't have much of."

Taryn tilted her head. "Like I say, you only get a finite number of heartbeats. It's best to spend them doing what you love."

Cassie raised her eyebrows and gave a hollow laugh. "That's a rather Utopian way of looking at things." She gestured toward the entrance. "Come on. I don't want to miss visiting time."

Taryn followed Cassie into the clinic, thinking about what she'd just said. There was a certain melancholy in Cassie's words, seemingly kissed with more than a little wistfulness or possibly regret. And as Taryn had uttered a version of her motto, she questioned the validity of her own choices. Did she still *love* the stunts and the shows? Over the last week of practice, even the levitated double globe of death hadn't offered its usual allure, and her mind had wandered to thoughts of what Cassie might be doing instead of laser-focusing on what she was doing. And that was dangerous. She counted herself lucky that her lack of concentration hadn't resulted in any incidents.

She flicked through the vast array of leaflets on the wall rack to give Cassie privacy while she made her donation. There seemed to be information for every type of cancer, disease, and physical ailment, as well as mental health assistance. The free clinic was trying to do what some of continental Europe and the UK offered, but with private philanthropic funding rather than money from the government. Taryn glanced around, trying to be as inconspicuous as possible, and her heart ached for what she saw. The waiting room was filled with people whose illnesses had gone hitherto untreated because they couldn't afford healthcare. Infected, undressed wounds; a woman with a growth the size of a watermelon on her side; and a father and son who looked in such a state of malnutrition, she could've mistaken them for starving Third World citizens—not citizens of one of the largest civilized nations on earth.

Cassie was donating her money, and she'd also talked about volunteering and giving her time and expertise too. Taryn thought about the money her parents had invested in her and her own lapsed license. She'd more or less renounced it because she didn't want to be tied to their business of perfection, but why hadn't she stopped to think about other avenues of medicine? Why hadn't she considered working at a clinic like this? She'd thought her desperation to escape her family, and by association, Miami, had been fueled by her wanderlust, but had the wanderlust simply been a by-product of her escape? She'd been feeling disenchanted with riding for a while and hadn't wanted to address or analyze it for fear it might bring to light what she already knew, deep down, in the shadows of her mind—that she was still lost and still looking for something special, but she didn't know what.

She filed the leaflet on testicular cancer back on the wall and shook the thought away. She loved traveling, and she was happily rootless. She *was* sure of that. But she was no longer sure of her current vocation.

"Taryn?"

Cassie's soft voice drifted into her consciousness, and she turned toward her. "Yep?"

"Do you want to wait in the car, or do you want to come with me?"

Taryn frowned. She'd already said she was happy to accompany Cassie to see Louise before they went shopping for Cassie's launch party outfit. "I'll come with you unless you don't want me to."

Cassie stepped forward and took Taryn's hand. "I want you to. I was just checking."

Taryn gently tightened her grip, enjoying the feel of Cassie's soft and strong hand in hers and liking how it seemed to fit so perfectly. She walked alongside Cassie to a single room where she was introduced to Sara and Louise, who wore a thin cotton beanie to cover her head, bald from the chemo's side effects. When Cassie had mentioned this situation and told her how Louise was only fifteen, Taryn hadn't known quite how to react. Seeing the kid now, along with her obvious distress at her appearance, Taryn knew exactly what she had to do. She excused herself to make a phone call and registered Cassie's wounded and quizzical expression but knew that would change if she could arrange what she had in mind.

She waited until she was in the corridor before she called. "Hey, Melanie."

"My favorite client," Melanie said. "You haven't set another wig on fire, have you?"

Taryn laughed at the unpleasant memory that had reinforced a valuable lesson about the inflammability of hairspray around cigarettes. That particular lover had cost Taryn five thousand dollars. "Thankfully not. I need a wig, but it's not for me." She quickly explained the situation with Louise. "Could you fly over with your magic box and help me out?"

"For you—and for this—I'll clear my schedule. I can be there tomorrow afternoon."

"You are a wonderful human being," Taryn said.

"Right back at you. Send me the details of the clinic and your hotel?"

"Sure thing. Thanks again, Melanie." Taryn hung up and re-entered Louise's room. She grinned at Cassie's raised eyebrow and slightly annoyed expression. "I don't know if Cassie's told you, but I wear a wig for my—"

"For your amazing stunts." Louise's face lit up. "Cassie's told us all about you, and we've been watching your videos on ZimTak. You're so brave."

Taryn choked back the ball of emotion that blocked her throat. "I think *you're* the one that's brave." She approached the empty side of Louise's bed. "How are you feeling?" she asked, putting off her news for a moment.

Louise put both hands on her head and pulled her beanie down a little farther over her ears. "Like an ugly duckling that'll never get to be the white swan."

Sara tapped her daughter's upper arm. "Don't say that, Lou. You're so beautiful, you can pull off any look."

Louise rolled her eyes and shook her head while still looking at Taryn. "I think she's talking to you," she said.

"Nope, kiddo. She was definitely talking to you, and she's absolutely right. You are beautiful."

Louise wrinkled her nose. "*She* has to say that. *You* don't. But thanks, even if it is total bullshit."

"Louise! I'm sorry, Taryn." Sara looked mortified.

Taryn laughed. "You're a straight talker, huh?"

Louise nodded. "May as well be. If this shit," she ignored Sara's mortified gasp, "is teaching me anything other than how to throw up and still be hungry, it's that there's too little time to not tell it like I see it."

Taryn flicked some breadcrumbs from Louise's bedsheets. "That's something I totally get. Most people don't realize how precious time is until they don't have any left."

Cassie groaned. "You're slightly obsessed with it, babe."

Taryn looked across at Cassie and didn't stop her grin from widening. *Babe*. She liked the sound of that. She focused back on Louise. "Anyway, I was saying. I wear wigs, and I've got a great wig woman. I just stepped out to see if she might have some time to pop in with her giant stock of wigs to see if she's got something you might want to wear while you're getting your chemo and kicking cancer's ass." God, she hoped Louise was going to beat this. "She'll be here tomorrow afternoon, if that's okay with you?"

When Taryn had begun to speak, Louise was frowning. That had turned into surprise, and now her mouth and eyes were wide open.

"No way!" Louise's gaze switched from Taryn to Louise and Cassie and then back to Taryn. "Are you actually serious?"

"I never joke about hair." Taryn ran her hand over her own sharply cut style.

"She doesn't." Cassie walked around to the same side as Taryn and reached up to touch Taryn's hair, but she ducked out of the way.

"Don't touch my mane." Taryn batted Cassie's hand away playfully. Of course, Cassie could put her hand anywhere she damn well pleased, but the kid was laughing at their banter, and Cassie seemed to be happy playing along.

"This is definitely happening?" Louise's eyes had gone glassy with unshed tears. "You're getting me a wig?"

"Sure am. And of course, you'll be like one of those Oscar actors who get all their outfits for free because you're going to look so good in it."

Sara clapped her hand over her mouth, and Cassie's expression... Taryn couldn't truly describe the look Cassie was giving her, but it was absolutely *all* good, and she had a feeling that her reward post-shopping would be *extra* special. Win-win.

***

Taryn waited on a comfy couch for Cassie to come out from the changing room in the next amazing outfit. Shopping had never been so much fun, and she was a *big* fan of shopping.

Cassie opened the dressing room curtain and stepped out in a slinky, figure-hugging, deep purple dress. She wiggled her shoulders, and the movement jiggled her breasts. With its plunging neckline, the dress struggled to keep them sheathed. Taryn gave a low growl.

"Now *that's* a look that can give a woman confidence in what she's wearing." Cassie gave a demure smile before she twirled around quickly.

"It's the woman *in* the dress that makes it that appealing." Taryn stood and circled Cassie slowly, taking in every inch of her. It was all she could do to keep her hands to herself. She leaned in from behind and whispered, "I want to drag you back into that changing room and take you right now." She could practically feel Cassie's soft skin under her fingertips as she mentally pulled up the dress and pushed Cassie against the wall.

Cassie shivered. "I want that too, but it's never going to happen."

Taryn came around to face Cassie and stuck out her bottom lip. "Spoilsport."

Cassie arched her eyebrow, instantly putting Taryn into a heightened state of arousal.

Taryn dropped back onto the couch and crossed her legs so she could squeeze her thighs together and control her response. "Woman, do you *know* what you do to me?"

"I know what I'd like to do to you," Cassie said, her tone dropping south into super sexy.

Taryn glanced away then returned her gaze to Cassie's. She knew exactly what Cassie was talking about, and she wanted it too. It had been a while since she'd surrendered her body to a woman's desires. Taryn was more than happy to give, but that didn't include giving herself to someone. She reserved that intimacy for women she had strong feelings for, and there'd only ever been a couple of those way back in her past, long before this stunt-show life.

But she couldn't deny her feelings for Cassie had developed unexpectedly. What she'd thought would be a one-time thing had turned into something regular, time she looked forward to, even craved. Time she didn't want to deny herself. When she'd gotten to Vegas, she couldn't wait to leave; now, the thought of leaving filled her with a sense of dread she didn't want to acknowledge. Deep down though, she knew that staying wasn't an option. She enjoyed traveling and moving from place to place way too much to give it up, even for...

She laughed at herself. It wasn't that. It couldn't be that. But that didn't mean she couldn't enjoy what they had right now and simply accept that her body and mind were desperate for Cassie to get on her knees and put her mouth on her.

"Do you want to see any of the other dresses, or is this the winner already?" Cassie asked when Taryn didn't respond to her overture.

"I want to see you in everything we picked out," Taryn said. "And then we should go back to my place so you can do whatever it is you want to do to me."

Cassie's eyes darkened, and she took three elegant steps in four-inch heels toward her. Taryn had gotten familiar with Cassie's various expressions, and this was a particular favorite.

Cassie shook her head slowly. She placed her finger under Taryn's chin and lifted it slightly. "We're taking this dress, and we're getting out of here right now."

Taryn swallowed and could do no more than nod. The pure

desire and lust she saw in Cassie's eyes weakened her ability to do anything else and certainly negated any notion of insisting on seeing the other outfits. It didn't matter which of the sophisticated dresses Cassie wore for the team's after party, she would look stunning, and Taryn would be proud to walk beside her.

Cassie returned to the changing room and was back out in magician-style time with the purple dress on her arm. After paying, she practically dragged Taryn out of the shop and jumped into her car, which was thankfully parked close by. Taryn tapped the location of her trailer and the team's camp into Cassie's phone and mounted it on the dash. Even with the top down, the air around them was thick with sexual promise, stifling any conversation and ramping up the tension. They'd had a lot of sex since they'd met, and Taryn had treasured every single time, but this already felt different, felt serious for both of them, like they were about to cross a line that took them into uncharted territory.

Ten silent minutes later, Taryn directed Cassie into the spot beside her trailer.

Cassie pointed at it as she got out of her car. "We'll talk about you lying to me about the size of this later." She came around the hood and pushed Taryn toward her home. "But first..."

She pressed Taryn against the door and kissed her. Taryn melted between the hard metal and the softness of Cassie's body. She let Cassie dictate the pressure and speed and surrendered to her passionate intensity.

Cassie broke away slowly, but not before she'd nibbled on Taryn's lower lip. "Let me in."

Taryn's lips twitched into a half smile. She was about to let Cassie in to more that her trailer, and though that made her chest hammer against her ribs, she pulled her keys from her pocket and opened the door. Cassie climbed up the steps, pulled Taryn in behind her, and slammed the door shut. She didn't look around or check the place out at all. She just looked at Taryn, and Taryn still couldn't find any words.

"Bedroom?" Cassie asked.

Taryn thumbed toward the far end of the trailer behind her, and Cassie ate up the space between them, guiding Taryn backward. She yanked Taryn's shirt open and began to unbuckle her belt before they got to the bedroom door. Taryn reached behind her as she was propelled backward and fumbled the handle open. They practically fell through the door, and Cassie pushed Taryn onto her bed.

"I can do anything I want?" Cassie whispered.

Taryn appreciated the self-restraint of Cassie's final check-in and nodded. "Anything."

"I wanted to do all of this slowly," Cassie said as she unzipped Taryn's jeans and tugged them down to the floor. She pulled off her shoes and tossed them aside. "I wanted to take my time and undress you item by item and wind you up like a clock."

Taryn lifted her ass from the bed to allow Cassie to tear off her shorts, exposing her most vulnerable self.

"But I can't." Cassie went down to her knees and pushed Taryn's legs apart.

She let out a quiet breath, and Taryn thought she might come right then. Cassie seemed to communicate all her unbridled desire, blatant longing, and yearning for Taryn in one simple but loaded expression.

"I like the way you look at me," Taryn whispered. Her latent, niggling fears of allowing herself to be laid wide open like this dissipated.

Cassie licked her lips and tucked her arms under Taryn's legs. She pulled Taryn closer and lowered her head.

She let out a guttural moan. "God, you smell good."

Taryn bit her lip and dropped her head back on the bed. But only for a moment; she didn't want to break eye contact, and she didn't want to miss a thing. She reached down and ran her fingers through Cassie's hair. "You're so beautiful." Her words weren't adequate, but they'd have to do. All Taryn wanted was Cassie's full lips on her, Cassie's tongue on her clit. "Please," she murmured, powerless and happily so.

Cassie's eyebrow quirked for the merest of seconds before she lowered her head and took Taryn into her mouth. Taryn sucked in a lungful of air as the sensation of Cassie's tongue on her lips sent her spiraling into a sexual freefall. She clenched her fists into the comforter and pressed her head back into the mattress. She felt Cassie's hands on her hips, holding her down though Taryn wouldn't leave this spot even if a tornado warning sounded. Cassie settled into a strong and forceful pace, falling into an easy rhythm with the movement of Taryn's hips.

Taryn placed her hands over Cassie's, and Cassie interlocked their fingers, sealing and reinforcing their connection as her tongue continued to tease and tempt Taryn to the precipice of profound pleasure. Taryn raised her head from the bed and locked eyes with Cassie. Unspoken words flowed between them as she seemed to understand exactly what this meant for Taryn, and for them. And as Cassie brought her to orgasm, Taryn fell, weightless and untethered from everything that was holding her back, everything that she hadn't even realized was doing so.

And she fell hard with a sliver of hope that Cassie might want to catch her.

Chapter Seventeen

"WHY CAN WE HAVE so much frivolous fun *and* seriously intense conversations?" Taryn plumped the pillows behind her and sat up. "I don't think I've had deep conversations like this with anyone but Andi—certainly not with anyone I've slept with."

"Maybe that's the difference; we're not doing an awful lot of *sleeping*." Cassie winked, and Taryn grinned. "If you want to redress the balance, you could sleep over tonight. If you wanted. I wouldn't force you, obviously."

Taryn glanced away and didn't respond.

They had only spent the night together once, after they'd fallen asleep exhausted the first time they'd gotten together. It was a different prospect entirely to *plan* to spend the night together. That was...intimate in a way that purely having sex wasn't. Did she want intimate? Did Taryn? If the past few hours were anything to go by, it seemed like she did. Unless what they'd just done had scared her off, and she was already looking for some way to back off. Which was hard to do right now since they were in Taryn's trailer. Maybe she should just leave and see if Taryn followed. "If you're going to overthink the offer, I'm rescinding it right now." Cassie looked at Taryn and smiled to show she was still trying to be lighthearted, even after what they'd just shared. She took a sip of water and focused on the door of Taryn's bedroom instead. She really hadn't expected Taryn's trailer to be quite this comfortable and spacious.

"No, please don't," Taryn said quickly then looked like she wanted to pull the words back into her mouth. "I'm just trying to work out what's happening, and if we're both okay with whatever that is."

"So you are overthinking it." Cassie put her glass down on the bedside table and placed her hand on Taryn's hip. "We're both competent adults, Taryn, and we know what we're doing. We're having an almost illegal amount of fun while it's available." She ran her hand along Taryn's stomach and stopped just below her chest. Was she pushing it, touching Taryn this much after only just being given permission to do so? "You've made it clear that you're a rolling stone, and as soon as your residency is over, you'll be off traveling around the world again with your stunt team. And I'm," she gestured to the window with her other hand, "happy here and at the hospital." She couldn't help the uncharacteristic hesitation and hoped that Taryn hadn't caught it.

"*Are* you happy here? We've never really talked about what you do or why you do it."

Cassie removed her hand and retrieved her water to take a large drink, vaguely wishing it was something stronger to cope with a topic like this. "I don't know that you really want to have that kind of intense conversation right now." Strangely, she *was* prepared to edge into that territory. She hadn't talked when Taryn asked her about having siblings, and Taryn hadn't brought it up again, but Cassie felt that was out of respect rather than a lack of interest or that she'd forgotten she'd asked when they'd been on the boat. Taryn had just laid herself bare for Cassie. Taryn already had complete access to her body, so the only way she could return the favor was by sharing her most sheltered memories and vulnerabilities.

Taryn turned sideways and tucked her feet into a meditation pose. She took Cassie's free hand and held it in her lap. "I do. I want to know all about you—and your family. You shut me down on the lake, and I've been waiting for you to open up, that's all."

Cassie smiled at the weird synchronicity of her thought process and Taryn's words.

"We can do the quid pro quo again, if that'll help." Taryn shrugged and scrunched her nose. "Though I think you know more or less everything there is to know about me and my family after the dinner at Cosmos."

"I doubt that, but there's no need. I think we're a bit beyond that now." And Cassie was beyond rolling back her feelings too. She knew Taryn wasn't offering anything long-term, even if she had just let Cassie loose on her body, but that hadn't stopped Cassie's heart from getting involved. And that was okay. She'd grieve their separation when the inevitable happened, and she'd get back to her usual life, grateful that she'd had the experience rather than wallowing in its ending. What she didn't want to think about was Taryn's show and all the dangers it presented. She could control that, surely.

"Okay." Taryn traced light patterns along Cassie's forearm and looked at her with a serious expression. "*Are* you happy with your life and job?"

"I thought I was." She took a long, cleansing breath and tried to relax. She hadn't even talked about this with her therapist. Cassie was grateful when Taryn didn't press for more and simply continued with her soft touch. Which would usually have led to more sex, but tonight, it was comforting rather than sensual. Did being comfortable mean she could finally share her darkest guilt with someone who wasn't paid to listen? And if it did, where should she start? She closed her eyes and was immediately transported back to that night. Pre-therapy, Cassie had relived it over and over, but now she was able to float above the room and watch. Detached but still so connected.

"Cassie?" Taryn whispered. "Are you okay?"

She opened her eyes, and the dam opened with them. Unable to stop the tears from flowing, she let them fall. "It's fine if you want me to leave. This probably wasn't what you had in mind when we tumbled into your trailer."

Taryn pulled Cassie's hand to her lips and kissed each of her knuckles gently. "I don't think anyone other than a psychopath hopes to be the cause of someone crying, but it's not a problem, honestly." She wrapped her hands tighter around Cassie's. "I adore having sex with you, but I also really love talking to you." She pressed her lips together and raised her eyes to the trailer roof. "Again, I'd rather you weren't crying but only because I hate to see you so sad, not because it makes me uncomfortable."

Cassie nodded slowly. She put her water down again and wiped her eyes with the back of her other hand. "You asked if I had any siblings, and I couldn't answer you at the time. I had a brother... but he died—he was killed." Died was such a passive term. Her brother hadn't just died. His life had been ripped away from him when he'd barely started it.

"I'm sorry," Taryn whispered and squeezed Cassie's hand.

"A drunk driver crashed into our bedroom." Cassie hovered above the scene, trying so hard to control old hurts. "He was only five, and I couldn't help him, Taryn. I couldn't get him out." A sob racked through her chest as the flames from the car engulfed their room. Her screams echoed in her head as her father dragged her out over the wall the car had decimated.

Taryn pulled Cassie closer and held her. She dropped her head onto Taryn's chest and released it, all of it. She hadn't cried like this for so long, and there was a peculiarly satisfying release to it. Taryn gently ran her hand over Cassie's head, stroking her hair slowly, and Cassie felt *held*, really *held* for the first time since the last occasion her father had held her before... "My father got me out, but he couldn't go back in. The fire was too strong, and the car exploded. He left home five months later. When the guilt got too much, and Mom's unrelenting blame was too hard to handle."

Cassie pulled in a huge lungful of air and sat back up. That's when she saw Taryn's empathy balanced precariously on the edge of her eyes. One blink, and her tears would overflow like the banks of a flooded river. Cassie had cried plenty of those for her brother, but she'd thought she had run dry.

"That's why you became an ER doctor—to save people?" Taryn asked quietly, and tears tracked down her cheeks. She wiped them away. "I'm sorry. I don't want to take away from your grief. Please, tell me why you became a doctor."

Cassie nodded, though Taryn's tears made her feel seen and heard. "Because I couldn't save him. I'm trying to assuage my guilt through helping hundreds of other people, but it's like the hole from a missing tooth. I keep tonguing it, and it never heals."

"I...I can't imagine what you've been through. What you're carrying with you."

This was where Cassie expected the pop psychology, the "you were too young to do anything," and "you shouldn't feel guilty," and "you were powerless." Instead, there was a refreshing silence, as if Taryn knew she'd heard all of it before, and there was nothing new to say.

"I have nothing to offer you, Cass. There aren't the words. Just let me hold you."

There. *That* was what she needed. That was what her mother hadn't done since the night of her brother's death, when she'd tucked them both into bed. It was what her father hadn't been able to do since he'd held her as she struggled through the flames and over the rubble... It was what she'd never let anyone do since, even though some had tried. The first person who really wanted to, the first person Cassie had allowed to, wasn't going to be around to do it for long either.

Cassie softened into Taryn's arms. So she may not be around for years to come, but she was here now, and Cassie could relax and accept what was currently being offered. For once, she had to live in the moment and forget the future, forget the past she was trying to make up for. She had to dwell in the possibilities of the now.

After many minutes of silence had passed, Cassie pulled away and settled into the full lotus position opposite Taryn. The outpouring of grief had left her both empty and fulfilled. Sharing the visceral details of her brother's death had brought them even closer together, and she felt less alone than she had for a long, long time.

"Show-off." Taryn prodded Cassie's knee. "I could barely get one foot on my thigh at your class."

"You'd be able to do this, no problem, if you came to BodyBalance regularly." She smiled at the ease with which they'd slipped back into gentle banter after such a profoundly difficult discussion.

"You think?"

Cassie nodded. "Repetitive practice can yield big results in a relatively short period of time. And it would help with your strength too." She dismissed the additional benefits of flexibility in the case of Taryn coming off her bike. More flexibility meant less chance of injury. Why was Cassie letting thoughts like that into her head?

Taryn tilted her head slightly and rocked on her butt cheeks. "I suppose I did think it was just about pretzeling yourself into strange animal positions, but my muscles ached like I'd done a real workout for the next few days."

Cassie pushed Taryn's shoulder. "Hey, they *are* real workouts."

"You know what I mean. Like cardio or muscle-building." She held up her hands when Cassie moved to shove her again. "But I'm happy to roll that back and admit it was a damned good workout." She gestured toward Cassie. "And it's obviously working for you. I might even consider doing it again."

"You're welcome to come with me when our schedules allow. I guess we're going to be seeing a lot less of each other once your shows begin." She tried to force the words out with her usual confidence, but she could tell by Taryn's expression that she hadn't managed it.

Taryn interlocked their fingers like she had just before Cassie brought her to her *first* orgasm a few hours ago. Mm, the recollection of the sounds she made and the way her body writhed beneath Cassie's mouth and touch made her throb. But this touch clearly signified more than an acknowledgment of the best sex either of them had ever had.

"It'll be harder but not impossible, right?" Taryn stared at their hands before looking up into Cassie's eyes.

"I don't know. I've been coasting a little these past couple of weeks." *That* was a bit of an understatement. She'd dropped from regularly working six twelve-hour shifts down to three ten-hour shifts. Both Rachel and Dinah had said Barr was starting to ask questions and that Fischer was on the verge of divorce. Her colleague's personal life wasn't her problem, but still, for the first time in her life, she'd put her career on the back burner and made herself a priority.

"You didn't say anything..." Taryn uncoupled their hands and began to trace light patterns on Cassie's palms.

"I was having too much fun with you." She shrugged. "And I needed a break. I was heading to burnout, working seventy-two hours a week and not getting enough sleep because I'm always too wired after a long shift to relax quickly."

"So I've been a necessary and timely distraction?"

Taryn grinned, but Cassie sensed the fragility in her words. Wasn't that all they were supposed to be to each other anyway? Somewhere along the way, that had ceased to be the case. "Yes, but you've been much more than that."

Taryn bit her lip and nodded slowly. "So we'll see each other when our jobs allow it. We've both been on an impromptu vacation, and vacations always end." She looked up and seemed hopeful.

Cassie grasped Taryn's hands. "*We're* not a vacation, and we don't have to end. We just have to do what most people do and find time for each other around our work commitments. That's all."

Taryn blew out a long breath. "Find time? That little fucker likes to hide."

Cassie laughed. "I think that's the first time I've heard you swear. It sounds strange."

"Oh, I curse plenty. I just don't do it in front of ladies."

"Oh my god, that's so archaic," Cassie said.

"I prefer the term chivalrous."

"I think the term you're looking for is *outdated*."

"Whatever." Taryn extricated herself from Cassie's fingers and got up from the bed. "Would you like something to eat? I'm starved."

She pushed through the door and left Cassie wondering what was happening. Were they still playing or had she actually offended Taryn? Cassie followed Taryn into the main area to find Taryn with her head in the freezer. "Whatcha doing?"

"Seeing if I can freeze my tear ducts. I've cried more today than I have in the past three decades." She closed the freezer door quietly. "Just tell me you want to see me, and that you're not going to use our jobs as an excuse not to."

Cassie frowned. "I'm not sure what I've done to make you think that, but no, I'm definitely not going to use my position to avoid seeing you." She hadn't been expecting this conversation and certainly not this reaction. It was little wonder that Taryn hadn't let Cassie touch her if this level of vulnerability and self-doubt was the outcome. It was extraordinary that even the most confident-appearing person could harbor such deep insecurities about being dumped, especially when they were only ever supposed to be a short-term thing. She cupped Taryn's face. "While you're in Vegas, I'll want to see you. Okay?"

Taryn placed her hands over Cassie's, pulled them from her face, and kissed them. "Okay." She gave a sheepish grin. "Sorry. I guess my post-O hormones got me all emotional and unnecessary."

"Well, you did have quite a few." Cassie wiggled her eyebrows, feeling quite proud of herself for hitting the spot more than once given that Taryn clearly didn't allow it to happen often.

Taryn shook her head slowly. "Feeling quite pleased with yourself, are you? You look like the cat that got the cream."

Cassie shrugged. "If we're going to be crude, that's exactly what I got." She laughed and pulled away gently, her attention caught by the many knickknacks scattered all over Taryn's trailer. Practically every surface except the sink had some sort of figure, rock, or miscellaneous item on it. In the center of the main table was a large and ornately carved wooden box, and curiosity got Cassie wondering what treasures were inside it and what they might reveal about Taryn—if she'd allow her to look, that was.

She wandered over to the side of the trailer and reached up to pluck a small Mickey Mouse painted with the American flag from a high shelf. But it didn't move.

"Most everything is stuck down," Taryn said. "That way, I don't have to keep packing it up every time I drive the trailer. Which is usually every couple of days while we're on tour."

"What's with all the trinkets?" Cassie ran her fingers over some of the shaped rocks and pebbles, wanting to know the story behind each of them.

"I collect mementoes from everywhere I go. Stones, ticket stubs, business cards, anything that'll remind me where I've been. I like to have them with me wherever I go."

"What about when you're not on tour?" Cassie sat at the table, her fingers itching to open the wooden box.

"Some of the time I'm at Andi's property in Texas, practicing stunts and trying to invent new ones." Taryn slid into the bench opposite and grabbed an apple from the fruit bowl. "I spend the rest of the time traveling the world."

"You take your trailer overseas?"

"No. I looked into it once, but it was crazy expensive. I rent cars or bikes or just travel by train." Taryn bit into the apple and juice dribbled down her chin, but she wiped it away quickly. "Are you sure don't want something to eat?"

Cassie shook her head. She *was* hungry, but that would wait while she sated her desire for more intimate knowledge of Taryn. "Is there one special thing you always take with you if you can't take everything in here?"

"Yes." Taryn indicated to the box between them with her gaze. "It's in there. But I don't think I should show it to you. I've done enough damage to my cool reputation today; you don't need to see it."

Cassie bounced on her seat, feeling a little like a kid hoping to see inside Santa's workshop. "I definitely *do* need to see it."

Before she could move, Taryn grabbed the box with both hands, pulled it across the table, and held it to her chest.

"You definitely do *not*. I can't have you thinking I'm any more sappy than you've already come to realize today."

"Huh." Cassie placed her hands on the table and inched toward the box. "And why would that be?"

"You like strong women who can carry you in their arms. I'm pretty sure you wouldn't be interested in a woman with a soft underbelly."

Cassie crept forward a little more. "Then you'd be wrong. I think it would be wonderful if you had a marshmallow heart beating beneath that extremely firm chest. A 'soft underbelly' protected by a rock-hard shell seems like the perfect combination for a woman."

Taryn raised her eyebrows and looked unconvinced. "Really?"

"Really. This isn't the 1950s. Showing you're vulnerable is more of a strength, in my opinion." Cassie focused hopefully on the box beneath Taryn's hands. "Will you show me?" she asked gently, sensing Taryn's reluctance hadn't been completely reduced.

Taryn opened the hinged lid slowly, but Cassie couldn't see inside from the angle she was sitting at. She pulled something out and clasped her fist around it before closing the box and shoving it across the table toward the window.

"Something small makes sense if it goes with you everywhere." Cassie retreated a little to give Taryn some space. She hadn't honestly expected this kind of softness from Taryn, but she liked it immensely. And that didn't stop her heart from falling a tiny bit more for the woman she hadn't anticipated getting to know beyond a few nights of wild and intensely satisfying sex. How cruel of the Universe to put someone like Taryn in her path, only to move her on after a few short months.

But that time was better than no time.

Taryn opened her hand slowly to reveal a small piece of metal in the shape of a dog bone. "It's the tag from my dog, Pepper. I had her when I was nine, and she grew up with me. It destroyed me when we had to have her... When, you know..." Taryn pressed her finger to her brow. "I still can't really talk about it. But I take this with me everywhere to remind me that there's never enough time but also that there are amazing things you can experience if you take the time to open your heart to them." She shrugged. "You got it right when you said I was obsessed with time."

Cassie ran her fingers along Taryn's forearm. "Thank you for sharing that with me."

"S'okay." She placed it back in the box and looked deep into Cassie's eyes. "Phew. That's been a lot of seriousness. Can we get back to the fun and sex?" Taryn grinned then launched herself over the table to pull Cassie in for a deep kiss.

When Taryn retreated, she left Cassie breathless, and the melancholy of the moment had been definitively replaced with their usual, more playful vibe. Cassie put her fingers to her lips; they felt almost bruised from their earlier passion. "I'm going to need food before I get back into bed with you."

"Do you want to go out or get something delivered? Or I could cook?"

Taryn showed no residual signs of the softer side she'd revealed with both their bedroom activities and their last conversation. But it was enough to know it was there, and that Taryn trusted her enough to be that open. "You cook?" Cassie hadn't expected *that* either.

Taryn leaned back and lifted her tank top. "You think I could look like this if I ate out all the time?" She slid out from the bench and opened the refrigerator. "I have fresh salmon and asparagus tips."

Cassie smiled at Taryn's apparent excitement and eagerness to cook for them. *Another string to her bow.* But she still hadn't answered Cassie's question. "Before I decide, I'd like to know your answer to my earlier question about you staying at my place tonight."

Taryn closed the fridge door and leaned back against the sink. "You could stay here..."

Different location, same outcome. That worked for Cassie. "I'll have to get up at five a.m. to go home and get ready for work. If that doesn't bother you, then yes, I'd love to stay with you tonight." She'd get as much of Taryn as she could, actually.

"So it'd be easier if I stayed at your place?"

Cassie nodded. "I wouldn't have to get up early, so we could play til later."

"Sold." Taryn pushed away from the sink and pulled Cassie to her feet. "But how about I pack the ingredients into a cooler and cook at your place?"

Cassie laughed and ran her hands through Taryn's hair, trying to straighten the bit that was stuck up from their afternoon's adventures. "I have no idea if my stove works, and you may have to peel the store stickers from the pots, but sure, you can be the first person in the world to cook something in my kitchen."

Taryn looked incredulous. "You've never cooked anything there? How long have you lived there?"

Cassie arched her eyebrow. "Hey, Judgy McJudge Bottom, I could cook if I wanted to."

Taryn wrinkled her nose and looked adorable. "Could you though?"

Cassie shook her head. "Absolutely not, no. Can't cook a thing. Never wanted to. Never tried."

"Will you sous chef for me?" Taryn asked.

"I can't possibly risk chopping off any digits, I'm afraid. But I will happily sit on the other side of the countertop, drinking wine and keeping you company while you rustle up something tasty for us."

Taryn smiled widely, and Cassie's heart warmed at the thought of that beautiful smile being the first thing she'd see in the morning.

Chapter Eighteen

TARYN COMPLETED ONE LAST circuit of the stadium before sliding to a halt in front of Gwen. She got off the bike and patted Gwen on the shoulder. "She's handling great, G."

"Excellent. And the new thumb throttle?" Gwen released the kickstand and began to wheel the bike back to her workshop area.

"Way superior to anything else I've ever used." Taryn followed alongside and nodded to Andi when she joined them. "You should trademark it and sell it to Honda or Kawasaki."

"Don't say things like that." Andi gave Taryn a hard shove. "We can't lose our genius."

Gwen tsked. "Even if I did do that, you should know by now that I'd never leave you... You guys are my family."

The resultant joy was unmistakable in Andi's eyes. "That's always been what I was hoping to create."

Taryn slung her arm over Andi's shoulder and pulled her into a bro hug. "Mission accomplished." More words nudged at her throat to escape, but she was still recovering from her bout of excessive emotion-sharing with Cassie and couldn't be sure her tears would stay put. She had never cried in front of Andi, and she didn't want to start blubbering in front of her *and* the rest of the team.

"Speaking of family and other awkward shit," Andi said as if she'd picked up on Taryn's discomfort. "I need to talk to you about something important, Tar." She gestured toward the Cosmos, its mighty height beginning to cast a monolithic shadow across the floor of the stadium. "Can we meet in Venus when you've freshened up?"

Taryn raised her arm and sniffed her pit. "Are you trying to say that I stink?"

"I'm not *trying* to say anything." Andi veered off toward the tunnel connecting the stadium to the hotel. "I said it."

Taryn waved her off and unzipped her leather jacket: necessary for safety but a killer in this heat. "I'll grab a shower and be with you in half an hour."

"Thirty minutes? You don't have to gussy yourself up for me, buddy." Andi laughed and continued walking away.

"Some of us don't like to walk around with bedhead, looking like rejects from the *Walking Dead* cast."

Andi turned around and clutched her hands to her chest. "Death blow." She chuckled and shook her head. "One woman's bedhead is another's stylish statement." She put both hands over her ears and sauntered away.

Taryn patted Gwen on the shoulder. "Thanks again for the bike adjustments. I can't wait to ride it in the show tonight."

"My pleasure."

Taryn jogged off to the changing room and took just ten minutes to "freshen up." While she headed toward the Venus bar, she video-called Cassie, the reason she'd told Andi she would be so long. "Did I catch you before you started your shift?"

Cassie's smile made Taryn's day brighter immediately. Going cold turkey on their time together had been as bad as Taryn had imagined it would be. She'd spent her life bemoaning the speed with which time passed, but the last five days and nights had taken an age. Snatched minutes of video and voice conversations didn't compare to holding Cassie in her arms, to breathing her scent, and touching her soft skin. And though it was probably good for her head to pull back this way—she'd be back on the road in no time—her heart did *not* agree.

"Yep," Cassie said. "The traffic was playing nice today. Did everything go well at your practice session?"

Before Taryn had the chance to respond, Cassie's friend

appeared on the screen.

"Thanks for arranging a room for me at your big celebration party next week. And for inviting me at all," Rachel said.

Taryn shrugged. "No problem." She tried to keep the irritation from her voice. It was bad enough that she had to get her fill of Cassie this way. Taryn didn't appreciate having that precious time interrupted by Rachel. She just wanted her gone.

"I saw Cassie's dress last night; it's phenomenal." Rachel shook her head. "Now we've got to go shopping for a new outfit, so I don't look out of place beside her."

There was so much wrong with that sentence, Taryn could've exploded. She doused her unhealthy jealousy with a bucket of metaphorical cold water. Cassie didn't have to spend every spare moment with Taryn, and friends needed time too. But Rachel wouldn't be the one beside Cassie—she would. She'd chosen a suit to match Cassie's dress perfectly.

She was probably wasting her energy worrying; Cassie had told Taryn that Rachel liked to enjoy herself, so as soon as she stepped into the VIP area, she'd be spoiled with potential playmates for the evening and would soon leave Cassie's side. "I'm sure you'll find something. If there's one thing this city does as well as its gambling, it's shopping."

Cassie jostled Rachel away. "Haven't you got some blood bags to prepare?"

She rolled her eyes at the screen, and Taryn acknowledged the immature plug of satisfaction that came with Cassie's dismissal of her friend. It was far harder to share Cassie when she wasn't getting enough solo time with her, and she was glad that Cassie seemed to share that sentiment.

"Sorry about that," Cassie said when Rachel moved out of view. "It's okay."

Cassie raised her eyebrow, clearly not fooled. "Oh, in that case, let me get her back for the rest of our conversation."

"No!" Taryn's forceful response left no room for misinterpretation.

"Sorry, I mean, no need."

Cassie gave a smug grin. "Want me all to yourself, do you?"

Taryn blew out her cheeks. There was little use denying it; Cassie seemed preternaturally able to divine her true thoughts. "You don't have to look *quite* so pleased with yourself."

"I think I do. So, did everything go well at the stadium?"

Taryn thought she detected more concern than interest in Cassie's question. "Yeah, great. We're ready for tonight... I wish you could be there."

"So I could throw a single red rose to the all-conquering hero?" Cassie blew Taryn a kiss.

She frowned. "If there were any roses to be thrown around, they'd be coming your way."

"So chivalrous." Cassie gave an exaggerated sigh and accompanied it with a flutter of her eyelashes. "My hero."

Taryn pouted. "I'm feeling attacked. I didn't call you so you could make fun of me."

"No? Are you sure?" Cassie held up her hand. "I better go then."

"You could wish me luck before you do."

Cassie tilted her head slightly and winked. "You don't need luck, superstar."

Taryn smiled widely, loving Cassie's faith in her ability.

"But, good luck, and don't break anything." Cassie's smile was strangely thin and tight. She offered her wrist to the phone screen. "I have to go. Let's talk tomorrow."

Cassie ended the call without a response from Taryn, who hesitated a moment too long. In deliberating how to sign off, she'd missed the opportunity altogether. She slipped her phone into the thigh pocket of her pants and pushed through the door to the Venus bar. Andi was seated inside one of the many booths enclosed by an amber-colored glass globe.

The door slid closed behind Taryn, and she sat down. "No soundproofing today?" she asked, still able to hear the ambient noise of the bar and its other occupants.

Andi hovered her finger over the sound station controls in the center of the table. "I can turn it on if you like, but you're not usually one for complete quiet."

"You can leave it off, thanks. I have no desire to pretend we're superspies having a 'let's save the world' conversation." Taryn pulled her glass of Coke closer and took a long drink. "Thanks for this."

Andi tapped the bottle of mineral water. "You need to drink this too." She poured it into a large glass and shoved it toward Taryn.

"I love how you look after me, *Dad*."

"Don't be a smartass."

Taryn emptied the water and refilled it. She was thirstier than she'd thought. "I like it." She liked it more than she cared to admit. Her parents had looked after her, of course, but they always wanted something in return and were never happy with anything less than perfection. She didn't envy Ralph and Jessica's inevitable battle with them over their baby. Jessica was a good-looking woman, but she didn't have the symmetry her parents considered the gold standard of beauty. Taryn believed their child would be beautiful but not beautiful *enough* for her parents. Thank God she'd never had a single maternal longing in her life.

"If you like me looking after you, this conversation is going to go nice and easy." Andi tapped the tablet set into the table. "Let's get some food. I hate heavy discussions on an empty stomach."

"Go ahead. You know what I like." Taryn watched Andi prod out their order for a few seconds then asked, "Is this about you and Bernice? Have you had 'the talk' yet?"

The smile that spread across Andi's face answered Taryn's question and the one she hadn't asked: how had it gone?

"It's partly about that, yeah." Her smile grew even wider. "This love thing kinda crept up on both of us."

Taryn nodded slowly. It felt like it was creeping up on her too, but she wasn't ready to give it the power of that label just yet. "She loves you too?"

"Can you believe it?"

Taryn wrinkled her nose. "Of course I can believe it. Why wouldn't she have fallen in love with you?" Again, the reflection of her own feelings for Cassie thrummed for her attention. Why wouldn't *she* fall in love with Cassie? Beautiful, intelligent, funny, and talented Cassie. The perfect woman Taryn hadn't thought possible and certainly hadn't been looking for.

Andi shrugged and took a long pull on her beer. They were silent for a while, and Taryn made no attempt to talk. This had always been how they'd communicated—long periods of silence punctuated by short and blunt sentences—and it worked for them.

Taryn saw the waiter approach with trays loaded with food. "Is all this heart stuff making you hungry?" She pressed the button for the door to slide open, and they emptied the platters onto their table. Taryn dropped ten dollars on one of the trays and thanked them. The door closed automatically behind them, and she and Andi dug in. "Bernice really did get the best chefs and waitstaff available," she said after she'd munched on a taste explosion of a Thai fish cake. "Everything we've eaten here has been amazing."

"There are two parts to what I want to talk to you about." Andi twirled her chopsticks in a plate of pad Thai. "And I don't want you to say a word or react in *any* way until I stop talking."

Taryn frowned. "Sounds ominous."

Andi shook her head. "Not ominous at all, but I need you to have an open mind and take the time to process what I'm saying before you respond." She wagged her chopsticks at Taryn. "I know that's hard for you. You're a gut-feeling, spontaneous person, but for the first time, I need you not to be quite so *you*."

Taryn downed another full glass of water. Being herself was something Andi had cultivated in Taryn from day one. "Okay." She thought about the meditation section of the BodyBalance she'd done with Cassie. Maybe this would be a good test of its efficacy. "Tell me what's going on."

"I took the advice you and Gwen gave me, and I laid my heart on the line." Andi flicked her glance to her plate and chased a piece of chicken with her chopsticks. "Lady Luck helped me out, and it turns out Bernice feels the same way. She wants to be my pillion passenger."

Taryn put her chopsticks down and raised her soda. "That's great news. Congratulations."

Andi smiled and clinked her bottle to Taryn's glass. "Thanks, Tar... Remember that you said we should get on with planning our future?"

"I remember, yeah." Taryn was beginning to get an idea of where this might be going. Whatever Andi had already decided or was thinking about, it directly affected Taryn. Of course she'd encouraged her best friend to follow her dreams, but she hadn't considered how it might impact her much. She'd basically fooled herself into thinking nothing would change.

"The pre-sales for the show have exceeded all her financial analyst's expectations. We're going to be the biggest show on the Strip since Celine Dion."

Taryn frowned. "Why would they compare our show to a musician's?"

Andi shrugged. "The content of the show doesn't matter. The gross profit does. Being compared to Celine Dion offends you?"

"Nah. I just thought it was strange, that's all."

Andi rolled her eyes. "*Anyway*, Bernice loves Vegas. It's always been the place she wanted to settle down." Andi wagged her finger. "And before you ask, no, she doesn't know why."

Taryn blew out her cheeks. "Curiosity is a good thing, you know. You shouldn't stifle it."

"It's like talking to a kid." Andi pinched the bridge of her nose.

Taryn chuckled. "I'm just messing with you. Spit it out; the suspense is killing me."

"Bernice wants to stay in Vegas, and I want to stay with her. She also wants to have a regular residency for the stunt show." Andi paused to take a big breath. "I need you to build a bigger team and lead them around the world with our traveling shows. I want you to be my business partner."

Taryn felt her mouth drop open, but she couldn't find the words.

"That's a first. Taryn Taylor speechless." Andi piled some spring rolls onto her plate. "I don't need an answer right away. I want you to really think about."

Maybe this was the answer she'd been looking for, and it would solve her current sense of ennui. She'd be responsible for... *everything*. Staying in the business but with a whole new direction and sense of purpose might be exactly what she needed. There was one big snag though. "I don't have the kind of capital you're talking about to become a partner."

Andi grinned and shook her head. "You don't need any capital. You've helped me build this team into something really special. Who knows if we would've even survived if you hadn't come along. You've put your blood and sweat into this family for nearly ten years—you've already invested more than enough capital. It's just a different kind."

"Wow... I don't know what to say."

"Good." Andi dipped a roll in the sweet chili sauce and shoveled it into her mouth. "I don't want you to say anything. I want you to process it and really think it over." She shrugged and waved her chopsticks toward Taryn's face. "But I think this is the perfect solution for everyone; you get to keep being a globe-trotting nomad, I settle down with Bernice, and the team can rotate in and out of the two shows if they want to. I think the money we make from the residency can supplement the traveling show income, so everyone gets equal pay no matter which show they work."

Taryn inhaled deeply, like Cassie's yogi had instructed. She didn't experience any sudden clarity, but she couldn't deny her rising excitement at Andi's proposal. "You've put a lot of thought into this."

Andi nodded. "Me and a lot of other people. But let's talk about something else now. How's it going with your good doctor?"

Taryn didn't know if she wanted a subject change. What Andi had set in front of her was mind-blowing, and it deserved her full attention, which had been focused almost exclusively on Cassie since they'd arrived in Vegas. And honestly, she wanted to see if she could think about something else for a while. If she said yes to Andi's plan—and why wouldn't she?—she'd be back on the road in five months. Wheels turning again, and her unquenchable thirst for new experiences and new people taken care of. Back to the life she loved. She'd be sad to say goodbye to Cassie, of course. They'd been intense for the past couple of weeks, and she'd loved every minute of it. But Cassie was a rooted willow, and Taryn was tumbleweed. There was no future for them, so enjoying the time they *did* have was what she was left with. And that was okay. That was life, wasn't it?

Chapter Nineteen

TARYN HELD CASSIE'S HAND and helped her into the Uber. "If this wasn't kind of *my* party, I would blow it off in a heartbeat and drag you back inside."

"So that's a 'yes' to liking my dress?" Cassie swung her legs into the car and fluttered her eyes at Taryn, who gave her a killer grin in return. God, she'd missed that smile over the past six days. Going back to sensible adulting and dedicated doctoring had been harder than she'd expected. Trying to convince herself that this was a healthy, weening-off process toward Taryn's inevitable departure hadn't worked at all.

Taryn closed the door then leaned close to the glass and mouthed, "Hell, yes." She came around the other side, slid in beside Cassie, and took her hand. "I have never seen you look more beautiful." She pressed her mouth to Cassie's ear and whispered, "Except when you're coming for me. Then you're at your *most* beautiful." She pulled back and wiggled her eyebrows.

"I've missed your flattery," Cassie said after Taryn had confirmed their destination with the driver.

Taryn leaned back in her seat. "It's not flattery when it's the god's honest truth."

Cassie had never received as much flattery or flowery truths as Taryn showered her with, and she'd grown happily accustomed to it. She'd become just plain happy. Her work still fulfilled her, but it didn't define her as it had prior to Taryn's arrival. She constantly cautioned herself against replacing one obsession with another, and her therapist had advised her of the same thing. But Cassie knew she wasn't doing that. Her meditation had become more focused, and she'd discovered a mindfulness she'd thought unachievable. Taryn had been good for her, and she wasn't going to be around for much longer, but Cassie knew she'd changed for the better, and those changes wouldn't fade when Taryn faded away too.

"How's work been?" Taryn scooted closer and placed her hand on Cassie's thigh.

They slipped into easy and comfortable conversation about their respective jobs for the rest of the journey to the hotel, something they were doing more of as they got to know other parts of each other.

When they got to the hotel, Taryn led them to what she said was Jupiter, the largest bar and restaurant in the hotel. Cassie thought she'd done enough fawning over Bernice's design choices, but the sheer abundance of travertine marble in this bar started her off again. It was clear that particular marble had been chosen because of its remarkable resemblance to how the surface of the planet looked from space. Complementing the marble was an effusion of lava-like moving walls, churning cyclones of fire. All the tables had the same effect. The result was hypnotic. "This has to be my favorite bar in the world."

Taryn nodded and handed her a glass of champagne from the tray of a passing waiter. "It's stunning, isn't it?"

Cassie followed Taryn around the space and was introduced to every member of Taryn's stunt team from the riders to the engineer to the MC. She didn't have a chance in hell of remembering any of their names, but she listened to their many stories of Taryn's death-defying escapades, even though they made her stomach churn.

"Are you okay?" Taryn whispered. "You look a little pale."

"Can we sit for a while?" She pointed to her five-inch heels. "These look amazing, but they're not the most comfortable things to stand on for any length of time."

"Of course." Taryn tucked Cassie's hand in the crook of her elbow and guided her toward an empty circular table. "You should've said something earlier. I've been oblivious to your pain, showing you off—sorry—introducing you to my friends."

"Though it pains me to admit it, I did like that." She shook her head. "You bring out all kinds of strange, archaic reactions in me."

Taryn helped Cassie lower herself onto the insanely comfortable seating and sat beside her. "You can't be telling me that your previous, uh, lovers haven't wanted to brag about you to their whole world."

Cassie shrugged lightly. "I told you, I haven't had any serious relationships, so I guess I've never given anyone the chance to show me off or brag about me." She pushed her champagne flute in a circle, following one of the cyclone shapes on the table. "And even if I had been with anyone long enough, I'm not sure they would've wanted to do that anyway."

"Are you kidding me?" Taryn asked. "When you're about to put on your makeup, do you not look in the mirror and see how beautiful you are?"

Cassie gave a small smile and traced gentle patterns on the back of Taryn's hand. "Beauty is in the eye of the beholder, and I don't behold any beauty when I see my reflection, no."

Taryn frowned. "It certainly didn't come across that way when I first met you. You seemed like the epitome of self-confidence; you were the queen of the club, and you could've had any woman you wanted in there."

Cassie leaned close to Taryn and kissed her. "That's not true, but I did somehow manage to *get* the woman I wanted, despite Erin's best attempts." She eased back, grinning, and wiggled her eyebrows.

"Erin?" Taryn asked before recognition crossed her expression. "Ah, the vampire you rescued me from."

Cassie nodded. "You've got to remember that I've always been too caught up with my career to have relationships longer than a few hours, and even those are only monthly, if I'm lucky. Attracting women takes effort and confidence, and I can usually fake it long enough to have those needs satisfied." She turned Taryn's hand over and ran her fingers over her calluses. "I don't really let people get to know me, and the real me isn't that super confident person."

"What about your work colleagues?"

"I don't sleep with them, so I just have to be good at my job, and that *is* one area in my life where I am confident. But I don't have to be sexually and physically self-assured. And apart from Rachel, I don't think they really know me either." She cocked her head slightly. "If I'm brutally honest, Rachel doesn't know me as well as she thinks she does, but she is the closest thing I've ever had to a best friend. Which is sad but unfortunately true."

"Mm." Taryn took off her jacket, rolled up her sleeves, and laid her forearm on the table in front of Cassie. She grinned. "In case you want to keep on using me as a fidget toy."

Cassie laughed and dragged her nails lightly along Taryn's skin.

Taryn withdrew her arm faster than lightning. "Oh, no way. You can't do that to me and expect me *not* to pull you out of this party right now and take you up to our room."

Cassie pouted. "Fine. No nails."

Taryn gave her a sidelong glance and narrowed her eyes. "Just fingertips?"

Cassie held out her little finger. "Pinky promise."

Taryn hooked her finger into Cassie's then placed her arm back in position. "No nails."

"You *want* the nails."

Taryn wrinkled her nose. "Of course I want the nails. But I have to stay here for another couple of hours, or that would be rude to our lovely host."

Cassie reluctantly began to use her fingers to follow the lines of Taryn's veins. "Speaking of Bernice, how are things going with her and Andi?"

Taryn bounced a little in her chair. "I'm glad you asked, and I've got great news, but first I want to get to the bottom of your unwarranted lack of self-confidence. You're a top ER doctor, you're smoking hot, and you've got a wicked sense of humor and stunning intellect. You're the whole package. If I had to pop-psychologize you, I'd say that your mom managed to undermine it somehow."

Cassie used her other hand to empty her champagne, and Taryn immediately gestured to a passing waitress for a refill. When the waitress had gone, Cassie arched her eyebrow at Taryn. "Are you sure you want a serious conversation on a night like this? Everyone is here to celebrate you and your rider buddies; the roadblock you're attempting to plow through isn't conducive to raucous revelry."

Taryn laughed. "I do love the way you speak, and yes, I'm happy to have this conversation. I'm enjoying being allowed to get to know the real you."

Taryn's choice of words didn't go unnoticed. Over the past few weeks, she had consistently given Taryn permission, and she'd given herself permission too. Every time they'd met up or talked on the phone or video-called, she'd allowed herself to be open and vulnerable in a way she'd never done with anyone. Her therapist had been impressed, especially with the boat trip story. If Cassie ever got on Taryn's motorbike, she was sure her therapist would have a coronary.

"First, I should thank you for all the lovely flattery—"

"It's not flattery when it's true."

Cassie tilted her head slightly. "Then I should thank you for all those lovely compliments. It's nice to be thought of that way, I'll admit that much." She ran her finger over the rim of her glass, not quite able to maintain eye contact with Taryn's intense gaze. "And secondly, you're right, and it took you way less time than my therapist to figure it out."

"Were you as honest with them as you have been with me?"

Cassie rolled her eyes and slapped Taryn's forearm gently. "You don't know me," she said, although her mock petulance was more a response to the dawning realization that actually, yes, Taryn did know her, and Cassie had actively encouraged that to happen.

"I never asked how your visit went last week..." Taryn tucked her leg onto the seat so she could sit sideways to face Cassie properly.

Cassie inhaled deeply and released her breath slowly. If only she could relinquish her mother's toxicity so easily. "It was horrible, and not because I cut myself and needed nine stitches." She raised her other hand to show Taryn. It was healing nicely; Rachel's handiwork was impressive, and there would be no scar. Taryn lowered her head and kissed the wound. It would've been a comforting and tender gesture had she not then looked up at Cassie with a particularly filthy look on her face. Cassie pulled her hand away and tutted. "*You're* incorrigible."

"*You're* welcome." Taryn smiled, but her expression quickly turned serious again. "What made the visit horrible?"

"My mom." It was a simple and brutally honest answer. It was the only one Cassie could offer. "Everything about her: the way she talks to me, and the things she talks to me about. The judgment. The entitlement. The complete and utter self-deception. Her victim complex." She thought of poor Buster, and how he'd looked at her. If he could've begged her to take him away from it all, Cassie was sure he would have. She remembered Taryn's story of her first dog and the tag she carried with her everywhere. She would likely be unimpressed with her mother's treatment and lack of care for him.

She looked up at Taryn, who hadn't spoken or attempted to prompt her to more words when Cassie had disappeared into her own head, into the dark silence she got so used to inhabiting as a child. "The only good thing was Buster."

Taryn's eyes lit up. "A dog?" The luminance flickered and faded as quickly as it had appeared. "I have the feeling she shouldn't have a dog."

Cassie shook her head slowly and sipped her champagne. "He's a boxer—an out of shape boxer because the only exercise he gets is loping around the yard. And that's if she lets him out."

Taryn clenched her jaw. "Some people shouldn't be allowed to have pets. Is she nice to him?"

Cassie's harsh laugh grated on her own ears. "I don't think she's nice to anybody. Although she says she has a new man in her life, and she certainly seems eager to please him."

"Was he there?" Taryn asked quietly.

"Thankfully not. And he had the new car I supposedly bought." She shrugged. "Could be that there *is* no new car, and she blew that money on something else entirely."

Taryn glanced at Cassie's hand. "I want to ask how you ended up with a sliced open hand, but I'm beginning to think that the answer might have me jumping on my bike to go confront your mom."

Cassie smiled. No one had ever come to her defense like that before or been so concerned for her health. The sting of Taryn's inevitable departure struck again. How was it that the one person who genuinely seemed to care for her would never consider sticking around to keep doing it? "I did it to myself. I'm afraid there's no story there, though I do like the thought of you being my knight in shining armor, much to the chagrin of my inner feminist."

Taryn narrowed her eyes, clearly unconvinced. "What happened?"

"I was trying to make coffee, and I slammed the glass jug in rather viciously. It didn't stand up to the rugged test." She smiled but knew it was weak and would do little to persuade Taryn.

"You don't strike me as someone who slams things around, but I guess we don't know each other that well yet..."

Yet... As if Taryn might spend more time overcoming that hurdle. "My mom mentioned my brother—used my brother to criticize me." Cassie offered a small shrug. "I didn't take it well." She lifted her injured hand and twisted it this way and that. "It did give me a great excuse to leave though, so it wasn't all bad."

Taryn took Cassie's her hand and tracked her finger around the stitches. "Can I ask you something? And it's obviously fine if you don't want to answer."

"Sure." They'd already delved into serious territory; how much deeper could they get?

"Okay... And I'm asking without any judgment at all," Taryn said. "I'm just interested because I can't see myself in your position."

"Out with it. You're building it up too much." Cassie waved her free hand, her nerves jangling on the edges of her laugh.

"Why do you stay in touch and keep going back to her?" Taryn pressed her lips together, as if to keep related questions from tumbling out.

"You mean, why keep subjecting myself to continued emotional abuse now that I'm a fully grown woman and don't need my mom for anything, not that she was any good at that stuff when I was a kid either?"

Taryn nodded but said nothing else.

"My therapist has asked me that same question." Cassie had been trying to figure out if she could distance herself from her mom for a while. And whenever they spent time together, getting to the answer became a little more urgent. "Logically, I know that all my mom has given me is her DNA. Even before my brother was...killed, I don't remember her as a great caretaker. I remember Dad taking us to school, cooking at night, making our lunches for school and breakfast in the morning. It was like she never really wanted kids." She exhaled a long breath. "I sometimes wonder why she didn't just give me away after Dad left." Cassie caught the sob in her chest before it reached her throat, but it didn't go unnoticed, and she found herself being drawn into Taryn's arms. She put her hands on Taryn's chest to stop her. "Please don't. If you hold me, I'll dissolve completely, and my makeup isn't *that* waterproof."

Taryn released her and pulled back. Cassie was relieved she could see no hurt in her eyes at the rebuff.

"I understand."

A comfortable silence stretched on between them, and Cassie recomposed herself. "I'm sorry. I don't think I've ever said that out loud."

Taryn shook her head slowly. "Please don't apologize. *I'm* sorry she made you feel that way." She gave a lopsided grin. "I hope you don't ever introduce us; I think I'd find it hard to stay silent if she was mean to you or put you down in any way." She raised her hands. "Ignore that. It's not my place to challenge your mom, especially when you don't, and you probably wouldn't want me to. Would you like to talk about something else?"

Cassie nodded. "We should get back to enjoying this fabulous party, and I shouldn't hog the guest of honor."

"I was joking when I said it was my party." Taryn slipped her hand onto Cassie's thigh. "This is a celebration for the whole team, especially everyone behind the scenes."

Cassie shuffled closer to Taryn so their thighs touched. "I'll answer your question about why I keep in touch with Mom another time, I promise."

Taryn rubbed Cassie's thigh gently. "Whenever you're ready. You'll never get any pressure from me." She slipped off the seat and held out her hand. Cassie took it, and Taryn draped her arm around Cassie's shoulders as they headed toward Andi and Bernice. "My parents weren't the best, but they were far from the worst, and I only spend occasional holidays with them if I'm not touring or haven't arranged to conveniently be in another country. If I didn't see them again, I'd be okay with that, but I think my outlook is pretty unique. Most people put up with their families, no matter what. But for me, time is too precious to spend it with people who don't see who you really are, or who don't *want* to see who you really are."

Cassie took another sip of her champagne. "Your time thing dictates your life, doesn't it?"

Taryn grinned. "Doesn't it dictate everyone's? It's just how soon you realize how precious it is that matters. Speaking of precious, how's Louise doing?"

Grateful for the sudden change in topic, Cassie beamed widely. "She adores her wigs, and Sara said that she doesn't have to force her to have her friends over anymore. You made such a difference with that gesture. Thank you."

Taryn glanced away, and even in the orange hue of the lights produced from the moving cyclones of Jupiter installations, Cassie could see her blushing.

"It was nothing," Taryn said.

Cassie pulled Taryn to a halt. "It was definitely *not* nothing. I know it might've seemed like a simple thing to you, but it meant the world to Louise and to her mom. Those kinds of small gestures can make such a huge difference to people." She ran her fingers down Taryn's tie then pulled her in for a deliciously deep kiss. "In fact, you've inspired me to make a difference too. I've signed up to work at the clinic."

Taryn pulled her bottom lip into her mouth. "God, you taste good."

"It's the champagne."

Taryn's eyes darkened. "Oh, it's you. It is *not* the champagne."

"I'm glad you mentioned Louise." She opened her purse and pulled out a small envelope that Sara had given her. "This is for you from them."

"Aw, that's sweet, but there was no need." Taryn took it and opened it.

As she scanned the letter inside, her eyes began to glisten, and her smile grew wider. Whatever Louise and Sara had written, it had certainly pierced Taryn's chrome-plated heart and melted the marshmallow inside. Cassie felt an unusual desperation to know what they'd written that had managed to have that effect on her.

Taryn closed the card, put it back in the envelope, and tucked it into the inside pocket of her jacket. She pressed her hand against her heart. "That's something I'll treasure."

"And will it be going in your special wooden keepsake box?" Cassie asked, trying to make light of the appeal of Taryn's soft underbelly and not dwell on how bereft she would feel when she no longer had that in her life.

"You're making fun of me." Taryn shook her head. "I knew I

shouldn't have shown you that box and told you the dog story. It could've gone either way, I suppose, but I took the risk anyway. It could've made you think I was super sweet and thoughtful. Instead, you now think I'm a sappy fool to be pitied and mocked." She put her head in her hands and her shoulders shook.

For a brief and mortifying moment, Cassie thought Taryn might really be crying, and she placed her hand on Taryn's forearm. "God, I'm sorry. I was just messing with you. I do think you're super sweet and thoughtful."

Taryn splayed her fingers open and peered between them. "You do?" she asked quietly.

Cassie took Taryn's hands, pulled them from her face and held them tight. "I do. I think you're amazing, and kind, and generous. You're a wonderful woman, Taryn. And I know that Sara and Louise will love that their card means so much to you." She kissed Taryn's fingers.

"And I was just messing with you." Taryn grinned and tried to pull Cassie toward her.

She put her hands on Taryn's chest and pretended to push her away. "No kisses for you."

Taryn pouted and gave a lost puppy expression that Cassie couldn't bear to resist.

"Oh, come on." Cassie gave in and pressed herself against Taryn's body. "That's not fair. You can't use those eyes after being naughty."

Taryn laid it on a little more. "I think I can."

"You two have got a room; maybe you should use it."

Cassie flushed and backed up a tiny step at Andi's intrusion.

"Don't think we're not tempted." Taryn put her arm around Cassie's waist and pulled her closer. "We're just trying not to be rude to our wonderful host."

She nodded toward Bernice, who flashed a bright smile and flicked her wrist. "I appreciate that, but don't concern yourself with what I might think. It's all I can do to keep myself from dragging

Andi up to the penthouse."

Andi wiggled her eyebrows and held up her hand, which Taryn high-fived. "There's life in the old dog yet."

Cassie arched her eyebrow. "You're not even fifty, are you?"

"She isn't. She's my toy boi." Bernice raised her glass, and Cassie clinked hers to it.

Cassie smiled, hoping she had the same verve for life and sexual appetite at her age, though Cassie had no idea what Bernice's real age was. She looked spectacular, and if anything, Andi looked older than her. "Congratulations on a successful first week," she said.

"Thank you. We've smashed all expectations. My CFO, Dade, has had a change of opinion and is suddenly *extremely* happy I followed my heart." Bernice hooked her finger in Andi's pocket, tugged her closer and kissed her cheek.

Andi grinned. "I think you were following a different part of you."

Bernice shrugged elegantly. "Initially, perhaps. But I had a strong feeling you were going to be perfect for me."

Cassie smiled along with everyone else but wondered how that was possible when Bernice had never previously met Andi. And she tried hard *not* to be envious that Bernice was getting to keep her idea of perfect when Cassie would soon have to relinquish Taryn like she was returning her to the store after a trial run. Though Bernice would have to deal with Andi going back on the road with her crew soon enough. Would she continue to view her vision of perfection so positively, or would distance dull the shine?

"And Dade is *so* happy that it didn't take much to convince her that the stunt show should be in permanent residency here."

Cassie's heart thudded against her ribs. *They were staying?* Was that the great news Taryn had bounced in her chair about earlier before they'd ended up having the dark discussion about Cassie's mom? Hope became something tangible in her heart, forming a bubble of potential joy for the future. If Taryn remained in Vegas, everything Cassie had begun to depend upon for her happiness would only grow.

Taryn squeezed Cassie's waist. "That was what I wanted to tell you about."

Cassie quelled the unfamiliar optimism that almost lifted her from her feet. She would've reprimanded herself, but her anticipation stood guard and shoved the negative thoughts back.

"Andi has asked me to be her partner in the business." Taryn's eyes sparkled with enthusiasm. "She wants me to build a bigger team so we can still have the traveling show as well as the hotel residency." She smiled widely. "Isn't that amazing?"

Cassie's ankles threatened to give way as the tentative ground she'd stupidly tried to build a potential future on began to shake beneath her heels. *No. No, it's not amazing, actually.* It was devastating, which seemed like the polar opposite of amazing. "Wow, that's wonderful." *Liar, liar.* She smiled as brightly as she could, though the result was likely dimmer than a solar-powered light installation in the middle of a Scottish winter. "You seem really excited about the prospect."

Taryn nodded, and her eyes widened. "I am... I am."

Cassie's hope temporarily reignited at Taryn's hesitation, but she dismissed it as swiftly as it had risen. She'd already made herself a fool in thinking that Taryn might make a sudden U-turn in her raison d'etre. She shouldn't hang onto her sinking dream and go down with the ship.

"I'm going to stick around for another four weeks," Taryn said, "so I can fully train my number one and make sure she's confident to take over my parts of the show. Then I'm going to concentrate on auditioning for new talent."

And the ship hit rock bottom, her dreams suffering a watery demise. Four months less time together. Cassie steadied her breath before responding. "Where will you do that?" she asked, trying to keep the desperation from her voice. From the way Bernice's expression turned to pity, she didn't succeed. Andi continued to grin however, so maybe she'd done enough to get away with it, and Bernice would be kind enough not to reveal her sorrow.

"At Andi's ranch in Ponder, Texas," Taryn said. "It's about eighty acres, isn't it?"

Andi nodded. "Eighty-seven."

"We set up a lot of tracks and jumps, so it'll be a great place to audition people." Taryn nodded toward their host. "Bernice is going to loan us her recruitment and marketing team for us to do a worldwide talent search."

"Yep, and we might even make our own reality show." Andi grasped Taryn's shoulder. "It's the beginning of a whole new era for us."

"That sounds like a lot of fun." And if it didn't signal the early end of her relationship with Taryn, Cassie would have genuinely been happy for the development. But she was already too deep in her emotional investment, and her devastation equaled, if not exceeded, their excitement.

"It's less than a three-hour flight from Vegas, and the ranch is about an hour's drive from Dallas." Taryn squeezed Cassie close to her. "Maybe you could visit?"

"Maybe." Cassie tried to find the positivity in Taryn's question; at least Taryn had considered Cassie in her future in some small way. She sounded genuinely hopeful and that was backed up with her expression, but really, what would be the point of eight hours' travel once or twice before Taryn set off around the world again? It couldn't even be called a long-distance relationship. "You know I'm really busy at the hospital though, and with the added commitment of the free clinic work, I'm not sure what spare time I'll have to combine a visit and that much travel."

"Oh. Yeah. Sure. Of course." Taryn glanced away.

Beyond Andi and Bernice, Cassie saw Rachel at the bar. "My friend's over there. I'll go say hi and come back." She slipped Taryn's hand from her waist and began to walk away. She wanted to walk all the way out of the bar and back to the safety of her apartment, but she didn't want to spoil Taryn's night.

Taryn caught her wrist gently. "Should I come with you?"

The confusion and uncertainty in Taryn's expression made Cassie's heart ache all the more. She clearly had no idea how her news bomb had raised and then obliterated Cassie's hopes for their relationship. Cassie forced a smile and touched her fingers to Taryn's hand. "I haven't spent much time with her recently." *And that's because I've been stupidly spending so much time with you and letting my heart fall for you.* "It'd be nice for us to catch up properly for a little while, if that's okay?"

Taryn's easy smile returned, placated by the half-truth. "Of course. I'll miss you."

Cassie turned and headed toward the bar, unable to find the composure to respond. She'd known this dream would eventually end, and she'd thought she was in control of her emotions, thought it was okay to get involved because a small amount of this kind of happiness was better than none at all. She blinked back her tears and repeated that affirmation in her head as she approached Rachel. Her time with Taryn *had* been wonderful, and if she was offered the chance to meet Taryn again for the first time, Cassie wouldn't do it differently. And she'd remember that for whatever time they had left. If her experience with Taryn had taught her anything, aside from the ability to cut loose and relax occasionally, it was that time was precious. And Cassie intended to treasure whatever time together she and Taryn were gifted. A broken heart was no fun at all, but it reminded her she was lucky to be alive. It was more than her brother had gotten, and it would somehow feel like a slight to his memory if she wasted any opportunities she was given.

For now though, she needed a moment to regroup and lick a wound she hadn't expected to tend to for some time. Rachel spotted her and waved, and her smile soothed Cassie's pain a little. Ten minutes of recuperation with her bouncy friend, and she would be ready to face Taryn again. She pushed away the quietly insistent voice that whispered four weeks would never be enough.

Chapter Twenty

Taryn fired off a last-minute text to Cassie before getting ready for her final stunt of the show, the aerial double globe of death. Over the past week, they'd managed to snatch a couple of nights together and Taryn had brought lunch to the hospital one day. Everything had been as wonderful as usual, but she was sure Cassie was holding on to a sadness Taryn didn't know the source of. Cassie's mom continued to be a cause of emotional stress for her, and Taryn warred with herself, vacillating between wanting to have a come to Jesus meeting with Cassie's mom so she could tell her exactly what she was doing to her daughter and that she should stop being such an entitled, evil bitch, and simply wanting to hold Cassie while she processed the debilitating verbal battles with the woman who should be holding her up, not dragging her down. But it wasn't her place to do any of it since Taryn wasn't Cassie's long-term partner.

The whole situation had caused Taryn to contemplate her relationship with her parents and siblings, but it hadn't changed how she felt. She hadn't had an epiphany which subsequently led to an emotionally charged meeting with them, where everyone forgave past misdeeds, behaviors, and judgments. Nor did she feel a burgeoning desire to seek a better relationship with them. But what her considerations *did* lead to was a concern that she might be some kind of sociopath, lacking in sentiment and unable to connect with people.

A chat with Andi and Gwen soon dismissed those fears. She'd connected with them and the rest of the team, and she'd quickly forged strong friendships. She loved them and would do anything for them. Sure, she hadn't fallen in romantic love, but she hadn't been closed off to it either. She locked her phone and placed it face down on the table when it became clear Cassie wasn't responding. *Cassie.* She closed her eyes and pressed her fingers to her mouth as though she could still feel Cassie's lips there. She wasn't closed off to their building relationship either, though it seemed more or less impossible for anything solid to come of it. When Taryn had extended an invitation to join her on Andi's ranch, Cassie essentially turned her down, and the underlying subtext was that there could be no possibility of a long-distance relationship.

Honestly, Taryn had no idea what she wanted when it came to Cassie, not without placing unfair demands on her, and Taryn wasn't about to start doing that. Andi was offering her the chance of a lifetime, to be part of a successful business without having to invest anything other than her time. It made sense to continue along the path she'd been doing okay on. Her current ennui would fade with this new challenge, especially when she began to audition for new talent. And the fiery intensity of her feelings for Cassie would fade too.

They had to. Because Taryn wasn't sure how she was supposed to reconcile traveling around the world with some version of a relationship with Cassie. She didn't want to mess up her own career or whatever it was she had with Cassie, so they should talk. They were never supposed to be anything other than a casual thing, but the deeper friendship that had organically developed had become important to Taryn. And she didn't want to lose it.

She took one last look at her phone—no messages—then headed down to the pit to get on her bike. It was time to focus and put Cassie to the back of her mind for a while, somewhere she hadn't spent much time since Taryn had met her. *Concentrate.* Their new finale had the fans and the media in raptures, and Taryn felt like she'd been riding the new bike all her life. Gwen's adaptations were some of her best work, and the result was so smooth, it was difficult to tell where Taryn ended and the bike began once she started to ride.

"They're calling your name again," Gwen said when she looked up from the bike and saw Taryn approaching.

She laughed. "They are devoted."

"If this continues, you won't be able to go anywhere without an entourage." Gwen got up and placed her wrench in its perfectly wrench-shaped foam nest in the second drawer of her rolling tool chest.

"Are you offering to be my bodyguard?" Taryn shook her head at Gwen's mortified expression. "I don't think you have to worry. I'm a stunt rider, not a singer or actress. Our fame is localized—and transient. Most of these people will have forgotten my name before their plane lands in their hometown."

Gwen frowned. "Jeez, Tar, that's dark and sad."

Taryn waved her away. "Anyway, I'll be looking out for someone else to take my place in the spotlight soon enough."

"I hope you're right about Fig; I worry about her." Gwen took her time wiping the grease from her hands with a fresh white cloth.

"I am. She's doing great in the globe, and that's a cauldron. Even the original globe has forged plenty of great riders. Your wife will be fine taking up my mantle."

"Talking about me again?" Fig asked as she clapped Taryn on the back.

"Just can't stop myself." Taryn looked up at the giant dual clock showing the time and the countdown to their stage entrance. She pulled on her helmet, climbed onto her bike, and started the engine, and Dee and the rest of the globe team followed suit.

The cacophony of sound from twelve bikes reverberated around the pit, and the ground shook beneath their feet.

Gwen stepped off the main area onto the raised platform where her many tool chests were situated and saluted. "Be awesome," she shouted over the thunderous din.

The other eleven riders circled until they were positioned in a perfectly straight line behind Taryn and waited. Taryn watched the bright green digits on the timer tick down, and time slowed. In her comms, she could hear Sally whipping the crowd's anticipation into a frenzy, and over that, she heard her name being chanted. Would she miss that if she gave all this up? She shook her head, puzzled as to why the question had popped into her head at all. Andi's offer sealed the rest of her career in this game; it was hardly the time to be thinking about giving it up. Now wasn't the time to be thinking about anything other than controlling her speeding bike around the globes in a figure eight as they rose and split into sections. *That's* what she should be concentrating on.

"Five, four, three..."

Sally's countdown floated into Taryn's awareness, and she revved her engine one last time before pushing the thumb throttle all the way down as she sped out of the pit in first gear. She shifted to second and emerged onto the stadium floor. She flicked her boot up to third, hurtling underneath the globes in the center of the stage area. She and the other riders did two laps while the globes were lowered to the floor, and each of them performed a variety of tricks to draw even more roars of approval from the audience.

Taryn rounded the corner and at the beginning of the long straight, accelerated to forty-five before she hopped up, rested her head on the tank, and raised her legs so she was completely vertical. She was back in her seat before the stadium curved again, and the applause increased a gazillion decibels. The audience stamped their feet in time with the music, though that was barely audible over the noise they were creating.

She saw the globes were in position, and she went in first, getting up to the correct speed, and winding around the reinforced glass spheres in a perfect figure eight. As she crossed the point where the two globes joined, she yelled into her mic to confirm she was ready for the next rider to enter. Dee was the next one in, and so it went until all twelve of them were inside the globes. The ramp closed and sealed them inside, and the hydraulics kicked in, beginning to raise them from the ground.

Even though the spheres were totally transparent, it made little difference to the view inside. Taryn had to keep her gaze fixed on the bike in front of her and those all around her. The riders separated into three groups: one set of four in the top halves of each sphere traveling in a circular motion, while the remaining seven riders stayed with Taryn in the bottom half, still going around in a figure of eight.

The two tops of the globes split slowly and rose toward the roof. The temperature changed slightly as the air rushed in to fill the space and cleared it of the exhaust fumes not removed by the custom-built venting system. Visibility improved slightly, and Taryn pinned her eyes wide open. Everyone was in perfect harmony, their speeds matching at the exact same points in their trajectories, and Taryn would've grinned if it hadn't been for the five-plus G-force pressing against her flesh. This life wasn't so bad.

A bike in the above half-globe Taryn was about to enter came into Taryn's vision, and immediately she knew something was about to go fantastically wrong. In a microsecond, the tires came too far over the edge of the higher globe, upsetting the delicate balance of velocity and centripetal force. The rider careened out of their path, heading through the gap between the globe halves, and for a nanosecond, Taryn thought disaster might be averted if centripetal force carried the bike and its rider out of the globes entirely.

The last thing Taryn saw was the rider jerking their handlebars at the last moment. The last thing she felt was the rider's helmet smashing into her chest...

Chapter Twenty-One

ICY COLD NUMBNESS STARTED at her heart and spread outward, traveling along her veins and arteries, threatening to bring her whole system to a standstill. Cassie prayed her ears hadn't processed the information correctly, that she'd heard the paramedic wrong, that their ambulance wasn't the first of three bringing in casualties from a stunt gone wrong at the Cosmos.

Because if she'd heard right, her worst and most frequently recurring nightmare was coming true. Her history was repeating itself in mutated form. Someone she cared deeply about had been harmed...and just like last time, she was powerless to save them. Her training kicked in, and she pushed away from the reception desk, taking long strides along the corridor. Maybe it wasn't Taryn; she didn't recognize the two riders the paramedics pushed into the ER. Cassie had met maybe twenty performers last week at their celebration party. Three ambulances meant six riders at most; what did that make the odds that Taryn *wasn't* one of them? She'd said she wasn't on stage for the full show. Perhaps she hadn't been involved in this stunt at all.

She pushed through the double doors, knowing she was grasping at straws when she should simply be laser-focused on helping the two already in treatment bays. Rachel joined her and matched her stride as Cassie headed toward the first rider to assess the damage.

"The first ambulance that left the scene had engine trouble a few hundred yards from us. They're pushing the riders in," Rachel said. "Jonny said they're the two riders who sustained the worst injuries."

Cassie flashed a glance at Rachel as she gloved up to inspect her first patient. Her feeble optimism wavered in the light of this new information. Taryn was the star of the show. Whatever stunt had gone wrong with so many riders *had* to include her, and she would've been at the heart of the danger. She let out a short breath. She didn't know that. She didn't know anything about the show; every time Taryn had mentioned something about it, Cassie had asked her not to continue, and Taryn had understood, knowing the thought of the risky stunts was a source of major discomfort for Cassie. All this conjecture wasn't helpful, and it was distracting her from the vital business of tending to the broken person on the bed in front of her right now.

"This is why I'll never allow my children to ride motorbikes," Dr. Fischer said as he strode past them to the second rider.

Cassie had no words to respond. Instead, she went into autopilot and almost removed her conscious soul from her body as she checked over the rider, talked to her, and assessed her injuries. Rachel operated in perfect unison beside her, administering the painkillers Cassie instructed her to and taking on the more human part of putting the rider at ease, the bedside manner Cassie had cultivated but which had currently deserted her as she struggled to maintain focus. As she and Rachel sliced through the protective leather clothing, much to the vocal chagrin of the rider, she concentrated on breathing in through her nose and out through her mouth. Long, deep, cleansing breaths to put her in touch with her body and mind, to center and ground her, and hopefully return her to the room.

Though perhaps it was best that she operated at a distance. Her heart pulsed strong against her ribs, each beat seeming to test the sturdiness of her bones to keep the organ in place. And her heart was the problem. Objectivity and emotional detachment had long been fine friends when it came to this part of her job—the real emergencies rather than the removal of vegetables from sexual misadventures or coins from the various orifices of curious children.

Those things had become second nature in her personal life too...
until Taryn came along. And now she was virtually paralyzed with
fear that the next gurney wheeled into her emergency room would
have Taryn lying on it.

Concentrate, damn it. She zeroed in on what she was doing
and was relieved to find that everything was proceeding as it
should. The compound fracture of the rider's femur luckily hadn't
nicked or pierced her femoral artery. She'd need to have surgery
within the next twenty-four hours, and she had a long recovery
process ahead of her. But the rest of her was relatively intact thanks
to her safety gear, most of which lay in a sad pile of giant leather
strips on the floor.

"Two more riders just came in," Dinah yelled from across the
ER.

Cassie's tongue felt enormous in her mouth and rendered her
temporarily unable to talk, like she was having anaphylactic shock
in response to the mere possibility of Taryn being one of those
riders.

Rachel placed her hand on Cassie's forearm. "Let me check,"
she said.

Cassie was glad for Rachel's instinctive protection and nodded.
The rider they'd just treated was still muttering about how expensive
her leather gear was even as the morphine kicked in and slurred
her speech. She was soon talking nonsense about vampires living
in Bluff County or some such place, and Cassie took that as her
cue to leave.

She turned into Rachel, and her concerned expression
confirmed Cassie's initial dread. "Taryn?"

Rachel swallowed and nodded. "Yes." She wrapped her arm
around her forearm firmly. "Blunt force trauma to the chest at high
speed—a flying motorbike smashed into her chest; everyone else
who couldn't get out of the way fell like dominoes."

The information, while it was scary, was also hopeful. "She told
you all that?"

"Yeah. She's pretty lucid." Rachel smiled and squeezed Cassie's arm. "She's obviously got a high tolerance for pain."

Cassie grimaced; she didn't need that final piece of information. As another paramedic wheeled Taryn past Cassie, she immediately noted the blueish color of Taryn's skin and heard her raspy breathing. *Cyanosis from lack of oxygen. Likely a pneumothorax from the blunt force trauma at high speed. Minimum three broken ribs, possibly more depending on the angle of the wheel when it hit.*

She moved to follow but found Fischer in her path. He shook his head and extended his arm toward her. "No, Dr. Kennedy, I'm sorry. You know the patient, don't you? It's the woman you've been dating, am I correct?"

How did he know that? Clearly, the hospital grapevine had been effective with the little gossip her sex life provided. She glanced at Rachel, who looked away. She hadn't pegged Rachel as a snitch. Cassie clenched her jaw and bit back the desire to spit something unnaturally venomous in Rachel's direction. She was just protecting Cassie from a possible malpractice suit if anything went wrong. When had the practice of medicine boiled down to life-saving decisions made with ambulance-chasing lawyers in mind? That wasn't what she'd gotten into this career for.

Her knees weakened, and she reached out for Rachel as the motivation for her job choice bounced into her consciousness. The same reason could end her career if there were complications, if Taryn... No, she wouldn't even think the worst.

But she'd become an ER doctor precisely so she could save people. She couldn't allow Fischer or Rachel to stop her from trying to save someone she cared deeply for. "I wouldn't call it dating as such," she said, mustering as much indignation as she could manage. "She's just someone I'm having sex with," she said, a little quieter. No one was listening, and over the shouted commands of nurses and the pained yells of a couple of patients, it was unlikely she would have been overheard anyway. But still, she didn't like to be grist for the rumor mill.

Fischer tilted his head. His expression softened slightly, and there was a kindness in his eyes Cassie had never noticed before.

"My dear Dr. Kennedy, that's exactly what I said about my wife twenty-eight years ago." He chuckled lightly. "If it were that simple, I don't expect you would've been as elusive as Bigfoot in these hospital corridors of late."

She opened her mouth to retort, but he held up his hand.

"No judgment, doctor. It's about time you found some balance in your life."

He smiled and turned in the direction of the bay Taryn had been wheeled into. Did everyone in the hospital know about her private life? Her thought was reinforced with the unwelcome appearance of Barr as Rachel gently took Cassie's arm to lead her to the rider who'd come in with Taryn.

"High profile, this mess," he said, his voice flint-hard. "No mistakes."

Barr focused his gaze on Cassie, and she narrowed her eyes, and her body tensed for retaliation.

Rachel leaned close to her ear and whispered, "You don't have the time to waste on him."

The muscles in her legs went jello-soft with the reference to time. Taryn was always so concerned with the concept, with making the most of what she had while she had it, of not wasting any of it. Cassie's muscles strengthened again, along with a rising anger. Taryn *was* wasting her time; how could lying on a hospital gurney with potentially life-threatening injuries possibly be viewed as a quality use of the finite time she had?

She allowed Rachel to guide her around Barr and pushed away the thought that she should find somewhere else to work. Barr had shown he was here to stay, and he was more concerned with making their hospital profitable than increasing the number of lives they saved.

Cassie entered the treatment bay and slipped into autopilot

once more, though she strained to hear any sounds of anguish and pain from Taryn in the adjacent bay. When her ears tuned in, Cassie immediately wished she hadn't. The tension and concern in Fischer's voice filtered in after she heard Barr repeat his warning. Every fiber of her being wanted to switch patients with Fischer, to hell with the rules. They could fire her after she'd saved Taryn's life. How was she supposed to stand here and ignore the possibility that Fischer wouldn't diagnose something fast enough, that he wouldn't act with enough speed, that he might nick an artery as he inserted the needle to remove the air from Taryn's collapsed lung?

She felt Rachel's steadying presence again, the touch of her hand more firm this time.

"Cassie. You need to concentrate," Rachel whispered.

Cassie squeezed her eyes closed briefly and tried to empty her mind of everything but the situation in front of her and the other woman who might need her expertise to save her life. She couldn't forgive herself if her inattention led to someone else's death. She opened her eyes wide, took in the scene in front of her, and set about doing her job... and praying to every god or deity that actually existed that Fischer would do his well enough to save the woman Cassie loved.

Chapter Twenty-Two

THE INFERNO OF HEAT spreading across Taryn's chest took her breath away, making it even more difficult to breathe than it already had been since someone's bike crashed into her chest at fifty miles per hour. She closed her eyes against the harsh lighting of the hospital ceiling and tried to use the tools she'd learned from Cassie's BodyBalance class.

It didn't work. Guiding yourself to a meditative state required deep inhalation and exhalation of air, and Taryn could do neither. In fact, the last thing she wanted to be aware of was her breathing, or rather, as it felt right now, her inability to breathe. Every molecule of oxygen she sucked in was like a collection of fireballs coursing down her throat. And when they hit her lungs, it was as if they exploded and coated all the cells in her body in a raging hell-blaze. She imagined this was what actually being in Hell would feel like, if she believed in an afterlife, which she didn't, despite how convincingly it had been depicted by that famous lesbian author from LA. Death did seem like she'd make a great buddy, but Taryn was in no hurry to find out if she was right or wrong about it all. The finite number of heartbeats she did believe in—she didn't want to believe that hers were all used up, and this was how it ended. This was how *she* ended.

A particularly excruciating shot of pain pulled her back into the room and onto the bed. Maybe the meditation had been working after all. Her eyes jerked open, and the fluorescent light flooded in. She could make out softly outlined shapes of doctors and nurses as they moved around her, barking out demands that sounded like a foreign language. Machines beeped and whirred all around her, and she became aware of cold metal against her skin, sliding from her stomach and upward. When she heard the accompanying snip of metal against metal, she realized what was happening. *Not my jacket.* She loved that jacket. Not because it had sentimental value or because it had been the jacket that she'd accomplished a spectacular stunt in for the first time, but because it smelled of Cassie. It was the jacket Taryn had wrapped around Cassie's shoulders and insisted she put on while they watched the Bellagio's water fountains one night after an early round of stunning sex. So it didn't just smell of Cassie and her sweet perfume, it had been infused with the scent of her most animalistic self. After Taryn had kissed Cassie goodnight and gone to her bike in the garage, she'd pulled it on, and her nose had been assailed by its intoxicating strength. It took all her resolve not to go back inside for more; Cassie had an early shift and needed sleep. Taryn had needed Cassie.

And in the past couple of weeks when they'd been unable to spend as much time together as they wanted, Taryn had fed her hunger by pressing that jacket to her nose, closing her eyes, and imagining Cassie in her arms. It was all very dramatic. And alien. And made her feel quite pathetic. But she didn't care.

Pain, along with someone repeating her name over and over, tugged her consciousness back into the cold, sterile room. The violent heat across her chest hadn't lessened, and she much preferred to be back in her head, alone with her musings and away from all this emergency nonsense she didn't want to be party to. *Fix me and let me rest.*

The same voice was asking questions, but Taryn couldn't make out the words. She squinted against the light in an effort to focus on the black hole where the sounds were coming from, but that didn't help. Their sentences simply wouldn't form any coherent connections in her brain that she could decipher. She let her eyelids close, the effort of keeping them open proving too much, and muttered at them to get on with it. She didn't have time to be lying around in an emergency room. She had things to do with her life, places to visit, new people to meet. She chuckled and regretted it immediately when the resulting vibration made her suck in another mouthful of fireballs and set her insides aflame.

When the pain subsided enough to remember why she'd laughed, Taryn stopped herself from doing it again. *New people to meet.* Hadn't she already met the most amazing person she could ever have hoped to meet on her extensive and unending travels? Wasn't Cassie everything good and right with the world? Taryn hadn't been roaming the planet in search of such a woman, but when Cassie had presented herself so memorably in the club that night, "protecting" Taryn from the wicked advances of vampy Erin, it felt a little like she could stop her wandering *because* of such a person.

But that had been the alcohol careening around her bloodstream, dulling every urge other than the sexual ones. When her most animalistic tendencies rose to the surface, she had always been quick to forget everything else that was important to her until those tendencies had been sated. Still, Cassie was a wonderful woman, and Taryn needed to survive this so they could spend more time together before she had to leave for Andi's ranch to get the next adventure in her life in motion.

If that was what she still even wanted. Hell, she still hadn't worked out why she felt so lost and aimless. What if this new development wasn't what she was supposed to be doing? Was she *supposed* to be doing anything? Maybe she was kidding herself that she had some dream to discover, to follow to the pot of contentedness at the far end of the rainbow.

She felt a sharp prick against the skin of her arm, then ice-cold liquid invaded her veins and blasted through her blood like frozen volcano lava. She took another sharp intake of breath that resulted in yet more chili powder cannonballs bombing down her throat. Moments later, something cold and hard pushed against the wall of her chest, and when it punctured, she couldn't hold back the subsequent scream of agony. Tendrils of darkness edged her eyeballs and began to close in, and she welcomed the black nothingness they promised.

Chapter Twenty-Three

CASSIE HAD COMPLETED HER work with the fourth rider and had also assessed the fifth and final patient who'd come in with the third ambulance. Her wife, Gwen, had ridden with her, and she'd been at pains to make sure Cassie knew her name—Fig, which was an unusual moniker—how old she was, and how they'd recently been talking about starting a family.

Cassie knew well enough the psychology behind the information dump; Gwen thought that if she could make Fig's doctor care about her, about them both, and about their life together, that Cassie would work harder to save her. With other doctors, the ones who had become jaded and tired, maybe that was necessary, but her tactics weren't required here. After her initial inability to focus, Cassie had pulled reserves from some deftly hidden place to shutter off the torrent of terror, anxiety, and fear threatening to overwhelm her, and she'd fallen into well-worn patterns to concentrate on the patient in front of her.

Fig had some contusions and deep bruising from her collision. But as the final rider to join the mangled pile of metal and bodies Gwen had described in disturbing detail, Fig had gotten off rather lightly. No broken bones. No trauma. No lasting damage. Cassie pushed away the unkind and selfish wish that Taryn had been in Fig's place rather than at the epicenter of the crash.

Gwen sat in the chair beside Fig in the temporary bay she'd been wheeled into. "Thank you, doctor," she said.

Cassie pulled down her mask and smiled. "You're welcome."

Gwen pointed to Taryn's treatment bay, where the curtain was still tightly drawn around it. "How's Tar doing?"

The somber note in her voice told of her worry, possibly exacerbated by the fact that she'd seen all of it happen firsthand. Cassie reminded herself that Gwen wasn't a medical professional, and crashes often looked worse than they were, especially when they involved loved ones. She then reinforced that with the assertion that Fischer was the best doctor Taryn could have asked for. His patient survival rate was 83% and second only to hers. She squeezed away the temptation to flick through his latest records to do the math. Was he due some of his 17%? *This is about people, not statistics.* Taryn was physically the strongest woman she'd ever met; she was tough, and she loved life. *Those* were the things that would pull her through this. Her survival wouldn't be at the mercy of quantitative numbers.

"Dr. Kennedy?"

Cassie tuned back into Gwen's voice and pasted on a professional expression. "She's in excellent hands. Dr. Fischer will let you know how she's doing as soon as he's able."

Gwen frowned. "I know you have to seem detached for everyone else in here, but you're talking like a robot, doc. I'm her friend... You're her...lover? From the little I've seen of you two together, I thought you were more invested in her well-being. Am I wrong? Don't you feel anything?"

Cassie gritted her teeth against the inference that she didn't care for Taryn, when she actually wanted to scream, and bargain, and whatever the hell else it would take to ensure Taryn was safe and healthy on the other side of that damned blue curtain.

"Give her a break, wife." Fig patted Gwen's hand then coughed.

Gwen immediately turned away from Cassie. She pulled an ice chip from a cup of them she'd just returned with and pressed it to Fig's lips. She sucked it for a while before crunching it into oblivion and giving a lop-sided grin.

"I'll give *you* a break," Gwen said. "What the hell are you doing getting yourself banged up like this?"

Cassie would've laughed had she not just been on the receiving end of Gwen's ire.

Fig lifted her arm to point at Cassie and her face crumpled in discomfort. "Not everyone is like you and me. Some people just hook up for the sex, you know that. Especially people in high pressure careers where they don't have time for real intimacy."

Christ. With Gwen's pop psychology and Fig's philosophy, Cassie felt like retreating to the on-call room now that the ER had calmed down. "I'll leave you to it."

Gwen widened her eyes and put her hands on her hips. "I don't think you will."

Again, Cassie had to fight the urge to laugh. She was maybe eight years younger than Cassie but was acting like she was the matriarch. Cassie idly wondered if that's what role she fulfilled for the not-so-little stunt family she'd met last week. "I have other patients to attend," she said calmly. "If you'll excuse me."

Gwen shook her head and stepped toward the end of the bed. "No, we will not excuse you. Do you care for Taryn or not?"

"Wife," Fig said and got a powerfully silencing stare from Gwen.

Cassie shrugged and pulled the curtain partially closed. There seemed to be little harm in answering Gwen's question honestly, particularly if it would serve to stop the interrogation. "I care for her deeply, and because of that, I wasn't able to treat her. The AMA Code of Ethics advises us not to treat family or anyone when our feelings might affect their care in some way." She admitted the formality of it sounded like a hollow, practiced excuse, but she'd also been physically prevented from treating Taryn. She was certain that any further attempt she made would've been met with security protocols, especially once Barr was in play.

Gwen waved her words away as if they were tangible stink in the air. "Pff. That doesn't mean you have to *act* like you don't give a shit."

Cassie pulled her shoulders back and stiffened. Enough of this. She yanked the curtain back, and Dinah gave her a questioning look from across the main room. She faintly shook her head to indicate there was nothing for her to worry about.

"Doc, please don't go just yet. Let me explain." Fig attempted to push up from the bed to a seated position.

"What are you doing?" Gwen rushed back to her side but helped her get into a more comfortable position. When Fig was settled, her indignant expression was restored. "And what do you need to explain?"

Fig took Gwen's hand and shook her head slowly as she let out a deep sigh. "You're projecting, wife."

Cassie bit her bottom lip to stop a smirk. The way Fig referred to Gwen only as "wife" was adorable, and even amid this tension, Cassie could appreciate something so tender and intimate.

"I'm sorry, doc," Fig said. "We're soulmates, you see. I know you're a woman of science and probably don't believe in that kind of thing, but we do, and we were meant to be together, to find each other."

Fig looked at Gwen in a way that made Cassie's heart ache and might even convince her that what Fig had said was true. She smiled and took a step closer to the bed to show she wasn't about to bolt, despite Gwen's attitude.

"Now that we've found each other, the thought of losing what we have... The thought of me dying is terrifying, and it's something she has to deal with every time I get on my bike for the shows."

Gwen's shoulders began to shake, softly at first, before she dissolved into a full sob and dropped into the chair beside Fig's bed.

"Aw, wife. Come on, it's okay. *I'm* okay." Fig reached over and gently rubbed her wife's back as Gwen cried into her hands.

In her peripheral vision, Cassie saw Rachel enter the ER with someone, another performer from the show if her leather outfit was anything to go by. As they drew closer, Cassie realized it was Dee, Fig's twin, and beckoned her over. Dee jogged across the room quickly and made her way to the other side of Fig's bed. They hugged then fist-bumped.

Dee jutted her chin toward Gwen. "What're you wasting your tears for, Gwenny? Our girl's invincible."

Cassie's eyebrow involuntarily quirked at the description. *Invincible.* That was the kind of attitude that was sure to get you taking risks that got you killed.

Fig rolled her eyes and frowned. "No one's invincible, Dee. We know that more than the average pumpkin."

That was a phrase Cassie had never come across, but she appreciated Fig's pragmatism.

"We want to start a family, Dee." Gwen straightened in her chair and wiped the tears from her cheeks.

"I know." She gestured toward Fig. "This doesn't change anything though, does it?"

Gwen blew out a long breath. "I don't know how much of this I'm supposed to take before—"

"Before what?" Dee chuckled lightly, but there was kindness in her eyes. "Before you ask her to stop stunting?"

Fig laughed and had to hold her chest to ease the obvious pain. "Don't make me laugh, butthead."

Even Gwen gave a small laugh, and Cassie frowned. "I don't understand," she said and looked to Gwen for an explanation since she wasn't a daredevil risk-taker.

Gwen rubbed her forehead and pinched the bridge of her nose. "I can't take this away from her, no matter how petrified I am every time she takes to the stage."

Cassie widened her eyes, still not fully grasping the situation, and waited for further explanation.

"If I stop, doc—if any of us stopped—you may as well just stop my heart from beating at the same time." Fig shrugged almost apologetically. "I live for this. We all do. We know the risks, and we take them anyway." She nodded toward Gwen. "The wife tries to mitigate the shit out of them, obviously, and she runs simulation after simulation after simulation to ensure she's eradicated as much risk as possible. But you can't account for bad luck, or a momentary lapse in concentration, or a freak engine malfunction. And if any of those or the multitude of other things happen, you just have to hope you survive so you can get back on your bike and get out there again." She pressed her lips together. "That's all I can tell you, doc. So I'm sorry my wife went all momma bear on you. She's just worried about me, and she's worried about Taryn. We're a family." She winked. "But you know that, don't you?"

Cassie nodded slowly and began to retreat from the room. She did know they were a family. She also knew she'd lost her own because of someone else's carelessness and risky behavior. And she knew she couldn't face that kind of loss again. It would break her in the places already broken, and she'd be beyond fixing. Fig's veiled ultimatum—be all in or all out—solidified her decision.

Taryn was one of them. She was exactly like the twins; stop her riding, stop her heart. And there was no way Cassie could begin to contemplate asking Taryn to give that up just to see where their fledgling relationship might take them. She'd resent it, and then she'd resent Cassie.

It was all moot anyway. They'd had a flippant exchange about Cassie visiting Taryn at Andi's ranch, and that was it. Clearly, Taryn wouldn't leave her life, and Cassie couldn't allow her heart to fall any more. She bid the trio goodbye and headed toward Rachel and Dinah. She'd wait with them until Fischer emerged from Taryn's treatment bay. And when Taryn was well enough, Cassie would let her know that she had to step back to protect herself. Taryn would understand, she was sure of—

The piercing scream echoed through the ER, and Cassie's heart lurched as if trying to escape through her mouth. She knew where it had come from, but she didn't know why. She glanced at Rachel, who shook her head and mouthed, "Don't" when Cassie looked back at the flimsy curtain separating her from Taryn. She looked back at Rachel again and nodded before walking toward her as steadily as she could despite her legs threatening to give way and send her to the floor in a crumpled heap. She didn't allow herself to falter and fall, because if she did, she wasn't sure she'd be able to get up. Not until she saw Taryn's gleaming smile again. Not before she saw those gorgeous, unusual eyes looking back at her as if they held all the love in the world.

Rachel put her arm around Cassie when she made it to the desk, and she held her tight. It took every ounce of professionalism, every inch of stoic determination not to break down in Rachel's comforting embrace.

Instead, she stared blankly at the lank blue material and prayed for Fischer to emerge, victorious and with a check in his 83% box. And time, that cruel mistress Taryn was obsessed with, slowed to an impossibly pedestrian pace as if taunting Cassie. She was out of control again, and the life of the woman she cared so deeply for, the woman she loved, was in the hands of someone else.

Chapter Twenty-Four

WHEN TARYN CAME AROUND this time, it was as if she were atop a fluffy cloud. She could no longer feel the dull, heavy burden of her bones nor the insistent ache of bruised muscles. The volcanic swell of searing pain that had swept across the whole of her chest had also receded. *Oh shit. I'm dead.* Taryn squeezed her eyes shut against the urge to discover where she was. Perhaps if she denied it, they'd drop her back into her skin; she'd tolerate the agony of the crash and the recovery process and the horrendous amount of time she'd have to sit doing nothing.

Maybe this was just a mini timeout, her body's way of dissociating from whatever the hell the doctors were doing to stabilize her. That was it; her brain had automatically triggered a special failsafe by disconnecting her mind from her body and the pain it was currently enduring. Made sense, really. She shuffled her butt into the soft marshmallow of her temporary sofa and took a deep inhalation. No fireballs. Yep, she was definitely not feeling what her body was going through right now. *Nice.* She didn't get much time like this just to think. No stimulus, no environment, no one else around her, and strangely, no sign of the thousands of thoughts that flitted through her brain at any given moment.

What to do then? Plan? She figured the effects of the crash were more serious than she'd initially thought. Sure, the pain had been all-encompassing, but she'd taken the fact that she'd remained conscious and coherent as positive signs, pointing to some badly bruised ribs and nothing more. Whatever. The docs were dealing with that. If she woke up to discover she wasn't able to ride for a while, she and Andi would just have to shift the timeline of the recruitment push. Fig was more than ready to take over as lead rider, and she really didn't need Taryn hanging over her anyway. Maybe Taryn could begin some of the prep work for their expansion instead, and maybe Cassie wouldn't mind playing doctor a little too.

What if you can't ride at all ever again?

Taryn laughed at the hoarse but vaguely familiar voice. *Don't be crazy.* There was nothing she couldn't come back from, and she wouldn't let anything beat her. A dark cloak slid over her optimism and tried to stifle it with the notion of paralysis. Okay, that was one thing she feared. After being so incredibly active her whole life, the thought of being unable to be one hundred percent independent was like bee stings to her eyeballs—unbearable. She shook that insidious thought from her shoulders, but it had already made her think about Louise and her cancer, about the free clinic and the great work they were doing, about—

A giant hand wrapped around her waist and yanked her downward, off the cloud. She slammed back onto a rubbery mattress with a yell, and her eyes sprang open.

"Welcome back, Ms. Taylor."

The man from whom the voice had come hovered over her and slowly came into focus. He had a nice smile framed by a ridiculous beard, though she could pack for a week's vacation in the bags under his eyes.

"How are you feeling?"

Taryn pulled in a quick breath and while there was a throbbing ache in her entire upper body, fireballs were no longer exploding in her lungs. "Pretty good. When can I get out of here?" She grinned and felt her lips crack. She ran her tongue along them, but before she'd finished, a nurse came into view by her side and offered a straw, pressing it gently against her mouth. Taryn took it and pulled in water that tasted like ambrosia. The nectar slid down her throat, cooling and soothing it to the point of bliss.

The doctor laughed. "Five days, if you're lucky. You'll be moved to the thoracic department where they'll monitor you and make sure there are no complications and no infections. They'll explain everything." He patted her shoulder softly. "You should rest now."

Before she could voice any more pertinent questions about how serious her condition was, he'd dragged back the privacy curtain and swept out of her eyeline. A far more pleasing visual greeted her in the form of Cassie's smiling face.

"Hey," Cassie said as she came to Taryn's bedside. "How are you doing?"

Now that Cassie was closer, Taryn could see her bloodshot and slightly puffy eyes. Had she been crying or had it simply been a long and tiring shift? "I'm all good." She grinned and tried not to show the resulting pain in her expression. The twinge of concern in Cassie's eyes told her she'd failed.

"What happened?" Cassie touched Taryn's hand, but the contact was all too brief, and she pulled away quickly.

Taryn exhaled and shrugged, an action she regretted immediately. Maybe she needed more drugs. "One of our riders in the top globe just...misjudged their circuit, I guess. The globes were slowly coming apart, and I saw a tire go over the edge. At those speeds, and with so many others around me..." She shook her head. "There was nothing I could do." As she'd continued to speak, with difficulty, she thought she saw sorrow in Cassie's eyes and hazarded a guess as to where it was coming from. But maybe she was wrong. It was egotistical to think that Cassie had dissolved into tears because of Taryn's crash. She saw hundreds of emergencies every month; there was probably very little that truly fazed her. Still, Taryn wanted to draw Cassie into her arms and comfort her, hating that she was in some sort of emotional discomfort. "How are you doing?"

Taryn saw Cassie apply the mask as clearly as if she'd watched her physically hold one to her face.

"I'm absolutely fine," Cassie said. "You don't need to concern yourself with me; concentrate on recovering and getting back out there."

The instant detachment and professional touch were like knives through Taryn's heart, hurting far more than anything she'd just experienced. But what did she want Cassie to do? Fling herself down on the bed and wail so loudly her sorrow would fly up to heaven? She played along anyway, deciding that Cassie had to project a certain way in her own ER. There were still nurses buzzing around, checking lines and fluids. "The other doc said I'd probably be out of the hospital in less than a week. When do you think I might be able to get on my bike again?"

Cassie blinked and glanced away, her chin trembling slightly. "You'll need at least two weeks before you think about anything physical."

Taryn was tempted to ask about *other* physical stuff, but Cassie's seriousness kept the thought in her head. "I don't feel too bad considering... How bad was it?"

Cassie smiled but not for long. "That'll be the morphine talking, I'm afraid. Did Dr. Fischer not discuss the extent of your injuries with you?" When Taryn shook her head, Cassie briefly raised her eyebrows. "I didn't treat you, so I'm not sure exactly what you've been through. I'm sure you have specific questions, so I'll ask Dr. Fischer to come back."

Again with the professional over the personal. Taryn struggled to reason with it, but she said nothing. It was her own issue, her need to know that Cassie cared for her. Which she knew was stupid. She could've saved herself a whole heap of pain and just asked Cassie how she felt about her, about them, before the accident. "How's everyone else?" she asked instead.

Cassie's face brightened. "Everyone else is stable. There are some broken bones: a wrist, a femur, and an elbow—two of which are on the same person. Considering the number of people involved, the speed, and the confined space in which the crash occurred, I think you've all been lucky." She shook her head. "Gwen and Fig are sweet."

Taryn wrinkled her nose. "That's one way of describing them. Did Gwen go crazy on you?"

Cassie smiled, and she seemed to relax a little. "That's one way of describing it," she said and winked.

"I'm sorry. She's all about two things: her work and Fig."

Cassie tilted her head. "She made that clear, yes. But she was also super worried about you."

Taryn grinned. "We've known each other a long time, and it's been a few years since our last..."

The last nurse in the room nodded to Cassie and left, finally leaving them alone.

Cassie perched on the edge of Taryn's bed. "Your last crash?"

Taryn swallowed, and it hurt far more than it should. Cassie reached for the cup of water on the small table and offered it to her. She sipped on the straw, enjoying the relief the cool liquid provided. "Since our last loss. Her name was Trig, and she died in a crash on Route 66."

"Oh." Cassie looked surprised. "Not during a stunt gone wrong then?"

Taryn shrugged. "Kind of. We think she was practicing to beat the record for the fastest headstand on a motorbike." Taryn didn't miss Cassie's subtle eye roll and clear disapproval, but she was respectful enough not to ask the same questions that had plagued her and Andi and the rest of the team.

"It's nice that you have this family," Cassie said.

The source of that sadness was unmistakable. "Speaking of which, have you heard from your mom lately?"

Rachel stepped into the bay and tapped Cassie on the shoulder. "GSW coming in."

Cassie nodded and stood. "Saved by the bullet rather than the bell." She squeezed Taryn's hand gently. "Get some rest. I'll swing by at the end of my shift; you should've been moved to the thoracic ward by then. And I'm sure Dr. Fischer will come and answer your other questions when he's free again."

Taryn caught Cassie's wrist as she turned to leave. "Then we can talk?"

"Sure."

She was gone without another word, and Taryn felt the loneliness deep in her soul. Yes, she had family. But she also wanted Cassie. Nothing like a brush with death to invoke a clichéd re-evaluation of priorities.

Chapter Twenty-Five

THREE DAYS OF DOUBLE shifts followed the multiple rider crash at the stunt show. In that time, Cassie had patched up two gunshots and three knife wounds, saved a woman from an accidental overdose, and treated a man with serious burns in an unfortunate place after sex play with a beeswax candle.

"Everyone knows you should use soy wax—or paraffin if you want the sting—but beeswax is a stupid choice." Rachel shook her head disapprovingly.

Cassie hadn't yet asked where Rachel's surprisingly in-depth knowledge of wax play had come from, but no doubt when they next went to the club, Rachel would regale her with an inevitably sordid yet equally sexy tale.

What Cassie hadn't done was spend any time by Taryn's bedside. She'd dropped in at the beginning of her shift a couple of times, but work had prevented them from spending any quality time together. That's what Cassie was telling Taryn anyway—it was the work keeping them apart. Really, Cassie simply couldn't handle being so close to her without resuming where they'd left off. But she'd made her decision. She had to break things off, but she didn't want to do it while Taryn was relatively fragile in her recovery. Once she was out of the hospital, Cassie would initiate the difficult discussion, and then she could get on with her life as before.

Though she wasn't going back to life exactly as before. Breaking things off with Taryn wasn't the only choice she'd made over the past few days. She'd also decided it was time to cut her mom from her life. She'd found a snippet of time to have a conversation with her therapist, mainly just to touch base. But it had precipitated her parental ruminations, as if her life had been plunged into darkness, and her path forward was now illuminated in neon green. Green for go, be free of the negative impact of her mom.

Cassie pulled into her mom's drive but left her car on the other side of the gate. Despite her sudden burst of courage, she might still need a quick getaway. Buster loped up to the gate as she closed it and almost knocked her over when he reared up and put his massive paws on her chest. Her back pressed against the metal and its heat seared through her blouse. She jumped forward, and Buster bounced around, thinking she was in full-on play mode. Cassie looked around and saw a chewed-up football. Buster glanced in the same direction before he leapt on it and sank his teeth into it. He thrust it toward her but wouldn't give it up when Cassie tried to grab it.

"You never were any good at sports."

Cassie looked up at the sound of her mother's voice. "Oh, I don't know. I fielded your shit pretty good when I was a kid."

Her mom's mouth dropped open, and her cigarette dropped to the floor. "What the fuck? Look what you made me do."

Cassie used the distraction to snatch the ball from Buster's mouth. "I didn't make you do anything, Mom." She hurled the ball down the yard, half imagining she was tossing it to a sexy butch quarterback for the winning touchdown. An image of Taryn's face pushed into her mind, and she flicked it away. One thing at a time.

Buster was back at her feet within seconds, a loopy grin on his face, if indeed dogs could smile. She rubbed his head and made her way toward her mom, who was in her trademark uniform of soiled PJs and dirty gray slippers that Cassie imagined were once pink.

"Well, aren't you full of piss and vinegar today?" Her mom stooped to retrieve her fallen cigarette and dusted it off before taking a long drag. She blew the smoke in Cassie's face as she got closer.

"No Fred?" Cassie asked, noting the absence of the car she still wasn't convinced her mom had purchased with the money Cassie had sent.

Her mom waved the question away. "You just missed him. The deadbeat left about twenty minutes ago, and yes, he took my car with him before you ask."

Cassie tried not to falter. She could do this. She'd practiced standing up to her mom hundreds of times in her dreams. But with Fred gone, her mom was already a wounded animal. Alone. *That isn't my problem anymore.* She shrugged and ruffled the folds of flesh around Buster's too-tight collar. "I wasn't going to ask." Because she was training herself not to care. If she could just button up her heart tight enough for her mom's barbs not to pierce it, she might make it through this final meeting.

"Two visits in three weeks." She mock-curtsied. "What have I done to deserve this?"

The way she said it made it sound like punishment rather than a treat. *Wrap the armor tight.*

"I could do with a new car." Her mom gestured toward Cassie's sports car. "You don't have to buy anything as fancy as that, obviously. It's a bit desperate anyway, that thing. Like you're filling in the hole that a man should occupy." She chuckled lightly at her own crude joke.

"I don't think so." Cassie unbuckled Buster's collar and saw a small box attached to it. "What's this?"

Her mom looked at her and then the collar and sneered. "It keeps him in line." She tried to take it from Cassie, but she pulled it away. "What's gotten into you today?"

Cassie took the time to look into her mom's eyes, to really look. For the first time, she saw a hint of a scared little girl, and she had to take a step back. *Stay strong.* She had to remember her mom was the queen of manipulation. She'd use whatever tool worked as long as she got the result she wanted. "You're electrocuting Buster?"

Her mom's resulting frown lines seemed deeper than ever.

They aged her in a way Cassie hadn't noticed before. It was like she'd thrown away the black-tinted glasses she'd always viewed her mom through, and now she could really see her, see her flaws and her vulnerabilities. She suddenly didn't seem as gargantuanly scary as she had for all of Cassie's life.

She liked it.

She looked down at the collar in her hand and tightened her grip to stop the slight shake. She'd read all the books, her therapist had given her all the tools, and she'd practiced this moment over and over. *All* she had to do was remember why she needed to do this. Her mom was—and always had been—toxic, and Cassie deserved to be free of her. Forever.

Her mom snatched at the collar again, and Cassie tossed it as far as she could into the yard. Granted, that wasn't very far, but it was symbolic. Buster somehow recognized the gesture because he watched it but stayed put, clearly happy to be rid of the torturous contraption.

"Since when do you care how I discipline *my* dog?" Her mom dragged her gaze back from the patch of dust-brown grass where Buster's collar landed. "And more than that, where do you get off thinking you can come here and *tell* me how to look after my dog?"

Cassie rolled her eyes. "If you actually looked after Buster, I wouldn't have to tell you, would I?" She gestured wildly toward the single-lane road beyond her mom's gate. "When was the last time you took him for a walk?" She pulled her arm back and pressed her palm to her leg, grounding herself and regaining control. She had to stay calm and relaxed if she was going to make it through this altercation *and* achieve the outcome she needed.

Her mom opened and closed her mouth a few times, but nothing acidic emerged. In fact, nothing at all emerged. She'd rendered her mom speechless, at least for a moment, which was longer than ever before.

"Have you come here just to find faults in my pitiful life?" her mom finally asked, though it lacked the vigor of her usual acerbic tone. "Perfect timing to rub it in—just after Fred has left, and I'm all alone."

And there was the gear shift from aggressor to victim. This was where Cassie was most at risk of veering from her course of action and letting her mom off the hook. She readied herself by imagining her blood turning to ice, making herself unable to feel or be affected by her mom's performance. That's all this was: a performance designed to keep her mom's world exactly as she wanted it and those in it under her power. *She's toxic, and I want to be free.*

"I'm not here to find fault, Mom." Cassie drew in a deep, empowering breath. "I'm here to say goodbye." The last sentence was like releasing the valve on a balloon and all the negativity whooshed from her body, taking with it her last chance to pull back and simply maintain the status quo. She pressed her feet into the ground, tried to feel her toes against the earth and find her strength to keep going. She could do this.

"What are you talking about?" Her mom flicked her cigarette butt into the gravel. "You just got here. Are you drunk?"

Cassie pinched the bridge of her nose, her mom's question triggering a sharp stab of pain in her head. "No, Mother, I'm not drunk. I'm completely lucid, and I've developed a clarity I never thought I'd achieve."

Her mom lit another cigarette. She took a long draw before blowing the smoke toward Cassie, who wafted it away and managed not to cough.

"Seriously, girl. Don't come knocking on my door with your fancy words, as if you're somehow better than me." She wagged her finger in Cassie's face. "You're not."

Her mom leaned close enough that the repugnant mixture of nicotine, whiskey, and gum disease invaded Cassie's nostrils. She exhaled in an attempt to clear the stench but didn't move back. She couldn't let her mom think she was backing down.

"You're still a white trash kid from the wrong side of the tracks who got a poor kid's scholarship, and your fancy doctor friends never forget it. Neither should you." She motioned toward Cassie's car. "Maybe you should leave."

Her mom's words hit their intended target, and Cassie's resolve wavered. Her heart chilled in her chest and vibrated against her ribs, spreading a sense of unease and instability through her entire body. College *had* been difficult, and other students hadn't let her forget her roots for a second. She carried that with her, just like she carried the rest of her past.

But that all changed once she'd proved her mettle at Spring Willow Memorial Hospital, and no one gave a rat's ass where she'd come from anymore. She was a respected and accomplished doctor, and her mother couldn't tear that down with her words, not if Cassie didn't allow it. "I will leave." She rubbed Buster's head, as if doing so might infuse her with the steel she needed to see this through. "But I need you to know that this is the last time you'll see me, Mom. I'm done. I'm done with pandering to your narcissistic personality. I'm done with enabling your dysfunctional behavior, and I'm through with giving you everything you ask for just because of my guilt for things that were never my fault to begin with. I'm done being your punching bag."

Cassie's heart continued to pulse hard, but the breath she pulled in tasted like the fresh, clean air at the center of a huge forest. It coursed around her system like it was the first breath of her new life, a life free of her mom.

Buster snuffled her hand, and his cold, wet nose nudged her back into the moment. Her mom stared at her, open-mouthed and astonished.

"Goodbye, Mom." Cassie moved to leave, but her mom grabbed her wrist roughly.

"You think it's that easy?" She snarled, curling her lip. "You think you get to just walk away from me?" She cackled. "You don't. I gave you life, girl. I gave you *my* life. I gave you everything you ever needed and then some. You *owe* me. You haven't even begun to pay me back."

Cassie calmly used her other hand to pry open her mother's grip and pulled herself free, literally and metaphorically. Everything her mom had just said, Cassie had needed to hear, if only to reinforce that she was doing the right thing. "This is over, Mom. I've given you more than I ever should have, and I've let you negatively impact my life for way too long." She began to walk away. "Don't ever contact me again. You're on your own."

"You *should* feel guilty," her mom yelled after her as Cassie strode up the yard, not looking back. "It should've been you who died. I should've given you up to the state and been done with you when you were a kid. Before you could turn on me like this. You ungrateful bitch."

She closed her eyes and squeezed them tight. Her mom wasn't worth expending the emotion; she'd shed enough tears for her to last a lifetime. She pulled the gate shut, and Buster jumped up, his paws landing on top of her hands. She opened her eyes and met the dog's soft, unassuming gaze. She saw the gentle pleading, deep in his soul.

Cassie yanked open the gate, and Buster dove through the small opening. But he didn't run for freedom; instead, he parked his butt beside the passenger door of Cassie's car and simply waited.

"Oh, that's just typical," her mom shouted. "Go ahead. Take the damn dog. That'll be one less thing to drain my wallet."

Cassie unlocked her car and opened the door for Buster. He jumped up onto the seat and immediately sat on his haunches, looking out the windshield as if he could already see his new life. She smiled a little at the way his ginormous head touched the roof, then she closed the door. She walked around to the driver's side and allowed herself one final look at her old life.

Her mom glared at her, and Cassie met the rage that radiated toward her with a complete sense of dispassion and distance. She didn't know whether it was a temporary or permanent state of being, but she was more than happy to take it on right now. She got into her seat, clicked the button to bring the top down so that Buster could have even more freedom, and she reversed out of the driveway.

Her hands trembled on the steering wheel, likely from the monumental effort it had taken to maintain her course. It wasn't that she'd felt sorry for her mom; it was more the obligation and responsibility that tugged at her core, screaming at her not to sever her sole remaining family tie. She recalled Taryn's philosophy on families and her consternation at the general inability of most people to make the decision to separate, the decision to put their well-being above that of their families.

As she drove away with a dog in the passenger seat that she had no idea what she was going to do with, she focused on the ties she had to cut with Taryn. And while they hadn't had long to form them, Cassie had a feeling they would be no less painful to sunder.

Chapter Twenty-Six

TARYN SHOVELED THE LAST spoonful of the Cold Stone Creamery sundae into her mouth and closed her eyes. "I would've crawled over broken glass for that. Thanks, buddy."

Andi laughed as she took the container from Taryn's tray and tossed it in the trash. "Lucky for you I just had to put up with a hellish twelve-mile round trip instead."

Taryn nodded to the discarded ice cream cup. "You should probably take that away with you. There are a couple of mean ass nurses in here, and I've got a feeling they don't appreciate the restorative value of Cake Batter Batter Batter."

"Ha. So good, they named it three times. I'll destroy the evidence for you." Andi retrieved the carton and wrapped it in a plastic bag. "So you've got Nurse Ratched, but doesn't Dr. Cassie far outweigh that negative?"

Taryn grumbled and ran her hand through her hair, which she'd noticed looked pretty frightful. The first thing she'd do when she got out of here would be to visit the barber.

Andi narrowed her eyes. "Trouble in paradise?"

"I think you've got me and Cassie mixed up with you and Bernice." She shrugged. "It's not trouble as much as a lack of contact. She's been busy pulling double shifts every day, and when she's not working, I'm sleeping, so I haven't seen much of her. A couple of quick visits before she starts her shift, but that's about it."

"Mm. She did look exhausted when she dropped CeDora at the hotel."

"Huh?" Taryn should've been happy that her best friend and her...and Cassie had hit it off well enough to see each other separately from her, yet she couldn't deny the illogical sting of missing out. Why could Cassie find time to see Andi but not her? "What's CeDora?"

"Not what—who. CeDora, née Buster, our adopted baby." Andi grinned and pulled out her phone to show Taryn a picture of her and Bernice with a giant boxer dog. "Cassie didn't go into much detail; she just said the dog needed a new home, and that you'd mentioned we both loved dogs. Isn't he gorgeous?"

Taryn nodded and smiled, immediately wanting to know the full story behind Buster's release. Cassie visiting her mom was never a pleasant experience, but how had she ended up with the dog? "I'm surprised she could fit him in her car."

"She had to put the top down to make room, and he left quite the slobbery mess on her upholstery." Andi tilted her head. "Seems like there's more to the story. Do you know something?"

Taryn shook her head. "Nope. She doesn't have a great relationship with her mom, and I know that the dog wasn't being properly taken care of, so it's great that you've got him... I love that you've renamed him after *the* CeDora. That's really cool."

"I know I'm misgendering the dog, but I think I can get away with it. I'm sure if he could talk, he'd confirm that being named after the most daring girl on earth would be okay."

Taryn chuckled then clutched her arms around her ribs. "Don't. It hurts to laugh."

"I'm sure," Andi said. "On that note, Sedge has left."

She frowned. "Why?" It had been Sedge whose helmet had made intimate acquaintance with Taryn's ribs when she misjudged the globe timing.

"She emailed me from the road saying that she was sorry, but she couldn't stick around. Too guilt-ridden to face everyone, especially you since you were the one most damaged by her 'inattentiveness.' I tried to call her cell, but the number's out of service."

Taryn pressed her head back into the pillow. Sedge had a lot of potential, but if she was already gone, there was nothing Taryn could do about it. "She shouldn't have left. Accidents happen. We know that in this business."

"And what about people *not* in this business?" Andi looked at her pointedly.

"What do you mean?"

"Cassie."

Taryn pushed herself back up into a sitting position. "What about Cassie? She's an ER doctor; she knows better than most how easily accidents can happen."

Andi's mouth twitched. "I don't think that makes it any easier when they happen to the person you're sleeping with... The person you're in love with."

"What are you talking about? Cassie's not in love with me. We're just having fun, that's all. She's the one who wanted casual," she grinned when she recalled exactly what Cassie had said, "and she said she only wanted me for my body."

"Laugh it up," Andi said. "You and I were oblivious at our celebration, but Bernice said that Cassie's reaction to your revelation about our business development was less than happy."

Taryn shook her head. "Bernice's imagining it. Just because you're both loved up doesn't mean that everyone else is. Cassie said it was great news."

Andi huffed. "What someone says out loud and what they're feeling inside don't always match, Tar. Bernice is sure Cassie is in love with you, and she's had more experience of that emotion than you and me combined."

Taryn thought back to first seeing Cassie after the accident. Had she been crying? And if she had, were her tears for Taryn and the possibility that she might've been seriously hurt or worse?

"You need to talk to her, Tar. But before you do, you need to really think about how you feel. Do you love her?"

Taryn shrugged. It felt like the kind of fun she could have forever, but what would that even mean for their future? "I don't know. How did *you* know—with Bernice?"

Andi leaned back in her chair and put her boots on the edge of Taryn's bed. "You're asking me to talk about my feelings?"

"If I have to, then you definitely have to." Taryn smiled, relieved for a tiny break from the seriousness of their conversation.

"Fine." Andi's eyes glazed over, and a wistful expression overtook her face. "I guess...I guess everything just feels so right." She frowned and rubbed at her forehead as if that might make the genie of love emerge from her ears and explain everything so that she didn't have to. "I'm not saying everything is perfect. Boy, when we argue, the roof of that hotel blows off." She smiled, clearly remembering one such incident. "But the makeup sex is amazing, and even the conflict feels *right*. Which is a stupid thing to say. Love has made me a soppy mess." She shook her head. "I know what life was before her, and I know what life is now. Basically, I can't even imagine going back to what it was before, and hell, I don't want to." She fell silent for a moment. "That's all I've got, Tar. You know Gwen is the one to talk to about this kind of thing."

"Gwen is all about soulmates and destiny," Taryn said. "I don't know if I can get onboard with that." She glanced out the window at the view of the desert. In some respects, that's what her life had been. Could it be that Cassie was her oasis? "We're in such different places, geographically and metaphorically. I can't stay here. I can't stay in any one place. And Cassie is obviously settled. Her life and career are in Vegas." She looked back at Andi. "And remember her reaction when I broached the idea of her coming up to your ranch when I'm recruiting for the expansion? She blew me off." Taryn shook her head. "So it doesn't matter how I feel. I think Bernice's wrong."

Andi tilted her head. "Don't you owe it to yourself to find out for sure?"

Taryn wrinkled her nose. "Maybe." Or maybe, definitely. Regrets were for convicts and convents. What was the harm in asking the questions, in having *the talk*? She and Cassie understood each other; they'd had so many serious conversations that this would likely be a walk in the park, and they'd be able to laugh about it no matter what the outcome.

At least that's what she hoped they could do. Although Taryn was still floating in a sea of confusion over what she wanted to do with the rest of her life, she was sure she wanted to take this chance with Cassie. Was she scared of being rejected? Frightened of having Cassie pull out her heart and stomp on it with one of her sexy heels? Sure, but wasn't it always better to know the answer than to be forever swallowed up in conjecture?

Chapter Twenty-Seven

TARYN'S RAPID RECOVERY DIDN'T surprise Cassie. After Dr. Fischer had told her the details of her injuries and projected at least a week before she was able to leave the hospital, it had been clear that Taryn saw that as a challenge and a deadline to be beaten. Four days later, she was discharged, and here she was at Cassie's door. Granted, she'd borrowed someone's car instead of coming on her bike, but still, Cassie thought she might be pushing it.

Or pushing her. The courage Cassie had summoned to face her mom had apparently been of finite reserve. So if she were honest, Cassie had been vaguely hoping Taryn's hospital stay would turn out to be the usual length, rather than the shortened version, thus giving her time to refill the well and prepare for *the talk*.

Taryn had said she wanted to talk too, and Cassie kind of hoped that she was thinking of breaking it off. They'd become far more involved than either of them had intended, and maybe Taryn saw that her traveling lifestyle and Cassie's settled career didn't gel.

Whatever had to happen was about to transpire, and Cassie could no longer delay it. She walked to her front door and opened it. Taryn smiled widely and held up a huge bunch of tulips and roses in several shades of red.

"Shouldn't I be bringing you flowers?" Cassie asked, taking the beautiful bouquet from Taryn and inhaling deeply. "You're the one who's just had a hospital stay."

"No, definitely not. These are just leftovers from well-meaning fans anyway." Taryn closed the door behind her.

"Oh..." The romance of the gesture ebbed away, but it was probably for the best. She'd read that roses were for steady relationships, especially red ones.

Taryn grinned. "I'm kidding, obviously. Of course I should bring you flowers."

"Come on in." Cassie turned and headed for the kitchen, suddenly feeling formal and weird. She sensed Taryn behind her and quickened her step a little. The desire to pull her in for a kiss had been almost too strong to resist when Cassie had opened her door. That smile and those eyes... But she was adamant she wouldn't be sending mixed messages, and as much as she wanted to press her mouth to Taryn's soft lips, she couldn't. It made her wish that she'd known that the last time they'd slept together would be the *last* time they slept together. She would've tried harder to memorize Taryn's body, the dips and curves of her incredible physique, the flat planes of L-shaped muscle leading down between her legs, the hardness of her chest, and her petite breasts... Mm, maybe she'd committed Taryn to her memory more than she'd thought.

She went around the kitchen island and busied herself with putting the flowers in a vase while Taryn gingerly took a seat at the breakfast bar on the other side. The vast chunk of marble and wood between them felt safe; building a wall between them emotionally was going to be especially hard, given the way Cassie's heart ached for Taryn.

As she snipped the ends of the stalks and placed each stem individually, and deliberately slowly, she noticed Taryn rolling the sleeves of her shirt up then down, as if she couldn't decide which look to go with. It was something Cassie had noticed Taryn do when she was nervous. If Taryn did want to talk about breaking up, it was sweet that she held a certain amount of anxiety about it. Even sweeter that she'd brought flowers to soften the blow. She was once again reminded how cruel the Universe was to put someone like Taryn in her path only to take her away when she'd thoroughly fallen for her.

"I wanted to ask you something," Taryn said after a period of silence and more sleeve-rolling.

Cassie fiddled with the twine on the neck of the vase, occupying the traitorous hands that wanted to pull Taryn close to her. The number of roses and tulips to be snipped was dwindling, but she continued to make them last, grateful Taryn wasn't cheap when it came to flower-giving. Another smack in the face from the Fates. "Is it whether or not you should have your sleeves down or up?" she asked, deciding that she wanted a last exchange of banter before they parted for good.

Taryn touched her shirt self-consciously and tilted her head. "Sorry. I guess I'm more nervous than I thought I would be."

"Mm." Cassie remembered what Taryn had told her about her lack of relationships and wondered if she'd ever even had to have this kind of conversation before. "So what's your question?"

Taryn bit her lip. "Can I have a drink?"

Cassie laughed lightly. "*That's* your question?"

"No. Apparently, that's just what I'm going to need to be able to *ask* the question."

Taryn smiled, and again, Cassie was taken with the raw and unguarded beauty of it. Damn, this was going to be hard. "You're driving—which seems silly considering your recent injury—so I can't offer you a drink. I hope this isn't a light beer or a hard liquor conversation."

"It could start as one and end up as the other." Taryn picked an orange from the fruit bowl on the countertop and began to roll it between her palms. "It's impossible to predict."

"Is it?" Cassie offered an encouraging smile. Did Taryn think she might go batshit crazy on her? Or had she pegged Cassie as someone who would dissolve into a puddle of tears? If Cassie was right about their mutual understanding of each other, Taryn wouldn't be thinking either outcome was possible. She went to the fridge, pulled out a bottle of water, and slid it across the marble into Taryn's hand.

Cassie knew she should just tell Taryn that she couldn't do this anymore; that would save Taryn the anguish she was clearly going through. She wasn't putting it off to torture her, though she was being incredibly sweet. It was for that exact reason that she couldn't yet bring herself to end it. It was relatively easy to make decisions when she wasn't in front of her, looking delicious, and vulnerable, and adorable. But now? She pulled on some of the courage she'd been trying to reclaim and got on with it. This wasn't fair to either of them.

"You know when you said you hadn't fallen in love with me and didn't want exclusive rights to my body?" Taryn asked.

Cassie nodded. "I think I remember saying something like that, yes." It was an unusual way to start a breakup speech, but whatever worked.

Taryn took a gulp of water. "Do you think... Do you think you might ever change your mind?"

"What?" The question was out before she could police her thoughts. That wasn't the direction she'd expected the conversation to take.

"Ah, shit." Taryn ran her hand through her hair. "I told Andi that Bernice was wrong."

"Hang on, slow down. What are you actually asking me?"

Taryn shifted her bottle from one hand to the other. "I actually want to tell you something, but I'm being a chickenshit by trying to find out where you stand first."

Cassie didn't interject, and the silence grew like a presence in the room.

"I'm falling for you, Cassie." Taryn gazed into her eyes and swallowed. "I was hoping we could build on what we've obviously got. You're an amazing woman, and I've had such a wonderful time with you. Maybe there's more to us than great friends with intergalactically phenomenal benefits. Maybe we could explore something...long term."

Taryn glanced away, and her face flushed. What she'd said would've been everything Cassie would want to hear *if* Taryn didn't personify everything that could split Cassie into a million pieces. "I'm sorry, Taryn, I can't."

Taryn's shoulders sagged. She pressed her lips together and nodded slowly. "I understand. You did keep saying this was just casual."

Cassie weighed the impact of telling the truth or keeping silent, and trying to figure out which Taryn would prefer, which would be the most comforting. "You don't understand," she said, deciding that Taryn deserved the truth. Honest was all they'd ever been with each other. "I care for you deeply, and my heart has gotten involved. And I thought that would be okay, that we could enjoy this time together, and then you'd leave, and what we'd had would be a special memory." She grasped the stem of a rose, and its thorns pierced her skin, but she barely felt it. The pain in her heart and the visible hurt and confusion in Taryn's eyes surpassed all physical stimuli.

"If you care for me, then I really don't understand." Taryn's eyes glistened. "Why can't we pick up where we were before the accident?"

Cassie pinched the bridge of her nose then pressed her palms to the cold surface of the counter. "It's the accident that's changed everything, Taryn. I thought I could ignore what you did for a career because we were just..." She stopped herself from saying, *making love*, and pressed on. "Because we were just having sex, and nothing more. But seeing you—hearing you scream... the other riders, the pain." She clasped her hand to her chest. Her heart felt bruised, and she had to protect it. She couldn't take any more. "It brought back everything I felt when my brother was killed. I can't go through that again. It would break me, and I'm certain I couldn't hold it together enough to go back to the ER again, to face more emergencies." She inhaled deeply, but it did little to calm the incessant needles of nerves across every inch of her skin. "I can't be your lover. I can't even be your friend. I have to distance myself completely from you, or I'll fall back into your arms. I can't watch and wait for the next freak accident, for the crash that might kill you. I can't be with someone who faces death with such a cavalier attitude."

"But this is the first semi-serious accident I've ever—"

"It doesn't matter." Cassie gripped the edge of the hard marble surface so tightly that her knuckles went white. "I can't live in the shadow of death anymore. And I would never ask you to give up what you love doing."

Taryn frowned and put her head in her hands. "But what's the point of living life if you're not sharing it?" she muttered quietly.

Cassie narrowed her eyes. Something about the way Taryn said the words made them sound like they were packed with judgment. "You haven't shared your life before. You can't preach to me about quality of life just because you're currently infatuated with me." She thought of all the women Taryn had said fawned over her at the shows. "Whatever this is will fade once you go back to your life on the road. This has been a novelty, something to amuse you and take your mind off your dislike of staying in one place lest you grow roots or become attached to someone. You can't begin to understand how I feel, how that car accident took so much of my life from me. You choose to be estranged from most of your family—mine was taken from me, and Mom just takes, because she blames everyone in her orbit for everything bad. I'm broken, Taryn, and no matter how hard I try, my past affects my present. The only way for me to move forward is to be with someone who values life, who doesn't take it for granted."

"You're right. I don't understand how it feels to lose a brother, but I've lost a close friend, so I know the pain of loss." Taryn rose from her stool. "I don't think you should compare our family situations. I won't tolerate negative energy in my life from my parents; you shouldn't judge my choice to be distant from my family just because you're not strong enough to step away from yours."

Cassie closed her eyes and fought back the tears that edged her closer to breaking down. "That's exactly it, Taryn; I'm *not* strong enough. I'm not strong enough to stay involved with you, all the while dreading news of a fiery crash you didn't survive. I can't do it, and I *won't* do it." She turned away and walked toward the window. "I need you to leave."

"I'm sorry, Cassie. I shouldn't judge you. I have no idea how hard that is for you. But it's because I value life that I do what makes me happy, and I don't waste it because of fear that it might end."

Cassie felt Taryn's presence behind her, but she resisted the overwhelming urge to turn into her embrace, to forego all her reservations and see where their path led them. "I've made up my mind, Taryn. Please respect that." She wanted to take one last look into Taryn's eyes, but she knew that if she did, she'd melt into Taryn's arms, and they'd end up in bed. But it wouldn't last. Cassie's fears were too ingrained, too gargantuan to overcome. She had to push Taryn away. "Please go."

She could practically feel Taryn's hesitation, so Cassie remained motionless, staring out the window and imagining her feet were immovable concrete blocks.

"Okay," Taryn whispered finally. "If that's what you want, I'll leave you alone. But you should know that this has been the best time of my life with you. If you ever change your mind, look me up."

The soft squeak of Taryn's boots indicated her retreat, and that was soon followed by the sound of Cassie's front door closing. Cassie's resolve deserted her, and she sank to the floor and wrapped her arms around her knees. She didn't recognize the sob that escaped her, and she made no attempt to hold back the rest that followed. Her tears fell onto her silk skirt and soon soaked through to her thighs.

She let it all go. Her sorrow, her loss, the possibility of love. The fear of death had a choke hold on her future, and she could see no way to release it. No amount of therapy could help her prepare for another senseless and monumental loss. It was better this way. And now, without her mom too, Cassie was truly alone, and she could get back to her career, without distraction. She could save hundreds of lives over the next few decades; her life's work could count for something. And by losing herself in that, she could also hope to bury her aching heart.

Chapter Twenty-Eight

TARYN GINGERLY FIST-BUMPED FIG and gritted her teeth a little at the resulting splash of pain across her chest. She smiled at everyone assembled to welcome her back. "Thanks, guys. It's so great to see everyone back in the stadium, doing our thing, and giving our ever-eager audience what they paid for. Fig—fantastic job with the shows this week. You've done me proud. But if you don't keep it up, I'll be back here soon enough to kick your ass into shape."

Gwen threw her an arch look. "You'll have to go through me, Taylor."

Taryn and the others laughed. "I'm only a little scared," she said and winked.

Bernice pressed her hands together and nodded. "You're all consummate professionals, and the way you've bounced back from this setback has blown me away. Thank you. Thank you for being you."

"The show must always go on," Andi said, and everyone cheered and began to disperse.

"I'm heading back to my trailer to rest for a while," Taryn said. Andi opened her mouth to say something, but Taryn held up her hand. "I need to be alone. I'll talk to you later."

Andi nodded, and Taryn made her way back to their ever-expanding base using one of the many Teslas Bernice had been kind enough to loan her. The vehicles practically drove themselves, so even though her ribs still ached, and she'd been advised not to drive, it was a better and safer option than getting back on her bike, which she could barely wait to do.

Their impromptu get-together hadn't been the celebration

they'd had after their first week of shows, but Taryn was just grateful that they'd made it through four days without incident since they went live again. And the support they'd received from the stunt community and the wider Vegas performance community had stunned Taryn. Though she wouldn't say it out loud, the sense of togetherness really vindicated Andi's desire to have a home for the first time in their history. And no one, other than Taryn, seemed to be missing the road much. She expected that would change by the end of the six months—there were plenty of the team who had a similar outlook to hers when it came to roots—but for now, the novelty *and* the bulging paychecks with attendance bonuses were dulling that desire.

She wouldn't be there to see them getting itchy feet though. Their plan for her to go back to Andi's ranch remained in place... though Taryn's enthusiasm for it had faded substantially. After the initial excitement ebbed away, she realized that it had been excitement for the potential of being happy again. She'd hoped that recruiting a new team would erase the tedium of her daily role, and that she'd be invigorated with the task of expansion. But she hadn't even begun yet, and she already felt that it wasn't the heal-all balm she'd hoped it would be.

Maybe the world-weary bone-tiredness that had set in was indicative of her general sense of displacement but being dumped by Cassie hadn't helped. Fueled by Bernice's insistence that Cassie was in love with her, Taryn had actually dared to daydream how a life together might work. She knew she wasn't able to curtail her urge for constant movement and travel. Sure, she'd enjoyed this time in Vegas, but that had mostly been due to Cassie. She was ready for her next journey and had already begun to dream of new adventures in other states and countries.

But she'd also been thinking of scratching that particular itch by renewing her medical license and joining Doctors Without Borders. The experience she'd had with helping Louise hadn't receded into her memory banks, and she'd been left with a sense of achievement and satisfaction that she hadn't felt in a while. Not to mention watching how the nurses interacted with their patients in the hospital. People needed people who gave a damn, and it had reminded her how good it had felt to be a junior doctor doing rotations.

But she couldn't begin to contemplate how difficult it might be to get her medical license back, if it were even possible. She assumed it wouldn't be after so long away from medicine. Likely, she'd have to start all over again, and the thought of having to go through all that again, in one place, made her bones ache.

That meant staying in the life she'd already cultivated. So be it.

Taryn parked the car, and as soon as she opened the door to her trailer, Cassie's scent assailed her senses. Cassie hadn't been in this space for a while now, but her presence persisted, teasing and torturing Taryn with visions of them together in her sanctum-sanctorum. This place that had always been just for her no longer provided a dark haven, away from the bright lights of fame and superficial adoration.

Which was why she never brought women back here, why she always went to fan hotels or their places for hook-ups. She yanked the makings of a PB&J from various cupboards and made herself a sandwich, knowing she was kidding herself. It had been clear from early on that Cassie was far more than just a hook-up. A drop of water landed beside her plate. *Not this again.*

She'd cried more in the days since Cassie had dumped her than in the rest of her life. Granted, she'd never had much to cry about. Her life had been relatively easy since she'd joined Andi, and Trig was the only person she'd lost and grieved for. But her emotions were running riot. And she'd disappeared to the restroom so often during practice and shows, feigning pain from her injuries, that Andi had taken her aside to ask if she'd left the hospital too soon and should be readmitted. She'd lost weight too, probably from the massive amounts of salt water she'd been ejecting from her tear ducts. The weight didn't matter now that she wasn't subjecting her body to the rigors of the globe of death, but her inability to control her abject sobbing *did* matter.

She dropped onto the bench and slid her plate across the table before pulling her wooden box of keepsakes closer. She couldn't open it, not right now, so she took her phone from her pocket and opened her messages. Taryn dropped her head back and squeezed her eyes closed. More stupid tears slipped down her cheeks. *Why am I doing this to myself?* It was a stupid question when the answer was so obvious. She wasn't ready to let go. She wasn't sure she ever would be.

She slowly scrolled through every missive they'd exchanged since their first dinner date and began to smile. Cassie's sharp wit was one of the most attractive things about her. Taryn recalled how Cassie's banter had knocked her off balance from the very beginning, and how she'd loved that. *Loved.* Past tense because Cassie had made it clear that she could never speak to Taryn again, and this bank of texts would be treasure much like everything in her wooden box and all the knickknacks glued to the various surfaces of the trailer.

Except the texts were more precious, more valuable than Taryn had ever imagined words could be. In every moment of desolate loneliness since Cassie had ripped them apart, Taryn had found immeasurable comfort in re-reading them over and over again, letting her emotions wash over her like a warm, cleansing rain, and reliving the joy, laughter, and happiness in each one.

And then the void Cassie had left in her life would kick in, and the tears would fall once more. How was she supposed to stick around this city, knowing that the woman who'd make her happier than she'd ever been before was only a few miles away, yet may as well have set up a hospital on the moon? Of course, Taryn understood why Cassie had torn their fledgling relationship asunder. She couldn't really begin to grasp the guilt and grief Cassie held in her heart and mind over the death of her brother. And of course, she understood that facing that kind of loss again was hard to reconcile.

But life couldn't be lived on a series of what-ifs. That would drive Taryn crazy. Cassie, on the other hand, was the polar opposite; if she lived regardless of the what-ifs, *that* would drive her crazy. Despite their intense chemistry and absolute compatibility in almost every other area, Taryn's career was too difficult for Cassie to live with, as was her constant traveling. And Taryn wasn't about to live a placid, danger-free life on the sidelines.

She figured her remaining time in Vegas would fly by, as time was wont to do. And once she was at Andi's ranch in Ponder, the distance would lessen the desperate loss, and she could lose herself in the new challenge of expanding Andi's business—now her business too. New people, new talent, new cities, and new shows. That was a lot of new to keep her mind occupied, to keep her thoughts from refocusing on Cassie. She hadn't given the venture half a chance, yet it was already losing its shine. Which was stupid, and short-sighted, and not her style at all.

Taryn pushed away the sandwich she'd barely touched, pulled her wooden box closer, and opened it. The check for their first meal together, the ticket stub for the boat rental, movie tickets, even the liberated hotel keycard from Cosmos... The items Taryn had thought would be beautiful reminders of wonderful times were now painful jabs at what she'd lost.

She replaced everything in the box and slammed the lid closed. She didn't have time for this. Moping around after a woman who didn't want her...when Taryn had let herself believe it was possible that someone wanted *her* rather than her stunt personality. Those— what were the kids calling them these days? *Situationships* was the word she'd heard bandied around on ZimTak—those situationships were safer and far easier on her heart. Perhaps they were all she could give herself to, given that her rolling stone attitude wasn't conducive to any kind of long-term relationship. Maybe Cassie had simply been a wake-up call, someone on Taryn's path for a limited time to highlight that she needed to make changes, and now she was gone after serving that purpose.

Problem was, Taryn had no idea where to start. She knew she was lost, but without a destination in mind, how on earth was she supposed to find her way? And whatever her journey was, why did she have to travel without Cassie?

Chapter Twenty-Nine

As she applied black eyeliner, the desire to cancel once again crossed her mind. Rachel would understand. Cassie wasn't ready to go clubbing, or dancing, or enjoying herself. She was content in her self-imposed purgatory. She slipped and almost poked herself in the eye. *Concentrate.* She steadied her hand and continued. Rachel *wouldn't* understand at all. Cassie had canceled their plans and been unavailable too many times recently.

Her phone pinged, and she opened it to read a text from Rachel.

I'm just pulling up to your place. Let me in x

Rachel knew her too well and was clearly expecting her attempt to cancel. What better way to circumnavigate that than to simply show up on her doorstep? She put down her makeup tools and padded barefoot to the front door, which she opened just as Rachel looked like she was about to knock.

"Your hot neighbor let me in downstairs," she said and hustled her way past Cassie.

She closed the door behind Rachel and turned to respond, but Rachel was already halfway down the corridor. Cassie followed her to the kitchen and sat on a stool at the breakfast bar while Rachel helped herself to a large glass of wine from the bottle on the countertop.

"Did you start without me?" she asked.

Cassie shook her head. "That's been open for a week. It might not be any good."

"Isn't wine supposed to get better with age? Like you are." Rachel winked, took a sip of the wine, and made an appreciative expression. "Tastes all right to me."

"So is this your proactive way of ensuring I didn't cancel?"

"Yes. That's exactly what it is." She took another glass from the shelf and filled it without asking. "I've missed you, and I want to be here for you." She pushed the glass a little closer to Cassie. "Even if you don't want me here."

She laughed lightly. "Of course I want you here. And you have impeccable timing since I was indeed contemplating canceling on you."

Rachel slapped her hand on the marble surface. "Ha! I knew it. Female intuition at its best."

She came around the counter and pulled Cassie into a hug. Despite being unsolicited, Cassie softened into it, grateful for the human contact. These were the times when you found out who your friends really were. She swallowed the rush of emotion that loomed large and promised more tears. It would be a long, hard night if she let them out this early.

Rachel released her and tugged her off the stool before guiding her to the couch. "If you don't want to go, let's order takeout from that fantastic Chinese place, and you can talk while you watch me drink your wine."

"You don't mind?" she asked, relieved that Rachel wasn't insisting on sticking to their planned evening. "Saturday night at home isn't really your speed."

"You're right. It isn't. But I'd rather do this with you than go out without you." She rubbed Cassie's forearm. "And a girls' night in seems like what you need right now, and what kind of friend would I be if I didn't recognize that?"

"Okay." A renewed energy coursed through Cassie's body momentarily before the weight of the past week's events settled once again. She pushed up from the sofa anyway. "Let me get my phone. The menu is on the side of the fridge."

She returned quickly and placed an order with Jade-Lai, who said Yan would deliver it personally, then she retook her seat, complete with the glass of wine Rachel had poured for her.

Rachel propped herself up on a little tower of cushions, and Cassie did the same on the opposite end of the couch so they could face each other.

"Should we start with your mom?"

Cassie nodded. Part of her didn't want to talk about any of it. A minuscule part of her briefly wondered how it might feel *not* to feel and to temporarily forget everything if she got obliterated. She scolded herself immediately for even considering it, then remembered her therapist's words about being gentle with herself. She was allowed to have all the reactions and emotions; it was how she acted on them that mattered.

Since she'd cut her mom from her life, she'd spoken to her therapist about it in one session and had only mentioned it in passing to Rachel. They'd both been incredibly busy with additional shifts and had managed little time for meaningful conversation. And this was a conversation that was bound to involve tears, something she wasn't eager to share with the rest of her colleagues. Cassie eased back into her cushion nest and retold the story of her final visit to her mom, finishing with the final death blow to their relationship: that her mom wished she'd died instead of her brother.

Rachel gasped and clasped Cassie's foot, the only part of her within reach. "The evil fucking bitch."

Cassie laughed, unable to stop her amusement at Rachel's summation. Laughing was a novel replacement to the tears she'd been shedding. Even though she fully recognized how toxic it was, the woman was still her mom. "That's a pretty accurate observation."

Rachel shook her head slowly, as if unable to process the events Cassie had described. "I moan about my family sometimes, but I never forget how lucky I am that I didn't end up with your mom." She sipped her wine. "And how are you feeling about it all? I know you've been heading toward this decision for a long time, but actually doing it... I can't imagine what you're going through."

"I've vacillated between devastation and euphoria since driving away from her," she said. "It felt so good to say goodbye and to believe I was removing her and all her poison from my life." She smiled, thinking of Buster, now CeDora. "And liberating the dog felt somehow symbolic too."

"I'll bet." Rachel looked around the living room. "I can't see any sign of a pooch. What did you do with him?"

"Taryn had told me that Andi and Bernice love dogs, so I reached out to them." Cassie twirled her hair between her fingers. "I admit I was a little panicky as I drove back to the city with a giant dog in my tiny little sports car, not knowing if I could find him a new home." She gestured around the spotless space, with its hardwood floors, glass tables, and sharp corners. "It's not like he would've liked it here."

Rachel grumbled. "And *you* wouldn't have liked him here, huh?"

Cassie tilted her head slightly. "The thought of having to home a giant dog in my pristine apartment did make me a little twitchy, yes."

"Okay. So that was part of the euphoria. What about the other bit?"

"I guess that revolves around the stark realization that I'm truly alone now—in terms of blood relatives," she said quickly when she saw Rachel about to argue. "Even though she's still alive, I have to think of her as truly gone, and that leaves me with no family, which is kind of scary. Floating around with no real roots."

"What about your dad?" Rachel prodded Cassie with her foot. "Have you ever tried to find him?"

She blew out a long, soft breath and blinked. *No tears.* "No, never. He left, and he didn't take me with him, and I can't see how it could've been any clearer that Mom didn't want me around. She still lives in the same place they moved to right after my brother was killed. I haven't moved far from the family home. I haven't changed my name. I have a social media presence—"

"Pah. Vaguely. *I* post more pictures of your life than you do."

Cassie smiled. "Fair, but still, I'm eminently findable, and he clearly doesn't want to. I don't know if he's got a new family or even if he's alive, but to care for myself, I have to *not* care about him or the reasons and excuses he has for never coming back for me."

"Wow, Cass. I don't know what to say, other than I'm sorry. You really don't deserve any of this. You're such a wonderful, caring person, though I'm not sure how you've managed to stay that way with everything that's happened to you."

Cassie shrugged. "I've never really thought of it that way but thank you. Sentiments like that will help get me through the bad periods."

"Because the bad periods will come and go?" Rachel asked, and Cassie nodded. "Okay, back to the good feelings. How are you making sure they outweigh the other stuff?"

"Hard work and mindfulness. The letting go is hard. And I suppose it will continue to be that way forever, like I'm making a choice every day to keep her out of my life. My therapist told me to list five good things that my mom had said to me or done for me." Cassie shook her head, almost ashamed to admit it and say it out loud, as if she wasn't good enough or worthy of receiving anything nice, or that she'd never done anything good enough to be praised. She thought of the millions of children with their scrappy finger paintings proudly displayed on the doors of fridges worldwide. "The thing of it is... I couldn't think of a single thing. Christ, I don't remember getting a birthday gift or even a card after my dad left."

She fell silent for a little while and was grateful that Rachel didn't try to make conversation. Cassie was glad to have the kind of friend who could engage in a deep conversation like this and not feel the need to try to escape from it with fripperies and shallow platitudes. "I guess when I really look at it," Cassie said. "When I step away and truly analyze my relationship with her, it's poisonous, and I'm not missing out by removing myself from it."

Rachel nodded. "Has she tried to get in touch with you?"

"Yeah. She's sent some texts, called, left messages. None

of them nice, and none of it an attempt to reconcile. There's no recognition of wrongdoing on her part at any stage in my life. As far as she's concerned, she's the victim. She's the one who's been burdened with a thoughtless, uncaring daughter."

"Is any of her bullshit getting to you?"

"I feel sorry for her, but I know that she's brought it on herself." Cassie put her wine glass down and wrapped her arms around her knees. "I've almost responded a few times. I've typed a response, but I haven't succumbed to her manipulations and actually sent anything." She knew she could change her number, but she didn't want that hassle. If her mom persisted, she'd block her. She looked up at Rachel. "That's good, right?" She knew the answer, but hearing it would provide some comfort, she was sure.

Rachel slapped her free hand down onto the sofa. "Abso-fricking-lutely that's good. You've worked so hard to get to this stage, and I can see how powerful her hold is and how hard it must be to resist. It's like being in rehab, but for parent addiction instead of alcohol or drug abuse. Going cold turkey must be so damn hard."

Cassie smiled, knowing how lucky she was to have just one amazing friend. "I'm so glad I didn't cancel on you."

"Huh." Rachel snorted. "I was never going to let them happen. Not tonight."

"And I'm through not being wanted."

"Mm, but apparently, you're also through with being wanted..."

Cassie frowned at the deliberately obtuse comment. "What are you talking about?"

"Taryn."

The apartment buzzer sounded. "Saved by the bell," she said and got up to receive their food. She had a sweet exchange with Yan but had to cut it short when he asked about the new woman in her life. It was nice of him to remember little details from their conversation nearly a month ago, but sometimes...sometimes, it just wasn't, and the anonymity of fast-food delivery became more appealing.

She returned to the living room and laid out all the containers on the table in front of the couch. Then she retrieved cutlery and plates from the kitchen. "This is way too much food."

"Nah. This is comfort food, and there can never be enough of that."

They loaded up their plates with the divine-smelling victuals.

"So. Taryn. She wants you, but you've pushed her away," Rachel said.

Cassie arched her eyebrow and swallowed the mouthful of food she had in her mouth. "Is there a question?"

"My question is why?"

Cassie rolled her eyes. "You know why."

"Okay. You're resorting to short, sharp answers... I get your logic behind your reason, but," Rachel wafted her fork toward Cassie, "are you going to live the rest of your life based on the fear of something that might never happen? Think about how fantastic these past few weeks have been—I know that because you've practically sparkled like a diamond since you met Taryn—and so, imagine what you're missing out on. You've just dumped a big part of your past. Maybe it's time to open up to your future."

Cassie looked away, unable to bear the intensity of Rachel's questioning gaze. She closed her eyes to shut out the mental image of Taryn being wheeled into the ER, into *her* ER. "I'm not strong enough, Rach. I've barely healed from the loss of my brother all those years ago, and I know it's not the same thing. What happened to my brother was an accident, and Taryn isn't a drunk, nor is she deliberately reckless. She just has a dangerous job—lots of people do, I guess, and she could die trying some new stunt. I couldn't take that kind of grief and loss again. If something happened to Taryn, it would destroy me, once and for all. I'm held together with hope, spit, and willpower, but I'd disintegrate if I let myself fall any deeper and then lost her."

Rachel grumbled. "You're a lot stronger than you think you are, but why haven't you asked her if she'd do something else for a career? If she knew that there was a chance of a future with you, I reckon she'd give up tearing around on a bike for you."

"Ha." Cassie shook her head. "There's no way I could ever ask her to give up her stunting. It's in her blood. I told you what Gwen and Fig said to me last week. If you take that away from people like Taryn and Fig, you're crushing their heart."

"What if her heart beats for you stronger than it ever did for what she does for a living?"

"No. And even if she did give it up for a chance at love, she'd come to resent me for it. She'd miss it, and she'd blame me, even if she didn't want to."

Rachel munched noisily on a spring roll and looked thoughtful. "So let me see if I've understood you. You're desperately in love with her, and you want to be with her. But the tiny possibility that she might one day land on her head and die is stopping you from enjoying all the beauty of the moments between now and then, which might be months, years, and decades you could have together?"

Cassie pushed her head back into the cushion. When it was put that way, it did sound weak. But that was her point; she *was* weak. "Yes. And it isn't just a tiny chance. What she does every single day is inherently dangerous."

Rachel put her plate down, shifted closer to Cassie, and grasped her knee. She looked deep into Cassie's eyes. "Here's the kicker, Cass. The fact that life is so fragile is what makes it so fucking beautiful. The fact that it's finite is what makes every moment special and unique, something to be treasured. You've can't *live* in fear of *death*. She comes for us all. Death *will* come for Taryn, and you, and me—though I'm going to live gorgeously until I'm a hundred and fifty. But it can't be avoided, and you can't hope to fall in love with someone who does a desk job and lives as carefully as humanly possible. Living in the shadow of what could have been the brightest love isn't living at all. You're just going through the motions, just existing and surviving. That's a terrible waste of the most wonderful gift of all."

"Jesus, that was a hell of a speech. Did you go on a Hallmark movie binge before coming here?"

Rachel laughed, and Cassie joined her until they were laughing so hard, they were crying. It felt good to be parting with tears of joy instead of sadness, but Rachel's words hit home. Was she betraying the gift of life that had been cruelly ripped away from her brother? What would he have done in this same situation? Would he have wasted an opportunity to love so deeply, to care so profoundly for another?

Rachel managed to stop giggling for a moment. "You'll think about it though?"

Cassie nodded, and she meant it. Rachel knew her well enough to know that she didn't make a decision on a dime or a whim. She needed to process, and process she would, but right now, she just wanted to eat and chat with her best friend as if she really was living life in all its glory.

Chapter Thirty

"AND YOU'RE SURE YOUR ranch could accommodate a camera crew?" Micki, bouncy marketeer number one, said.

"Easily." Andi nodded. "The ranch house has eight bedrooms, and there are ten yurts on the property. And I've got hook-ups and plenty of space to camp—under canvas or with RVs."

"I bet that influencer Sage Samara would be interested in hanging around for a week or so," bouncy marketeer number two, Lisa, said. "She's got a huge following on ZimTak, and that would hit a younger market and potentially a whole seam of unmined talent."

"She follows quite a few of us already, including me. I could reach out personally if you think that would help." Taryn tapped the end of her pen on her notepad, not that she'd used either item. Her heartbreak daze continued to affect every aspect of her life, and she was increasingly unhappy about it... Which added to her high-intensity sorrow that was vibrating harshly, barely hidden beneath her skin.

"That's excellent," Micki said and gestured to Lisa.

Lisa scribbled on her iPad, adding to the list that was cleverly projected onto the wall of the huge boardroom space Bernice had arranged for them to use. Everyone was excited. Everyone except Taryn. Mustering anything like enthusiasm had been proving too difficult for over two weeks now, and she feared she was slipping into a low-level depression, something she'd been grateful never to have experienced before. Something she didn't have time for either. Though what she was supposed to be doing with the rest of her time on earth still eluded her. And her irritation with herself over *wasting* her time added a layer of anger onto her fully loaded emotion cake.

"Taryn?"

She looked up at the sound of Andi's voice. "Yeah?"

"The camera crew?" Andi widened her eyes and looked expectant.

Taryn shrugged. "Yeah. They'll fit in at the ranch, and I might even cook for them." Maybe being a chef would be fulfilling... "What's the problem?"

Andi chuckled and shook her head. "I asked if you'd want to work with the crew who shot our last ZimTak promo? I remember the director really enjoying it. What was her name?"

Taryn knew what Andi wasn't saying, but the last thing Taryn wanted to think about was sex with another woman. "Helen." They parted on good terms; both had known it was nothing serious. "Yeah, she and her team were really professional, and the finished content is our most-watched video."

Andi looked at her contemplatively for a moment, then she turned to everyone else gathered in the room. "Okay, let's take a break and get some fresh air and something to eat."

The two marketing bunnies looked puzzled at the abrupt break. "How long should we be gone?" Micki asked.

"Go wild; take an hour," Andi said and grinned.

They collected their purses and left. Taryn got up too, but Andi put her hand on Taryn's shoulder and pressed her back into the chair.

"Not you."

Taryn blew out a long breath and relaxed back into the plush leather seat. She flicked at the thick cotton stitching, trying to decide what she'd do if this was an intervention. "I know I'm being a wet blanket," she said. "I'm just feeling a bit...melancholy, that's all."

Andi sat on the edge of the table beside Taryn. "Melancholy? Is that what you're gonna call it?"

Taryn shrugged. "It's a good word. It was good enough for a

whole ode from Keats, so it's got to be good enough for me."

Andi rolled her eyes. "I don't know who that is or what the hell an ode is," she held up her hand to stop Taryn from responding, "and I don't need to know, before you try to distract me with an English lit lesson." She punched Taryn's shoulder lightly. "But I do know you look like you need a break. Maybe an extended one."

Taryn scowled. Another waste of time. "And what would the point of that be? Especially when we've got so much going on. We're on a timeline, and that doesn't include me disappearing for no reason."

"It wouldn't be for 'no reason' though, would it? And since the whole development revolves around your *active* participation, there's no 'point' in having a timeline if you're not fully engaged. Is there?"

Taryn didn't appreciate Andi's repetition of her own excuses. Echoed back at her, they sounded weak and easily dismissed. "Okay. I'll buck up." She didn't know why she was promising something she had no idea how to do.

"You're not hearing me." Andi laughed gently. "The show is under control. Fig is on top of things. This development can wait a couple of weeks while you rest and recuperate."

Taryn didn't meet Andi's gaze until the silence became awkward. She looked up, and Andi stared at her with an irritatingly all-knowing expression. "I don't need to rest. I need to work."

"Do you? I don't think you're going to be any good to anyone until you get your doctor off your mind. Visit Ralph in Miami, hook up with some women, spend some time with your family to remind yourself it's not so bad back here." Andi laughed again, but her expression was serious.

"You think it's going to be that easy?" Taryn pushed out of her chair and stalked toward the floor-to-ceiling windows, unable to cope with the itchiness Andi's scrutiny was causing.

"It should be," Andi said, "since you're not in love with her."

Taryn clenched her fists and pressed them against the cool

glass. The vista of the Strip stretched out as far as she could see. Just beyond the Stratosphere hotel that she couldn't quite make out, Cassie would probably be tearing around her ER, saving lives and not really living her own. She punched the glass half-heartedly.

"You *are* in love with her, aren't you?"

Taryn leaned against the glass and rested her forehead against it. "It doesn't matter. Love isn't enough this time. Cassie cares for me, but she won't let herself fall any deeper because of her brother's accident and because of what I do. I could die in any one of our stunts."

"You could die if a chunk of ice fell out of a hotel window and whacked you on the head," Andi said. "Or if a tired bus driver mounted the sidewalk and ran over you. Bernice is a little scared that something might happen to me too, but that doesn't stop her from loving me. It doesn't stop her from taking advantage of whatever time we have together."

"You don't understand." Taryn wished she didn't really understand either. If she could lever even a modicum of apathy toward Cassie's past, maybe she could begin to get over her. "She says it would break her if anything happened to me."

"Running away on the basis of an 'if' is nonsense. And if you truly love someone, you're supposed to break if you lose them. That's the way we were designed."

"I can't argue if you're going to make so much sense," Taryn said and bumped her head repeatedly against the glass. Perhaps a gentle concussion could erase Cassie from her memory. Nah, she wouldn't want that. Though their time together had been all too brief, Taryn wouldn't change a second of it.

Andi came up beside her and grabbed the scruff of Taryn's neck roughly. The familiar gesture almost made Taryn crumple into Andi's arms, but she held fast.

"I hate to ask, because it would fuck up everything that we're in the process of planning, but would you give up the stunting for her, for the possibility of your love?"

Taryn pressed the heel of her palm to her forehead. She hadn't expected the conversation to go in this direction, but now that it had... "What would you think of that if I did?"

"I'd be devastated. Obviously." Andi's expression was blank for a moment before she grinned. "But if that's what you have to do to be happy, Taryn, then I'd support you." She clasped Taryn's shoulder. "You should know that."

"Look who I found in the lobby."

Taryn and Andi turned quickly at Bernice's voice, and Taryn's legs weakened beneath her. "Cassie," she whispered.

"Andi, let's go," Bernice said. "You need to come to my office... for something very important."

Andi visibly melted at her commanding tone. "Duty calls." She clapped Taryn on the shoulder. "Whatever happens, I'm here for you, Tar, and I always will be," she whispered so only Taryn could hear.

The burden of expectation lifted as Andi's words landed and sounded like *do what you've got to do regardless of the consequences* to their business partnership. But she had no idea why Cassie was here. Friendship. Sex. Love. Taryn's desperation clawed at her heart and told her to take anything she could get.

Bernice bundled Andi out of the room and closed the door behind them quickly. Cassie hovered awkwardly between the door and Taryn. Was the distance between them that great already? "Hi. This is a nice surprise," Taryn said. "I thought you didn't want to see me again."

"I thought that too." Cassie took a couple of steps into the room. "I've tried really hard to convince myself. But it turns out that I can't stop thinking about you."

"I'm not surprised. I am unforgettable," Taryn said, deciding that a return to their original banter was the best way not to make a fool of herself by dropping to her knees and begging Cassie to change her mind. But Cassie was here of her own accord, so she must've already changed her mind about something. She took a steadying breath, not wanting to get ahead of herself.

"You are." Cassie laughed, and her smile brightened the room better than the noon Vegas sun ever could.

Taryn pushed away from the window and walked around the huge oval desk. "What do you want to do about that?"

Cassie stepped into the space between them. "Honestly, I have no idea. I hate the thought of something happening to you and not being able to do anything about it. But I also know that maybe nothing bad will ever happen to you; you could live to be a hundred, and I missed out on a lifetime with you—or even a few years. And all my fears could remain scary monsters locked in a dark cupboard. My nightmares might never see the light of day."

She took a final step toward Taryn and tentatively reached out. Taryn matched her courage and interlinked their fingers. Emotion strangled her vocal cords, stifling her ability to speak. But silence was likely her friend right now; this had to be Cassie dealing herself into the game, because Taryn was already all in.

"I don't know how this might work, especially with you traveling all the time, but I get some time off, and I could visit between shift blocks when you're only a short flight away." Cassie grasped Taryn's other hand. "But I'm willing—no—I have to try...if *you* want to. If you haven't changed your mind about me coming to find you now that I've changed mine. I love you, Taryn. And I'm not living in fear and missing out on what we might be together." She bit her lip and looked into Taryn's eyes. "What do you think?"

"I think that I've been dying little deaths every day without you." Taryn smiled and pressed her lips to Cassie's hands. "Whatever your terms are, I'll take them. I'm in love with you too. Do you remember that I told you I believe each of us only has a finite number of heartbeats?" She waited until Cassie nodded. "However many I've got left... they beat for you."

"Such pretty words. Any chance we can get out of here, and I'll show you how fully I appreciate them?" Cassie arched her eyebrow. "I've *really* missed you, and I would love to finally take the time to enjoy you slowly and properly."

"So you *have* fallen in love with me and want exclusive access to my body?"

"Apparently," Cassie whispered and pulled Taryn into a long overdue and deeply passionate kiss.

Taryn lost herself in the sensation of Cassie's soft lips on hers, and gravity seemed to become guidance rather than a rule, with her feet lifting off the ground in euphoric joy. She tugged Cassie hard against her, forgetting her recent injuries, and when their bodies slammed together, she groaned in pain.

Cassie pulled away slightly and laid her hand gently on Taryn's chest. "Easy, tiger," she whispered. "Let's go somewhere you can just lay down and relax while I have my wicked way with you."

Taryn grinned. Andi had given permission for Taryn to follow her heart. She thought about the research she'd been doing into Doctors Without Borders and how it might work for them both. But there was Cassie's mom, Rachel, the hospital, her new work at the free clinic... But she didn't want to think about that right now. "I have a feeling we could get a room in this hotel. I know the owner quite well."

"Indeed." Cassie ran her finger over Taryn's lips. "And she does seem to be rooting for us."

"Let's go." Taryn led Cassie out of the meeting room and headed for Bernice's office. Hopefully reserving a room wouldn't take long, because all she wanted to do was jump into bed and let Cassie make love to her until her bruised body could take no more.

And when those hours had passed, they could spend the rest of the day figuring out their future.

Chapter Thirty-One

"NICE TOUCH TO GIVE us the same suite we first had sex in," Cassie said as she led Taryn inside.

"Is that what we're going to be doing now—just sex?" Taryn closed the door behind them, then slipped her arms around Cassie's waist.

"No." Cassie walked backward, drawing Taryn with her. "I'm going to make love to you. Slowly." She pushed open the bedroom door with her heel. "*Very* slowly." Cassie stopped a few feet before the bed. "I'm going to take my time undressing you, so I can fully take in every inch of your godlike physique."

Taryn laughed lightly. "Or we could get real naked real quick." She glanced away, almost shy. "I'm not sure I can take this level of adoration."

"You'll have to get used to it." Cassie unsnapped the top stud on Taryn's denim shirt and kissed her collarbone. She leaned back and popped the next two, then ran her hands across Taryn's chest and murmured her appreciation. She opened the last few down to the large buckle of Taryn's belt and pulled her shirt out of her jeans.

Cassie bent slightly to press delicate kisses around Taryn's stitches, careful not to apply too much pressure near her bruised skin. "You're going to have some scars, I think," she said as she ran her fingers around the waist of Taryn's jeans.

"Scars are free tattoos with a good back story," Taryn whispered and ran her fingers through Cassie's hair.

Cassie extricated herself from Taryn's grip and moved around to her back. She pulled Taryn's shirt slowly over her shoulders, kissing her well-developed traps and rear delts. She traced her nail across the tree at the top of Taryn's full back tattoo. "You never did tell me who this woman is and why you've immortalized her on your back." Cassie held no judgment for it; people did crazy things when they were young or in love or in foreign countries, and the art was truly beautiful work.

"You never asked."

Cassie raked her nails along Taryn's biceps and forearms as she dragged her shirt further up, revealing the full extent of the tree, the stunning long-haired woman, and the geometric designs surrounding her. She pulled Taryn's top off completely and tossed it on the bed. "It didn't seem my place to ask about it before. But now that you're mine, I'm asking."

"There's nothing to be jealous of," Taryn said, her voice husky. "She's Gaia, the creator and protector of the earth, brought forth from nothingness and chaos."

"Mm, that seems fitting." Cassie followed the fine lines of a complex symbol with a single nail, enjoying the response of Taryn's shivering body beneath her fingertips. "You've brought me back from a black hole and certain chaos. What about the symmetrical shapes?"

"Sacred geometry. It's all about the flow of energy and changing negative to positive thoughts… Your touch is making my knees weak."

Cassie pressed her body to Taryn's naked back and gestured toward the chair by the desk. "Straddle that. There's no way I'm rushing this. You've let me have you twice before, and both times, I was so desperate to get my hands on you that I rushed right in. And I have to be careful with you while you're recovering." She ran her fingers in the hard ridge between Taryn's abs. "I'm savoring every second and every inch."

Taryn grabbed the chair and sat astride the seat. "Tease."

Cassie sank to her knees behind Taryn and ran her tongue from the base of Taryn's spine to her neck. "You won't call me that when you're in my mouth, coming for me."

Taryn muttered something Cassie didn't catch and grasped the top of the chair hard enough for Cassie to see her knuckles turn white.

"This is so beautiful." Cassie used her tongue, nails, and fingers to follow every line and curve of Taryn's back and the intricate tattoo. Taryn shuddered and murmured beneath her touch, and Cassie grew wet with the anticipation of making love to her. She rocked back on her butt. "Turn around."

Without a word, Taryn did as Cassie asked her.

"There is something incredibly hot about a butch woman like you, half naked like that." She let out an appreciative sigh. "Men get to parade around shirtless all the time, but women don't. But when you've got a body like yours, all muscle and perfect breasts... my god." She swallowed hard and bit her bottom lip. "You really are something." What she wouldn't give to wrap a strap-on around Taryn's hips and ride her until she was too sore to take any more.

"What are you thinking?" Taryn grinned. "Because from the way you're looking at me, it must be dirty."

Cassie arched her eyebrow, still taken with the mental image of Taryn's hands on her waist, pulling her in deeper and deeper, while she pushed harder and harder. She revealed her thoughts unashamedly and smiled.

"We've got enough time to do that on as many chairs as you want to sacrifice. We can make that our first joint purchase."

"That's a deal." Cassie unbuckled Taryn's belt slowly and opened her jeans. She pulled back again to admire the incredible fucking sexiness of what was before her; Taryn looked like she'd been pulled from an explicit photoshoot for a lesbian calendar. How lucky was Cassie that she'd get this every month? Schedules willing, of course. But she didn't want to think about any of that now. She only wanted to be in this amazing moment with this unbelievably sexy and sexual woman, someone she wanted to spend her lifetime exploring, appreciating, and constantly rediscovering.

Cassie kissed Taryn's stomach, and ribs, and up to her chest.

She stretched to meet Taryn's mouth, and Taryn wrapped her hand in Cassie's hair. Cassie moaned lightly as their kiss took her places a good orgasm would. The simple sensation of their lips pressed together, moving as one and drawing energy from each other, shouldn't feel this good, but dammit if it wasn't the best kiss in the world. All their previous kisses had been intensely arousing, but this one, with all its promise and love, felt better than most orgasms Cassie had ever had.

And the whole time, she got to stare into Taryn's beautiful open eyes, which were focused entirely on Cassie. She felt the love, the adoration, the promise. And she hoped Taryn saw those feelings reflected back at her.

Cassie pulled away and tugged at Taryn's jeans. She lifted her ass from the chair, and Cassie peeled Taryn's jeans and shorts down to her ankles. Taryn's heavy engineer boots protruded from the inside of the jeans, and Cassie swallowed. The calendar shot had taken a turn toward filthy sexy, and she was glad she was already on her knees, because seeing Taryn like that made her want to worship at her throne of leather and steel for hours.

She pushed Taryn's knees apart, and the scent of her arousal rose up to greet her. Cassie licked her lips, barely able to stop from diving in and devouring her. They locked eyes. "Goddamn, what was I thinking, denying myself this?"

Taryn's eyes half-lidded, and she held onto the chair. "I don't know," she whispered hoarsely, "but please don't deny yourself now."

Cassie took Taryn in her mouth and murmured against her skin when she found Taryn was already rock hard. She grasped Taryn's hips and sucked her in, licking and flicking her clit until she settled into a steady rhythm that Taryn responded to.

"Fuck, that's perfect."

Taryn's hips rose and fell gently, and Cassie shifted her hands to grab Taryn's ass so she could pull her in closer.

Taryn wound her hand in Cassie's hair. "Please...don't stop."

Cassie returned her lips to Taryn's solid clit and sucked her in hard. She circled her tongue over and over, in time to the beat of Taryn's movements, and kept her eyes open. She didn't want to miss a single second of Taryn's surrender. The way her hips moved, the way her stomach tensed, the noises she was making... Cassie thought she might come from the immensely sexual vision of it all.

Taryn pulled her hand from Cassie's hair and gripped the backrest of the chair. She opened her eyes and looked down, and Cassie arched her eyebrows, hoping to communicate her desire. She thought about stopping, just for a second, to tell Taryn how fucking unreal she was, how it seemed that she stepped out of Cassie's fantasies, the embodiment of sex in flesh. But the desperate plea in Taryn's eyes was crystal clear, so Cassie controlled her smile and continued to suck and lick Taryn's sex. Taryn slowly closed her eyes and rested against the chair, murmuring Cassie's name quietly.

Cassie took one hand from Taryn's hard ass and trailed her nails over the L-shaped muscle below her stomach. She ran one finger between Taryn's lips slowly before she slipped inside. Taryn gasped and her eyes sprang open. For the briefest of moments, Cassie thought she might've overstepped and gone too far, but the pleasure in Taryn's expression and her loud moan indicated otherwise.

"Oh, fuck... Yes."

Cassie contained her delight that she'd managed to discover something new Taryn clearly enjoyed and risked another finger. The resulting expletive and guttural sound of desire spurred Cassie on in her exploration. She pushed her fingers in and out of Taryn's slick pussy and continued to lick her clit. Taryn wrapped both hands around Cassie's head and pulled her closer, and Cassie responded by pushing in deeper and harder. She kept her eyes open, not wanting to miss a single movement of Taryn's body. Cassie was no pillow queen; she'd given her fair share of sex and enjoyed it, but this was so incredibly different. The mental connection she now

shared with Taryn, the love Cassie held in her heart, made this feel
so much more profound. She'd known she was falling before, but
knowing now that Taryn had fallen with her amplified the sensation
of every nerve ending and multiplied the pleasure she took from
Taryn's body. No longer just sex, this was making love. Connecting
and reconnecting, over and over. It wasn't even about getting off; it
was about maintaining their intimacy.

"Keep doing that... Please," Taryn murmured in gasps.

Cassie watched as Taryn let herself go, watched the contraction
of her stomach muscles as she ground down on Cassie's fingers,
saw the subtle change in the fullness of Taryn's lips—lips she wanted
so badly to kiss but dared not change a thing about what she was
doing.

Though Cassie thought it impossible, Taryn grew even harder
in her mouth, and she held Cassie firm against her. There was no
need; ten-ton trucks couldn't have pulled her away. Taryn lifted her
hips from the chair, moaned and writhed, cursed and murmured
while Cassie controlled the pace of her tongue and the pressure of
her fingers. Cassie felt Taryn's climax approach, felt the quickening
of her pulse, gripping her deep inside.

"Oh, fuckshit."

Cassie almost laughed but kept her rhythm as Taryn flushed,
and she peaked with a final expletive. Her body shuddered and
vibrated her orgasm through and into Cassie, who moaned into
the softness of Taryn's lips as if she'd come herself. Cassie stayed
inside Taryn, liking the intermittent contractions that squeezed
her fingers hard and the slow softening of Taryn's clit against her
tongue. It was such a beautiful moment, and Cassie's desire to cry
didn't surprise her. She fought against it, not wanting Taryn to think
something was wrong. Especially when they were tears of esoteric
euphoria. In taking everything Taryn had offered her in this moment,
her body and her vulnerability, Cassie had released the doubts that
itched to hold her back. She wanted this. She wanted Taryn. And
Taryn was giving herself freely and wholly, and the beauty of that

transfer of power was breathtaking, sealing their bond forever.

Cassie used her other hand to trace slow strokes over Taryn's hip, and she shivered in response. She lifted her mouth from Taryn's clit and kissed along Taryn's thighs, enjoying the softness of her skin that disguised marble-like hardness beneath.

Taryn gazed at Cassie and shook her head slowly. "That was... I don't think there are words for what that was."

Cassie grinned and nodded toward the bed. "How about I do it all again and see if that prompts your vocabulary?"

"Yes, and yes." Taryn got up from the chair and helped Cassie to her feet. "I'd love to scoop you up in my arms and carry you to bed, but I have a feeling that might not be a good idea for my ribs."

Cassie pressed her mouth to Taryn's chest then took her hand and led her to bed. "Why don't you lie back, relax, and see if you can get used to this."

Taryn eased onto her back and shuffled up the bed. She opened her legs wide and beckoned Cassie to join her. "I've got a feeling it's not going to be that hard to get used to."

Cassie smiled widely. "I like the sound of that... And I do like the sounds you make when you come."

"Well, who am I to deny you anything?" Taryn put her hands behind her head. "I'm ready for you."

Cassie joined Taryn on the bed. She was ready too. Ready for love, and ready for forever with Taryn. They had stuff to work out, but Cassie's heart told her mind to trust. With a love this strong, it would always be enough to overcome anything.

Chapter Thirty-Two

TARYN TWIRLED CASSIE'S HAIR in her fingers, contentment settling deep in her soul. "I'm pretty sure I haven't had that many orgasms in my life, let alone in a few hours."

Cassie laughed lightly, and her breath cooled Taryn's nipples, still wet from Cassie's attention.

"Yay for me," Cassie said, her touch gentle as she stroked Taryn's ribs.

She kissed the top of Cassie's head. "Yay for *me*. I didn't think I was built to have pleasure like that."

"Maybe your body has just been saving them up for me."

"And I was already wishing I'd met you sooner." Taryn traced slow patterns on Cassie's naked back, feeling a peace so solid and profound, it was almost overwhelming. "I think we should lock the door and stay like this forever."

Cassie pushed up and readjusted herself to lay her head on Taryn's stomach. "Won't that go against your policy of not staying in one place too long?"

She shrugged then nodded. "I guess, but being with you has made this long stay in Vegas bearable."

Cassie narrowed her eyes. "Bearable but not viable?"

Taryn gave a small smile. "You already know me too well."

"I don't think so, but I'm going to enjoy getting to that stage."

Taryn's heart expanded in her chest with the mere concept of longevity Cassie's words implied. "I hope so. About how that might work..." She cupped Cassie's breasts and lazily ran her thumb over Cassie's nipple.

Cassie swatted Taryn's hand away. "There's no way I can have a serious conversation with you if you're doing that."

She returned her hand and continued to play. "Really? Why not?"

Cassie shuddered and clasped her hand over Taryn's. "Because of the insane effect you have on my body. I can't concentrate on actual words when you're touching me that way."

Taryn grinned, feeling rather smug, but her smile faded when she thought about the obstacles they had to overcome to truly be together.

"What's wrong?" Cassie asked. "Why do you suddenly look sad?"

She stilled her hand. "I'm not sad. I just... We've got a lot to talk about, and I don't know what the outcome will be."

Cassie took Taryn's hand and kissed her knuckles. "We're going to work it out. We have to." She pressed her hand over Taryn's heart. "Remember, the beats that are left in here are mine, and I'm not letting them go. So let's figure out our future together."

"Okay. Well, I kind of have an idea that I want to run past you, but I need to get it all out before you respond." Taryn glanced out the window. Maybe if she saw a shooting star, she could wish that their future together was simple. "Would that be okay?"

Cassie smiled widely. "For you? I can do that."

"Cool. So... I haven't really mentioned it, but I've been having a mini mid-life crisis. I haven't been happy—no, scratch that. I'm happy with the people around me. I just haven't been fulfilled with the job itself. Traveling is somehow in my blood, even though my family has lived in Florida for four generations. I love being on the move and not having roots feels good; it feels natural to me. But I don't get the same rush from the shows that I used to get. And even this new development and business partnership with Andi hasn't solved this feeling of being...*lost*. I was excited about it initially, but that's worn off, and I'm still left bouncing around like a pinball in a never-ending game."

Taryn focused her gaze on Cassie, and she nodded but said

nothing. "Spending so much time with you has saved me from disappearing into a total funk, and you also indirectly introduced me to something that might just be the thing I'm supposed to be doing with my life."

Cassie pressed her lips together, clearly struggling not to respond or ask a question.

"It started when you took me to the free clinic and introduced me to Louise and Sara, and also when you asked if I'd thought of doing something other than plastic surgery with my medical degree." She shook her head. "I hadn't, which was so short-sighted and narrow-minded of me. I'd wanted so badly to get away from my family and what they thought I should be doing with my life that I associated medicine with something undesirable and superficial. But after helping Louise and seeing the huge difference something relatively small could make, I got to wondering what a difference I could make if I actually went back to medicine."

Cassie's eyebrows arched so high, Taryn thought they might touch her hairline. She suppressed a laugh, and though it was tempting to put Cassie out of her misery and allow her to speak, it was too funny to see her struggle with staying quiet.

"I think I want to get my license renewed, but I don't want to work in a system where profits are prioritized over people. Obviously you've heard about Doctors Without Borders. My crazy idea and a solution for us to have a real life together is for us to apply to join them. I've got research to do; I don't know how long it will take to get my license back. But we could both practice medicine. We could be together. And I wouldn't be terrifying you daily..." Taryn ran her fingers through Cassie's soft hair, delaying the inevitable onslaught of questions. "I know you've got your mom and Rachel to think about. And there's your job and the work at the free clinic. But I'm hoping we can work around all that somehow, so we can be together—properly together. What do you think?"

Cassie didn't speak for a long moment, and Taryn dropped her head back into the pillow. Of course it wasn't a solution. Asking

Cassie to leave everything and everyone she knew behind was too great a request, even for love.

"My mom isn't the problem," Cassie said finally.

Taryn listened as Cassie told her that she'd cut her mom from her life. She dared to let her hope grow as it sounded like Cassie's decisions and actions were final. Her mom's parting shot made Taryn nauseous. How could a mother say something so vitriolic to her own flesh and blood? Her parents were no role models, but she was grateful they'd never said anything like that. Cassie's breakout of Buster, though, made her laugh. "So that's how Andi ended up with your mom's dog? I thought you'd convinced your mom to give him up; I would never have pegged you as dog-napper."

"Me either." Cassie grimaced. "I don't know what I would've done if Andi hadn't taken him."

"You could've used him to commute to work. He's the size of a small horse," Taryn said.

"I hadn't thought of that."

"I'm sorry about your mom." She twisted a strand of Cassie's hair and dragged it along her own skin, enjoying the soothing sensation of its silky softness. "And I'm sorry I wasn't there to help you through it."

"Don't be," Cassie said. "It was something I needed to do by myself. And I feel stronger because of it. That strength is part of what made me realize I couldn't walk away from you."

Taryn recalled Cassie's exact words. "You said the problem with my plan wasn't your mom..."

"I love Rachel. She's my best friend. But she'll always be that regardless of where I am in the world."

Taryn's heart jumped into her mouth. Was Cassie really working toward saying yes to her proposal? She tried to slow her racing pulse.

"And I don't like the direction the hospital has taken since Barr took over. He couldn't care less about the patients, and that's getting harder to ignore *and* keep doing my job properly with the

Stunted Heart

cuts he's making." She nibbled her lower lip and fell silent briefly. "I want to do the clinic work, but that's not something I could do full-time because I have to eat. And I love my apartment but after seeing your trailer..." She shook her head. "It's no home. It's just a place I sleep." Cassie fixed her gaze on Taryn. "I want to be wherever you are."

Taryn sat up and put her arms around Cassie. "Oh my god. Are you saying what I think you're saying?"

"What do you think I'm saying?" Cassie asked and grinned.

"That you'll give the travelling doctor thing a try with me?"

Cassie nodded. "The only problem with it is the danger. As long as the places you take me to aren't super dangerous, I'm in. But, you know, if my heartbeats are finite, maybe I've got the same number left as you. If we're meant to go in a blaze of bullets trying to save lives, maybe that's okay." She winced. "But somewhere that wouldn't be the case would be better."

Taryn chuckled. "I'm pretty sure the vast majority of their work isn't that dramatic, but I like your thinking. I love you so much." She pulled Cassie into a kiss and closed her eyes to sink into the dream-like feel of the past few hours. All her negativity and dread had fallen away, and the path ahead promised a life Taryn couldn't have begun to imagine before she met Cassie.

Taryn opened her eyes to see Cassie looking back at her, love and longing bright and unabashed in her soft gaze. She pulled back and smiled. "So we're off on a new adventure together?"

"I'll adventure with you anywhere. You're my home now."

Epilogue

Two years later

"I KNOW I'VE ALREADY said it, but this really is the only way to travel."

Taryn wasn't wrong. This had been Cassie's best trip ever on a plane. She leaned across the substantial gap between their seats and kissed Taryn. "Don't get used to it. We'll be back in suspension-challenged vehicles in two weeks."

Taryn rolled her eyes. "I won't. But it's okay to admit I've missed comfortable seats and a smidge of luxury, right?"

"If you can call a private plane a 'smidge of luxury,' sure," Cassie said.

Taryn grinned. "Having a friend with a billionaire wife has its perks."

"Did you say Andi is meeting us at the airport?" Cassie took a sip of water and placed the glass back in the cooler situated in the armrest of her seat.

"Yep. Ralph, Jessica, and Sammie are coming in on a later flight, and they'll meet us at the hotel."

It still stung that they'd missed Sammie's birth while they were overseas. "I can't wait to meet the little one," Cassie said. "Seeing her face on a screen is no substitute for the real thing."

Taryn tilted her head and narrowed her eyes. "Exposure to tiny humans can activate long-dormant maternal instincts. You have to promise me that she won't replace me as your favorite person on the planet."

Cassie shrugged. "You know I don't like making promises I can't keep." She laughed when Taryn frowned.

"Then I'm turning this hunk of tin around and heading back to the Ukraine."

Cassie laughed. "I don't think you need to be jealous of a baby."

"I'm jealous of anyone who gets your attention instead of me." Taryn winked and reached for Cassie's hand. "I've had to share you with hundreds of people for months; I'm looking forward to some us time so you can focus just on me."

She shook her head, but truthfully, she couldn't wait for that same alone time. "Babe, even if I'm not with you, I'm always thinking of you."

"And I love that. But I love your eyes on me more." Taryn ran her fingers over Cassie's palm. "It's your fault. The way that you look at me... Mm, I'm addicted to it."

The captain announced their imminent landing. Cassie gave Taryn's hand a gentle kiss before fastening her seatbelt. They hit the tarmac and were unloading in no time.

Cassie laughed when Taryn bounded down the plane's steps and ran toward Andi, who was leaning against a black Humvee. CeDora was in the back seat with his giant head hanging out the window. When he saw Cassie, he clambered out of the car and loped toward her. He stopped just short and reared up on his hind legs then planted his paws on her shoulders, looking happier than she'd ever seen any dog look. She was glad life with Andi and Bernice was working for him. She registered the tiny stab of guilt as she recalled the day when she freed him, and when she thought of her mom, who still invaded her mind occasionally. But it wasn't too often, and with time and distance, the memories were no longer quite as painful.

She gave him a cuddle then headed over to join Taryn. Bernice had gotten out of the car, and they took turns hugging.

"So, was two hundred hours of retraining worth it?" Andi asked. "Or are you ready to come back to the show?"

Taryn blew out a long breath, and Cassie squeezed her hand. Studying to catch up on ten years of medical education and development had been intense and incredibly difficult for Taryn, but Cassie held her hand through it all. She was so proud when Taryn finally got her license to practice reinstated. According to Ralph, their parents were equally proud, though Taryn still had no desire to reconnect with them.

"That was nothing compared to the grilling the Credentials Committee gave me." Taryn smiled. "But every painful second of it *was* worth it, yeah. I'm loving it." She put her arm around Cassie's shoulder. "We're both loving it. And I'm not missing my wigs and stuffed bras either."

"I'll bet." Andi laughter bellowed across the airstrip, then she smiled genuinely. "That's amazing. I'm really glad you've found your calling. Your potential was always a bit wasted with me."

Taryn punched Andi's arm. "Don't ever say that. I loved every minute of working with you, and I'll never forget what you did for me when I was just floating through life."

Cassie smiled inwardly at the awkwardness of the exchange as Taryn pulled Andi into a bro hug. She found it baffling that Taryn was able to share herself so completely with her but still struggled to show her emotions to her best friend. "How's Louise doing?" Cassie asked to dispel the weirdness. Sara, Louise's mom, had kept in touch. She'd been as shocked as Sara when Louise had said she wanted to follow in Taryn's footsteps and learn to stunt ride.

"She is a younger, prettier version of your fiancée." Andi prodded Taryn's arm. "She might even be better on two wheels than you were."

Bernice nudged Andi. "You shouldn't be noticing how pretty someone is when they're more than half your age."

Andi huffed and drew Bernice close. "As if I'd look at anyone else that way when I'm married to you."

"I'd pretend to be sickened by your loved-up nonsense," Taryn said and looked at Cassie, "but I know the feeling well."

Cassie kissed her cheek. The love in her eyes seemed to grow every day, and Cassie never grew tired of seeing it.

Andi gestured around the side of her SUV. "I brought your bike and your leathers in case you wanted to go for a ride."

"Aww, man. You're the best." Taryn raced around the Humvee and jumped three feet in the air in excitement.

Andi looked a little guilty. "Sorry, Cassie... I hope it's okay."

Cassie patted Andi's shoulder and went around the hood to watch Taryn fawn over her sleek-looking machine. "Don't be silly. Of course it's okay."

Andi tapped the trunk. "I brought a second helmet and some leathers in your size in case you wanted to ride with her."

Taryn chuckled as she straddled her bike. "I don't think she'll want to... Do you?" Taryn sounded hopeful. "I know you don't like the risks on two wheels."

Cassie huffed. "I've just spent the last six months working my way around the Ukraine, dodging the occasional rogue Russian. I think I can go for a ride on the back of your bike."

Taryn's eyes lit up. "Are you serious?"

Cassie nodded. "I really want to."

"Wow, this trip is getting better by the second. Next thing I know, you'll be wanting a tattoo."

"Don't be crazy," Cassie said then followed Andi to the rear of the Humvee to pick up her leathers. Taryn pulled off her jeans, obviously desperate to get back in her gear.

"I won't be doing that," Cassie said. Apart from them, the airstrip was empty, but she still wasn't about to strip down in front of Andi and Bernice.

"I'll show you to the restroom," Bernice said.

"Thank you." Cassie followed her, and Bernice told her all about their upcoming first wedding anniversary celebration, the reason for Cassie and Taryn's visit.

"I'm so glad you were able to come," Bernice said as they headed back toward Taryn and Andi. "It means so much to Andi that Taryn's here."

"Taryn wouldn't have missed it, you know that." Cassie hooked her arm through Bernice's. "And neither would I." Even with the distance between them, Bernice had become something of a surrogate mom to Cassie, and she felt closer to her than she ever had to her real mom. Bernice's presence and support had made the separation from her mom that little bit easier to manage too.

Cassie saw that their luggage had already been taken from the plane and loaded into the back of the Humvee. She added her sweaty travel clothes to the pile and walked around to Taryn, who was ready and waiting beside her bike. Cassie bit her lip at the sexy sight of Taryn in her leathers. It had been a while since she'd seen her in anything other than a T-shirt and fatigues, which, though not an unattractive outfit, was functional. This, however, was like she'd stepped out of a lesbian fantasy calendar *again*.

Bernice touched her arm. "See you back at the hotel." She winked. "Take your time." She got into the Humvee, and they pulled away, waving as they went.

Cassie put her hand on Taryn's thigh. A bolt of desire soared through her.

Taryn grinned. "We can find somewhere to stop on the way back to the hotel if you want," she said, having clearly registered Cassie's expression.

"I definitely *do* want, but I wanted to ask you something before we get going."

"Shoot." Taryn put her helmet over the handlebars, turned to Cassie, and put her hands on her hips. "You look amazing in full leather gear, by the way."

"Stop it. I'm trying to be serious." Though, goddamn, Cassie couldn't wait to pull off on the road somewhere and have sex over this bike. "We've been in the same place for six months. I just wanted to check in again and see how you're doing with less traveling."

Taryn opened her legs wider and pulled Cassie between them. "I've told you; I'm fine."

Cassie wrinkled her nose. "Fine isn't great."

"Then I'm great." Taryn shrugged. "I think my wandering heart was just in search of you. Now that I've found you, I don't care where I am or for how long. And I'd be happy to settle down and become a number of any population sign you want, when that time comes. For now, we'll see parts of the world together and help make it better. As long as I'm with you, I'm happy."

"God, I adore you." Cassie's heart filled with love and almost lifted her from her feet. Wanted. Cherished. Loved. Everything she'd ever desired and everything she didn't know she needed— she'd found it all with Taryn *and* her extended, chosen family. And it was hers, forever. The happy-ever-afters of romance novels and movies had nothing on this.

Other Great Butterworth Books

An Art to Love by Helena Harte
Second chances are an art form.
Available on Amazon (ASIN B0B1CD8Y42)

Stolen Ambition by Robyn Nyx
Daughters of two worlds collide in a dangerous game of ambition and love.
Available on Amazon (ASIN B09QRSKBVP)

Dark Haven by Brey Willows
Even vampires get tired of playing with their food...
Available on Amazon (ASIN B0C5P1HJXC)

Where the Heart Leads by Ally McGuire
A writer. A celebrity. And a secret that could break their hearts.
Available on Amazon (ASIN B0BWFX5W9L)

Green for Love by E.V. Bancroft
All's fair in love and eco-war.
Available from Amazon (ASIN B0C28F7PX5)

Call of Love by Lee Haven
Separated by fear. Reunited by fate. Will they get a second chance at life and love?
Available from Amazon (ASIN B09CLK91N5)

Cabin Fever by Addison M Conley
She goes for the money, but will she stay for something deeper?
Available on Amazon (ASIN B0BQWY45GH)

Zamira Saliev: A Dept. 6 Operation by Valden Bush
They're both running from their pasts. Together, they might make a new future.
Available from Amazon (ASIN B0BHJKHK6S)

The Helion Band by AJ Mason
Rose's only crime was to show kindness to her royal mistress...
Available from Amazon (ASIN B09YM6TYFQ)

What's Your Story?

Global Wordsmiths, CIC, provides an all-encompassing service for all writers, ranging from basic proofreading and cover design to development editing, typesetting, and eBook services. A major part of our work is charity and community focused, delivering writing projects to under-served and under-represented groups across Nottinghamshire, giving voice to the voiceless and visibility to the unseen.

To learn more about what we offer, visit: www.globalwords.co.uk

A selection of books by Global Words Press:
Desire, Love, Identity: with the National Justice Museum
Aventuras en México: Farmilo Primary School
Times Past: with The Workhouse, National Trust
Young at Heart with AGE UK
In Different Shoes: Stories of Trans Lives

Self-published authors working with Global Wordsmiths:
Steve Bailey
Ravenna Castle
Jackie D
CJ DeBarra
Dee Griffiths
Iona Kane
Maggie McIntyre
Emma Nichols
Dani Lovelady Ryan
Erin Zak

Printed in Great Britain
by Amazon